Cornish Village School - Happy Ever After

Kitty Wilson lived in Cornwall for twenty-five years having been dragged there, against her will, as a stroppy teen. She is now remarkably grateful to her parents for their foresight and wisdom – and that her own children aren't as hideous. Recently she has moved to Bristol, but only for love and on the understanding that she and her partner will be returning to Cornwall to live very soon. She spends most of her time welded to the keyboard, dreaming of the beach or bombing back down the motorway for a quick visit! She has a penchant for very loud music, equally loud dresses and romantic heroines who speak their mind.

Also by Kitty Wilson

Cornish Village School series

The Cornish Village School – Breaking the Rules
The Cornish Village School – Second Chances
The Cornish Village School – Summer Love
The Cornish Village School – Christmas Wishes
The Cornish Village School – Happy Ever After

KITTY WILSON

The Cornish Village School

HAPPY EVER AFTER

CANELO

First published in the the United Kingdom in 2020 by Canelo

This edition published in the United Kingdom in 2021 by Canelo

Canelo Digital Publishing Limited
31 Helen Road
Oxford OX2 0DF
United Kingdom

A CIP catalogue record for this book is available from the British Library.

Print ISBN 978 1 80032 268 4
Ebook ISBN 978 1 78863 906 4

Look for more great books at www.canelo.co

Printed and bound in Great Britain by Clays Ltd, Elcograf S.p.A.

For Rob and Andrew, the best wedding of the year. ♥

Chapter One

Marion glanced at the kitchen clock as she was prepping supper; her son Rafe was later than usual. He was out walking Darcy – a Weimaraner, who was the size of a small tank and possessed a similarly destructive nature – and it was unlike him to be more than fifteen minutes. He had been gone nearly an hour.

However, nothing was going to bother her this afternoon, neither her sons nor Darcy, whom Richard had bought as a puppy to keep her company whilst he was working away. Today she was thoroughly loved up, happy to indulge her husband's bizarre thought processes, happy to turn a blind eye to her son's tardiness, so excited was she about the upcoming anniversary weekend she and Richard had planned. February was such a romantic month for the two of them, with their anniversary followed by Valentine's Day the week after.

She was still staring into space when Rafe wandered in, the dog bounding beside him, unspeakably grubby as if he had been rolling in every slurry pit within a five-mile radius.

'Rafe, no! Take him into the garden; he can't come in like this.' Just as she was gesturing at a muddy footprint – Disneyesque in its perfection – upon her wall-to-wall white carpeting, a howling scream came skittering through the house. It was rapidly followed by a *thud,*

thud, crash down the stairs, as if an escaped racehorse had become trapped in one of the bedrooms and was making a run for it, risking its ankles on every step and going heavy and fast to get it over with.

Only it wasn't a racehorse, it was a small boy followed by a slightly larger one. Loud words, hard to decipher, tumbling over each other as both raced to be the first to get to their mother.

None of which was helping Rafe control the dog, who, at the sound of the other two Marksharp boys, had begun to whirl around, his tail thrashing from side to side, trying to join in the rumpus. Mud flew from him as he scampered around the room barking with joy, his lead still attached.

'Boys!' Marion bellowed, to little avail. Why was it that she was respected in this village, could quell an entire school with an eyebrow and shape a whole community into doing what she wanted in under five seconds, but marshalling her own sons – Rafe, who was twelve years old, Rupert, who was ten, and Rufus, the baby, at six – felt like a task akin to Napoleon attempting to invade Russia? If the members of Penmenna PTA could see her now, they wouldn't believe this was her home life. They may never follow another order.

'Boys!' she shouted again, one more attempt to halt the noise, mud and general hubbub occurring in her living room.

Nope, nada.

Rafe was trying to drag the dog out, far from easy with Darcy weighing as much as he did and blessed with a determination matched only by her sons. Rupert was trying to grab hold of his younger brother, Rufus, who was enjoying evading him, giggling as he nipped here and crouched down there, turning and twisting just out of the grasp of his increasingly frustrated sibling.

She took a deep breath, counted to ten and prepared herself for battle.

'I swear to…' Marion rarely actually swore. Only in a dire emergency where her humanity took over from her innate and embedded sense of control. Control that sadly wasn't extending to her offspring at this moment.

Her words were interrupted by the high-pitched call of the laptop, open on the table.

Like a siren to a sailor it pierced the chaos and the three boys spun to look at it.

A video call from their father. A rare treat at this time of day.

Rufus, small, wiry and with a twisty form that Houdini would have been proud of, was first to reach the table, the other two and Darcy – who Rafe had now completely given up on getting outside – shortly behind him.

'Dad!' came the chorus of three as they clicked the answer icon and Richard's beautiful face filled up the screen.

Marion indulged in a brief sigh at the sight of him. Things were so wonderfully back on track at last, something she had feared could never be after the run-up to Christmas last year. Then her eye caught the state of the living room.

This would not do.

She hauled the dog – whose excited turn up and down on the sofa had given it a unique print pattern – and booted him unceremoniously out of the back door whilst the boys talked to their father. A man they all equally adored, to the point that when they were little Marion felt that if they could have unzipped his skin and climbed in they would have done and still not felt close enough.

The unexpected video chat was extra special as Richard was a man *very* frequently absent these days. He'd been working away in the city for the last couple of years, leaving Marion the joy of parenting practically by herself but without the support network that other single parents in the village seemed to have created.

Dog dealt with, she quickly grabbed the lipstick sitting on the mantlepiece. She applied it perfectly and in under two seconds before heading to the table, patting her hair into place as she went.

She joined the boys at the laptop, glimpsing her husband's face through a gap between Rafe and Rupert's shoulders and able to catch his smile as his eyes lit upon her face.

'Boys, I'm sure you've got a whole heap of homework to be doing,' Richard said as Marion utilized her very best serene agreement face, successfully masking the truth that chance would be a fine thing. It normally took her a good ten minutes to round them up just to leave the house. Getting them all to sit down to do their homework took a good half hour.

'Go make a start and be good for your mother, you know how lucky you are to have her. I love you all so very much but right now I need to have a chat with Mum, just her and me. I'll be back next weekend and we shall do something wonderful just the five of us. With any luck the sun will smile and it will be glorious; you can think of things you'd like to do.' Richard always managed to make everything sound as if they still lived in a world in which the Famous Five reigned supreme. Mind you, he did keep a picnic basket in the car, along with lashings of ginger beer, so maybe in his they did.

Like perfect Stepford children, the boys brushed their fringes out of their eyes, and chorused 'Of course, Dad, that'll be awesome, love you, see you soon' before heading up the stairs far more decorously than they had come down, aware that their father's eyes were tracking them across the room as they did so. Marion didn't know how he did it but was grateful that he could. She just wished he was home a bit more often, using his magic for everyday good.

'Such good boys, a credit to you, darling, I don't know how you do it.' Richard smiled at his wife as she pulled out a chair and sat down, holding his eyes and grinning right back.

God, she loved this man.

She had been attracted to his tall frame, tightly curled short hair and overall nerdiness when she first set eyes upon him, all those years ago, during her first term at Oxford. He had embodied geek chic before such a thing even existed, with his thick-rimmed glasses, love of books and stuttering discomfort around women.

The last couple of years though had been tricky, not because their love – which was strong and passionate and true – had dimmed over time but because his work necessitated his absence, despite his promise that he'd be able to take early retirement any day now. A hope that hovered over them and their family as his absences were prolonged, the promise never fully realized. Marion felt more and more isolated, abandoned, desperate even as she struggled in this village raising the boys and presenting the archetypal picture of the perfect family.

There had been a couple of low points, points where she had seriously considered leaving him. Where she had begun to believe that things would be easier if she were on her own; she'd know that everything was on her, without the burden of disappointment, failed expectations of another person contributing. Maybe the people in the village would help more, take off some of the pressures that she piled upon herself.

In summer, her resentment had built so high that she'd escaped to where she knew she would be welcomed and had jetted off to Morocco, boys in tow, to spend the summer with Hector, a mutual friend from their uni days; but her love for Richard had brought her right back again. Determined to try one more time.

Then this year at Christmas, she had been on the receiving end of a particularly spiteful campaign by another mother at Penmenna School who had told her that Richard's colleague, Claudia, was desperately in love with him. Her husband, who was now staring out from the screen, running his fingers around his collar and smiling at her nervously. The husband who spent every day in his office, over two hundred and fifty miles away with Claudia's raven-haired beauty beside him.

'Darling, how have you been? Sorry to be calling at this time of day but the Texans are landing later and I'll be tied up with them all evening. Not tied up, you know that's just for you and me...' Richard gave her a wink – she felt a shiver trail down her spine – and then changed the subject. 'What's new? I see the boys are thriving.'

'They are.' She angled the laptop screen slightly away from the muddy footprints she spotted on the sofa, just to the top right of the screen. That bloody dog. It was going to take her ages to brush all that out. She wondered

6

if there was anyone she could call to come and do it for her.

'I'm fine, everything is running smoothly here. But…' She dropped her voice, making it sultry, promising. 'I cannot wait until this weekend. We are going to have the best time.' She gave him her most practised look, the one that normally had him fumbling at his belt buckle as if he and she were still twenty.

She meant it. After a big blow-up at Christmas he had promised her this weekend to show her how much he cared, how she was his everything, had been since he was nineteen and continued to be now.

'Oh, Marion.' He drew out her name in the same way he had always done, a word that when said in that tone had a languidity to it that conjured up decades full of loving. Then he broke eye contact, looking down at the keyboard just for a second before bringing his eyes up to meet hers again, jiggling his glasses as he did so. That was a tell. 'Marion, I don't know how to say this so I'm just going to come out with it. Look, this is crucifying me, I wish it were different…'

'Nooo!' Marion heard herself let out a low sound before sharply trying to pull herself together, but it was a struggle and she couldn't contain the words that followed. 'Not this weekend. Oh, Richard, you promised.'

'I know, sweet pea, I know. I said I'd hand in my notice before I let anything stop us from celebrating our anniversary, I know I did. But honestly, it's just *this* meeting. The Japanese have finally agreed to fly in and negotiate terms face to face. I tried, I did try, I told the CEO that he needed to reschedule, that I couldn't possibly be here, that I ran the risk of losing my wife.'

'And?'

'And he said that my wife could... well I won't say what but he suggested something most unpleasant and he still wouldn't let me skip the meeting. He said after this deal was finished I could afford five wiv... um... yes, maybe not... but I begged, I really did. And he's right, he is. We've been working on it for so long now and this meeting is pivotal; if we can just pull this off then that will be it. I can come home and we can be together, like I always promised. One more weekend. I'll make it up to you, I swear.'

Marion took a deep breath. She could have predicted this, *had* predicted this and then told herself off for being so pessimistic. He couldn't help it, and as she looked at the deep brown of his eyes she knew he was feeling as bad as could be, knew he wouldn't have done this on purpose.

'Marion, I love you so desperately, please understand, please don't be angry at me. It's tearing me to bits.'

And she knew it was true. She knew it. The very bones of her knew it.

It was just that after all the rumours of an affair last year, she had crowed high and wide about this special anniversary away, triumphant about how Richard was choosing her over work. She had told anyone that would listen. And a fair few that wouldn't. Childcare had been arranged, the dog-sitter had been booked. She couldn't bear not to see him, but even more she couldn't bear the look of pity on people's faces when she cancelled. The look of superiority of the Serenas and the Jennys of this world, with their ever-present husbands. She couldn't and she wouldn't.

An idea formed in her mind, an idea where she could still be the perfect wife, still see her husband and keep the respect and envy of those catty-tongued women in the village. She smiled at Richard. God, she loved him. Of course he couldn't help it.

'Darling, I understand. It's not your fault. I know you'd be with me in our hotel, in our plush five-star four-poster bed, watching me take off the most insane lingerie I have ever bought or in the private hot tub out on the decking if you could…' She lowered her tone suggestively again; no harm in getting in what he was missing out on. 'Of course you can't help it. I understand, I really do.'

Her husband gulped and she thought she saw a tear well in the corner of his eye.

'Marion Marksharp, I love you. You are the best wife any man could ever have.'

She smiled knowingly; after all she couldn't help but believe that he was absolutely right.

Chapter Two

Marion stood on Jenny's doorstep waiting for her to answer the door. She wasn't sure what was taking so long – the woman knew she was coming and Marion was never late. Surely the least she could expect was that the person she was entrusting her children with for the weekend could answer a door promptly.

She glanced across at the boys and wondered, just for a millisecond, if she should brief Jenny on the worst possibilities that could occur whilst she was away. But having surreptitiously checked the boys' bags thoroughly before they left she figured that she would carry on maintaining the perfect-family myth. No need to explode what she had worked so hard at maintaining over the years. If anything, she took comfort from the fact that her boys were bright enough to cover their tracks effectively.

Rupert didn't seem to have any matches, lighters or any other implements upon him and she was fairly sure he had grown out of his brief dalliance with arson. She suspected the vicar's shed going up the way it had a couple of years ago had been enough to put paid to that. Or at least she hoped so, if just for this weekend.

Rafe was banned from going to Whispering Pines, the old people's home up the road, and had been respecting the ban for a few months now. Indeed, he was banned from going anywhere where he could fleece people of money or otherwise engage in gambling. His fear she would tell his father had proven a very useful deterrent. He didn't need to know that she already had. The two of them had no secrets. However, she had set up parental controls on their tablets that Edward Snowden would have trouble getting past, and changed her bank details again to be on the safe side.

And as for darling Rufus, the baby of the bunch, he seemed to have stopped biting and Jenny *had* received the same training at Penmenna School that she, Marion, had.

She could hear voices approaching the door, at last!

'But no one likes her, and she's mean to you.' The muffled words came from inside the house and were hard to make out. Marion cocked her head to see if she could hear more but all she heard was Jenny's entreaty for her daughter to be quiet and then a fumble at the door. Was the voice referring to her? More than likely. You couldn't please all the people all the time.

'Ahh, hello, sorry. I was in the garden.' Jenny pulled the front door wide open and bestowed a smile upon the Marksharp family as they stood there, ushering them all in with a wave of her hand.

In the garden? When she *knew* she was arriving? Marion had trained Jenny up to the highest of standards and she had proved the quickest and most reliable of all her PTA ladies but even now, sometimes, she had her doubts about the woman's competence.

As she entered the hallway Jenny leant forward and the two engaged in the traditional air kiss, double-cheeked, at least six inches away from actual flesh and as false as Serena Burchill-Whyte's perfectly perky bosom. Marion had seen Jenny's husband, a local fisherman, so there was no way she would ever allow Jenny's lips to come into contact with her own skin.

'Well, you're here now.' Marion could afford to be magnanimous, especially today. She couldn't wait to be on the road, to arrive at her destination and show Richard how she was indeed the perfect wife in oh-so-many ways.

'Do come in and make yourself at home, boys.' Jenny showed them through to her lounge, which would be so much nicer if she just got rid of some of the clutter, invested in a new sofa and some darling little chairs and threw out that hideous table. Marion would help her with it after her road trip.

Marion gave the boys her fiercest behave-yourself-or-I-will-rain-Armageddon-down-upon-your-heads look – it was one of her favourites – whilst Jenny's back was turned as she quickly fussed with the magazines on the coffee table, looking to Marion for approval as she placed *Tatler* and *The Lady* on the very top. Marion nodded in acknowledgement, and cocked an eyebrow at the copy of *Take A Break* peeking out behind some god-awful cushion, revealed as the boys demurely took a seat.

'Oh that was my mother-in-law.' Jenny rushed out an excuse and Marion nodded, prepared to let her have this one. She was on such a high and wanted to get on her way. 'You must be so excited about your trip away; did you say you were staying at Belmond Manor? I looked it up, it looks amazing,' Jenny gushed in an attempt to make up for the faux pas.

'Belmond Le Manoir aux Quat'Saisons.' Marion corrected Jenny's pronunciation with her own faultless French; she had always been proud of her language skills. 'We're so very excited, it has a fabulous reputation and the food is to die for.'

'You'll have to take photos,' Jenny encouraged; Marion shut that down with a look. There was no way she was admitting that the booking had been cancelled – far better to imply that she and Richard were above selfies.

'What a ghastly concept. Although you are very sweet. Now I'll be back in Penmenna late Sunday as we agreed. You are quite sure on all their dietary requirements, aren't you? No one wants to have to undergo a trip to Treliske in my absence.' Marion named the hospital in Truro, just to make sure Jenny knew that any deviation wouldn't be acceptable.

'Absolutely, I have everything ready as per the menus you planned and gave me last week, Marion. I must say I'm very excited. My two have never had snails before so it's going to be quite an adventure.'

'*Escargots*, Jenny, *escargots*. There's no need to make it sound as if you're digging them out of the garden. I'm sure everything will go smoothly; I have no worries about my boys. I expect the weekend will fly by very quickly indeed. Now I must say goodbye or I'll be late to meet Richard – we thought it would be romantic to drive to Oxford together, save him catching the train. You know how dreadful it can be getting into London.' Jenny didn't look like she did but then Marion understood she had never been much further north than Plymouth. She'd have to sort that out for her at some point in the future. After all, education was key; she was the living embodiment of that.

Rufus, Rupert and Rafe all stood up in a neat line as she took her leave, kissing her on the cheek and asking her to send their love to Richard.

Jenny clasped her hands together at the demonstration of affection. 'How lovely. I can't even get Sophie to talk to me most days.'

Marion wasn't surprised. Up until today, she had always thought Sophie a girl of exceptional good taste.

Chapter Three

The journey to London had been torturous, the traffic absolutely dire. It seemed the roads these days were filled with incompetents and lunatics. Marion had always thought driving in Cornwall at the height of tourist season was bad enough, but London these days was something else. They really should develop an IQ restriction for those allowed on the M25 or inside London itself.

Things hadn't been helped by this god-awful underwear she was wearing. She knew it looked utterly fantastic on but it was halfway up her bottom and not in a good way. Mind you, such was the price she was willing to pay for love. And she knew Richard would love it.

She pulled up near his flat, the one he rented for when he was working, and decided to ignore the double yellows.

One quick fix of Fuchsia Crush applied to the filthy grin already upon her face and she stepped out of the car, clicked the lock button on her keys and headed in to surprise her man.

She tapped in the security code that powered the lift and guided it to the correct floor, its jolt marking its ascent, suddenly felt queasy. She was nervous for some reason when she shouldn't be. But she was used to feeling this way and masked it exceptionally well, confident in the belief that if you lined up a hundred people that knew her and asked them to describe her in as many words as they could, nervous or anxious would not come up. Not even once.

She gave her shoulders a little shake as the lift continued upwards. There was nothing to be worried about. Richard was her husband; she loved him very much. He loved her very much. He was also a creature of habit and she knew nothing would change his routines. If Richard was due out tonight with the Japanese then he would be having a wash and a change first. And around about now. She had always been very attracted to his cleanliness.

There was nothing here for her tummy to be worried about. Richard would be in the shower now then would wander into his bedroom to pick out a fresh shirt and tie. The only difference was this time she would be waiting for him, splayed out and in scarlet on his large king-size bed wearing her best come-hither look and underwear that currently felt like it was extracting a kidney.

The lift halted and there was a short pause as it settled into position before the door opened. Marion took a deep breath as she prepared to scamper out and across to the bedroom, to position herself in readiness.

One, two, three and g…

She stopped.

No.

This made no sense.

There had to be a good reason.

What the hell was Claudia doing walking down the hall and dressed in nothing but a robe, her hair wet and her face smug?

No.

Marion blinked. She was still there. Marion felt her shoulders sag, her spirit, her conviction drained. Richard had never been a man of surprises. Never. And this was one hell of a surprise. Maybe she didn't know her husband as well as she thought. She couldn't bear to be one of *those* women, the women that were clueless about the type of man they had married, yet the evidence in front of her was suggesting that may well be the case.

Claudia turned, as if she sensed Marion's eyes upon her. But she turned slowly, deliberately, a flash of satisfaction in her eyes. Of triumph. She knew the lift had arrived; it always made that little settling noise, impossible to hear from the shower, impossible not to notice when in the hallway.

'Marion, darling.' She headed towards the indubitable Queen of Penmenna, the real Duchess of Cornwall, her chin angled, ready for the faux air kiss.

Marion tried to pull her shoulders up, to launch herself into her finest offensive mode, to watch this woman with her perfect skin, her lustrous cascade of damp jet hair turn into a quivering jelly whose only recourse was to slink out of Marion's husband's apartment, too scarred, too scared to ever show her face again. Marion could do this. It was her number one skill, her most refined talent.

And yet her body wasn't responding. Wasn't drawing itself up to its full height, ready to spit venom and tear out eyes. Her legs were suddenly clay, stolid damp clay impossible to lift as they clung to the floor. Her heart slowed, opiated into slothfulness rather than hammering through her chest, raising her adrenaline and pushing her forward. *Come on*, she tried to shout at herself, *what is happening here?* Even the words in her head were slurred, lacking their usual incisive, acerbic wit; everything was in slow motion, as if it weren't real and she was stuck in a bad dream, her body refusing to wake from slumber.

'Oh dear, you don't look very well. Come in and I'll get you some water. Or some fizz, perhaps you'd like some fizz, we've got a bottle in the fridge. I hear you're *very* fond of it and, well' – she paused – 'you do rather look like you need it. Richard is *still* in the shower I'm afraid but I'm sure he'll be out in a minute.' She smirked that cat-like smirk favoured by all evilly seducing, immoral, husband-stealing jezebels since the dawn of time. 'I can go and let him know you are here if you like; I know he's been meaning to talk to you.' She tied the tie on her robe a little tighter, a proprietary move, showing Marion exactly how comfortable she was in this flat, forcing Marion into position of guest, of supplicant. As she did so she also flicked her hair, a movement of unrepressed exultation, of victory.

Marion stood, a droplet of water from Claudia's hair landing on her face and instantly dissolving the sluggishness that had overpowered her up until now. She felt her spirit return, flood through her and finally give her the power she needed. The power she had always relied on to get herself out of any situation in which she felt in danger, challenged. That had saved her skin more times than she cared to admit.

'You…' She took a step forward; her lips moved, imbuing her with power as she looked at Claudia as if she were no more than a mere irritant. '*You* are going to go and tell my husband that I am here? I don't know who, or what' – she let out a little chuckle, mirthless and pitying – 'you think you are, *Claudia*, but the only thing you'll be telling my husband is that I *was* here, and that you are welcome to him.'

Chapter Four

Marion turned the key in her car, her fury keeping her body rigid, powering her through until she could get to somewhere safe, somewhere Richard couldn't find her, chase after her and spill lies from his duplicitous, cheating mouth. She'd just get away from here and then she'd let go, let out the emotions clashing around her body, the feelings screaming in her mind. Somewhere no one could possibly know her, recognize her, watch her give in to the overwhelming sense of heartbreak that was coursing through her.

How could she have been so stupid? So naive? She had been secretly pitying the foolishness of those women for years, the ones whose husbands worked away from home, installing mistresses in their little flats, their secret urban love nests. She had never dreamt her husband would do the same. Never dreamt that the man she had shared her bed with, her life with for the last twenty plus years, could be so stupid, so selfish.

And now it seemed she had been fooled as well. The indignity.

No, she would not get sucked into this now. She needed to drive the car, and she needed to be out of here before Richard appeared, all wet from the shower, muttering apologies and excuses, with that cute little look of devoted helplessness that he was oh-so-good at, trying to justify the truth of his double life now it had been revealed.

Bastard.

–

She had surprised herself when, after two-and-a-bit hours of racing out of London and up the M1, she pulled the handbrake on and turned the engine off. She hadn't thought she would ever come back here voluntarily, ever come back full stop. But it seemed shock did strange things to the body, for here she was. This was where her autopilot in a time of emergency had brought her.

However, it was fair to say that no one here would recognize her. Here she looked out of place, bearing no resemblance to the girl who had lived here all those years before on the sixteenth floor of the tower closest to her. Here she could do – feel – anything and it would never bleed into her current Cornish life. If she wanted to suddenly turn into the Class Three teacher from Penmenna School, the hideous Harmony Rivers, and march up and down the streets engaging in primal screaming and waving a sage smudge stick about, she could, and no one would bat an eye. Unless they were impressed and approached her for the name of her dealer.

She looked out of the car window disdainfully. It looked even worse now than it had on the last day she had been here, the day she had packed her bag, headed out of the estate and onto the main road where she had hitched a lift to Oxford, to her brand-new life and the future it held, at barely eighteen years old. Not once had she looked over her shoulder as she left, not once had she looked back, until now.

The three tower blocks rose into the sky, grey and grim and dank. Behind her was the canal, a smell rising from it that Marion was grateful she had managed to erase from her memory.

As she got out of her car someone shuffled towards her, hood up, jeans slung low. She held her breath as he approached. If she hadn't escaped this, the chances that this could be her son in the near future would be so much higher. His acned face, gaunt and yellow, came close, muttering, 'Brown, ket, spice.' She closed her eyes and took a deep breath, shaking her head decisively as he passed.

What was she doing here?

And did he really think she looked like a drug addict? Surely more like a magistrate or high-ranking detective than someone wanting to score drugs from a teen on a towpath?

She took a step forward and headed down the canal path on autopilot. So why had she brought herself to this place? Was this her subconscious telling her that without Richard she could well still be here, trudging up a thousand wee-stained stairs with her shopping rather than prancing around her chi-chi Cornish village in tailored printed dresses and designer make-up, breathing the bracing sea air? Was her mind suggesting a course of action, reminding her that women since the dawn of time had turned a blind eye to their husbands' affairs to maintain their lifestyle, to keep their homes together for the sake of the children?

She approached the bench that she used to escape to as a child, when the noise of the flat became too much, when her mother was at her very worst. It was still there. Missing a slat and covered in graffiti, nettles beginning to spring up around it. She gingerly sat down, flattening her hands on the boards first and then perching on top of them before she realized she was being ridiculous. She was hardly going to die from siting on a blooming public bench. Her nostrils slowly adjusted to the stench of the canal, although not enough to be able to take the great big lungfuls of air her body was craving, as she recalled her past.

She had been the smelly child in school, the one ostracized by the others but nothing, *nothing*, had ever actually killed her. And today was no different. You win some, you learn some, they say. Her childhood had certainly been a learning experience. She hadn't expected her marriage to be one too.

What other women did was not for her to worry about; what she needed to do was work out what *she* was going to do. What was right for her? She was interested by the fact that she had come here instead of heading straight back down the motorway to the safety of Penmenna. But if her subconscious *was* indeed telling her that she *needed* to stay with Richard then it could do one.

For the first time this evening a glimmer of a smile crossed her face. That's what she needed, some of her Marion spirit. That would help her decide how she was going to react. She had long believed that you couldn't control the things that life threw at you but you could choose how you reacted once you had processed the inevitable emotion. Today was one of those times.

And she didn't choose settling, turning a blind eye; she didn't choose pretending over time that she wasn't feeling utterly hurt and betrayed, riven in two, by her husband. She had genuinely, for years, believed that they were different, that they would be inseparable, together until death.

She felt the tears begin to stream down her cheeks and brushed them off angrily; she would deal with that later, for now she knew she had made her decision. She would not be standing by her man. The very idea that he had... that his... that they... She could barely formulate the thought, it was so repulsive. That he had slept with another woman... No, that was it, for her. What was right for others was not okay for her. She didn't want to look at him over the breakfast table and see Claudia's face in her head. See him coming out of the shower in the mornings, his towel draped around his waist and replay the scene with Claudia in his flat. No, that she would not do.

She had tried her absolute hardest to be the perfect wife to him, fulfil every fraction of every conceivable role: to be his friend, his lover, his helpmeet. She was there for everything he could possibly want or need, often before he was aware he had it as a want or a need. She made sure his life ran smoothly and as the boys came along the same applied.

Actually, the more she thought about it the angrier she became. How dare he? How *dare* he? She had repeatedly put her needs on hold, her wishes, desires paused so she could be the perfect wife and mother, so she could ensure her boys got the very best start, be wrapped in security, in love, in a family that was aspirational and supportive, that could help them shape their futures in a positive way.

And he had threatened that with one simple selfish act... maybe not simple and probably multiple, but with his actions her hard work and devotion over the last two decades had all been sullied. Now it all risked tumbling down. Just so he could get his end away with a younger model. Oh, Richard.

She took a huge gulp of air despite the stench, her hurt once more overwhelming her before her anger kicked back in again. All risked, for what? And now she had to go home and tell the boys that their life was going to be very different from now on. That her life was going to be very different from now on.

For a start she was going to have to earn a living. How could she possibly carry on her usual levels of activity and find work? She couldn't run the boys to all their clubs, run the PTA, organize everyone else's social events *and* take on Richard's role as breadwinner. It wasn't humanly possible, not even for the superhuman she had trained herself to be.

And what would she *do*? She hadn't worked since she was a student, and running a bar and a student newspaper umpteen years ago wasn't going to help her cover the mortgage and her boys' refined eating habits.

What *could* she do? She knew one thing: she knew she wouldn't be leaving Penmenna, that was for sure. She hadn't found the country's most perfect village for her boys to flourish in and then uproot them and bring them… well, anywhere else. She had a responsibility now to minimize the shock as much as she could. Divorce could do terrible things to children, and her boys were at such impressionable ages as well. No, she'd have to stay in Penmenna and try and get a job locally, keep them in their schools, within their friendship circles, in the same house. There was no way she was giving up the house.

But if she were to stay locally where could she work? There were limited jobs going in Cornwall for a woman with a First from Oxford in Classics. Not a huge call for her ability to read ancient Greek. Everything down there was seasonal or in the public sector. She didn't have the professional qualifications to work for the NHS or teach, plus she'd need something that would pay well enough to keep the boys in the lifestyle they were used to, and that didn't come cheap. She considered politics – she thought she'd make a rather good member of parliament – but the general election wasn't due for a while and she couldn't gamble on winning. No, she needed a certainty, something she could control, that guaranteed her what she needed.

A woman with a small child and a pushchair came up to the bench next to her. The child had a ring of chocolate around her mouth and a can of Red Bull in her hands.

'Now sit down, and drink your drink whilst I sort out the baby.'

'I don't wanna sit down.'

'Sit down or I won't let you go to Kayden's party.'

'I don't want to go to Kayden's stupid party, he's weird and his house smells. I wanna go McDonald's!' The little girl threw her can of drink at her mother before opening her mouth and screaming a scream that would wake the dead at the bottom of the canal, an arc of the drink careering out as the can flew through the air, splashing Marion's new Max Mara skirt that she had bought especially for this weekend.

Marion automatically gave the child a look, a look that would have stopped an entire class in Penmenna in its tracks, made them cry and sob an apology. But it was a brief one, for this child had sowed the seed of an idea, no, not a seed, a great big beanstalk of an idea. So, Kayden's mum may not know how to throw a party, but you know who did? Marion.

Marion knew how to throw a party. Everyone loved her parties; she was the queen of party-throwing. All she had to do was work out how to monetize that. She got to her feet and threw another look at the woman next to her, but this time of gratitude. Well, gratitude and a little bit of disdain – it didn't matter where you came from, no one in their right mind would let their pre-schooler drink caffeine. Actually, she didn't care. This was genius. It was so obvious; she could events manage. She could do it from home, use all the contacts and the skills she had and still be there for the boys.

'And you can sod off too, you stuck-up old cow. Sneering at me when you're sat 'ere sobbing on your own. No mates, is it? No one to talk to, well we don't want you 'ere neither. Go on, fuck off back to London or wherever you're from.'

And do you know what? Marion thought that wasn't a bad idea either.

Chapter Five

Marion let herself back into her home after two whole nights spent sobbing and plotting in a B&B a couple of miles away from her childhood home. To say it was not up to her usual standards would be the understatement of the year. It had non-ironic floral borders for a start and the toiletries provided were so bad she had wondered if it were a deliberate policy to stop the guests from washing so they fitted in better with the staff.

Her feedback had not been well received.

This was followed by a five-hour journey, most of which she had driven powered by rage. She had spent two nights now sobbing her heart out, and it was unlike her to be so emotional – the last time, just before Christmas, had been over Richard as well! He had had enough tears spent on him now; she must have cried ten buckets' worth this weekend and was very thankful this morning to have her trusty aviators in her handbag. Red-rimmed eyes were not a look Marion was ever prepared to sport, not even for her husband and especially now she had discovered he was an errant one. Completely sobbed out, she was happy for anger to become her dominant feeling instead.

Returning home was not the happy occasion it usually was. Although she was most impressed as she caught a glance in the mirror that she didn't look as drained as she felt. Concealer and bravado made an awesome pairing.

She had already picked up the boys – they were trailing in behind her – having pretended to both them and Jenny that Mummy and Daddy had had a lovely weekend and that everything in their world was just as it should be.

Jenny had wanted to know all the details of the hotel and Marion had forgotten what she had seen on the website before she had been forced to cancel her chi-chi night away, the horrors of the peach chintz from where she had actually stayed in the forefront of her mind instead. The last thing she needed was to out herself, the end of her marriage and the admission that she had spent the night in a two-star B&B on the outskirts of nowhere-ville.

Jenny had looked perplexed as Marion explained that she was simply too tired to possibly tell her all about it in that moment, then gave her a slow wink and a nod in the hope that Jenny would assume she had been overly vigorous at the weekend and thus needed to get home for an Epsom salt bath and a rest. Jenny may love hearing all about Marion's travel experiences but she would have to forgo that treat until Marion had time to double check Belmond Manor's website again.

As she managed to whisk the boys out of Jenny's and make her escape, her phone had pinged with a message from her friend, Angelina. She had used a snap of Angelina and Chase's house, all lit up and sparkly, for the business cards she had ordered – a perfect chic aesthetic to present her new events management business. She was sure she wouldn't mind.

If she could land Angelina as a client, along with her brother, celebrity gardener Matt Masters, who was due to marry Penmenna School's headteacher, Rosy Winter, this summer, then her diary would be filling up before she had begun any campaign proper. Ideas had come thick and fast whilst she was away; emotion was obviously good for creativity. Perhaps that was why all those starving-in-a-garret artist types chose a garret in the first place whilst proclaiming poverty – misery really did get you thinking.

She checked the text as soon as she was in and through the door.

> Darling, would love to see you, but I'm desperately busy. St Bart's is unbearably crowded in February, heading back tomorrow. Could have a quick lunch Thursday? Kisses.

Perfect, her plan was ready to put into action. She wasn't pleased that she'd have to wait until Thursday but she supposed that was the price one paid for being friends with the glitterati. Or the clitterati as Richard called them… no, she wasn't to start thinking about Richard now and certainly not with a giggle. She needed to hold on to rage for a bit; it was a great motivator.

There was another noise too, coming from upstairs, familiar and yet not quite right. Marion shook her head to dispel it; she didn't have time for nonsense right now – there was nothing alarming it could be. That was the joy of Penmenna. No fear of the unexpected. It seemed London was the place for that.

She dampened down her crossness – this was time for focus – and pulled out her phone to call Rosy as the boys unloaded all the bags and dragged them upstairs.

'I have the best idea so I thought I could come and see you and the darling Matt this evening…' She found it was better to launch straight in; no need to waste time on irrelevancies.

'Oh hello, Marion. Well it's Sunday, can it wait until—'

'Quite, no time like the present.'

'You see the thing is—'

'Now, now, don't be silly. It won't take long and it's Sunday evening, you're not going to be doing anything other than watching some period drama and sighing whilst Matt does Matt things. Actually, that's a point, you'll need to tell Matt to be there too. Honestly, you'll be so excited when you hear my ideas, Rosy darling, I'm going to revolutionize your life. See you in thirty minutes or so.' Marion thought she heard Rosy gulp as she hung up the phone, but with it being February there were a lot of winter colds going about.

'Oh, thank goodness for that...' a male voice sang out from the top of the stairs, causing Marion to freeze to the spot.

'Daddy, Daddy!'

She heard Richard's laugh as Rufus came bounding out of his bedroom like a springer spaniel puppy and launched himself at his father's legs. She didn't need to turn around to see the scene playing out here. Rufus would be clinging to Richard's leg, Richard would ruffle his hair before disentangling himself and walking over... stop. This was not okay; Richard was *not* the man she thought he was, and now he appeared to have turned up in their house, after all his protestations of how he couldn't possibly get away because of the sodding Japanese and yet, now his secret was rumbled, he seemed to have time to come home and cover things up. Well, she could tell him now how that was going to go.

She spun on her heel to face him, the man she had loved with all her might, the man who had betrayed her, the man who was currently wrapped up in a hug with their youngest son and looking for all the world like there was nothing, no one he loved more than his family.

Curses.

She couldn't shout at him in front of the boys; this was a house of domestic harmony and would stay that way if it killed her. Damn it. She watched him walk down the stairs, Rufus trailing behind him, Rupert and Rafe having left their rooms to see what the commotion was.

'Darling, I'm so glad to see you safe and home. I was so worried about you – where have you been?'

Rupert looked at his dad oddly. 'She's only been gone ten minutes, she whirled us out of Jenny's like a hurricane. Made Rafe pretty cross. Did you have a nice weekend?'

Rafe went to hit his brother around the head but caught his dad's eye and paused his hand mid-air, bringing it back to scratch his shoulders as if that had been his intent all along.

Bloody Richard; if he hadn't been here the boys would no doubt be wrangling on the carpet by now. She'd have that joy to deal with by herself once she was officially a lone parent. A lone parent? That hadn't been the future she pictured for herself.

'Yeah, actually, Mum, I have to go and meet Sophie now.'

'You've just spent the weekend with her. What on earth could be so important that you need to see her again?'

Rafe paused and caught his mum's eye. 'Um… algebraic fractions. She doesn't understand them and we didn't get through all of her homework.' Marion softened a little; he was a good boy, just as she always told people. These boys were going to do alright in life, she knew it. As long as they didn't turn out to be cheating weaselly philanderers like their father.

She fixed Richard with her evillest stare, one she hadn't dished out to him since he was pursuing her heavily in their undergraduate days and she hadn't taken him seriously.

'I don't understand what's going on?' he said, looking confused and a little hurt. Pah! Of course he did; he was shameless.

'Boys, go to your rooms for a bit and yes, Rafe, you can go and see Sophie but don't work too hard or stay too late. Tell Jenny I said it's okay.'

'But you've seen each other all weekend, we want to see Dad too,' Rufus cried plaintively, oblivious to the bemusement on his father's face.

'And you can, but not right now. I need to talk to him… um… about birthday surprises…' Marion wracked her brains for something to say to get Rufus out the way.

He looked at her sceptically.

'Rupert.' Marion cast around desperately.

'Yes, of course – Rufus, come with me.'

He said in his sweetest of voices, 'Thing is, Mum, I'm trying to play *Fortnite*, I *need* a new skin and it's not accepting your card details. Have they changed?'

Marion looked at him. Computer games. Surely he could find something else for them to do? And then she remembered the recent *Fortnite* World Cup that had been all over the news, and the prize fund. Maybe it wouldn't be the end of the world, just for today, plus Rufus *was* scampering up the stairs in anticipation. Sighing, she opened her bag, undid her purse and wordlessly handed him her debit card.

Once the children had gone, Richard walked over to her and tried to take her hand. She started as if she had been burnt. She didn't want to even think where those hands had been and now he was laying them on her. He may be fresh out of the shower but it was going to take more than a quick wash before he was ever allowed to touch her hand again. She didn't think even a metal brush and some Jeyes fluid was going to be enough. Cleansing by fire was tempting though.

'Marion, what is going on? I don't understand. Claudia said you were in the flat but then you were gone, you didn't wait to see me, you didn't pick up when I rang. Why did you come up, why did you leave? When you didn't answer I pictured you upended and in a ditch. What is going on?' His tone was confused; Marion *used* to think that was adorable.

Marion raised her eyebrow at him and pinched her cheeks in, her lips forming the shape beloved of fishwives of old. It was really tempting to put her hands on her hips, but she still had a modicum of decency. But seriously, this was how he was going to play it, was it? As if she were a complete fool and he was an innocent. He really did know nothing about her, nor care, if he thought that was the best way forward. Fool of a man.

'If you *think* about it, Richard, it makes perfect sense. I came to surprise you for our anniversary, an anniversary you promised was as important to you as it was me, and yet I was the one surprised, I was the one with her world blown to bits. And all this time I have believed every word you have said, about how you'd be coming back to Penmenna, about how it was the Japanese deal that was keeping you away. I know better than that now.'

33

'What are you talking about? I am in Penmenna, I've driven here to check you're alive and safe and now I'm asking if we can sort out whatever is going on but I can't talk to you if you speak to me in riddles. You've been weird ever since last summer, Christmas was bizarre and now this. Look, Marion, I love you, I have always loved you, but I don't know what's going on.' Richard's arms were waving up and down with the energy of a windmill in a storm, and then he stretched them outwards as he tried to pull her towards him.

She resisted.

'We can get you help if you need it, if you need to talk to someone. You've always been so strong, so unbreakable but sometimes it's the boughs that don't bend that snap. If that's what is happening, I'm here for you.' He nodded his head to reinforce his point, his hands raised again as he tried to stress his concern. 'We can get you the best help available, you just have to say.'

Marion could feel her own frame shaking, shaking like his so-called bloody boughs in a force ten gale. How dare he? How *dare* he?

'Are you standing here in front of me now suggesting that, I don't know, that I'm in the midst of some kind of nervous breakdown, that my reaction makes *me* the mad one?'

'Noooo…' Richard drew out the word, in that way people have when they want to say yes but are worried about the tsunami of shit that would be unleashed if they did.

'Oh wow. I know I have many faults and for some reason, Richard, apart from what I had assumed to be a general sense of naivete, I thought you were pretty perfect, and now you are revealed in your truth, aren't you? Now we see you standing there trying to transfer the blame to me. Gaslighting, it's called, Richard, and I will not put up with it. *Will not.* The example you set and the way I react to your behaviour is what will shape our boys, the most important thing in my life. I will not have you shaping the attitudes they have towards women and relationships for the rest of their lives. They are not going to see me being manipulated and played like this; they will only ever see me behave with dignity and be treated in the correct manner. They are not going to see—'

'Mum… Mum…' A little head peered out amongst the polished white oak of the bannisters on the landing.

'Not now, Rufus!' Marion snapped. 'I'm busy!'

'He won't let me have a turn, he says I'm a baby.'

'Well, if you're going to come running to me then you are. Stand up for yourself; go and make him give you a go. Marksharps don't quiver.'

Rufus did quiver a bit and then dashed up the stairs again, making a war-like cry as he went.

Richard's mouth fell open. 'You talk about setting an example – why don't you just tell him to whack his brother and be done with it.'

'Oh do shut up, Richard, I have had just about enough of your nonsense. If you were any type of real man you would stand here, admit what you've done and we could carve out a plan but instead you just try and tell me I'm crazy. Not a good move, *Mr* Marksharp. Not a good move at all.'

'This is insane…'

'And there you go again.'

'I don't know what I've done!' Richard looked defeated, the frustration clear in his tone, then he became pensive. 'Is this about last summer when you took the boys to go and stay in Morocco with Hector? Is this what's going on? You've had an affair and now you're trying to blame me so you can jet off to Hector and his harem and live the life of Riley in the sunshine whilst I've been working my guts out with the Japanese...'

'Really? Really! If the damn Japanese were so important to you, why are you here now, huh? If you haven't been able to leave the Japanese for months, then how come now they're finally here you can hotfoot it down to Cornwall? Don't even answer the question. It's because of a guilty conscience, clear as day, and then you attempt to brainwash *me*. I don't know who you are any more but I do know you are not the man I thought I had married.'

Marion raged, still shaking and partially aware of the bedroom door decisively shutting upstairs, all her years of hard work and now this, her own boys hearing their mother shriek like a banshee at their father. It was fury that was driving her now, not guilt; she would not feel bad about this. She had worked herself to the bone on this marriage and this family and it was collapsing all around her through no fault of her own. He sleeps with his colleague and she gets accused of adultery! She wanted to launch at him, actually launch herself at him, stamp on his glasses and scrape his eyes out with her nails, pull his tufty hair until his face was streaming with blood and he was revealed for the weak, inconsequential man he really was.

'Marion, love...'

'Don't you dare.'

'Marion.' Richard drew himself up. 'I am here because I was worried about you. I have left the Japanese and come here to find you. I stopped at our college on the way down, spoke to all our old friends to see if they knew anything and then I drove down here to find you and yes, I have to drive back. I may get the sack for leaving and I very definitely will if I'm not back in the office at eight sharp tomorrow with cap in hand and penitent smile on and all I'm getting is the screaming madness of a woman who is making no coherent sense. If you're not having an affair or a nervous breakdown then I don't know what is going on. I just want to help you but I can't help you if you don't talk to me rationally. Look at you – you have lost all composure and I'm not sure who this woman screaming like a vixen and standing in my living room is.'

His living room? Did he carefully choose the exact shade of blue on these walls, did he scour the land looking for the perfect sofa, the just right accents that made it feel both stylish and homely? Did he feature in those articles for *Cornish Living*? Did he arrange for half the PTA to give up their spare time to paint this house so beautifully when that useless firm of decorators cocked up their diary? His living room? Was it, hell!

He took another step towards her, his face still the picture of confusion. Under any other circumstances it would have her grabbing him by the hand and racing up the stairs, or at the very least her heart swelling with love as she swore to protect this man from the cruel realities of life that he had always been so cushioned from with his cotton-wool privileged upbringing.

No longer.

No longer would she be fooled by outward appearances; that was her mother all along – as long as her suitors had a plethora of hair gel and honeyed words, no attention was paid to character. Well, Marion was not her mum and she was not prepared to be fooled for a second. Her whole life she had tended to this man, and look where it had got her. Being treated like a fool, and then being accused of insanity. No more. He could sod off with his plaintive looks, puppy-dog eyes and perfected air of confusion. Richard Marksharp was an astute businessman, he was pin-sharp in financial markets; she would not go along with his I'm-not-madly-emotionally-intelligent-but-I-am-madly-in-love-with-you bollocks any more. She looked at his hand, outstretched again, obviously thinking he could win this.

'Marion... love, maybe, maybe this does make sense after all.'

'Oh finally, does it. I'm glad. So, Richard, tell me now, tell me here and now what you think the matter is?' Her heart sped up, feeling like it could burst through her chest any moment. If he could just admit his wrong, if he had the respect for her to be honest now then they could forge ahead, put the needs of the boys first and work out the best plan of action. She didn't want to do battle; she just wanted a bit of respect and acknowledgement of all she had done and how badly he had betrayed her. Her breath caught in her throat. Was this going to be it? Could they find a way to be adult about this?

'I can't believe I didn't see it before but, Marion, you mustn't be frightened; we can see this through together – obviously me saying you were... um, well, struggling was wrong. And of course I don't think you've slept with Hector, not if I really think about it. But, Marion, if we're both just strong and firm in our love for each other we can see this through. After all it happens to every woman, to every relationship...'

Marion started to snarl; where was he going with this? This did not sound like the heartfelt abjectly remorseful apology she needed.

'Marion, it's only nature after all; every woman eventually hits the menopause.'

Chapter Six

Richard stood out in the street rubbing his head where Marion had broken her favourite vase over it. He wondered if he had a concussion. It was quite possible. He had always known his wife was a volatile woman; you only had to spend the night with her – or morning or afternoon – to know that. A rueful smile crossed his face; volatile was different to raging and aggressive and today she was very definitely the latter.

It had come from nowhere.

Normally she valued every item in the house far too much to destroy it; it was her overly emotional attachment to things that was one of the traits he found so endearing, an indication of her hidden vulnerabilities. But the wife he'd faced today, she hadn't seemed particularly vulnerable, and what's more, she had the aim of Eric Bristow.

He knew other people found Marion difficult at times, sharp, rude, overbearing, but he had always respected her. There was so much more to her than met the eye. But violent? She had never been violent before. That was never acceptable. If she was cross she drew up an action plan and exacted revenge in a way that benefitted her. She wasn't a shelf-sweeper, or a plate thrower. None of this made any sense at all.

He had felt dreadful cancelling their anniversary plans at the last minute, but Marion knew him, knew how much he loved her, appreciated the way she kept their home running whilst he was away. The plan was to earn enough money to enable him to retire early and spend the rest of his life with Marion, their boys and the dog doing exactly as they wished. He was so nearly there and had thought they agreed about this, that she had understood. *He* certainly didn't want to be doing a weekly commute to London from Cornwall; it was hideous. Exhausting. *He* would have been happy in a job earning less with more time spent at home. If, after retirement, he never had to step foot on a train or see a motorway again he would be very happy indeed.

But for Marion he was willing to do anything and if this was what it took for them to have their perfect life then so be it.

He knew she felt isolated on her own during the week; that was why she kept herself and the boys so busy. He had even bought her a puppy because he didn't want her to feel unsupported, left all on her own through the week. A puppy she could cuddle into in the evenings and see it as a daily reminder of how much he wished he could be at home.

His colleague Claudia had recommended the Weimaraner, promising him that they were the last word in dogs at the moment, the absolutely number one fashion for all in-the-know families. It had sounded like exactly the sort of dog Marion would want, even though he thought it looked as if it would grow rather large and dribbly. Mind you, far be it from him to understand what women wanted when it came to things like this. He had learnt a long time ago to just do as he was told. His mother had been very like Marion, a force to be reckoned with, although nowhere near as loving. She

41

had been cold whereas Marion's devotion to her boys, her family, shone through.

But something had changed recently, shifted. Their happy balance was suddenly off-kilter. Marion had become noticeably discontent with things. It had started off in small increments; instead of being as encouraging as she could be when they chatted in the evenings, she had started to lose her normal sangfroid, became upset, almost – she was very wary of letting her mask slip, even to him – when he had to cancel visits home. Then she had dashed off and spent all summer at Hector's house in Morocco, barely waiting for the boys to be finished in school before she had them on a plane and out of there.

Hector was a good friend; they had been to school together and then on to university and he trusted him with his life.

Just not his wife.

Hector had a mad crush on Marion when they were younger, when she had long blonde hair down to her bottom and the shortest shorts man had ever seen, which, combined with her nothing-can-touch-me attitude, was like catnip to a gaggle of privately educated boys from a single-sex school. But it was he, Richard, who had caught Marion's attention, though Hector had had a hankering ever since.

He rubbed his head again; there could well be a bump there the size of an ostrich egg by morning. Knowing that he had to hotfoot it back to London again and face his boss's wrath at him for skipping out on the weekend, there was a high chance the bump may soon become one of a matching pair.

Chapter Seven

What a day! Richard stood in the lift to his apartment really quite grateful to be there, ready to fall into bed after an epic journey back to London. He may not have solved the problem of his wife but at least he knew she was alive and safe, thus he could relax a little before tomorrow's big telling off, which would no doubt be accompanied by his P45. Then he could drive back down the motorway and try and resolve what needed to be resolved with Marion. As soon as he worked it out.

Tonight at least, what was left of it, was a comfy bed and no confusing messy emotions. He had never been sure how to respond to such things; it seemed in situations like these that whatever he said or did only made things worse. Although right now, he wasn't sure what could possibly be worse. He had spent the best part of twenty-four hours driving up and down motorways only to have the woman he loved more than anything else in the world bosh him on the head with a vase so expensive that the price alone would be enough to make most people's eyes water, let alone the impact.

As the lift came to a halt he couldn't help but think how lovely it was going to be having the flat to himself for a bit. His colleague, Claudia, had been there for ages and treated the apartment as her own, wafting around in negligees and silky dressing gowns with no apparent thought of Richard's presence at all as she sprawled across the furniture in the unseemliest positions.

Originally, he had let her stay when she had told him she had the decorators in and was planning to crash at a hotel for a few days whilst they were there. But after she had tearfully confided that she was having a bit of a cashflow problem he felt morally obliged to offer her a place to stay; that's what Marion would do. She was always the first to look after those in Penmenna, jumping in at all times to try and improve the lot of others. Claudia certainly seemed overjoyed that he had, so he had been pleased that he had called this right.

Then after the decorators she said it made sense to get the fumigators in, although she had never actually specified what she was trying to get rid of. She certainly didn't look like someone that lived somewhere with hard-to-beat infestations, but presumably that was the point of fumigators. That had been four days ago so he figured she would be home now, he would have the flat to himself and grab a few hours' sleep, a few hours where he wasn't plagued by women, either the one he had married or the one he worked with.

Sweet blessed relief.

The lift door opened and he walked into the hallway.

Eh? What on earth were these… were they rose petals?

What on earth were rose petals doing in his hallway? He followed the trail that was leading to his bedroom and his heart sped up. Could this be Marion's way of apologizing? Was she here to say sorry for being wildly unreasonable for no apparent motive? Reason kicked in to kill his momentary hope. No, not unless she had somehow chartered a helicopter. Had she chartered…? Of course not, and judging by the look on her face this evening she wouldn't be making an apology any time soon. There was bound to be an explanation of some sort. He just had to turn the handle and find it.

He placed his hand on the door, took a deep breath and pushed it open.

'Oh my good God! What do you think you're doing?'

There on the bed was Claudia, Claudia from *work* wearing very little, very little indeed. This would not do.

'Oh my goodness.' It occurred to Richard that he sounded like a frightened Miss Marple, only he figured Miss Marple may have a better idea of how to respond.

'Hello,' Claudia purred; it really did sound like a purr but one he imagined a lioness may make as she eyes up dinner. He shut his eyes.

'I think you should get out now,' he said in his politest voice. 'I don't know what you're doing or who you're waiting for but I really do need to… um… go to sleep.'

'Oh, Richard, I'm waiting for you, you silly boy. Always so proper; open your eyes and come over here. I promise I know a way or two that will help you sleep like a baby – it's just that I am rather stuck, you see.' He heard the rattle of metal upon metal and half opened an eye, his head cocked to one side. Oh my goodness, she had cuffed one of her hands to his bedstead. If Marion ever found out about this! His heart felt like it would burst through his chest any minute. What if Marion *had* chased him up the motorway to make amends after all? What if she walked in on this? He had to get Claudia out.

She sat there smiling like a cat eyeing a mouse, stretched one long leg out and dangled the key in her unbound hand. Aha, the key. That had to be the first stage. He had to get the key. Warily he opened his other eye and gave himself a pep talk; he had survived cross country at school – he could very definitely survive this.

'Um… I don't think I'm going to do that, can you… um… can you… oh dear, I don't think you're going to be able to angle yourself… oh dear.' He realized there was no way she was going to be able to undo the lock on her own and it occurred to him from the look in her eye she had no intention of untying herself and quietly leaving. *Waiting for you*, she had said. How on earth had he got himself into this situation? 'Um perhaps you could… um, throw me the key?'

'Well, perhaps I could.' She smiled. And then she dropped the key into her cleavage and winked. 'But then I've never been very good at doing what I'm told. In fact, I'm a very bad girl, very bad indeed. I need someone to punish me.'

Richard gulped. He suspected she may well be right. He also knew that he was not the man for the job. Neither was he brave enough to go over there and fish the key out of her bra. Truth was he suspected she may well overpower him and do goodness knows what. He had heard about women like this; they had been the fodder for many an adolescent dream. He just hadn't realized he wouldn't be so keen as an adult.

He'd have to think quick. What could he do? Perhaps he should ring Marion and ask her; she always knew what to do. No, no, that was a stupid idea, of course he couldn't do that. Um… um… arghhhh.

How could he have been so stupid? Of course! This was why his life had suddenly been tipped on its head. He opened his eyes wider as the realization dawned on him. Claudia must have been planning this all along. He wasn't sure why; he had spent hours after her last break-up

46

reassuring her that not all men were pigs and that he himself was devoted to Marion, how it suited him to have a wife he adored, that he could look after every day for the rest of her life. She must have said something to Marion when she came in the flat the other day. Must have.

That was something he could sort out easily enough. If this was why Marion was so cross, he could rectify it. He had never even as much as looked at another woman; he would just have to explain that Claudia was lying and, looking at the scene playing out in his bedroom, clearly completely bonkers.

His attention focused in upon the woman responsible for the stress of the weekend, currently writhing her bottom half across the covers as if she had ants in her pants, not that they would fit, and making the oddest moaning noises.

'Claudia...' he said tentatively. He thought he ought to check that she wasn't in any real pain, that the noises were just an effect she was trying to create rather than an actual medical condition.

'Yes, Richard,' she breathily replied.

'Claudia, I don't know what is going on here.' He made his tone firm as if he were disciplining one of his boys. It was discipline she had asked for – that he could do, just not the kind she wanted. 'Claudia, I am going to leave and find myself a hotel room for the night. I suggest you phone a friend' – he nodded to her mobile left out on the bedside table and within easy reach – 'and get them to come and unlock you. I will not be coming any nearer. And then I suggest you take all your stuff and go back to your apartment at once. I will see you at work tomorrow and we can pretend this never happened. However, should you ever, ever try this sort of thing again then I will not tolerate it. I shall… I shall take it to HR.' And with that bold and threatening speech made, he turned his heel on the woman currently dressed in not much more than a shoelace's worth of purple silk and for the second time in one weekend a member of the Marksharp family flounced out of the flat, temper high, into the waiting elevator.

Chapter Eight

Marion huffed out of the village towards Rosy's house the minute Richard had gone, channelling her fury to get her up the hill, not pausing to stop and look at the fields around her as the early signs of spring were appearing. Not for her the time to dally at the sight of the very first lambs out in the fields, standing close to their mothers, nor the early buds on the trees and the hint of hope, of birth, of new beginnings in the skies. Oh no, today may be Sunday – and a jam-packed one at that – but for the new reborn Marion, today was a day of business.

She grabbed a breath as she opened the little gate to the path up to Rosy Winter's cottage. Rosy was the headteacher at Penmenna School, where Marion's two youngest boys went and that Marion herself had been, up until this weekend, very actively involved in. Marion had never thought that much of Rosy – she seemed a little young for such a responsible post and a little too apple-pie. Marion never fully trusted anyone who looked as if butter wouldn't melt. But the battle to save the primary school from forced enclosure had arisen and at that point Miss Winter had showed her mettle and fought a jolly good fight, and they had gone from comrades-in-arms to sort-of-friends.

As they had been saving the school, Rosy had fallen in love with the very eligible Matt Masters, TV gardener and all-round good egg. Of course, Marion knew that when Matt had moved to the village he couldn't help but take a shine to Marion herself – he was a man with very good taste and Marion was such good friends with his sister, whom Matt had raised from when she was eight years old. But with Marion clearly devoted to Richard then Rosy Winter made a very good second best.

She chuckled to herself; her naughtiness did amuse her. And now she was on their doorstep ready and willing to make all their wedding dreams come true.

'Oh hello, how lovely to see you, shall I come in?' Marion greeted her hostess as Rosy came to the door and gave the headteacher a quick double air kiss before heading into the living room, a great big granite fireplace a nod to its Cornish history and two richly coloured but old sofas, both riddled with dog hair.

Ah, and there was the culprit. Matt and Rosy didn't have children yet so Marion bent down to make a fuss of their dog. It really could do with a good brushing. She beamed her friendliest hello at Matt, who smiled at her and put the garden supplement he was reading down.

'Who's a good boy, hey, good boy.' She ruffled the dog on the top of its little head and then beamed again at Matt as Rosy gestured with her arm to the opposite sofa. The dog just stared at her, unresponsive to the fuss she was making, is tail remaining perfectly static, its lip curling up a little at the corner. Perhaps it had been dropped on its head as a pup?

'So, Rosy, Matt, thank you so much for agreeing to see me.' Marion bestowed her most ingratiating smile as Rosy cut her a wedge of cake from the tin on the table. Cake? One hardly kept svelte with cake but she took the plate with just the right amount of jollity.

Matt quirked an eyebrow. 'From what Rosy said you didn't— ow!' Rosy dug her elbow into her fiancé and gave Marion a please-carry-on nod. She was a sensible girl.

'I've been putting a lot of thought into many things, life in general and just between us friends' – she grinned inclusively – 'I have decided the time may have come to change direction. All the boys are settled and in full-time school and as dedicated as I am to Penmenna School' – Rosy nodded in acknowledgement; there was no one in the surrounding community that didn't doubt Marion's commitment – 'the time has come for me to spread my wings.' Marion took a deep breath; did she want to admit the change in her marital situation just yet? She hadn't told the boys so should she now tell Rosy and Matt?

She decided against it. She didn't want to secure this job because they pitied her and whilst she chose to see herself leaving Richard because of his philandering as a strong move, a symbol of her unwillingness to put up with being messed around, she knew that society in general – no matter how much it had moved on – still seemed to see the wronged woman as an object of pity. Decision made to keep private things private for now, she ploughed on. 'So I have decided to start my own business and it occurred to me that the timing couldn't be better for either you or me.'

She looked across at Matt and Rosy, who were sitting opposite her and who both had smiles plastered on their faces but didn't look as enthused as she had expected. Did they not understand the opportunity she was offering them?

'That sounds like a fabulous idea, Marion, I'm very excited for you. But I am, um...' The headmistress swapped what could only be described as an anxious look with her partner, and Marion used the opportunity to slip a small piece of the cake onto the floor.

Scramble moved closer.

'…am unsure how we can help?' Rosy continued.

'Oh, dear, I don't want your help, oh no. On the contrary, I am here to help you!' They weren't looking convinced. 'Let me explain how. I have many skills as you know, but I excel at organizing events, making sure everything runs smoothly and pulling things together, preventing problems before they occur and adding finishing touches that make an average event extraordinary.'

'You do, that's undeniable. The Valentine's party you threw at Chase's house was outstanding. Do you remember, Matt?'

'I didn't really look at the décor that night but I do remember people talking about it for a long time afterwards. And I can't fault you in helping with the Save-our-School campaign; you were a… um… a force, that's for sure,' Matt added, swapping another look with his partner. More cake down.

'Thank you, Matt, and this is how I can help you. You and Rosy both lead very busy professional lives, but with love in the air and a wedding coming up I expect you are worrying about how you will manage to fit everything in.'

'I'm not really that w—' Matt yelped again; Rosy was most uncoordinated with her elbows.

'Sorry, Marion, please do continue.'

'As I was saying you must be worried about the huge responsibility for someone with your public profile, but if I stepped in as your events manager and, in this instance, wedding planner then all of that organizing would be off your hands. Ta da!' She imitated someone with a magic wand before continuing, 'All the bother-some details, dealing with the invitations, accommodation for the guests, seating arrangements, tricky relatives…' At this Matt's ears pricked up.

'Just a minute, Marion, are you saying if we have any guests that could be a little… um… demanding that you will take them in hand? Deal with all of their nonsense?' Matt leant forward. A sleight of hand and the last of the cake was on the floor.

Scramble came up and sat right next to her.

'Oh yes absolutely, all part of the service. Look, see how quickly your dog has warmed to me.' Taking in Hand was one of Marion's top five skills. 'I'm very skilled with people and dogs, particularly the difficult ones. But all the enjoyable bits, the bits you want to do then obviously you get to do those, you know, choosing the dress, picking the cake, the colour scheme and then I do absolutely every-thing else. You, Rosy, could drift through summer term without a single worry about your upcoming nuptials and you, Matt, could concentrate on the next series of *Green-fingered and Gorgeous* rather than having to worry about groomsmen suits, buttonholes or seating plans. Both of you enjoying the summer and knowing that the most important event of your lives was in *the* most capable hands.'

She paused for breath. Matt was sitting up straighter and looking at her with a very definite gleam in his eye. 'Now as you know I am well versed in making things look high-end; my eye for quality is unmatchable, I'm sure you'll agree. So, I can envision the perfect wedding for someone of your social standing, Matt, with your profile and your sister's. We can make it glitzy and glamourous, the wedding of the year and all completely stress-free and with zero inp— effort from you. I will find you the most perfect location, easily able to cater to all your showbiz friends.'

'I think we were rather hoping for a small intimate affair, Marion. We were going to have it in the village church. We've already spoken to Dan and Alice has offered to help...' It was Rosy's turn to lean forward to catch Marion's attention.

'Pshaw... Alice, what does she know? I mean, lovely girl, far more spirit than I ever realized but do you really think she has the skill set for this sort of event? Hmmm?' Marion paused to let that sink in. 'If you insist in having it in the church, um, let me think... romantic, country-living, traditional plus it's got the capacity for about two hundred guests I should imagine, we could easily fit in a string quartet if we tucked them at the back, yes, yes, we can make that work.' She pasted a grin on, but really. Alice as an advisor? That freezing cold smelly old church? Dear me, oh no, this would not do at all. This was to be her debut, her moment. Her own wedding had been a very small affair, bare and in no way the lavish extravaganza she had always pictured symbolizing the change from her old life to her new one.

'I'm not sure we'll have two hundred guests,' Rosy said.

'I'm fairly sure we don't want a string quartet,' Matt added.

'Oh, you are sweet.' She sighed and clasped her hands together, deliberately designed to conjure up images of weddings and marital bliss that would put Disney to shame. 'Of course you will. Everyone will want to come. And Matt, you may not *think* you want one but that's what I'm here for, to show you all the possibilities and then get them in place with zero stress to yourselves. It's going to be fabulous.' She just needed to get them to agree for now; the finer details could be sorted out later.

'But maybe a stuffed swan or two, could you do that for us? Five should do. Ow! Stop that!' Matt doubled over as Rosy faux-walloped him in the stomach.

'Marion, this is all very kind of you and there is nothing Matt and I would rather do than support you in your new endeavour, however...' Rosy interrupted her fiancé and her facial expression was not filling Marion with hope.

'I'm sure I could get you stuffed swans, Matt. Nothing is too much trouble.' How on earth was she supposed to do that? She was bound to be a crack shot but even she wasn't prepared to take on the Queen!

'I don't know, Rosy,' Matt moved a gentle hand to his fiancée's leg. 'I think this could work; I think this could be a *very* good idea indeed. Marion, no to the swans but as to the rest of it let us have some time to think it over and we'll get back to you in the next couple of days. How does that sound?'

That sounded like it was in the bag. Marion grinned and patted her knees with joy; she *knew* he had always had a soft spot for her. You could see who had the brains in this relationship.

Chapter Nine

With Rosy and Matt's wedding practically secured and lunch scheduled with Angelina for Thursday, Marion's nascent business was looking better and better and she couldn't resist feeling very pleased with herself. However, she still needed more clients. Nothing was secure yet so she wrote up a list of all potentials. Maybe she could check out Penmenna Hall, where Matt's TV programme was filmed, and see if they had anything planned that she could turn her hand to.

There was no harm in harnessing local events along-side the celebrity ones she was hoping to bag. They'd be writing features about her in the Sunday supplements before the year was out. Marion Marksharp, the events people's events person. She could see the strapline now, and the photoshoot. She quite liked working so far; she should have started this years ago.

Whilst she didn't really want to be dwelling on the matrimonial heartbreak that had led her to this point, she couldn't help but think that weddings seemed like a very good starting place. And with the romance that had been blossoming in Penmenna over the last couple of years, why should she stop at Matt and Rosy? Perhaps she could give some other couples a nudge, play Cupid alongside wedding planner.

And with Cornwall still being terribly chi-chi, she had the most perfect backdrop. If she could get Alex and Sylvie married, and maybe Pippa and Kam then that would be a strong start. Perhaps push Alice and Dan down the aisle; after all, he was a vicar – he shouldn't really be living in sin. Alice was staying at The Vicarage most nights and Marion doubted it was for further bible study. Ooh, at this rate she would have a drop-dead stunning portfolio of different types of weddings before the year was out. If she could just get Rosy and Matt to ditch their stupid idea of a small wedding then she could set them up at Penmenna Hall and throw a full-on country house, local gentry type of affair. She rubbed her hands in glee at the thought of all the media attention that one wedding alone would garner.

However, with the school disco this week, she needed to get into school and make sure everything was running to plan. Her ladies were well trained now, with Jenny having worked alongside her for the last five years; she felt they could organize the events seamlessly without her monitoring every last minute, although Marion did like popping in to keep them on their toes. A couple of times she had actually made them screech when she came in through the door or crept up behind them. She knew it shouldn't be so much fun, but it really was.

However, when her new venture really took off, and she had no doubt that it would, she may have to relinquish her PTA crown and trust the running of Penmenna School events to someone else. And unfortunately, despite having been her deputy for so long, she was not convinced that Jenny was queen bee material. An excellent worker bee but she just didn't have the verve, the spark that leadership required. No, Marion would need someone with bite and she was going to have to consider her replacement very carefully.

She pulled into the school car park and got out of the car when she spied another parent parked up, albeit sitting in the passenger seat and playing on their phone. Really.

She marched up and tapped on the window.

'Parents are not allowed in the staff car park; it's always been made quite clear. These spaces are needed by those with urgent business at the school or the staff. Please remove your car at once or I shall call the clampers.'

'But I—'

'No, no buts, a successful world is not built on buts, it's built on yes ma'ams – skedaddle, go on.'

Honestly some people. She marched into school to check in on how her ladies were doing and passed Alice, who was guiding one of the children and a parent into the car park. The child did look a little peaky; a greenish tinge accompanied a sick bag and worried-looking father. Alice… aha! She did need to speak to her about her new plans, but no, she'd let her get on for now. She had other people on the list to tackle first; it made no sense to go out of order.

She wandered into the corridor where the store cupboard was located, tucked at the back of the school where the PTA kept all the decorations, trestle tables and so forth. The Valentine's disco was one of the easier of the year's festivities, beaten only into second place by the harvest festival. There wasn't much that needed to be done: the decorations from last year were perfectly okay to be reused; they had been made out of fabric rather than paper and she had sent them home last week with Sarah to be washed and ironed, the jelly sweets needed to be bagged up, and Serena was overseeing her idea for Cupid's cupcake delivery.

'Jenny!' She didn't have anything to say particularly, but the woman jumped on the spot and dropped the red table decorations she was holding. Marion smirked.

'You need a bell.' Serena, the other woman standing with her deputy, turned and grinned.

Serena and Marion had not got off to a good start, with the two women going head to head over how the PTA was run and by whom when the younger woman joined as a new parent in the school. Marion had only won that battle because Serena was the woman behind the poison pen letters that had told her, truthfully as it was now proven, that Richard was having an affair. Serena's realization of how appalling her actions had been, albeit at the behest of that Claudia cow, and the knowledge that Marion had no qualms about trumpeting that far and wide had meant the woman agreed, reluctantly, to toe the line and accept Marion as the queen.

The meekness hadn't lasted long but Marion was developing a sneaking fondness for the woman that was peeking out; her determination reminded her very much of herself.

'We've everything under control here, Marion. We've bagged up the sweets into bags of ten, no more than one per child, and the tablecloths and floral decorations are ready to lay out in Kam's classroom. Jenny has all the decorations ready to hang as soon as Sylvie has finished in the hall.'

'Sylvie's in the hall?' Quick as a whippet, Marion spun on the spot and headed to the hall. Ah, she spied Sylvie teaching PE with Class Three in the hall. She had been number one on her list to see today.

'Hello, Sylvie darling.' She marched towards her and the whole of the class stopped to watch her. She knew she was a primary role model for the children in this school; they often stopped what they were doing when she came into a classroom.

'Hello, Marion. Carry on everyone, please.' Sylvie shot a smile across at her but kept her eyes on her class.

'Sylvie, I'm so very pleased to see you – I have some news that could very well make your life a lot easier.'

'Ah… okay, the thing is, Marion, I am teaching now.'

'Music and movement, is it? Very well – you, Harry, you're a good boy, aren't you, dear? How's that lovely father of yours, hmm?' It occurred to Marion that she was single now; all those delicious men she had admired from afar were now free game. That was a silver lining she hadn't considered before. It was a shame that Sylvie had captured Alex; after Matt he was by far the most sought-after man in the village. But such was life, and at least now they were an item she could use that to her advantage, which was exactly why she was standing here right now.

She felt herself gulp. Neither Alex nor Matt were a patch on Richard. The endearing little quirks of the man she had married filled her mind and she wanted nothing more than what she'd thought she had with him. She wasn't going to capitulate to her emotions now; she was doing brilliantly. She was *not* going to burst into tears in front of these children.

'Don't look so scared, boy. Here, you come to the front and be Simon says – you know, Simon says wave one arm and rub your tummy, that sort of thing. Excellent. Off you go.' She called one of the pupils to the front, her voice giving no hint of the turmoil coursing around inside her. And by using such a brisk tone she managed to pull herself together, focus in on what she needed to achieve in this moment.

'Marion, can this not wait?'

'Oh dear, no I don't think so. You see, I'm getting terribly busy already and I'd hate for you to miss out.'

Sylvie took a deep breath before asking, her eyes almost closed as she swung her head around, 'And what are you worried I'd miss out on, Marion?'

Marion moved her to the corner of the hall. Harry was doing a great job – only two children had fallen over so far. 'I've started up an events management company and we're getting booked up terribly quickly and I would hate for you not to be able to take advantage of me for your big day.'

'My big day?' Sylvie looked quizzical.

'Yes, dear, you've been dating for a while now, I'm sure wedding bells aren't too far off in the future, you know, you and Alex wanting to set the date.'

'Marion, Alex and I have no plans to get married. Is that what this is about? I must get back.' Sylvie's tone was firm; most unusual – she was normally all fey and fairylike.

'Aha, but you could have.' Marion had planned for this; she herself was fired up at the moment so happily launched into the offensive. 'This is the twenty-first century, a revolution in the time of sisterhood, of women taking power back, of standing up to be counted, to be heard. This is our time, Sylvie. This is your time.' Marion wondered if she should pound the wall to reinforce her point. Goodness, if the suffragettes had had her around, they would have achieved the vote at least twenty years earlier.

Sylvie's eyebrow went from mildly quizzical to sky high.

'Marion, do you need to sit down?'

'No, no, there's nothing wrong with me.' She batted Sylvie off her. 'I'm fine. I am merely fired up on the notion of sisterhood, of us banding together, taking back control.'

'Never did I not have control of my ow—'

Marion cut her off, her oratory high along with her passion, whether it be for her subject or her business it would be hard to call. Marion herself wasn't sure but she was enjoying herself. 'Moving forward, Sylvie, moving forward. There may have been no talk of marriage yet, but why wait for him to propose, why give him the power? Don't you want the security, the tax breaks?'

'I'm not waiting for him to propose, between us we have—'

'*You* ask *him* and then this is where I can come in and help. I can help you arrange the most beautiful marriage proposal, something that would speak to him, blow his mind, bowl him over so much that the only thought running through his head will be yes, yes, yes.' Sylvie wasn't looking convinced and had started to cast desperate looks over Marion's shoulder towards the class she was meant to be teaching.

Marion needed to refocus her and do so by appealing to a memory of when Marion's help had been personally useful. 'It will be even better than the time I helped Alex out with the belly dancing, the gesture that got you both together in the first place,' Marion said triumphantly. Sylvie couldn't help but smile and Marion could taste victory. 'And then I could help organize the wedding, take all the stress away and before you knew it you'd have a ring on your finger and all would be right with the world,' she finished, putting her most convincing facial expression on and cocking her head to one side as she waited for Sylvie's gratitude to pour forth.

'Well, Marion. That is all very interesting but I do need to get back to the children...' As if on cue, another three toppled in unison after being told to hop on one leg and clap behind their back. 'And I have no intention of proposing to Alex. You're quite right, this is the time for women to stand up, make their voices heard and be counted as we have been doing for a while and do you know what? I don't need a ring on my finger to do that.'

Chapter Ten

Monday morning was here and a bleary-eyed Richard wandered into the office, leaving behind streams of people racing from the Tube, the buses – schools of fish swimming with the tide. It made him wish, not for the first time, that he could spend his mornings waking up in Penmenna, walking the dog and making breakfast for Marion and the boys rather than being jumbled into the Tube, sweaty armpits and hefty bags walloping him in the face, carried along on a wave of bad temper and resentfulness.

Reaching MH Capital Holdings, he entered and took the lift up to his floor in the terribly chic streamlined glass building and wished for once that it was a little less modern, less open and visible, a little more Victorian.

He was dreading today. Not only would he have to face Claudia, who would probably want a public and bloody revenge after his rejection of her last night, but also Scott. Scott was his immediate boss, whose management style involved shrieking and waving his hands around wildly as flecks of sweat flew around the room, whilst everyone present held their breath in case he keeled over with a heart attack – more than likely when one considered his penchant for pork scratchings, doughnuts, call girls and cocaine. Hence the wish to hide, just for a minute or two, behind some dust-covered ledgers and perhaps arm himself with a pointy quill or two.

Meghan, his executive assistant, who resembled a young librarian with a smidge of Heffalump and a smudge of hair, was already at her desk. She had a sharp mind he admired and was a willing listener to his tales of a desperate weekend, how he had failed to meet with Mr Nakamura for drinks on the Saturday and instead spent his time trying to find his wife.

'But you met him in the office that day – what on earth happened between then and meeting them at the Ivy for seven thirty? You had it in the bag.'

'All sorts of craziness happened, that's what. I ended up chasing Marion down the motorway...'

'Marion, your wife?' She paused as he nodded in confirmation. 'You chased your wife down a motorway? What, like those crazy car chases you see on American news? Like OJ?'

'No, not exactly, not at all! It's a long story but I had to try to stop my marriage imploding so I raced to Cornwall on a bit of a wild goose chase.'

'Did you find her? Did you save your marriage?' Meghan sounded intrigued.

'No, no I didn't.'

'You're joking?' Meg's face fell. 'Not after your romantic dash and everything? Was she not bowled over by the romance of it?'

Richard shrugged and gestured to his forehead to show the remnants of where she had bashed him with the vase.

'Ah.'

'Yes.'

'Looks painful.'

'Uh-huh.'

'What did you do?' The concern was gone and there was a mildly affectionate men-of-your-generation-are-so-clueless expression on her face.

'I offered to get her help, I thought it might be the, you know...' he whispered, '*the change.*'

'And you said that whilst *not* carrying a tray with a cup of tea, some flowers, six bars of chocolate and a little bag from Tiffany's? Can I assume you had none of those things?'

'You can.'

'So boosh, you got a bump on the head. I'm fond of Marion and I know she's a sucker for a romantic gesture, you two are my relationship role models, but what on earth did you do that was so bad that she couldn't forgive?'

'It started when I cancelled our anniversary break because of the Japanese thing...'

'But she understands that, she's always been so supportive, far more than I would be under the circumstances.'

'Hmm, she did, she was. She decided to come up to London and surprise me in the flat so we didn't have to miss out on our weekend together, I think...'

'Oh, let me guess how this ends.'

'Go on.' Richard raised a brow. How could Meghan guess what happened next when it had only begun to form a clear picture in his own mind last night?

'You still had Claudia there, didn't you? Marion saw her and...'

'Exactly that. Do you know what, talking to you about this is really focusing me. All sorts have been running through my head, worrying about work, wanting to be with my family. But you're right, Marion has always been supportive, and now I'm left thinking what on earth am I doing with my life? Why am I back here? Mr Nakamura has signed the contracts despite me not being there, my bonus for landing him is ridiculous. I think I'm in the wrong place.' He looked at her. Why was he only just realizing he could change this, he could change it now? He had always said he'd take early retirement after this deal. He wasn't sure he was prepared to do that but there was no reason for Scott to know this.

'I think this has little to do with me; I think you came to that all by yourself. But you know what, sometimes you have to throw it all to the winds, mix it up a bit.'

'You do. I am. I'm going to be bold. I know what I want; I'm going to make sure I get it. Meghan, I'm going to miss you. If you ever need a bed in Cornwall…'

'I think that's what got you into trouble in the first place!' Meghan winked, safe in the knowledge of their friendship. 'Now stop cluttering up the place. Go see Scott, be bold, be brave, be free!'

Chapter Eleven

Persuading Sylvie to get married and quickly may not have gone exactly as she had hoped, and Marion had spent the last couple of days tracking down other potentials. She had accosted Alice with her we-are-women–hear-us-roar wedding proposal plan and had been laughed out of the staffroom as Alice pointed out that she and Dan had only been dating a couple of months and as committed as the two of them were, that was a bit quick.

Pippa had disappeared from the face of the earth, despite Marion checking every classroom and all the cupboards and loos, so she'd pencilled in nabbing her later.

But right now she was in one of Cornwall's swishest restaurants with her celebrity gal pal, Angelina Masters. She should have been having the best time but the truth was she felt as if she had used up all her bravado already this week. With Valentine's Day tomorrow, Richard repeatedly ringing her and her repeatedly refusing to pick up, she was feeling the strain of maintaining the pretence that she was starting a business merely because the boys were old enough now. When all she wanted to do was scream, so loud that it jettisoned the moon out of its orbit, that this business had begun because her husband was a duplicitous toad.

This feeling of gloom, resentment and unending sadness wasn't helped by the fact that she had the locksmith coming to change the locks this afternoon and that she, unlike all the other people in the village, didn't seem to have a girlfriend that she could confide in, pour her heart out to. She had never felt the lack of this beforehand, always smugly reassuring herself that she was lucky enough to have a husband for that sort of thing; that had come back to bite her on the arse.

She had hoped that when she saw Angelina this lunchtime the woman may offer her a shoulder as well as satisfying her new business needs but alas they had been here for half an hour and so far Angelina had kept up a relentless steam of '…and then we went… and I said… and I bought… and I demanded and I… I… I… I…'

The monologue was broken by the beep of Marion's phone. Her heart sped up as she looked at the message, only calming when she saw it was Matt and not Richard. Matt was texting to confirm he and Rosy would be very happy if she would help them with the wedding. She felt like punching the air. She was up and running!

She broke Angelina's monologue to tell her the news.

'Oh, darling, how fabulous, although such a bore that you have to work. I'm not surprised my brother has said yes; for someone so constantly muddy he can at times be quite brilliant. We'll have to make it the most glamorous… scratch that, he's marrying Rosy, isn't he? Okay, vaguely glamorous wedding Cornwall has ever seen – you and I will just have to step up, be the glitterati. Mind you, that shouldn't be hard.' Angelina cackled as she threw her head back to quaff the glass of champagne in her hand and Marion felt another flash of sadness.

This was how it was now. She had found that as long as she kept busy during the day she was coping until she would suddenly be caught by a wave, a memory triggered by a word, a phrase, a view. It would be as if someone had dealt her a blow to the solar plexus, the memory accompanied by a sharp intake of breath. The nights were far worse.

Angelina didn't notice and carried on talking in her high-pitched tone. Marion had noted before that her pal lacked any kind of empathy.

She continued to squawk for another five minutes before saying, 'Now let's stop talking about me.' Finally. Marion tried not to sigh with relief. 'It was lovely to lunch, it's been simply ages, but you did say you were hoping for a favour? As you know, darling, time is precious – what was it you wanted?'

Before Marion had a chance to answer, Angelina had turned to one of the young waiters walking past, waving her glass at him as she spoke and pointing to the champagne bottle on the table. 'This was finished some time ago and now so is my glass, so I'm having to take time out of my conversation to ask you to do your job. Another one please. And preferably within the next few minutes – no nipping off for a fag or flicking through the *Beano*, there's a good boy.' She turned back to her friend. 'Honestly, Cornwall. One wonders what the point is? I have no idea why Chase insists on spending so much time here.' She waved her hand extravagantly around her and Marion fought to keep her eyebrow in place. She was very fond of Angelina; the girl was a raging success in everything she did, her perfume had just become the number one bestseller on the high street and she was currently designing a range of sunglasses. But honestly!

They were sitting in a restaurant that was three sides glass, overhanging the ocean and surrounded by the majesty of the cliffs and the rocks, the sky bright blue and crisp, the reflection of the sun making the sea sparkle. It was pretty damn perfect. Marion knew she had her faults but she was loyal to this county. Her own beginnings meant she loved every inch of this coastline, every crag and rock, every sandy beach. Why, once she and Ri— boom, and there it was again. She took a hefty swig, emptying her own glass as the terrified teen brought another bottle over, a bead of sweat running down his brow as he popped the cork. Marion did hope this was the last bottle of the day. Angelina liked a drink and was particularly fond of ones at everybody else's expense whereas Marion was going to have to cut her cloth according to her means for a while.

'I'm glad you brought it up, I wanted to talk to you…'

The boy slid the new bottle into the ice bucket, and walked backwards, as if they were dangerous beasts he had to keep his eye on. He could be right.

'Ha, I expect we made his day. It's not often they get a mega star in this shabby little place.' Marion wasn't so sure. Rumour had it that Robbie Williams and Ayda Field had hired this venue for a private party just last month on Elton John's recommendation, Kylie had been spotted in here at the weekend of her Eden Project gigs and the restaurant did have a helipad attached.

'Quite, I expect he'll be talking about it for years to come,' Marion managed to say. She was a born business-woman; schmooze should become her middle name.

'Probably.'

'I asked you here today because I am about to break into something new…' She flew into her spiel about being a brave independent woman that knew the world of business, Angelina was absolutely right, Cornwall did need a little livening up and that she, Marion, was the woman to do it. 'And I am not a stupid woman, I know

71

the key to any kind of success is having that special sparkle...' Oh shit, she shouldn't have said that – what if Angelina thought she meant drugs? She did *not* mean drugs. 'That... um... X-factor that only the very select few can bring. That *je ne sais quoi* that *you*, Angelina, are the absolute queen of. So, I'm asking you to throw a huge party, a great big event and let me do it for you. Then you can tell everyone how wonderful I am and the world will bow at your feet for throwing the party of the decade. I can and will get you everything you want to ensure, *ensure* it is the most talked-about event of forever!'

'Let me think. It's Valentine's Day tomorrow, isn't it? That would be cute, could you throw Chase and I a Valentine's party? It's the anniversary of when we met, when you got us together. Wouldn't that be lovely?'

Marion's heart sank; she may well be a superwoman, the new queen of every ball, barbecue and blow-out on the block, but a Valentine's party tomorrow, with Angelina's friends in attendance? Because woe betide her if any of Angelina's guests couldn't make it to Cornwall with one day's notice; that would definitely be considered her fault.

However, Angelina Masters *was* hot property and she needed her onside. Suddenly inspiration hit. Why not? The idea was pure genius – the trick was to sell it to Angelina. The woman didn't like sharing the limelight with anyone, but if she could persuade her to marry Chase, and not just marry him but have a shared wedding with her brother then the celebrity exposure would be huge. It genuinely would be the wedding of the year, like a royal wedding but bigger, better. The TV gardener that everyone loved to love and the opinionated celebrity that everyone loved to loathe, two siblings respectively marrying a schoolteacher and a multi-billionaire self-help guru. This would make TV gold; she could sell the rights and live off the merchandising for years.

She turned to Angelina, her face alight with possibilities.

'You've perked up; you've been very bleurgh since you arrived today. Can I take this to mean you'll have a party for us in place for tomorrow?'

No, it blooming didn't, but what she would have time to organize, if she didn't sleep, was an intimate, private engagement. A moment just for her clients alone – with an announcement that would break Instagram and rack up a whole heap of followers for Marion.

'Possibly, but I have a much simpler idea, an idea that could shape your life forever. An idea that would be the final step to shaping you into an international icon for the ages. An idea that would mean when people searched for the words perfect, romantic, feminist, bliss, inspirational and so on, then a picture of you and Chase would come up. You and Chase under an arch of love accompanied by all the people in your life who love you, adore you, idolize you, even.'

Angelina sat up and put her drink on the table as she held Marion's eye keenly. Marion fixed her gaze upon her friend and then leant over and whispered, so as to make her come closer and really listen. 'Let me talk to you about womanhood in the twenty-first century.'

Chapter Twelve

Marion sidled around the staffroom door. Aha, as she had thought! Jenny and Serena were there, the latter cutting out the last of the hearts for this evening as Jenny served her coffee. Marion smirked at the scene in front of her. She needed to choose between these two, decide which one was suitable for succession and so far Jenny seemed to be unable to step out from second in command. Marion's theory was reinforced as Jenny passed Serena the coffee with an obsequious smile. Serena accepted graciously and carried on cutting out the hearts, making sure each one was perfect.

'Are you finished?' Marion hissed from behind the door jamb. Jenny let out a scream but only for a second before she put her hand over her mouth.

Serena didn't even look up.

'Hello, Marion, yes, pretty much done. We can never have too many hearts.'

'Excellent, in that case can you delegate all the finishing touches to someone else? If I remember rightly Rosy likes cutting out heart shapes, does a fabulous job. Then come and meet me outside in the school car park for A Very Important Job?'

This did cause Serena to react, placing down her scissors and turning in her chair. 'Now that, Mrs Marksharp, is something I like the sound of. A job that sounds like an adventure – Jenny?'

'Yes, yes, of course, Serena, Marion. How long will we be out for?'

'For goodness' sake, woman, as long as we need to be. I'll see you by my car in five.'

Marion marched away, irritation clear in her step. As if Jenny was going to have anything more important to do.

It was becoming increasingly clear to her that Jenny, despite having been groomed for the top dog role for the last few years, just wasn't going to make the grade. Jenny was good at barking out instructions when given permission to do so, fixing people (other than Marion) with forceful stares and collecting money. But leadership skills, they were something very definitely lacking.

Serena was shaping up to be far more interesting.

By rights Marion should hate her vehemently. Serena had committed heinous crimes against her. But Marion had learnt a thing or two over the past few years and was trying to apply it to life. Especially now she had learnt that everything could turn upside down in a fraction of a second.

She had never been a woman with many friends, certainly not female friends – either at school or university. She had always been drawn to men, enjoying their humour. Men were easier to understand; there seemed to be fewer complex codes shooting between them. If they liked you, they liked you, and if they didn't then they didn't bother. There was little of the covert one-upmanship that she associated with women. Men just bought bigger watches or cars if they had something to prove. Women were far more nuanced: they would pretend to be your friend and stab you in the back. Claudia being a perfect example.

Being involved in Penmenna School had taught her something about friendship, how it was formed over time and over events shared – ooh, she'd have to use that in her marketing. Everyone had different skills and brought something else to the table; the female friendships she'd seen here were collaborative and supportive, undermining the assumptions she had made before.

Some of the women working at the school had started to pierce her armour – she liked Rosy, respected Sylvie and had learnt that Alice was far more gutsy than she had given her credit for. And whilst she was still firm in the knowledge that she was the most efficient, and probably the smartest of them all, she now appreciated there were many ways to success that didn't necessarily include having the loudest bark.

Not everything was black and white, and Serena was a great example of that. At first glance Serena looked perfect. A deeper look revealed considerably more. Marion knew that Serena was insecure in her standing in the village as a relative newcomer but was willing to sacrifice her own reputation to ensure her child got the best care and education. Playgroup had labelled her a troublemaker and Marion knew from experience that didn't happen unless you were prepared to do battle.

If you applied those principles deeper – for Serena, Marion had – and looked at the poison pen letters Serena sent last year, a first glance would reveal someone who gained pleasure from inflicting pain. But at second glance those letters showed a woman who had placed loyalty to an old friend over doing what she thought was right.

Marion could understand loyalty.

What you saw with Serena wasn't necessarily what you got. And even better, the woman had sass. She did her duty and did it well, efficiently and with a smile but baring her teeth when required. Marion liked that. She wanted to know more. And today she was going to.

Chapter Thirteen

'We've got an awful lot to do,' Marion informed Serena as she sat in the car beside her. Jenny had been given the keys to the van and told to meet them at Chase and Angelina's. Jenny had been to the hard-to-find house before when Marion had staged a massive Valentine's party when Chase moved to Cornwall two years ago. She'd been harping on about a repeat invitation ever since. So now she had one, albeit only in the capacity as Marion's helper – the event she was planning for tonight was only for an audience of two.

And it was going to take a lot of help.

'Then it might be useful if we get there alive,' Serena retorted as she clasped the dashboard. 'Seriously, Marion, slow down.'

'It's quite alright, dear. I do know these lanes like the back of my hand.'

'Yes but whatever is coming the other way may not. And I don't think 60 mph is a sensible— arggghh...' She paused, closed her eyes and let out a long sigh as Marion sped around a hairpin bend. '...sensible way of driving down them.' Her voice got louder, and faster, as the sentence continued. 'Seriously, has no one ever told you this before? I swear I'm going to make you stop this car and get out and walk... oh my God, brace, brace!' Serena's right arm flashed out in front of Marion – that age-old trick of mothers across the world when in a car and sensing imminent danger – as a tractor suddenly came from a side road.

'I never had you down for a wuss,' Marion countered as she hit the horn heavily in fury.

Eventually, Marion turned into the driveway that led to Chase's house. Serena's mouth dropped and her eyes widened as they drove down the long, long driveway, pulling into a traditional half-moon gravelled entrance in front of an exceptionally modern, large building that screamed wealth, exclusivity and status. Three of Marion's favourite screams.

'Right, let's get out, chip chop. We've got an awful lot to do and not much time. Ah, Jenny, good of you to join us. Serena, do close your mouth, I know it's very grand but you'd better get used to it. You're in the A-Team now.'

Serena raised an eyebrow at Marion but couldn't help herself. 'I do love it when a plan comes together.'

'I'm Hannibal, dear, you can be… um… any of the others. If you both make a start unloading the van, I shall go and find the client.'

'The client?' Serena asked. 'Is this not school stuff?'

'Ho ho, dear, oh no, we've left that with the other ladies. You two have been specially selected to help me today, me and my very special celebrity friend. I haven't had a chance to tell everybody so I would appreciate if you didn't just yet, but you see standing before you Marion Marksharp, Cornwall's latest business mogul and premier events manager.' She flexed her muscles and giggled. This was all so exciting.

'So not school stuff then?' Serena did not look pleased or particularly excited, folding her arms and cocking her head to one side.

'Oh, how exciting, Marion, of course I always knew you'd be brilliant in business. What are we doing?' Jenny, on the other hand, was reacting properly, jumping up and down on the spot and clapping her hands. A little bit like a seal that perhaps wasn't as bright as his brothers, but suitably enthusiastic nonetheless.

'Thank you, Jenny dear, you've always been so loyal.' The blonde woman puffed up with the praise. It was a rare occurrence.

Serena arched an eyebrow. Marion decided to ignore her surliness; some women didn't appreciate an opportunity when it was presented. Such a shame – if only she could somehow meld the two women together then she would have the perfect person to take over her PTA crown when she retired.

She directed the women to unload the things from the van and pointed out the entrance to the winding path down to the beach, hidden in the shrubbery, before running in to check that Angelina was still keen on the plan. She was, although making a dreadful fuss about the importance of having her hair exactly so. Whilst Marion attached huge import to personal grooming, she was finding Angelina particularly irritating today. Although she supposed it must be quite a nice thing to be so secure that the only concern you had when you were about to propose was that your fringe wasn't sitting right.

With her client suitably reassured, Marion headed back to join Serena and Jenny to make sure everything was set up perfectly for the evening.

It was as she was on the beach, the wind building up and whipping around their heads, amplifying the tang of seaweed and the squawk of seagulls, that her ringtone pierced the air. She saw Richard flash up *again*, his brown eyes and slightly hapless look filling the large screen. This face had so endeared him to her when they first met; he always looked as if he needed rescuing when the truth was he had been *her* rescuer.

Hold on, him? Your brain and hard work! You didn't just pitch up at Oxford because of chance; you worked hard. She needed to change the narrative here. As much as she liked the idea of teenage Marion being rescued by her very own Prince Charming, it wasn't strictly accurate and if she was going to feel a pang of heartache every time his picture flashed up on this screen then she needed to change that as well – maybe to a picture of someone drowning kittens or socks with sandals, something that would repulse her every time he rang.

'What?'

'Marion, darling…'

'Don't darling me.'

Richard sighed. 'Look, I'm standing outside the house, the keys aren't working. For a second or two I doubted myself, but you've changed the locks. Changed the locks to *my* home, Marion. That's harsh. I wanted to be here to see the boys when they got in; I've got some good news to share. News that might change everything.'

'Pfft. Of course I've changed the locks, and unless your news is that you've dipped your willy in so much TCP that it has dropped off, I don't want to hear it, and even then you still wouldn't be getting a key. You have your love nest in London. Why on earth would I let you see the boys?'

'Because they're my children. Honestly, Marion, if I thought a quick TCP wash was the solution then I'd happily bathe in the stuff, drink it even. But I know you're going to want more than basic-level torture so let's talk…'

She fought to keep the smile that was playing at the corner of her mouth at bay. He was right. There wasn't a single soul in the world that knew her as well as he did – knew her, understood her, and celebrated it. She drew on all her self-control to stay silent because if she spoke, teased as she wanted to, he would hear the smirk and recognize it as a chink in her armour.

Richard continued, 'We're both adults, we want the best for the boys and that means doing this civilly. Could you come and let me in? Please.'

Marion wasn't a complete monster. He *was* the boys' parent too; they loved him. She was a big believer that her relationship with Richard would set the tone for the boys' formations of relationships later in life. Plus, she needed someone to sit with them tonight whilst she helped Angelina with her proposal. But if he thought he was back in and sharing her bed then that wasn't happening. Not a chance.

'Right, yes. Give me an hour…' She looked at Jenny, who was winding red roses around the Bali bed that Chase and Angelina had on the beach. 'Give me an hour and a half and I'll meet you and we can talk. And if you want you can see the boys this evening, I won't be in anyway – I have a very romantic evening planned…' She said the last bit airily; no harm in making him think that she was an international woman of mystery. It *was* going to be very romantic so it wasn't a lie-lie. 'But you cannot, absolutely not stay there. I am finding this difficult enough; it's been very traumatic for me and we need to talk things out and you moving back in and acting as if nothing has happened will not help either of us long term.'

'But nothing did happen! I never moved out!' The exasperation was clear in Richard's tone. 'It's my home…'

She heard his deep breath and knew he would now centre himself; he was not a fan of emotional outbursts and this phone call was enough to finish him off. 'It's okay, I'll ask Chase if I can stay for a few nights.'

'No!' Marion squeaked. 'No, you absolutely cannot stay with Chase.' Trust Richard to come back to Penmenna after all these months away and immediately throw a spanner in the works of her new business. 'You'll have to stay with Alex, just for tonight.' She changed her tone. Barking at him wasn't going to work as effectively. If she wheedled he'd be more receptive; he'd think it reflected a softening. 'Please, ask Alex, just for this evening.'

'Okay, and I'll see you at home in an hour and a half, spend the evening with the boys and tell them a bit about what is going on. They must be so confused.'

Marion thought they probably hadn't noticed much of a difference – Richard had been absent and she had been doing all the work. Fairly standard. The boys would need to be told, when it was appropriate. Today was not that day.

'Yes, we can talk, that sounds sensible. I'll…' She was about to say *look forward to it*, but it wasn't true, so she stopped the words in time. 'Um, I'll be there. Goodbye, Richard.' She pressed the red icon, ending the call, but there was a poignancy to the *Goodbye, Richard* that threatened to overwhelm her if she didn't get control of it very soon indeed.

She closed her eyes and counted to three. She could do this. She could do all of this; she was Marion Marksharp.

Opening her eyes, she saw that Jenny had got all the roses at the wrong angle – dear Lord, help her. She was working with imbeciles. 'Jenny White, what on earth do you think you're doing? Were you really born this stupid or does your brain just leak out of your ears in small increments? Perhaps if I attached a bowl each side like earmuffs we could keep the bulk of it in, hmmm? Hmmm?'

Chapter Fourteen

Richard stood outside of the house feeling a bit of a fool. He quite literally didn't know where to put his hands and feet to look as if it were perfectly natural for him to be waiting outside his house for his wife to let him in. Even the pint he had just sunk in The Smuggler's Curse wasn't making this any easier, although it had been good to catch up with Alex and Chase.

Both had been in the village when he messaged them, and as luck would have it both were together at Alex's house looking at this year's fundraising plans for Alex's foundation in South Sudan and how they could best support everyone as the country struggled with a huge influx of locusts. Both were very happy to break and join him in the pub for a quick pint.

There had been a tricky bit when the assumption was he was back to take Marion out for Valentine's Day, and he had not only had to correct it but tell them he was booked into a hotel in Treporth Bay and that he something else that she had disclosed was romantic and very definitely didn't involve him. When Marion had spoken to him on the phone he realized that he couldn't really stay with either Chase or Alex tonight because of the day it was.

There was only one thing worse when your marriage was disintegrating in front of your eyes and that was spending time with people who were still madly loved up, which both of his friends currently were. Alex he could understand: he was bowled over by Sylvie, who worked at the school, an ex-ballerina; she was pixie-like but had a strength to her that belied her tiny stature and wispy red curls. But Chase's girlfriend was a nightmare, and Richard was used to high maintenance. Each to their own and all, but still. Watching either couple this evening would be horrible – feeling like a spare wheel and wishing he was curled around Marion, revelling in their crisp white sheets and smugness of a relationship that spanned twenty years.

But now he was here on the doorstep and she was not.

Just as he was thinking this, he saw her car pull up, careering around the corner in that terrifying way Marion had of driving when she didn't have the boys in the car.

'Had to drop Serena off.'

'I thought you hated Serena?' Richard was puzzled as she stood in front of him, her body angled away so he couldn't make any kind of move to greet her, give a cuddle or even a chaste peck on the cheek.

'Well it turned out she knew more than I did. Lots of things aren't as they were, Richard,' Marion muttered at him darkly as she held the door open. 'I suppose you had better come in.'

As they walked into the living room the dog came bounding out and nearly knocked him over as he jumped up, placing both paws on his shoulders and trying to lick his face.

'Get down, Darcy.' He laughed. 'So good to see you.'

'He thinks you've got food. Get down now,' Marion said dismissively, before using her sternest voice on the dog, who slunk down and lay at Richard's feet instead, fixing him with mournful eyes as if to say *please come back and rescue me*.

Richard wondered if he should just slink down and lie on the floor as well until Marion forgave him.

'Right, do take a seat.' She gestured towards the sofa and used her most formal tone. He knew Marion. He knew the barkier she got the more insecure she was feeling. He gave the dog a ruffle on its head and then held his hand out to Marion, a let's-just-stop-all-of-this-right-now gesture. A plea. She ignored his outstretched hand and gestured briskly at the sofa instead.

He decided his best bet was to play along. He thanked her and perched on the edge of the seat and fiddled with his glasses.

'Aren't the boys going to think it's a bit weird that we're not spending tonight together, that I'm with them and you're out?'

'Nope, not at all. Rupert and Rufus will be at the school disco until seven o'clock and will be far more concerned about whether they can get Sarah to break the no more than ten sweets per child rule.'

'And Rafe?'

'Rafe is almost a teenager, in case you had forgotten; he doesn't think of anyone other than Sophie White at the moment. They know I have a new business to run and won't be at home as much as I was for them. They're fine with that. It's important to show them that women are dynamic, forceful innovators in the workplace and not limited to being stay-at-home mothers.'

Had Richard entered some kind of parallel universe or something? Was the myth behind science fiction actually proving itself here and now, unravelling the world order here in Penmenna in February?

'What new business?' He was fairly sure no one would ever think of Marion as anything other than dynamic and forceful. It had definitely been said, although perhaps not quite so politely.

'Well, now I'm a single parent…' Marion sniffed and perched on the other end of the sofa, pulling herself up to her full sitting height as she did so.

'You're not a freaking single parent – I'm here. I am right here.'

'I am actually and I have been for a while. It is rather typical that now as I'm embracing it you decide to turn up in the village mid-week. Always contrary, Richard.'

Richard was many things and, he hoped, a man aware of his flaws. He was fairly sure contrary wasn't on the list. He decided to change tack.

'How have you explained changing the locks to them?'

'A recent spate of burglaries.' Marion's lips shot straight back into their pursed expression when she had finished talking, nose still held high in the air. He had to give credit where credit was due. She played wronged wife beautifully.

'Has there been a recent spate of burglaries?' he asked, a little alarmed. 'There hasn't been one for a few years, and even then we both knew that Rafe had everything that had gone missing stashed in the shed.'

Marion fixed him with a narrow-eyed glare. 'Such a good boy. *So* kind of him to look after his things for his friend. His worst mistake there was being too loyal to a bad sort.'

'Oh come on, Marion, it's me. I am in the circle. I know the truth of our sons.'

'Not any more you're not.'

'Right, okay.' Richard felt a huge sigh leave his body. He was trying to be reasonable, but easy was definitely not Marion's middle name. Her feisty fighting spirit which she twinned with an air of insouciance was both contradictory and so goddam appealing. He was so proud that she hadn't diminished as she aged. If anything, she had become more Marion, although one would never have thought that possible. And he *loved* her.

'Look, let's start again. We have lots to talk about and we need to deal with what is going on here, the important stuff. Maybe just put our egos to one side and try...'

'I think it was putting our *ego*s in places they shouldn't be is what got us here in the first place, Richard.'

'Well, it wasn't mine! I haven't done anything I shouldn't have.' He was exasperated.

'It was certainly something of yours, and I find it hard to believe ego wasn't involved. Albeit not as much as your d—'

'Marion, please. Let me talk — I think I know what's going on now. I came home the other day to find Claudia tied to the bed...'

'Are you joking me? You're sitting here, expecting me to listen to this? Oh my God Richard! I always thought for all your faults you had a degree of sensitivity and now you're regaling me with tales of your sexual—'

'No, no, no, no!' Maybe that wasn't the best way to have started what he was trying to say. 'I realized that on the day you came to the flat...'

'On our anniversary weekend?'

'Yes, yes. On our anniversary, I realized that Claudia was present and that she must have said something to you. You know me, Marion, you know me better than any other person on this planet.' He made a grab for her hand and for a second she let his fingers curl around hers, trying to hide the fact that she had gulped a little. Then she shook her head decisively and pulled her hand away. Richard ploughed on.

'You know I'm a bit naive, a bit stupid, sometimes too trusting; that's one of the reasons we are such a good match – you protect me and I soften you. On that day Claudia must have said something to you and I don't know what it was but recent events have given me an inkling and I promise you, I promise you there is nothing going on.'

Marion turned to him, a tear running down her cheek and he could feel himself beginning to well up, seeing her so upset. His wife, the boldest and bravest of them all was now sitting in front of him upset and he thought it might break him.

This was not something he was used to dealing with. He took his finger to the tear to brush it away and she shook her head again, pushing him off. 'You can't believe her over me, Marion, really you can't.'

–

Marion wanted to believe him so desperately, so, so much. To turn the clock back, to go back to the way they were, but she didn't dare. She was not going to be that woman who forgave her husband time and time again as he shagged all around the country. Safe in the fact that he could so with impunity, confident in his good wife waiting uncomplainingly at home. She would not do that.

She remembered the letters Serena had sent:

Your husband doesn't come home for a reason.

She remembered the words the woman had spoken when she described the love Claudia had for her husband. No one felt like that about someone without something going on, not unless they were completely unhinged, and

Claudia was a very successful hedge-fund manager so she had to be pretty damn stable.

She remembered her mother's upturned face as she forgave waster after waster.

She remembered Hector, Richard's best friend, saying over the summer how he had always respected Richard for being faithful for years when, as far as he was concerned, it went against the basic fundamentals of male sexuality. She had pooh-poohed him at the time, pitying him for being of such a mind, of lacking the depth, the maturity of her husband. Maybe Hector knew more about it than she did.

'I'm sorry, Richard, I don't believe you. I wish that I could but the facts speak for themselves. If you're here to tell me that you have evidence that you haven't done anything wrong then fine, show me. I've an awful lot of evidence to suggest that you have.'

'I don't know what to say. I'm innocent. I can't provide evidence of something that didn't happen, because it didn't happen! It's an impossible task. Why... how could you believe her over me? You and me forever, come on.' He pushed his glasses up his nose.

'Richard, I want to believe you, I do.' She paused; everything she was saying was true, absolutely true, and she was crumbling inside knowing that the weaker she felt the stronger she had to appear. 'But I can't take the gamble. I haven't got it in me to go through this another time. We're done. Done. There is no trust left.'

And with that there wasn't much more to be said.

Chapter Fifteen

She managed to get him to agree to not tell the children yet – who wanted Valentine's Day tarnished with memories of their parents announcing their divorce? Talk about impacting future views on romance, and at the moment they were doing quite nicely.

She knew Rufus had taken a teddy bear clutching a heart for Freya in his class today – she knew because she had bought it. She had also paid for Rupert's vast array of cards – her second son had sent out about ten cards all with a question mark inside; he had always been a boy who liked to hedge his bets. He'd also popped his initials on the back. He figured the smart ones would work it out and approach him, thus cutting out those not capable of critical thought.

She was less sure about Rafe but with the amount of time he had spent with Sophie recently and the moony grins on his face when he walked home afterwards, she was fairly sure he would have prepared something for today.

Richard's attempt at a present this year was far too little and far too late.

Ooh, Marion could feel her temper rising as she thought of Richard and Claudia and tried to talk herself down. She'd just done her make-up and had needed to slap a little more on than usual, meaning she was a bit *Real*

Housewives, but make-up had been a weapon of hers for some time, providing her with a confidence, a swagger, that she often only faked. She was not leaving the house looking as if she was out of control of anything.

It was a weird feeling, driving out of Penmenna. Usually she would be entrenched in the school hall by now, making sure that the Valentine's dance ran as smoothly as it could and that none of the children were so hyped by being in the school after hours that they were hanging off the climbing bars or walloping each other with rulers – two things it seemed primary school children really liked to do when excited.

It was nerve-wracking leaving it in the care of the other members of the PTA, but this was her life now; she was going to have to step away. Some of these women had been in training for years now. They should be able to cope.

She hoped she had come across as independent and determined, rather than just coping, as she sat next to Richard on the sofa and tried to talk things through, but truth was she had found this meeting difficult. And when he had brought his hand up to wipe her tears away the whole of her had wanted to curl into him, to open herself up and sob it out alongside the one person in this world that had always seen who she was.

It was unfortunate that the one person who had always seen who she was, was the one person who had utterly betrayed her.

It was hard to believe their relationship and thus Marion's whole life had been blown to bits by this man in front of her, by his actions, by his lies. And for all her fury – and there was fury consuming her, exploding out at times she didn't need it and then hiding, submissive when

93

it could be really helpful – today she just felt sad. A heart-wrenching sadness that this should have happened to them and their perfect family.

She had had to use all her powers of self-control to not reach out and stroke the crinkle from his brow, not pull him close and murmur into his hair that together they could get through this. The sadness coursed through her as she witnessed the pain and frustration of the man whom she had always helped with any struggles – as he had her – but for her to do so now, for her to comfort him and make everything right, would involve sacrificing herself.

She may have done it for this man, had it just been her. But she wasn't simply Marion Marksharp *wife*, she was Marion Marksharp *wife and mother*. If she forgave the boys' father now, she would be giving them permission to do the same in the future and there was no way on this green earth that she was going to give her three boys any excuses to grow up into the weak, selfish sort of man that she had despised from childhood. She hadn't realized at that tender age that things weren't quite as black and white as she had assumed, that things were more nuanced, but still, she would not have her sons thinking that cheating, along with lies, duplicity and the dishonesty that accompanied it was ever, ever alright.

Step bold, lip firm and eyes determinedly blinked, she left their home and headed over to Chase's house.

The fact that she had to oversee a wedding proposal now and do so enthusiastically was not an irony that was lost on her.

However, she couldn't afford to dwell on ironies, or may-have-beens or what-ifs. She had a business to build, three rather large and gaping mouths to feed and feeling sorry for herself was not going to achieve any of that. Hard bloody work, on the other hand, just might.

–

Hard bloody work currently involved hiding in the grasses at the top of Chase's private beach and waiting for her two friends to appear so she could help cement their bond in the most romantic of moments. She supposed she was rather like the Cornish seaside version of Cyrano de Bergerac, only with a tiny microphone, much more attractive nose and no real burning passion for either of the people in the couple she was helping bring together.

She was safely in her place now with the torches lit to create a flaming path down to the barbecue and Bali bed. The bed was strewn with rose petals and long-stemmed roses intertwined around the frame. It looked fabulous.

The table had been set and Jenny had done a fantastic job; even Marion struggled to find a flaw, but then she had spent a whole two days a few years ago trying to teach Jenny about the importance of a perfect place setting. Not everyone was born with the knowledge, Marion knew that better than most. How one got to the age of thirty without understanding that a glass should be clean and the cutlery sparkling, Marion would never know.

The salads were set out and covered, the fish prepped and in a cool box ready to be put straight onto the gas barbecue. The cushions were all at the correct angles and the blankets were folded and draped exactly as Marion had wanted, the checks placed precisely so. Based on this it was impossible to see who was the strongest contender at the moment out of Jenny and Serena; she'd have to hear what was said about the Valentine's dance and make a decision then.

'I don't know why you want me out here, darling, you hate the cold and it's practically blowing a gale.' Chase's American accent carried, thanks to the wind, and Marion ducked down again. It was unlikely that she would be seen, but even though she was here at Angelina's request, she was aware that hiding in some tall beach grass with a microphone attached to her as she spied upon a couple's romantic dinner could be considered a little weird. The last thing she needed as she was building up her business was to be outed as Penmenna's peeping Tom – especially when she had a strong feeling that Mickey, who frequented The Smuggler's Curse, deserved that title.

'It's a Valentine's surprise, darling… Ta-da!' From the sounds of it they were now on the beach.

'Oh wow, I didn't expect this. Angelina, you are full of surprises.' Marion could imagine the delight on her friend's face in response to this; she couldn't see it because her head was still tucked down and curled into her lap until Chase got settled.

There were some kissy squelching noises – she did hope they wouldn't be doing a lot of that. Especially as whilst Chase had been looking around at the scene laid out, Angelina had very quickly grabbed her secret earpiece through which Marion could instruct her, and right now the kissing was being amplified far more than any person would ever, ever want.

Chapter Sixteen

The wind was picking up and Marion noted with pleasure that the Bali bed, barbecue and table all had piles of large stones and slates piled up around the legs in an attempt to secure them. The chairs, however, looked as if they were about to take off, and she uttered a quick prayer for the wind to die down.

'Now, now this is important. Let me light the barbecue.' Oops, this was the code sentence she and Angelina had discussed. When Ange said this, that would be Marion's cue to jump in and start feeding her lines. The one advantage to the wind was that it may mask Marion's whispering into the headpiece. What to say... um... what could you say when two people were gathered together for a romantic moment? Ah, of course!

'Dearly beloved we are gathered here today...' she began. Oh shit, that wasn't a romantic start; that was what vicars said. Must have been all that prayer. Um...

'Dearly beloved, we are gathered here today...' Angelina parroted.

Oh gosh.

'Sorry,' Marion hissed, 'I was nervous. That's not what I meant!'

'Sorry, I was nervous. That's not what I meant,' Angelina said gaily, waving around the long barbecue lighter. It wasn't responding well to the wind.

'Here, if I shelter you.' Chase stood to the side of Angelina, blocking the wind and allowing her to successfully light the barbecue. 'Are you alright?' He looked at her with both tenderness and a little alarm. 'You don't sound very like you.'

'Now, now this is important,' Angelina said again desperately, clearly not knowing how to respond to Chase's question. The woman never normally had trouble speaking – could she not think of something better than that?

'I'm fine, I'm just excited. Now let me get this fish on the barbecue and we'll be ready to go,' Marion hissed into the mic.

Angelina repeated it. Marion didn't need to be close to know that right now the woman's face would be scrunched up tighter than a cat's bottom as she picked the fish out of the cool box and placed it on the barbecue.

'Now I am worried,' Chase joked. 'Have I just watched you touch fish with your bare hands? Okay, what have you done with my actual girlfriend?'

'I know, it's absolutely bloody disgusting. I am never, ever doing that again,' Angelina spat, forgetting her role for a second and reverting to her actual girlfriend form.

'But it's a testament to how much I love you,' Marion added quickly, leading to Angelina, unusually obedient, saying so.

'Really?' said Chase, perplexion clear in his tone.

'Yes,' said Marion. 'It's two years to the day since we met, thanks to Marion; she's fabulous, isn't she? Such great clothes and hair and generally lovely…' She knew it was naughty but she couldn't help herself. 'So I wanted to mark the occasion and make it romantic because it's Valentine's Day.'

Angelina repeated Marion's words, snorting with laughter at the clothes and hair bit before composing herself for the more serious sentiment.

Then Marion watched as Angelina turned and wiped her fishy hands on Chase's jumper. Marion winced; she knew him well and in all probability any sweater he owned wouldn't cost less than £300. Mackerel on cashmere was not a particularly Chase look.

'Oi!' he objected mildly. Marion's mouth dropped open, her eyes widening as Chase gathered Angelina into a cuddle and ruffled her hair. Okay, he valued Angelina more than his clothes; that was a sight she never thought she'd see. And boded well for this proposal. 'Romance does not start with fish guts,' he chided.

'I couldn't agree more, and yet you seemed to think mackerel fishing was a great idea for a first date so I thought I'd return the favour,' Angelina retorted quick as a flash, her voice a little muffled as she whispered into his fishy jumper.

They were cute. She had never seen Angelina as cute before. Pushy, loud, neurotic and, she admitted with more self-awareness than she would have liked, a little like herself, yes. But cute, not so much.

'It was a good idea – it worked didn't it? You're here now.'

'Hmpf, only because I have the patience of a saint and quite frankly I was so bored of staying with my brother and his ever-increasing crush on that dreary goody-two-shoes.'

'Hey, I like Rosy, and she's good for your brother.'

'She is,' Marion hissed into the mouthpiece; she didn't want to lose the romance of the moment as Angelina started to be Angelina. Being nasty about others was never a good look for a wedding proposal. 'She makes him happy. And *you* are very good for me and look like you mean it.'

'She is. She makes him happy. And *you* are very good for me and...' Angelina paused devilishly as Marion hoped she wasn't going to repeat the whole sentence. '...I mean it. Which is why I have prepared all of this for you.'

'You prepared it?' Chase looked sceptical. 'I've lived with you for two years and at no point have you ever shown any smidge of domesticity. *You* wound those roses around that?' He pointed at the Bali bed. 'And you can skin and gut a fish?'

'Well I had some help, obviously; I can't do everything by myself. Do you know how long it takes to look this good?' She waved her hands down the length of her body.

Chase laughed. 'Phew, that's my girlfriend. I was beginning to worry that you had been replaced by some sort of clone. Shouldn't you have turned the fish over by now?'

'Oh, sod the fi...' Angelina stopped mid-sentence.

'Of course, thank you,' Marion barked. This woman was her own worst enemy.

'Of course, thank you,' Angelina obediently repeated.

'Now plate up the salads.'

'Now plate... oh. Here, let's put the salads on the table.'

'You made salads, as well?'

'I did admit to having help.'

'This is possibly the most romantic thing anyone has ever done for me.'

'Good,' Angelina purred. 'I want to be *the* most romantic, I want to be the most everything. I want to be the best girlfriend you've ever had.' She drew out the e's in *ever* and it reminded Marion of quite how young she was.

'Will you stop going off-script,' hissed Marion into her mic.

'Will you shut up a minute,' Angelina hissed back.

'Eh?' said Chase.

'Nothing. I am the longest and the best girlfriend, aren't I?'

'Um, yup. Should I flip the fish and pop it on the plate?'

'Yes, and I'll open the champagne – that is something I don't need any help with.' She sniggered and Chase chuckled too.

'You're supposed to be serving him, not getting him to do the work,' Marion reprimanded.

'Oh, hush up, this is the twenty-first century. He likes it.'

'Hmpf. Do you want my help or not?'

'Probably not if you're going to constantly nag me.'

Marion wanted with every cell of her body to rip the microphone off and storm off home, back to central heating, back to her three own boys, back to Richard.

No, not back to Richard, that wasn't an option any more. But dear God, they said not to work with children and animals, and Marion had experience of both, but celebrities should definitely top that list. Mind you, celebrities may be annoying but they had a lot of disposable income and a huge amount of followers on social media. Two things that Marion's new business would be very keen on. She made her tone slightly more saccharine and played ball.

'You are quite right, I'll pipe down and let you take the lead. Just use the key word, um… windy… when you want some help.'

'Okay.'

Chase brought the fish over, having placed it upon the plates next to the barbecue. 'Are you okay? You seem to be mumbling to yourself a lot this evening.'

'I'm fine. Oh, this actually looks quite good, doesn't it?'

'You sound surprised,' Chase commented.

'Well, to be honest I thought it was a bit of a shit idea…'

'I thought you said this was your idea.'

'Yes… um… it was, it is… um… wind… wind,' Angelina finished, more than a hint of desperation in her final word.

Marion rolled her eyes before helping Angelina out. 'So let's eat our food and then we can… flick your eyes over to the Bali bed suggestively and say… and then I have something to show you.'

'So let's eat our food and then we can flick… Oh no sorry, not that bit, let's eat our food and then I have something to show you.' Angelina was good at suggestive and from her viewpoint Marion could see her toss her hair and lick her lips. What would look cartoonish on normal people looked perfect on Angelina. It was no wonder she had so many Instagram followers. It also made Marion very grateful she had boys, who as far as she was aware were not currently under any pressure to perfect duckface whilst wearing not much more than a bit of netting and a thong. But then with the world, her world, moving so fast, who knew what the next year would bring?

'Do you indeed?' Chase said suggestively, and without being able to see him Marion knew he would be doing his double eyebrow lift.

Marion could see him reach out his hand to cover Angelina's as they both ate, Chase's supper – served in an

Angelina-sized portion – only taking six bites to finish. Marion shifted her angle slightly and with the light from the torches flickering across his face could see the adoring glances he was bestowing as Angelina pushed her food around her plate, taking tiny Barbie-doll mouthfuls every now and then.

There was little conversation as they finished their meal, or as Chase watched his girlfriend very slowly pretend to finish her meal, but Marion was quite grateful for the time free from thinking and sat back, casting her eyes up to the sky spotted with stars, inky black and stretching into the forever, the unknown. The crash of the waves pulled her back and refocused her on the beach. But even the waves themselves, like the sky and space and far away galaxies, seemed never-ending, reassuringly relentless. Dangerous if disrespected but eternal, there, reliable.

Angelina's voice jerked her back to the here and now. Good, let's get this proposal signed and sealed so she could throw the biggest, most showbiz wedding Cornwall had ever seen.

Her friend pushed her plate away and clasped Chase's hand in hers.

'Chase Cooper.' She took a deep breath, a sigh that every romantic heroine of the golden era of Hollywood would have been proud of. Marion forgot that despite all her many flaws, Angelina was a consummate actress. Then she felt immediately guilty. Angelina did love Chase; Marion did believe that. 'I love you more than... more than... diamonds.' That, not so much.

'Wow, and you love diamonds.' Chase laughed.

'I do. And you're about to see how much.'

'Ooft, that sounds expensive.'

'You wouldn't have me any other way.'

'To be honest there are quite a few ways I like to have you.'

'Chase, I'm trying to be serious.' Angelina giggled as Chase rose slightly to lean over the table and give her a kiss, which rather like the earlier one went on a little bit too long. Marion shut her eyes, wishing that she could drown out sound as well.

'Oh, I'm very serious.' Chase said and Marion opened her eyes again to see him being gently pushed back into his chair by Angelina.

'I'll tell you what, let me come around there.' Angelina pushed her chair back and walked around the table to sit on Chase's lap. Marion thought she might vomit.

'Oh, I like this idea.'

'You need to listen to me a minute.' Angelina slipped her hand underneath the table and fidgeted a bit on Chase's lap. Marion didn't want to look at her friend's face; she could only imagine what a wriggling, fidgeting Angelina on your lap would do to any man.

'I can do that,' Chase remarked in a slightly strangled voice. Marion gave her pal top marks for being respectful. She imagined there was quite a lot more he'd like to do, but she really would prefer he didn't whilst she was watching from the sidelines.

There was a crow of success as Angelina found what she was looking for and spun on her bottom to look Chase in the eye. Marion had been particularly proud of her idea of sticking the engagement ring under the table with a bit of tape, meaning that it would be hidden from view and the proposal would be a real surprise. No ring boxes saturated as they hid in the ice bucket, for example; no chance of something so expensive becoming buried in the sand for sand fleas and baby crabs to wriggle over.

She was slightly less proud of the fact that Angelina had overnighted herself a giant diamond engagement ring but seemed to forget to buy one for Chase. But when challenged, the blonde superstar had merely pointed out that by saying yes he would have her for life and that was prize enough.

'So, it's Valentine's night...'

'It is.'

'And we've been together two years...' Angelina was going off script again but then Marion had suspected that when it came to the proposal she would probably take charge; Marion's presence was required more for morale than anything else.

'We have.'

'And there is no one I would rather spend my time with.'

'Me neither.'

'Will you let me get a word in? This is important!' Angelina snapped as Chase chuckled and then nodded solemnly and silently, indicating that she should continue.

'I love you, Chase Cooper, more than I've ever loved anyone before...'

'That's just as well; from what your brother has said, everyone you have loved before has been a nightmare. Oops, sorry, I'll be quiet.' Chase raised his hands in an admission of guilt and Angelina gently punched him on the arm. They were quite sweet in a dysfunctional sort of way.

'As we know I'm not really a traditional sort of girl, and neither do I necessarily follow the rules.' Chase's mouth grew wide as he mimed struggling to keep the laughter in.

'So seeing as I know my own mind, I know how I want the rest of my life to be. And I know that I want to spend it with you. You're my best friend, you make me laugh and you listen to me, like really listen, and you make me a better person, or so Matt keeps telling me, and we have the best holidays and I really like your taste in everything, cars, food, houses, clothes, me!'

Dear God! Marion buried her head in her hands again, but then she supposed Chase did love Angelina and this was pure Angelina.

'Chase Cooper, seeing as I have decided that I would like to spend the rest of my life with you and I sure as hell don't want anyone else to have you, I think the time has come...' She paused and dotted his face with little kisses. Chase had stopped grinning and looked a little shellshocked, but as Marion squinted she could see that it was a pleased kind of shellshocked rather than a God-help-me-get-me-out-of-here face.

'...to make an honest woman of me.' She revealed the ring box in her hand and flicked it open to reveal, as Marion knew from earlier, the biggest diamond ring known to man, which sat sparkling on the velvet screaming ostentatious, conspicuous consumption.

'Chase Cooper, will you marry me?'

There was a silence for a minute as Chase looked down at the ring box, looked up at Angelina, who was slightly higher than him as she sat in his lap, and laughed, laughed loudly before reaching up and kissing her full on the mouth.

'Yes, Angelina Masters, yes, I will marry you.'

Angelina squealed with joy and the kissing began again, but only for a minute or two until Chase pulled his head back and nodded at the ring box.

'Seeing as you're not a traditional kinda girl,' he quoted her from earlier, 'is it safe to assume that this ring in front of me is not for me but for you?'

Angelina nodded excitedly. 'Isn't it beautiful? Conflict-free diamonds, you know. See, you're making me a better person.'

Chase took the box from her hand, removed the ring and looked her in the eyes as he slid the ring onto her finger. 'Angelina Masters, you have made me the happiest man in the world; I cannot wait to be husband and wife.'

'Oh no, Chase Cooper, *now* I'm going to make you the happiest man alive,' she drawled as she slid off his lap, held out her hand to faux pull him up – he needed no encouragement – and started to lead the way to the Bali bed.

No! No, no, no, no, no!

It was bad enough to have to hear the kissing; what was she going to be subjected to now? Had Angelina forgotten she was here? Of course not, she wasn't stupid – was this what she meant the other day when she said there hadn't been a decent celebrity sex tape in ages? Did Angelina expect Marion to record this?

To be fair it wasn't a bad idea as such. It would certainly push her and Chase's profile through the roof. The wedding deals they would get would be increased tenfold if Angelina anonymously released an engagement sex video.

Marion had never filmed someone else having sex before; she was fairly sure angles were of paramount importance. Should she crawl closer, make sure that everyone looked as good as possible?

No, that was too much; she could just hold the phone out and keep her head down. She didn't need to watch it, just film it. A grainy, furtive quality would probably increase its value. She shuddered. This was about putting food on the table – the boys' clubs did not come cheap and they were used to two holidays a year. She had better bloody well get the best, and she meant the best, recommendation from the shameless Miss-Masters-soon-to-be-Mrs-Cooper for this, she really had.

Her mouth screwed up mulishly as, with reluctance, she pulled her phone out of her bag, clicked open the camera, set it to video and held the phone up in the rough direction of the Bali bed, which now had two beautiful blonde people beginning to writhe upon it.

She pulled out her earpiece; Angelina clearly didn't need her any more and Marion was dammed if she was going to have this amplified into her ears, especially as she now lived in a world where she may never have sex again.

Holding the phone up, looking down at the sand, she wondered how on earth her life had come to this when suddenly she felt her whole body being lifted through the air, someone's big sweaty paw on the collar of her coat.

What the hell?

'What on earth do you think… well, fuck me, Marion Marksharp, you dirty little hussy. I always suspected as much.'

'Put me down!' Marion said forcefully, aware that Angelina and Chase had stopped what they were doing as she stood there, now upon her own two feet, glaring at Hector, the man who had found her filming from the sand dunes.

Chapter Seventeen

Richard tossed and turned in the hotel sheets. It was a very nice room but it wasn't his; his was currently occupied by his wife, whose behaviour was becoming increasingly bizarre by the minute.

He had assumed a simple chat would have resolved all the misunderstandings and he'd be curled up back in the marital bed, happy in the knowledge that at some point early in the morning Rufus would jump upon his torso and peel his eyelids back to see if he was awake. Enhanced interrogation professionals could learn a thing or two from his youngest son.

But alas, this had not been the case. Marion was immovable, like a very stubborn mountain but icier, and it was apparent that she did not believe him when he protested his innocence. Which was ridiculous. He was a one-woman man and with that woman being Marion he was quite frankly too exhausted to even contemplate taking on another. He adored his wife and, having seen how devastated his mother used to be by his father's habitual playing away, he had always vowed never to behave as his father did with extra-marital shagging being his number one hobby.

It seemed particularly unfair that he was now tossed out of his house for a crime he did not commit, did not even consider, whilst his father had happily got away with doing whatever and whomever he wanted for the whole of his adulterous life.

However, it wasn't just the unfairness of this that was keeping him awake now. It was this evening that was bothering him.

Marion had been very mysterious about where she was going and he'd had high hopes that she was attempting to send a message by being out somewhere else on Valentine's Day this year, less than a week after she had claimed their marriage had disintegrated beyond repair. He had hoped she may be parked up in a layby somewhere, reading a book or plotting future world domination, or even sobbing a little bit about the state of their marriage and wishing they could sort it out – he never wanted Marion to be sad but any remorse over their current situation would be helpful right now.

Either way he'd imagined that she would eventually return, having punished him enough, and he would have got to spend a pleasurable evening with his boys before she returned home, punishment served and relationship, hopefully, resumed.

It had appeared that every part of that belief had been a little optimistic. As far as the boys were concerned, it would appear something called *Fortnite* was far more compelling than he was. Although all three of them had been pleased to see him at first, the novelty dimmed some point soon after they had persuaded him that Valentine's Day was expensive, that Mummy had left them with barely any pocket money at all and his wallet had been opened and emptied.

He had then been left on the sofa all alone with nothing but a stream of romantic movies playing on the television, an over-sized dog trying to lick his ear and video games making his boys completely audio-impaired.

When Marion had returned home, he'd reported back on how the boys were faring; she had barked something about how he wasn't a babysitter, he was their father, how his friend Hector was in the village and how sometimes the bloody beach was overrated before storming up the stairs and shouting down to him that he'd better return to Treporth Bay as she didn't want him setting a bad example to Darcy by sleeping on the sofa.

He had stopped in the hotel bar to have a glass of whiskey before he headed to bed in the hope that it would help him sleep and forget the thoughts that had been spinning around his head since Marion had walked back into their house.

It hadn't worked.

He had always admired her for many things, one of the more superficial being that no matter what happened to her she always, always thought enough of herself to be well-groomed. She could have been mud wrestling with the women from school – there was a thought – and she would still not have a hair out of place or smudged lipstick. She could bring up three boys and look as beautifully groomed as she had pre-motherhood; it was not a skill he had. He tended to be a little on the ruffled side.

The reason he appreciated this was because the only time she looked anything other than cool, calm and collected was in the throes of passion, when she would become softer, tousled and red-cheeked. It was this Marion that he loved the most, with every heightened fibre of his being, the more relaxed version, the one that didn't suck her tummy in or purse her lips but the one that relaxed and laughed and loved, the side of Marion that only he got to see. The side he doubted anyone else in the world had *ever* seen.

Which was why her entrance tonight had been so suspicious.

His wife had walked back into their home with her hair very definitely out of place; windswept would be a fair description, but he couldn't think of any innocent reason Marion would be outside on an evening like tonight with the wind picking up and howling its way through the village. This was a night for setting the fire, wrapping up and staying cosy.

That by itself may not cause anything other than a flutter, the *mildest* flutter, of concern. But the seaweed she had stuck to the back of her jumper, that was an almighty red flag, one waving so ferociously that the flag itself may jump from the stick it was attached to, grow legs and run around the living room shouting *look at me, look at me.* Marion never had anything stuck to her, nothing: not for her an unfortunate bit of loo roll attached to the shoe, or one of those sticky stems of goosegrass, picked up from the school field or hedgerow and attached to a cardigan or skirt.

On top of which she was shedding sand left right and centre. A perfectly normal thing to do in Cornwall, and there was barely a house in the county that did not have a thin layer of sand coating the inside of it and bunging up the shower in the summer months. But it was not summer, it was February, it was dark and Hector was in the village. This was the final and most damning piece of evidence yet. This was what was really making his spider senses tingle.

His wife had clearly spent the evening on a beach, been secretive about where she was and Hector was in town. Richard had never had any pretensions to be the next

Hercule Poirot but quite frankly Yogi Bear could piece this conundrum together in under five seconds.

Hector epitomized everything about Richard's own upbringing that he had tried to avoid. He was a walking, talking public-school cliché with his booming voice, outdated and downright offensive opinions about the place of women and the British Empire and a fashion taste that only a certain, entitled type of man dared to try. Richard had spent his life avoiding salmon pink and mustard, simply because it reminded him of his father, while Hector embraced both shades with gusto.

However, despite his dubious fashion sense and his vile opinions, time and shared memories had bred a kind of camaraderie and Richard had learnt that as loathsome as Hector appeared, he did have the odd redeeming feature. He was remarkably generous and played a caricature of himself because he didn't know how to be any different.

Thus, Richard could forgive him most things. There was one thing, though, that Richard had always been uneasy about and that was Hector's determination that he should have anything he ever wanted. And he wanted Marion.

Hector was used to getting his own way and boy had he tried. He had tried throughout university. He had tried after Marion and Richard had married in their twenties, he had tried when they were having children; apparently Marion when pregnant was like a ripe goddess, glowing with fecundity and a rich sexuality that only a true man could appreciate. Thankfully Marion at the time had pointed out that a true man *was*.

It would appear that wasn't firm enough as he hadn't given up.

Marion liked to flirt but Richard had long suspected this was tied somehow to a desire for male approval, born from seeing her mother's need for the same. Richard was no psychologist and had no pretensions of being one; what he did know was that his wife had a bit of a reputation for draping herself over any man that caught her fancy, occasionally purring as she did so and batting her eyelids in a way that most people found quite frightening.

What he also knew was that she didn't mean any of it. It was just programmed, an instinctive reaction to anyone entering the room and possessing a willy. That whilst Marion flirted like she was Cleopatra saving her empire, she actually saw the sexual act as one of such intimacy, such bonding that he *knew* she would not cheat, would not share that with someone else, not after the years they had put into building their marriage, carving out a life for themselves. It was a pity she did not believe the same of him.

As he lay in the sheets of the hotel room, the moon so full that it was sitting on the tideline, he couldn't help but think that Marion's seaweedy, sandy, dishevelled form and her decades-long suitor turning up in the village on Valentine's Day, were very much related.

Chapter Eighteen

Despite a somewhat sleepless night, Richard grinned as he walked past the window of The Smuggler's Curse and saw the flames of the fire roaring – Roger, the landlord, did like a good fire. The regulars were standing at the bar laughing raucously and no doubt his friends were sitting down and tucked in the corner. He thought he could see Alex's dark good looks and beaming face and half of Chase's ear.

He had known this set of friends for so many years they were like brothers. At university they had a sense of confidence that emanated from them, whether it be Hector's boorish entitlement, Chase's all-American good looks or Alex's sense of masculinity and purpose. It was no surprise they had all gone on to be raging successes in their field. The only surprise to him was that they wanted him as their friend. And still seemed to.

With an upbringing that centred around his very controlling mother, adulterous father and golden boy older brother, Richard had, until he met this particular little gang, never been particularly sure of himself or what he had to offer other than getting under his mother's feet and being a nuisance – both phrases direct quotes. Whereas this lot had helped shape the man he had grown into, given him the bravado to pursue Marion with the ferocity of a mountain lion. He loved them all so much and was excited to see them – bar Hector. Hector he would not be excited to see and, if he did, wondered if this was the time he would actually have to throw his first ever punch. Did he have the knuckles for it? Did it take some special skill?

He pushed the door open, the tattiest piece of wood you had ever seen. The locals claimed that Roger refused to replace, burn or at the very least paint it, because he didn't want to risk anyone who wasn't local coming in. You would think that profit was more important to a publican, and to most it was, but not Roger; with The Smuggler's Curse being at the centre of the community, regularly packed with events and people throughout the year and a table for Sunday lunch practically impossible to get unless Roger's great-great-great-great grandfather had gone to school with yours, then it didn't need to be. The landlord saw no need to drive the locals away by encouraging the emmets – tourists that scurried around Cornwall in the height of season, sunburnt red and bustling like the ants they were named for. And in this moment Richard was glad for it, knowing that as he walked through the door, he was home.

As ever, the chatter and laughter in the pub stilled when anyone walked in as every head turned to see who was joining them. Richard grinned and Mickey and Andy at the bar raised a hand in greeting – the apocalypse could come and those two could still be relied upon to prop up the bar – before continuing their conversation, and Richard's heart filled with warmth.

He spotted Ethel sitting in her usual spot and having her tea-time sherry. She was accompanied by another woman dressed in brightly coloured clothes and cackling loudly as the two played dominos. His beam widened; he did love this village.

He glanced over at Chase and Alex and his heart sank as he saw that they *were* joined by Hector. Marion had been right; he was in the village. His face fell. He had a few things to say to him.

'Pint of Tribute please, Roger.' He approached the bar to get his drink first. The low hubbub that had resumed once everyone had ascertained Richard was one of their own was suddenly pierced by the wah-wah voice of his old friend, and new enemy.

'I say, Richard, good to see you, old boy. Have to say, always knew that wife of yours was a cheeky little mare but my God, last night proved it. That woman has no shame!'

Before Richard was even fully aware of what was happening, he was standing in front of the table with his arm pulled back and his fingers curled into a fist, until Chase, up on his feet and standing next to him, firmly gripped it. He could feel a muscle throbbing in his forehead, his jaw was clenched and he felt as if he had the strength of a testosterone-filled bull.

Hector was very much the red rag. Red in the face years before his time and soon to be bloody-nosed as well.

'Woah, woah. He didn't mean anything by it. Calm yourself, sit down, here next to me.' Chase spoke quietly but firmly as he indicated the empty banquette, still holding onto his friend. Richard lowered himself into the space Chase had highlighted, his brow furrowed as he maintained silent, and he hoped menacing, eye contact with Hector. He had never glowered before; he was fairly sure what he was doing now was glowering.

But seriously, how dare he? Who the hell did he think he was?

'I think that was badly worded, Hector,' Chase said as he relinquished Richard and sat back down next to him, hemming him in, encouraging Hector into an apology.

And failing.

Richard felt someone pat him on the back as Roger brought his pint over and put it on the table at the same time as Alex turned to Hector, shaking his head. 'You are such a dick, why would you say that? Just what did you hope to achieve?'

'It's true. I always have been and she was. Let me tell you the full story.' Hector maintained his bravado, knocking back a swig of red wine as he did so, unperturbed by his friend's intense scowl. Richard felt himself begin to rise out of the seat again. He wasn't sure who this new macho Richard was – he had never thrown a punch in his life, but now he was feeling it, now he felt he could not just throw one punch but maybe two or three.

It was better to focus on that rather than the realities of what Hector's words may mean. Going with anger was best because he'd been keeping an unbearable ball of sadness curled inside him ever since Marion had kicked him out and believed him capable of things he could never do, revealing what she really thought of him. A ball threatening to grow and grow and grow until it took the whole of him over.

And if he thought about Marion and Hector – he gulped; he couldn't even think it. Deep breath, and a reminder to stick with the anger. Whilst his friends – most of them – weren't the outdated chauvinistic type that didn't believe in men experiencing a gamut of emotion, he knew he sure as hell didn't want to cry in the middle of the village pub. Once he started he'd weep a river that would inevitably squelch Roger's fire out and he would be no longer in possession of either a home or welcoming local.

'Hector saw Marion at mine last night,' Chase explained gently. 'He's just being an ass about it. Angelina had proposed and for God knows what reason…'

'Angelina proposed?' Alex interrupted. 'Mate, that's… um… epic.'

Richard was pleased for his friend as Alex was, despite the latter clearly struggling for an appropriate congratulatory word. Chase may love Angelina desperately but his friends couldn't help but have reservations – she was not an easy person. But then Richard supposed, with a sudden flash of empathy, neither was Marion; it was only he that saw the true her, the more vulnerable her. Maybe that was what Chase had with Angelina. It would explain a lot.

'Congratulations, Chase. I'm really pleased for you,' he added.

'You are?'

'Yes, of course I am. I assume you said yes?' Richard smiled but, despite wanting to be happy for his friend, he couldn't help that the primary thought in his head now was that maybe it wasn't just him that saw Marion's' vulnerabilities; maybe now Hector had as well. He shot another evil look at Hector, who was clearly made of Teflon.

'I did.'

'So how come Marion was at yours?' Alex asked the question Richard was building up to.

'Um… honestly, I'm not entirely sure. When Angelina and Marion get together a world is created where nothing much makes sense.'

Richard couldn't help but bark a laugh at that. 'Isn't that the truth.'

'When I found her, the little minx...' Hector began as the three other men whipped their heads around, all with warning looks upon their faces. 'Oh, do calm down.' Hector took another swig of his wine and waved the empty glass in the air, no doubt expecting magical mini butlers to come and fill it for him. Irritatingly Roger did.

'When I saw her, she was hidden in a sand dune...'

'She what?' Alex questioned.

'Well, quite.' Hector's eyebrows were waggling with ferocity. 'Quite. Hiding in a sand dune, video recording Chase and Angelina in a compromising pos—'

'No? No!' Alex's mouth dropped open as Chase scrunched his face and nodded confirmation.

'My wife spent her Valentine's evening recording, or trying to until you stopped her, Chase and Angelina, you know... um... well, you know? Is that what you're saying? And she was *hiding* in the sand dunes as she did it?'

Hector met Richard's eyes for the first time that evening. 'Yup, pretty much. She was so engrossed she didn't hear me approach. I had flown into the UK the day before and thought I'd come and check in on you all.'

'Didn't occur to you that of all the evenings to drop in, Valentine's isn't the appropri...' Alex started to say but Richard tuned him out. All he could feel was a huge wave of relief that this explained all of the things that had concerned him last night. However, his eyes narrowed as he looked across at his old friend. Marion may have been innocent last night but still, having Hector in the village when Marion was newly single, well that was like having a fox in the henhouse. He was going to have to keep a very sharp eye out indeed.

Chapter Nineteen

Marion supposed the one bonus to Richard being back in the village was that he could at least make up for some of the time he had missed over the past couple of years and keep an eye on the boys for her as she swung the next stage of her plan into action. They had both sat the children down during half term and explained that they were separating but that they loved them and would still be a family, just one where Mummy and Daddy lived in different places. The boys had taken it in their stride and had asked remarkably few questions, though Marion wasn't sure whether that was because it was the same for so many of their peers or because they were used to Richard being away. Whatever the reason, she was relieved it had been done and that no blame had been assigned. It had been civilized and they had done it together.

Today she'd be using her persuasive powers to talk to Rosy and Matt about her wonderful idea. She was aware it may be quite a hard sell, but thought it might be easier pitching it on her own with full control of the way she spun the narrative. Angelina, helpfully, had point blank refused to be part of the meeting, saying that with a wedding imminent she needed to stay as stress-free as possible for the next few months and visiting Rosy was not going to be stress-free. Then she muttered something about Scramble and her shoes; Marion didn't quite understand but the gist was very much that she was not a fan.

In truth, Marion was surprised that Angelina had agreed to her suggestion of a double wedding; she had expected that the star would be reluctant to share her big day with anyone, especially the headteacher of Penmenna School, whom she had always written off as a country mouse. But what made Angelina a star – apart from her utter lack of boundaries, decorum and remorse – was her ability to play the game. She knew that her wedding to Chase would be a huge draw but if she combined it with her brother's nuptials, added his stardust to the mix and combined it with an 'orphans together' narrative, then it had the potential to blow sky high and worldwide. The money to be made would be staggering and Angelina was very, very keen on money.

She clearly also knew that she didn't want to be the one who suggested it to her brother.

Marion was in the school office berating Sheila, who seemed completely unperturbed that the PTA cash box was missing, when she heard a burst of laughter coming from the headteacher's office. Was that Matt? Perfect! They couldn't make too much of a fuss if she suggested the joint wedding idea in the workplace.

She gave Sheila one last meaningful look as she rapped at Rosy's office door, which the school secretary completely ignored as she rustled through some papers, muttering, 'Now what was it I was looking for?'

Her mouth suddenly dry, she found herself rubbing her fingers against her palm as she waited for Rosy to call her in. This would be fine; it was a good idea, it was. Although if she could be infused with magical powers of oratory to prevent Matt throwing her out in the first five minutes that would be great. She ran through the mental checklist she had in her mind for why a joint wedding would be such a good idea, but she had to admit she wasn't convinced any of the reasons were strong enough to do the job.

She'd have to rely on the sibling bond thing and stood there repeating that to herself as she waited.

'Hello, Marion, everything okay?' Rosy held the door opened wide and beamed at her. 'I was surprised not to see you at the Valentine's disco.'

'Well, I wanted to give my ladies a chance to shine. Sometimes if I'm there they fade a little into the background so I thought the decent thing would be to let them take the lead. But I thought I heard Matt; I had hoped to catch you both today.' She peeked around Rosy to give him a little wave, her face falling as she realized the laugh belonged to Kam Choudhury, the only male member of staff. Drat!

Rosy motioned her into the office, but left the door open.

'Matt's not here, I'm afraid, but Dan is coming over tonight to discuss the wedding. I was going to ask if you'd like to join us? And yes, the dance went very smoothly.' Rosy continued, 'I think everyone had a wonderful time and Jenny certainly seemed very pleased with the takings at the end. And the cupcake secret delivery, what a fabulous idea, that was new and seemed to go down very well indeed.' Rosy referenced the latest fundraising idea of sending a cupcake from a stall to your crush and having it delivered anonymously.

'Fine, yes, I'd love to join you, and I think a little romance does us all good. The cupcakes were Serena's idea to give credit where it's due. Such a dear friend.' Both

Rosy and Kam looked at her, eyes wide. 'And how do you think she did? And Jenny?'

'Oh, um… yes… they both did well; as I said, a great success.'

'Hmm.' Marion looked pensive. 'But which one did better?'

'Oh, I didn't realize it was a competition,' Rosy responded.

Honestly, some people were so naive.

'When one is looking for a leader then a bit of competition is healthy, don't you think? I'd argue it was imperative in order to find the best candidate.'

'Hmm. I don't like the thought of you gone; you say it with such finality,' Rosy said. 'The school won't be the same without you.'

She looked genuine enough, and Marion knew Rosy wasn't the type to say things just to be polite so she relaxed her shoulders again and felt a little bit of warmth course through her body.

'Ooh, I'm sure you'll still see a lot of me. Fledgling days for the new business so I'll be about for a little while yet. Now I do need to track down the cash box so I shall nip over to yours at seven and we'll have a wonderful evening. I just know you're going to love my ideas.' That bit was a lie but maybe before the evening was over they would.

Her ladies were having a Valentine's Day debrief in the staffroom so that was her next stop: swizz in and check and assess for herself who was leading in the stakes to take over her role. By rights it should be Jenny but she couldn't help the increasingly sneaking fondness she had for Serena.

She was approaching the staffroom when she heard her name and, as was only human, paused to hear what was being said. She knew there'd be a big gap in the school when she couldn't be there as frequently as she used to be – Rosy had just said so – and assumed they were pondering this. Carefully she crept along the wall and then leant back against it, just to the edge of the door frame so she could hear clearly.

'Marion?' she heard Jenny say.

'I'm a bit worried about her; she's more absent than usual and when she's here she's racing faster than a jaguar through the school and making even crazier demands than normal. She tried to force me into marriage with Alex earlier this term to suit her schedule and Alex didn't give much detail but said her and R—' Sylvie was speaking. Crazier demands than normal – how rude!

'Marion is fine,' Jenny snapped with a frostiness that Marion was proud of. Yes, pull the drawbridge up; don't you dare let them whisper about me.

'It was just that I wanted to ask how we could best support—' Sylvie was cut off again, but this time by Pippa, the teaching assistant from Class One.

'Richard is back, I saw him after the dance the other night, in Treporth Bay when I was with Kam.'

'Oh my God, he wasn't at Claudia's, was he?' Serena's shock was clear in her voice. Marion knew why she was asking. Claudia had her second home in the same apartment block as Kam, so if Pippa had seen him, that was probably why.

Ooh, she could feel her temper rising. If he had come back to Penmenna and then when she'd kicked him out gone and stayed with Claudia... Marion felt her blood begin to boil. If he was still treating her like a fool and in their own back yard, she was going to have something to say. She toyed with storming in and asking for a clear answer, hoping the shock of her presence would stun them into an honest response.

'No, no. In fact, I'm fairly sure I saw an estate agent whacking in a post and a for sale sign up in her window; she's not been down for ages so definitely not there. I saw him going into The Cormorants – it was quite late.' Pippa named a hotel in the bay.

'On his own?' Jenny questioned, her earlier determination to close the conversation down clearly disappeared once there was a whiff of scandal. Marion wouldn't be surprised if her ears had popped up and stood to attention. 'On Valentine's Day?'

'Yup.'

There was a brief silence as everyone digested this fact.

Marion calmed herself down and splayed her whole body against the wall, holding the position tight as well as the breath in her body as she leant over to hear more. Her body angled like a question mark, her ear was as close to the door as she could get it. It wasn't the easiest position to hold but she figured it was the best way to hear every last word.

'Oh, that doesn't bode well.'

'Exactly, so I wanted to know how we can help. I'm fond of Marion. To be honest it took a little while, and her conviction that I was some sort of stripper didn't help…'

'Ooh, I remember that,' Jenny answered gleefully. Dear God, that woman would sell her own babies down the river for some gossip. And how cruel of Sylvie to bring up the exotic dancer thing; everyone leapt to assumptions – it was human nature. How was Marion to know she was a prima ballerina? She hardly dressed like one and Marion had seen the way she shovelled food in – not the actions of someone classically trained.

'So, you're saying that Marion might need a little bit of nurturing – we can do that. She still drives me wild but I know you like her, Sylvie, and so does Rosy, and I don't like to think of anyone being upset. We should get Alice involved; she's always good at this sort of thing.'

This sort of thing? She was hardly a *this* or a *thing*! Marion was leaning so hard now she feared she may topple over.

'Mrs Marksharp! Why are you bending over like that, are you alright?' A child's voice came from nowhere, loud, really loud, and startling Marion so much that she almost lost her balance.

'Are you in pain, Mrs Marksharp?' came the second voice, slightly quieter, but as Marion heard a hush descend over the staffroom she knew Ellie's voice, the first child's – loud enough to pierce a drum – had been heard and she had just been caught eavesdropping.

'No, no, dear, it was nothing. Shoo now.' She flapped her hands at them in an attempt to drive them away as she hissed quietly but as firmly as was possible.

'Oh, are you being a cat? Your uncle Tom's cat rubs itself against the wall all the time, doesn't it?' Ellie pronounced loudly as she looked at her friend.

'It does, to get rid of the fleas.' Sam nodded as he offered his explanation.

'I hardly have fleas!' Marion was indignant. Why did children have so many questions? For a second, she wished the children in Penmenna School weren't taught to be quite so confident.

'Well what *were* you doing then?' Ellie was inquisitive and clearly not prepared to give up. 'My dad says lots of people are a bit odd and we have to be understanding about people being different to us. Were you just being differ—'

Ellie's questioning was halted as Sylvie came out of the staffroom. Sam was her son and Ellie was Alex's so she was the obvious person to respond to their voices.

'Children, what are you doing here? Oh, Marion, hello, are you alright?' She echoed Ellie's question as she looked at her with sympathy. As well she might, clearly having just caught her in the act of listening intently to the conversation about her.

'Absolutely fine, thank you, Sylvie.' Marion was aware her tone was brisk but she was a little embarrassed. 'I was just heading into the staffroom; I'm hoping some of my ladies are in there and preferably with the cash box from the Valentine's dance or we're going to have a bit of a problem.' She barged her way past Sylvie and into where the others were all gathered, Sylvie following behind her, the two children agog at the door.

'Hello, everybody, lovely to see you. I've come to find out about the Valentine's dance. I assume it couldn't have gone too wrong.' There was a chorus of *hello Marion*s from the PTA as Pippa raised her eyebrows and shook her head at Marion's entrance. She'd always had a tendency for stroppiness, that one. Marion had no idea what the Class Two teacher, charming Mr Choudhury, saw in her. Maybe Ellie's dad was right.

However now was not the time for that. She caught sight of the cash box on the table in front of Serena.

She beamed at the PTA members sitting around the table. 'Thank goodness for that, I was beginning to worry. Nice to see it so full. I hear the dance went very well indeed, even without me.' This was okay, she could do this; no one had said anything about her eavesdropping and neither did they have looks of pity on their face after hearing Richard was in a hotel. That was a bit of a relief. It was hard enough dealing with the realities of her life right now; being spoon-fed faux sympathy was not going to help her. However, if gossip was spreading maybe now was the time to halt it, get the facts out there. She took a deep breath and looked at the faces around the table. 'I overheard a snippet of what you were saying so it seems timely to let you all know that Richard and I are now separated, we are both very happy with the decision and will continue to parent our boys amicably.' Then she sat back, folded her arms and gave her most terrifying look to all present, just in case anyone mistakenly thought she needed to hear any more of their opinions or their commiserations. There, it was done, everyone knew now. And she hadn't melted into a puddle on the floor.

Chapter Twenty

'Hello, hello, hello. Only me.' Marion didn't bother ringing the doorbell and waiting; with the amount of time she was going to spend with them over the coming months and the trust they had put in her to organize the wedding she knew they wouldn't mind her letting herself in. 'Coo-ee!'

'Marion?' Matt popped his head around the living room door and looked shocked as he saw Marion in his hallway. She couldn't blame him; she was wearing a beautifully fitted tweed dress today.

'Hello, darling, thought I'd let myself in, save you getting up. Are you ready?' She brandished her tablet at him and walked into the living room. 'I have oodles of fabulous ideas for you and Rosy to consider. I was so pleased when you agreed to have me as your wedding planner; it really will take the burden off the both of you and you know you can rely on me to deliver a top-notch event.' She paused to grin at them, because it had said to do so in the plan she had put together in preparation for this meeting. Marion was fond of plans; they took away any anxiety about an event by having a step-by-step guide to controlling the action. Next step was to let them know that she was grateful for their custom and fully prepared to make their wedding the best day they could ever hope for.

'I listened very carefully to what you said last time we met and I have thought of some ideas.'

'Um… we don't really need ideas; we know exactly what we want. We just need you to—' Matt interrupted her.

'And that makes my job so much easier, thank you for that, Matt.' Her ears were going to fall off if she faux-grinned much harder. 'But there may be things that haven't even crossed your mind, that I have thought of so if you hear me out then I think you'll find I have some very exciting news.'

'Go on.' Matt dragged the two words out, looking at her as if marauding hordes were likely to come through the door any minute at her command. He didn't have to be so suspicious; she had his best interests at heart.

'No doubt you have spoken to your sister and she has shared her fabulous news with you.'

Matt broke into a genuine smile at this and grabbed Rosy's hand as he grinned.

'Yes, it makes me so happy. Chase is good for her and knowing that she is secure and settled is an amazing feeling.'

'It must be. I understand how close the two of you are, how you brought her up after your parents died. It can't have been easy and you have done so superbly if I may say.'

Matt inclined his head.

'He really did. And he was so young.'

'Quite. Angelina told me that you had always said that you couldn't really settle down until she had and now, ta-daa, it looks like you both are happy and ready to tie the knot this summer. So knowing how important Angelina is to you, Matt, what better idea—'

'No!' said Rosy forcefully, in a tone that Marion had never heard her use before. Then she looked as if she had thought twice and turned to Matt, scrunching her eyes up with self-sacrifice as she did so. 'Of course, if you want to…'

'If you'd let me finish.' So rude to interrupt. 'What better idea than to have the two of you combine forces and have a Masters wedding extraordinaire. I have a whole list of positiv—'

'No!' said Matt.

'But the advantages, not to mention the emotional satisfaction—'

'NO,' Rosy and Matt said, unanimously this time. Both holding Marion's eyes with a very firm look.

Damn, she had known this would be difficult but thought she could convince them how perfect it would be. Perfect for them as a family and perfect for her profile as an events coordinator. Drat. She was going to have to pull out the big guns.

Matt looked at her. 'Rosy and I have told you we know exactly what we want. Tonight is about letting you know the full details an—' He was interrupted by a bark from Scramble, who had been stretched out on the floor in front of the fire, with everything on display. Most distasteful.

'That must be Dan.' Rosy jumped up and headed to the door as someone knocked on it. Clearly the vicar wasn't on good enough terms with them to just let himself in.

'Dan? Oh goodie.' Marion couldn't help the worlds slip out of her mouth; the local vicar was an absolute dish. Too squeaky clean for her but perfect for his girlfriend Alice, and it did no harm to look. She wondered if he'd be in his dog collar – there was something extra special about forbidden fruit.

'Hello, Dan, do come in and take a seat.' She patted the space on the sofa next to herself as the vicar entered the room. 'We're going to have such fun. Now if we're all settled let's get to it and I can tell you how I see the day itself panning out.'

'Hello, Marion.' Dan smiled. Ooh, he was delicious. She breathed in, a default response to an attractive man; it made her look thinner and she'd been doing it automatically since she was fourteen. Would she have to breathe in twice as deep now she was single? She supposed that was something she could have to think about late at night when her mind was awhirl. She needed to fill it with this type of nonsense rather than flitting between wondering what she had done wrong, what she had done to alienate her husband and drive him into Claudia's arms and what a bastard he was. It was exhausting, utterly emotionally draining and not particularly conducive to sleep.

'Dan.' Rosy touched a hand to his arm. 'Come and sit down, and let's slow down a bit and…'

'No time to slow down, dear; if you want to get married this summer then we do need to get a wriggle on, especially if we want to make this a double Masters wedding extravaganza.'

'We don't, we made it quite clear,' Matt said immediately.

'Well, I know you said that…' Marion tittered to mask her irritation. 'But you didn't really give me a chance to explain. To paint a picture of just how gorgeous it would be. Give me five minutes and I will wow you with the romance, the majesty and the glamour of it all.'

'I think Rosy and Matt have a very clear picture of what they want, and from what I've heard majesty and glamour aren't really on their wish list. Small and intimate is what they are after,' Dan said.

Honestly, if he wasn't going to help!

'Well, if their only advisor to date has been the village vicar, forgive me, Dan, then maybe that would explain why they are limiting themselves. Hmmm?' She tried to put it nicely, but the trouble with the clergy was they had no vision, always harking back to the past. Last time she had checked Dan wasn't even on Instagram.

She couldn't help but conclude that he didn't understand exactly what was at stake here. Dan may be trying to look after their souls, but these two were so good he didn't really need to worry. He could spend his time with practically anyone else and have more of an effect. She quickly flashed through her mind to see how she could suggest him leaving in a way that didn't cause too much offence.

She scanned the room; their faces did not look as if they understood she was really trying to be nice. Okay...

'Let me try and rephrase that...' They all raised their eyebrows; Dan quickly lowered his and nodded supportively. Truly, once the novelty of his good looks wore off, his presence was a bit of a downer. 'Let's look at the bigger picture here.' She started again, throwing her whole self into her pitch. 'Yes, your wedding day should be all about the two of you declaring your love, your commitment for the world to see, for everyone to know that from here on in the two of you cannot be torn asunder, that you are a team with an unbreakable bond that will last well past any of the nonsense that life throws at you, two souls joined for a lifetime...' She could feel tears prickling at the corners of her eyes and she blinked rapidly; what was wrong with her?

You couldn't let emotion interfere with business. She'd thought she had more backbone than this.

And now she needed to sniff. How could she sniff in the middle of such an impassioned plea? It would kill the mood completely. She inhaled deeply and blinked her eyes hard in a last-ditch attempt. Okay, now she could continue. 'But the thing is, neither of you are spring chickens; both of you have a past.' She felt Rosy stiffen beside her. This was not going as it was meant to – she needed to think quickly, get that happy mood back. What did these two like to do other than good? Ah, that was it – they liked to do good! 'This wedding has the potential to generate a lot of interest *and* therefore a lot of money, even once all the costs and my fee are covered. With that revenue you could do *so* much good. Donate it to any number of charities. Think of all the unfortunate souls you could help, children, animals...' She flicked a look at Dan, who didn't look as supportive of this as he should. 'Um... the deserving but destitute vicar's fund?' The words came tumbling over each other at speed. So much for cool, collected and professional. She'd be on her knees begging in a minute if she didn't get a hold of herself.

'Marion, what are you talking about? How did we get from planning our wedding to destitute vicars?' Matt always had to hark back to the practical. She supposed he was a gardener; she couldn't expect him to be too cerebral. Millions of viewers didn't tune in every Friday night because of his brains.

'The thing is, Matt...' She needed to stop babbling, slow down and present her clearest self. 'It's not just the good you could do. You and Angelina have done all your growing up together; I know how you looked after her, sacrificed everything to give her the best upbringing when your mother, you know your mother...' Marion was flustered but felt that talking about maternal suicide at this time was not going to be okay. She didn't know how much Rosy knew and certainly not Dan. 'The point is that there's a really nice symmetry to this: the two of you survived together and you both get your happy ever afters together. It's not just a case of you seeing her happily wed, and thus less of a burd— um, responsibility to you. But the two of you getting married together, at the same time. It has a beautiful synchronicity, a final ceremony that ushers in a new life, new priorities for each of you.'

Matt did not look particularly captivated by her argument but she could see Rosy, absent-mindedly patting Scramble, looking as if she understood the point.

'On top of which, I saw how you rose to the save the school challenge when you two first met.' Rosy and Matt exchanged adoring looks and Marion tried not to gag. 'I know how important giving back is to you. How you like to use your current status as television's darling of the nation... now, now, don't blush, we all know it's true.' She leant forward and tapped him playfully on the leg and Dan and Rosy nodded in acknowledgement. 'Well, this is your finest opportunity to give back; this is worth even more than sucking up the name *Green-fingered and Gorgeous* for the sake of the pupils in Penmenna School, Matt.'

'How did you know...?'

'I know everything that happens in this village; you should know that by now.' She heard the laugh escape her lips, but it was genuine and good-natured this time. She did know everything, it was a fact; knowledge was important when one wanted to hold a community together as she did.

'What you're saying, Marion, is that if Matt and Rosy chose to get married in a double ceremony with his sister and her partner then they could donate large sums to the charities of their choosing,' Dan outlined.

'Yes.' Marion sat back smugly. She knew it would work.

'Which means that you will have raised that money by selling our wedding to the tabloids, or whomever proves to be the highest bidder and our wedding becomes a circus,' Matt countered.

'No, well, a bit, but I'm sure if we made it an exclusive then we could limit that.'

'So, if we sell it as an exclusive, we only have one or two photographers there and we give a substantial sum to charity?' Rosy asked, bless her. Marion knew Rosy would have her back on this. See how important this day was to Marion. But before she could answer in the affirmative, Matt had butted in.

'The thing is, I don't want what Angelina wants, and I'm fairly sure neither does Rosy. It's still a big no from me.'

'Well.' Rosy laid her hand on Matt's leg. 'You're right of course, I don't want that. Not at all. But if we could raise some money, we could donate it to Alex's foundation and it's only one day, one day and then we have the rest of our lives together to do exactly as we want. And it would make Angelina happy; that has to be worth almost anything.'

'Of course it'll make Ange happy, because she'll have all the attention and that's what feeds her. She's like a gremlin; just because she asks to be fed doesn't mean it's wise to do

137

so. More importantly, it's *our* day, our wedding day. The first, the last, the only, and I don't want it hijacked by my sister. That may sound selfish, but it's true. I want this day to be about just you and me. That's not so wrong, is it?'

'Not wrong at all.' Rosy reached over and held both of Matt's hands with hers and there was a pause as they looked at each other lovingly.

Dear God, today was proving rather testing. She'd better let them have their moment. Even the poxy dog had sat up and cocked his head to one side in adoration.

Dan was the first to break the silence. 'Why don't you see what Matt and Rosy want to do for their day and then go from there. There may be a way to work out a compromise that suits everyone.'

'There won't be,' Matt said, still looking lovingly at his fiancée but perfectly capable of making snide comments out the side of his mouth. 'Have you met my sister? Actually, you probably haven't; I'm ready to bet money that she has not set foot in the church since she arrived here two years ago. The fact that it's still standing is testament to that. I'm fairly sure she would have burst into flames and taken out a pew or two had she tried.'

'Matt!' Rosy giggled and faux slapped him. That was almost as annoying as the whole staring into each other's eyes thing. Even when she and Richard were together they never made a public show of themselves like that!

A quick memory flashed into Marion's mind of herself and Richard in a coat cupboard the very night that Chase and Angelina had met and she felt, just for a second, a flicker of guilt. Of awareness that Chase that night certainly saw more than was fit for public consumption but then that was hardly their fault. They had shut the cupboard door; it was he who had rudely pulled it open.

'Why don't we go through the order of the day, what you two have already decided that you want and go from there,' Dan said, breaking Marion's reverie. She supposed anything that made a start would be something. She did need them on side and maybe listening couldn't hurt. That way she'd know their plans and be able to show how if they had Angelina and Chase involved it could become even better than their wildest imaginings. Which she now realized were very limited. The last thing she wanted to do was alienate them even more.

Marion took another deep breath; there was more than one way to skin a cat. 'What a good idea, let's do that. So, Rosy, Matt…' She leant forward, her tablet poised, most professional and amiable smile on. 'Tell me, what is it that you would like?'

Chapter Twenty-one

The meeting hadn't gone the exact way she had planned it. Marion had walked back from Rosy and Matt's with a list on her iPad of the wedding they wanted and it was very different to the one she had hoped for. She wasn't sure how she was going to turn this around and get their wedding and the wedding Angelina would undoubtedly want into any kind of correlation, but she had faith in herself. If anyone *could* do it, it would be her.

Then she had come home to find Richard in the house with the boys, all upstairs gathered around the laptop screeching and shouting in communal joy at the screen as Rupert played his game. This was how a lot of the previous week, half term, had panned out, and it hadn't been easy. She knew the boys loved her; they may be little rotters a lot of the time but when it came to the outside world her boys had her back like no other. But did they ask her to play video games with her? That was a definite no.

She had dotted each of the boys' heads with a kiss and then headed into the kitchen where the most delicious smell was emanating from the oven. Peeking through the oven door she saw it was a lasagne, presumably one with butternut squash and goat's cheese, her absolute favourite that Richard used to cook for her on a Saturday when he felt she needed a lift after running the boys around all day.

She heard footsteps behind her and turned to see her husband standing in the doorway, sheepish grin on his face.

'I thought after your long day, the least I could do whilst I was keeping an eye on the boys was to have something warm for you in the oven.' She looked at his little face, the crinkle around his eyes and knew he was worried that he had overstepped. He had always been respectful of boundaries and was aware she may feel it was an invasion. She allowed herself a small half-smile of thanks and a grin spread across his face, presumably thankful that she wasn't reaching for something to throw at him. She had felt a little guilty about the vase she had cracked over his head. It was hard to be cross with this face that she had loved for so many years; it would be a lot easier if he just sodded off.

'There's a good half hour or so before it's ready. If you want to go and have a quick bath, the boys and I will have everything ready when you come out. Although I won't stay for supper,' he added, the last sentence an afterthought.

'No, that's okay. You can stay. The boys will be cross if you don't. And a bath, that would be nice. Thank you.'

'My pleasure.' He reached over and touched her shoulder, tentatively. 'I've got lots to tell you. I'd love it if we could go out this week, maybe for lunch, and I can fill you in with all my news. Lots of changes.' She may appreciate a lasagne and a bath but a lunch date? With the man whose actions had tipped her family upside down? Pfft! 'The main thing is I will be in Cornwall full-time now, just as we had always planned. It means I can support you lots as you get this new business off the ground,' he continued.

'Better late than never I suppose,' she snapped. He did have a cheek. She had been desperate for him to come home and then, typically, he had finally managed it a little too late.

–

Supper had been lovely though. It was a snapshot of everything she had ever dreamed of, her whole family around the table on a regular weekday, the boys and Richard laughing and joking as they ate, discussing what they had done at school. She had found herself taking a backseat, too scared to join in, in case she ruined the mood.

She was grateful that the boys were so accepting about the situation and tonight, when Richard left, Rafe had come down the stairs and rubbed her back silently as she stood at the front door. Her sons really were special.

Marion decided to get comfy and cuddle down on the sofa with Darcy and watch reruns of *The Wedding Planner*, to see if there was anything she hadn't thought of – unlikely, but one had to keep one's sword sharp. She popped on her pyjamas and dressing gown – a look she would never normally sport but her whole world was far from normal these days, and other women seemed to make a big fuss about it so she thought she would try. She was just beginning to get comfy when the doorbell rang.

Shit!

No one ever visited Marion in the evening, not without it being pre-arranged and at Marion's behest. Trust that the first ever time she decided to slob out and watch reality TV, she would have a visitor. Did she have time to run upstairs and change?

The doorbell rang again – argggh! She turned the television off and went to see who on earth had decided to disturb her.

She peeked through the spyhole. For goodness' sake! It was Alice. What was she thinking? Marion yanked the door open and fixed Alice with one of her fiercest looks. One of the things she respected about the teaching assistant was that Marion's looks slid right off her. Alice was made of stern stuff and Marion quite liked it. Still, it amused her to try.

'Yes!' she barked.

Alice smirked, in a you'll-have-to-try-harder-than-that manner before saying, 'Is it okay to come in?' *as* she was walking in. One of Marion's tricks. For a minute Marion forgot that she was in pyjamas and smirked back. This might be interesting.

She wasn't batting an eye at Marion's attire so Marion decided to relax a little.

'You'll have to be quick,' she snapped. There was relaxing and then there was being a pushover. 'Why *are* you here?' Marion felt her eyes narrow as she quizzed her unexpected guest, widening only as she spotted a bottle of wine peeking out of her tote.

Alice followed her line of sight and wiggled the bag. 'I thought we could have a drink, a catch-up, a chat.'

Now Marion was suspicious; no one nipped in for a chat. Was Alice grooming her? And what for? She'd better not be looking for volunteers for Sunday School again.

But maybe now she was single, this was when people started coming out of the woodwork. Was this part of the plan she had overheard in the staffroom? She supposed it could do no harm just to have one drink. Free wine was free wine and Marion was savvy enough not to get caught into anything she didn't want to be.

She motioned Alice to the sofa, the dog to his basket and went to get a corkscrew and a couple of glasses.

'So, how are you?' Alice asked.

Marion fixed her with a look and stayed silent.

'What about those lovely boys of yours, how are they?' Alice flashed a huge grin.

'Just that, absolutely lov—' There was a huge crashing from upstairs, followed by a slapping sound and a loud 'Muuuuum!'

Both Alice and Marion's heads whipped around.

'Should we...?' Alice gestured to the stairs.

'Oh no, nothing to worry about. They're just practising their karate, such diligent children,' Marion fibbed. She really didn't need the myth of her perfect family life smashed at the same time as she was slumming about in pyjamas.

Alice didn't look convinced.

'Muuuum!' the bellow came again, this time from Rafe, and with a distinct note of panic in his voice. Then some kicking and owwwing from what sounded like Rupert.

This time Marion didn't even try and gloss over it. The two women jumped from their chairs, racing up the stairs to the bathroom to find Rupert in his pyjamas on the floor rolling around like a professional football player, his older brother Rafe in front of the bathroom mirror with his hand atop his head but at the oddest angle and Rufus laughing hysterically whilst pointing at Rafe.

'Boys, what is going on?'

'They're little shits, Mum, little shits, look what they've done.'

'Language,' Marion reprimanded sharply.

'I think this merits it.' Rafe's vocabulary had always been so adult, bless him. Rafe, however, didn't seem particularly bothered about his vocabulary right now. But he did spot Alice behind Marion in the doorway.

'Oh, I'm sorry, Miss Pentire, I didn't see you there. But look, look what they've done!'

'Rupert, get off the floor; there's nothing wrong with you. Rufus, pull yourself together. If your brother is distressed that is not a thing to giggle about. What have they done, Rafe, darling?'

Rafe tried lifting his hand from his head but it didn't appear to come away. Although his hair, despite being short, raised up with his hand.

'They put superglue in my hair gel. How am I ever going to get it off? I'm never going to be able to leave the house again. I'm meant to be FaceTimeing Sophie in a bit and…' Rafe's voice was spiralling getting higher and higher and more and more angry. He kicked out at Rupert again, who was getting up off the floor and who bounded out of the way just in time.

'Why would I put superglue in his hair gel?' Rupert said, an expression of faux outrage on his face. An expression that didn't fool a single person in that room.

'Rupert Marksharp, I cannot believe you have done this. Why would you do this to your brother?'

'Because he's an idiot?' Rupert answered as if his mother was stupid for asking a question to which the answer was so obvious.

'I'm gonna kill…' Rafe turned around to attack his brother again, but could only do so one-handed; the other remained firmly attached to his head.

'It wasn't just me!' Rupert giggled as he skipped out of the way again. He had always excelled at his country dancing classes, Marion thought with pride before she remembered the situation she was in, and all in front of Alice as a witness. Mortifying. She threw a glance in Alice's direction but the woman was tapping away on her phone, a half-smile on her face.

'Shut up, shut up, shut up!' Rufus jumped up and also tried to attack Rupert, who was still busy laughing, his words coming out between giggles. Rufus was landing blows on his brother but not enough to stop him from speaking.

'Rufus weed in your Lynx shower gel,' Rupert said triumphantly.

'Mum!' screeched Rafe. 'That's disgusting, disgusting.'

'That is too far, boys, really too far. Rupert and Rufus, get to your room now. No video games for two weeks – you're both grounded and I will be drawing up a list of chores to keep you busy and they will involve so much scrubbing you may lose your fingerprints,' Marion said firmly. The skirting boards could do with a good clean; every cloud and all that.

'I don't want to lose my fingerprints,' Rufus sobbed.

'I don't want your wee in my shower gel, you disgusting little toerag,' Rafe shouted in response over his mother's head, still with only the one arm flailing wildly.

'What's disgusting is that he hasn't worked it out yet. Rafe put it in there three days ago and he's clearly not showered in that time. I thought having a girlfriend would make him want to wash at least,' Rupert shot over his shoulder as he tripped out of the bathroom towards his room.

'For the last time, she's not my girlfriend,' Rafe shouted, tears welling in his eyes at the unfairness of life. At that moment, his phone began to ring on the side, his not-girlfriend's face flashing up on the screen.

'Oh my God, oh my God, she can't see me like this, it'll be all around school. What am I going to do? Mum! What am I going…'

Marion grabbed the phone, angling it away from Rafe so all that could be seen as she answered was her face and the shower behind her.

'Oh, hello Mrs Marksharp. Is… um… is Rafe there?' Sophie's face popped up on the screen.

'I'm afraid he's very busy with important family business,' Marion said sharply.

'But we had agreed to…'

'Yes, that was before the important family business and now he is too busy to come to the phone. I shall tell him you called.' The matriarch of the family used a tone that brooked no disagreement.

'But…'

'Do I need to speak to your mother?'

'No, no, of course not. Well, if you just tell him I ca—'

Marion cut her off. 'Yes, quite. You can see him in school tomorrow. Goodbye.' She ended the call and Rafe looked at her, tears fully streaming down his face now.

'Mum, why? Why would you do that? I can't have my mum answering my phone, that's so embarrassing.'

Marion walked over to him and started to rub his back in a circular motion, as he had her earlier in the evening, trying to calm him. 'Look, everyone knows I'm a nightmare. Your friends certainly do. So, let me take the blame on this one; no one is going to mock you just because I'm being difficult, and certainly not Sophie. If she does then

147

she's not worth it.' Rafe didn't look convinced. 'You had three choices: you could have me being a difficult parent, you could just not answer and incur her wrath or you could let her see that your hand was superglued to your head. Which would be worse?'

'Your mum is right, Rafe. I think she's just saved your bacon.' Alice finally spoke. 'And if it's superglue, we can get that out no problem, thanks to Google.' She held her phone aloft to back up her point.

'There, see. Now, Miss Pentire and I...'

'Alice.' Alice smiled warmly.

'Alice and I are going to sort this out. Everything is going to be okay.' Marion gave Rafe a steely glare full of promise of a future so brutal she would be amazed if he could sleep, then guided her eldest son downstairs to the kitchen where she and Alice set to work with a large bottle of nail varnish remover, an old comb and an awful lot of patience.

It took almost two hours. Two hours of Rafe constantly shrieking *ow* and vacillating between self-pity and anger as they teased his hair away from his hand. But eventually they did it, finally managing to free him and sending him upstairs for a shower in the hope that when his hair was washed it wouldn't look as if it had been mauled into tiny little patchy bits. Marion dreaded the fallout that was going to occur if he did come out of the shower with his hair all uneven.

Alice looked at the bottle of wine, measuring its contents with a beady eye. There was probably about one glass left each – both had been sipping as they worked – and she poured out the remaining content into their glasses as they sat around the kitchen table looking at the debris, the comb and little bits of sticky stuff, solidified into round balls with small amounts of hair stuck to it.

'You did really well. I can't imagine what would have happened if my mum had been in charge of that,' Alice sympathized.

Marion bristled. 'I did as any mother would do. It was most unusual. My boys are never normally badly behaved.' Alice quirked a brow and Marion decided to change the subject. It was going to be hard arguing the my-boys-are-angels viewpoint after what Alice had just witnessed.

'You really didn't. I was an only child so didn't have the whole siblings arguing thing but my mum banned superglue in our house, alongside anything else vaguely creative – painting, Play-Doh, sand. It just wasn't allowed in case it caused any mess at all.'

'Your mother is a very sensible woman. How is she? Still in Dubai?' Marion was genuinely curious. Alice's mother had the most perfect life, was remarkably well put together and as different to her daughter as could be.

'Yup. And no she wasn't, isn't, a sensible woman. Truth is, she was and is a very frightened woman who depends upon male approval for her *raison d'être*. She couldn't cope with any suggestion that her house and child – and thus by extension, her – were anything less than perfect. Appearances are everything to her, but scratch the surface and it's an empty, fearful existence. You were fab up there. You were calm, you didn't make it about you and I suspect those boys are in for a hefty punishment.' Alice didn't seem fazed by giving such a candid answer, one that dived down straight past the surface level of small talk and into honesty. Marion suddenly felt comfortable; she knew about difficult mothers. Alice's praise for her parenting was a rare jewel and made Marion feel far more at ease than she had been five minutes ago.

'Oh yes.' Marion nodded. 'They most certainly are. I don't mind making allowances for them in terms of sibling rough and tumble; I was an only child and desperately craved a brother or sister so I never wanted to punish them for creating the bonds that I missed out on. But there are limits.'

'I think weeing in the shower gel is probably a very sensible limit,' Alice responded.

'Quite,' replied Marion with a smile. 'My mother had some similarities to yours. Not the house-proud bit; she was as slovenly as they came. I mean blow-her-nose-on-banana-peels-then-shove-them-down-the-back-of-the-radiator bad. Old cups of tea as ashtrays because she could never be arsed to get up. She didn't have a washing basket; she would just chuck her knickers, all her dirty clothes, onto the kitchen floor once she had worn them, waiting for a time that laundry was done. A job that I can promise you wouldn't have even happened if it hadn't been for me. I'm not sure how we managed when I was a toddler and too small to reach the washing machine dials. This scar here...' Marion lifted her fringe and leant forward so Alice could see it better. 'That was when I went head first into the units because my foot got caught in a thong. I was six.'

Marion silenced herself as she realized how frank she had just been; she had shared a detail she had never shared with anyone, not even Richard. But as she snuck a look at Alice through her eyelashes, she saw that the woman opposite her didn't look revolted or even particularly surprised, just sympathetic and understanding. She had to admit that in all her dealings with Alice she had recognized that the woman seemed inhumanly free from judgement. Marion found herself continuing. It was like a valve that had been rusted shut for years was suddenly twisting open.

'Until she had a new love interest; at that point she could drag herself away from watching game shows all day and do a bit of tidying up. She truly believed that one day she would be a contestant, win a fortune and it would make up for her never working. I think she viewed watching those shows as some sort of training for the life she believed she deserved yet had never quite happened for her. Anyway, when she did get a new love interest, well, you should have seen them. She liked the ones dripping in gold best, a sixty-a-day Embassy Number 1 habit and preferably with cars they would rev up and down the estate as if they were at Silverstone in a fully tricked-out Formula One racing car, rather than zooming around the Merryfield... talk about a misnomer' – Marion barked out a sarcastic laugh – 'around the Merryfield estate in a clapped-out Ford Capri with a pimped-up exhaust. Then she'd learn how to tidy. My God, did she whizz around with the Pledge then. Any toys I had would be hidden, any evidence of me expunged and her sexiest knickers would be dangled over the radiator as if they were drying, to show what a racy woman she was. I remember one set, it had a basque...' Marion paused. What was she doing, telling someone who worked at the school all of this? What was she thinking sitting here chatting about maternal promiscuity and detailing her mother's underwear to a woman who was dating the bloody vicar? Yet now she had started it was like a compulsion. She picked up her glass to have another sip and realized it was empty.

Wordlessly, Alice got up and moved to the kettle, flicking it on as if she were in her own house and for some reason Marion didn't feel like taking umbrage. She did feel like talking, though; the floodgates had opened, so to speak. Alice hadn't interrupted her yet and seeing as she had put the kettle on clearly was set to stay for a bit.

'They weren't all bad. Some of them were kind to me, would bring me little treats but that wasn't the point. The point I guess was that my mother wasn't. She never showed a millimetre, a fraction of a millimetre of pride in me and my achievements. And by God did I achieve, thinking I guess that one day I would do something so great that she would have to praise me. Do you know I won the awards for the most hard-working child in school every sodding year, and not once, not once did my mother turn up to the celebration assembly? Not once. I don't think school knew what she looked like; secondary school certainly didn't. By that point I'd stopped striving for her approval, I just wanted an escape and figured that being the exact opposite of my mother was the best chance I had of getting the life I wanted. I got myself into Oxford, you know. That's where I met Richard, and the last words she said to me as I packed up my stuff and got ready to make my own way to university was that I was a lazy bitch who hadn't taken the bins out.' Marion took a sip of the tea that Alice had set down wordlessly next to her. 'I was so conditioned to it, I went back and did them before I shut the door for the last time.' She heard a little *hmm* noise escape her lips as she finished speaking. A reflective *hmm* that fully captured the essence of how foolish doing the bins made her.

'I'm so sorry, Marion, that's dreadful. What did she say when you graduated?'

'I didn't tell her. What was the point?'

'And now, how are the two of you now?'

'I never went back. Once I was out, I was out. I haven't gone back to Merryfield since. No, that's not strictly true. I went back for the first time this month. When I found out that Richard was cheating on me and for all my hard work, for all my choices, I had ended up choosing a husband as unreliable as the many lovers of my mother. The only difference being that he never turned up with a kebab or called me sunshine.'

'I'm sure that's not the only difference.' Alice leant over and placed her hand upon Marion's. Marion allowed it to stay. Alice had never said a word about the ridiculous scenario in the run-up to last Christmas where Marion and Serena had a full-on old-fashioned cat fight, well worthy of her Merryfield heritage, and Alice had doused each of them with a basin of water to break them apart. Marion had a feeling she could rely on Alice not to say a word about what had happened here tonight. Trust was not something Marion had really applied to women before but this woman, the one with the thick reddish brown hair that could do with a brushing and a frame that could do with losing a few pounds, this woman Marion trusted, and before she knew what she was doing, a tirade about Richard, his betrayal and her love gushed forth from her lips – *I miss him, I love him, I'd do anything to have him back but once a cheat…* It was as if she were a dam that had just been destroyed, her past and her emotions a raging torrent unleashed.

Chapter Twenty-two

Marion was back in Penmenna School the next morning. She pushed open the big old Victorian front door and entered the building, reaching the office where Sheila, the school secretary, was based.

Chatting with Alice last night had had an impact upon her. Alice hadn't left until gone eleven and Marion had found that not only did she not mind, but she had quite enjoyed herself. Marion had talked for hours about how much she missed Richard but could never forgive him. She'd found herself going on and on about how she loved his outdated sayings, how he could sing beautifully but only after a couple of drinks, how he knew what she needed before she did. She talked about how his freckles made her smile, the scent of him used to make her feel safe.

She had gone on a bit.

She also learnt that having someone who sat, listened and made encouraging noises was soothing. Alice hadn't jumped in to try to problem-solve, try to offer solutions so that Marion would shut up and move on to the next subject; she had just listened.

It had made Marion wonder when she woke up this morning, fully rested for the first night in *ages*, if perhaps listening was an undervalued skill that people needed to utilize more. If being listened to was responsible for making her sleep well and wake up this invigorated then maybe it was something she should give more credence to. It was certainly a skill she was prepared to utilize in her nascent business. She had sent a text or two to make sure people were aware that she was a Very Good Listener these days. And now she was going to practise on Sheila.

The last thing she expected to see was Richard in the office, comfortable as comfortable could be sitting behind Sheila's desk, his glasses slipped partly down his nose as he looked at Sheila's laptop screen. The woman was known for many things; her wizardry at IT was not one of them.

For goodness' sake! She knew she couldn't get too mad; he was chair of the governors so was entitled to be in the school from time to time. She would have just preferred it not to have been today, the day she had woken up perky and positive rather than exhausted and wrung out. And now his very presence was liable to make her mood plummet. It didn't help that Sheila was leaning over him, cooing about how clever he was, whilst wafting a plate full of biscuits, complete with doily, under his nose. Who had doilies these days? Marion was fairly sure none had been sold since 1972 and certainly knew she had never been on the receiving end of one in all her years in the school.

'Ooh, hello, Mrs Marksharp. Aren't you lucky to be married to such a clever man?'

For God's sake, he was hardly Einstein. It would also seem that the news hadn't made it back to Sheila quite yet; that was a relief, albeit an unexpected one.

Sheila suddenly gasped. 'Oops, sorry. Awkward…' She giggled to mask her embarrassment. Okay, the gossip had reached her, as had her granddaughter's language skills. Sheila tried to cover up her blunder by more talking. 'I just couldn't get the laptop to work after the latest update but Mr Marksharp is being terribly kind and sorting out the whole thing for me.'

Marion felt herself suck in air and without meaning to she could feel her lips begin to purse. Great. Here was Richard Marksharp, laptop saviour, and Mrs Marksharp, sour old lemon. She could practically hear the whole village thinking *it's no wonder their marriage failed*. She tried really hard not to growl and instead stalked through into Rosy's office, the door of which was open, and which she very firmly closed so she wouldn't have to hear any more cooing.

She wondered how Sheila would feel if she knew the terribly clever Mr Marksharp had been caught cheating with a colleague. One would hope she wouldn't see him as a towering genius then. Although knowing Sheila's ability to gloss over anything she didn't feel was particularly pleasant, she would probably start rattling off some nonsense about boys being boys. Marion flinched a little as her scathing inner monologue reminded her that it was one of her default phrases for her sons' misdemeanours. She wouldn't be using that again. In fact, she had a feeling she may be tightening up on that score immediately. She had been lucky that Rafe's hair recovered remarkably quickly and had been fine this morning, but the pendulum of her liberal parenting had obviously swung too far. She would have those boys back on schedules before they knew what had hit them.

It took less than ten minutes for Rosy to agree on colours and designs for the bridesmaids' dresses, to okay stationery, schedule the cake tasting and adamantly refuse to consider writing vows – she and Matt wanted it to be as pressure-free as possible and no, having their wedding planner write the vows for them was definitely not an option. Marion smiled as she left the room. She could see she was going to get good at listening.

'I can't believe you've done it. You really are a marvel, Richard, so lovely to have you back in the village. I didn't know how I was going to get through the working day without my Candy Crush running; it breaks the time up so nicely. And then we had this silly update on the network system…'

'It was an absolute pleasure, Sheila. Everyone needs a little bit of downtime through the day. If you'll excuse me a minute – Marion! Marion…'

Marion had already opened the door and was heading down the granite steps at speed. It had been tough having him around last night at supper; it cut a little too close to the bone. She really wasn't keen on him turning up at school as well. For a man who had spent the last few years rushed off his feet he seemed to be finding a remarkable amount of leisure time.

'Marion!' He wasn't giving up easily.

'Yes?' she snapped, turning and facing him.

'I was hoping you might be coming to the PTA meeting in a bit?'

'I hardly have the time, Richard, not these days.'

'I thought I would go.' His chin dipped into his chest. He had always been rubbish at hiding his emotions but Marion wasn't going to take the blame for his disappointment.

'Jolly good, see what you think and feed back to me later.' It would do no harm to have eyes and ears there when she wasn't. She wanted to get to St Michael's Mount today and have a talk with the family there. She was sure they could easily monetize such a fabulous setting much more efficiently than they were.

'Later?' Richard's face perked up. 'Yes, I could do that, shall I pop home... um, to yours,' he corrected, and Marion knew how that would cost him, 'afterwards? I could take you to lunch?'

'I said no to lunch yesterday, Richard. I meant feed back by text; there's no need to give the boys false hope by turning up every day. I think perhaps if you limit your visits to the weekend and when I need you, that would be best. Now if you'll excuse me, I really do have to be getting on.' Marion wished she had a fan she could clasp shut firmly or a velvet cloak she could sweep around her in a movement of dismissal but alas, she would have to rely on what was at her disposal, and that was bucketloads of sass. She turned pointedly on her heel, huffed down the school steps and stalked back to the car park, aware of his eyes watching her every move as she left.

Chapter Twenty-three

Well, so much for that plan. Richard had thought Marion would be leading the PTA meeting to which he had invited himself. Now what?

Being back in Penmenna permanently meant he could get far more involved in his family's life and he figured helping out in school was a good first step. It would send a message to the boys that this wasn't a fleeting visit and, he hoped, would enable him to spend a little more time with Marion outside of the house, which was now an area of uncomfortable pauses, constant fear of stepping over the line and feeling distinctly not welcome. All of which had to be balanced by pretending to the boys that this separation wasn't something to worry about.

Yesterday had gone well; he knew she loved that lasagne but he wasn't a fool – he didn't think the odd supper cooked was going to win his wife back. He was worried that it may actually be a task beyond his solitary skills. He needed to assemble a crack team, and her friends at the school were a jolly good start. The dinner party Chase had planned for this evening would be a good second. Richard had never thought of himself as particularly Machiavellian, that was his wife's forte, but he was realizing that after almost two decades of marriage he had learnt a trick or two.

'Hello, I thought I heard your voice, how are you?' Rosy popped her head around the door just as he was walking back into the school after Marion had scarpered.

'Oh hi, Rosy. All good, thank you. Happy to be back in Penmenna full time.'

'Fabulous, that's great for us. How come you're back?'

Richard explained as briefly as he could how his firm had offered him consultancy work that he could do from home, which enabled him to spend more time at the school. Rosy listened politely, made no mention of the fact that he had been thrown out by his wife, and invited him to take a wander around the school whilst he was waiting for the meeting at breaktime.

'Oh no, that doesn't seem fair, I don't want to interrupt anyone's teaching.'

'I'm sure no one would mind; it will give you a far more accurate picture of school life rather than just relying upon the timetabled observations.'

'Won't everyone hate me popping in? I don't think I'd be keen if I was a teacher with anybody just wandering in and out.' Rosy laughed at this and as soon as he said it he realized that he knew Marion had spent the last few years doing exactly that. Rosy still didn't mention her though.

'I think everyone is very comfortable with you. I've experienced some scary chairs in my time, and you are not that. You are reasonable, understand it can't be awe and wonder every minute of every day and genuinely want the best for the school. I don't think anyone will mind, and quite frankly it's tough if they do. It does Harmony no injury at all to be surprised occasionally, curbs her worst excesses as it were. I do it at least once a day or she'd have the children painting protest placards every day and never get around to anything maths or science-based. She's great at all the humanities, citizenship and so on, but does need a firm hand. Today, you can be me for a bit.'

'I might not be a very good Miss Winter; not sure I'm going to fool anyone. Talking of which, congratulations are in order. I heard that you and Matt are getting married – that's lovely. I'm sure the two of you will be very happy. You must be busy with all the planning.'

Rosy placed a hand on his arm which was full of unspoken messages; he just couldn't work out exactly what.

'Actually, Marion is taking over the body of the work; she's already saving me loads of time. I tell her what I want, she researches all the options and then sends me the details. I couldn't see the wood for the trees before and she's bringing a clarity and ease that makes everything a lot less stressful. Or at least she is this week; she was pushing for a joint wedding with Matt's sister but she's quietened down about that now. We haven't run into any major problems yet but knowing Marion will intercede if anything goes horribly wrong is such a relief. I'm genuinely looking forward to it.'

'I'm so glad to hear that; she is definitely someone you want fighting your battles for you. I've never met anyone that Marion couldn't subdue or a problem she couldn't solve,' Richard said, very aware that right now he was both the person she had subdued and the problem she had solved.

'Quite; she has Harmony in a perpetual state of anxiety.' Richard knew he looked alarmed when Rosy giggled. 'I'm only joking, well I'm not but I protect Harmony and she does bring a lot of it upon herself. Marion is much easier on the other teachers.'

The phone rang; Sheila answered it and then asked Rosy if she were free to take it. Rosy ducked back into her study for the call to be put through and Richard decided he had better do as he was told – years of training – and headed into the main part of the school.

It was unfortunate that as he walked through into the school hall, admiring the colourful displays up on the walls, the first person he saw, sitting on one of the wooden PE benches at the side of the room with his teacher next to him, was Rufus. Rufus looking shamefaced and Richard wasn't quite sure what to do. He didn't want to embarrass anyone, either his son or Kam Choudhury, but with the hall door slamming behind him loudly, there was no way he could quietly back out of the room now.

At that moment Kam looked up and made eye contact. Shit, he'd have to go over now. He knew if Marion was here she'd start a great long spiel about what a good boy Rufus was and how there had obviously been a mix-up. Richard had never been convinced this was the best policy.

He knew, as Marion did, exactly how mischievous his boys were but unlike her, didn't hide behind the my-boys-can-do-no-wrong style of parenting so beloved by the Krays' mother. He understood why Marion was the way she was but he couldn't help but feel a slightly more honest answer was usually more helpful.

He approached the two, and as soon as Rufus saw him he could see the boy beginning to well up. Rufus quickly looked down at the floor and tried to hide his emotion by surreptitiously wiping his hand on his sleeve.

'Mr Choudhury, good to see you.' Richard stretched his hand out to shake Kam's. 'Everything alright?'

'Hello, Mr Marksharp.' Kam was the newest member of staff and as such didn't know Richard very well yet. And vice versa. But Richard knew he wouldn't have been hired if Rosy didn't have complete faith in him and Marion had very good things to say as well. 'Everything's fine, Rufus and I were having a little chat. There was a bit of a misunderstanding this morning but I think we're just about to clear it up, aren't we, Rufus?'

Rufus nodded slowly, his blonde curls tumbling down his forehead giving him massive cute appeal. Then he rolled up the bottom of his sweater and started sheepishly unhooking a row of sewing needles he had woven onto the inside of his school jumper.

'We've been doing some sewing, as part of the DT curriculum, making bags for special treasures. Everyone has been working really hard, haven't they?'

Rufus nodded, eyes still down on the floor.

'And Rufus was in charge of counting the needles back in, weren't you? But he decided he had further use for them and very cleverly stashed them inside his jumper. Unfortunately for him, he was clever but not tidy and I could see little glimmers of silver giving the game away so we've just come out here to talk about it.'

All primary school teachers spoke like this, but it still always took Richard back to hear a fully-grown adult talk as if they lived in a land of unicorns and sparkles. Mind you, he supposed it was better than whipping out the cane or slipper at every possible opportunity. His school had been very regimented and he wouldn't wish that on any of his sons, ever. In his day, it seemed that there was a belief that the crueller people were to you, the better prepared you were for adult life.

Richard crouched down on the floor and reached for his youngest son's hand. 'If you take something without asking, even if you plan to give it back later, then that's stealing. And you're a clever boy, you know that stealing is wrong, really wrong. If you were a grown-up you would have the police come and arrest you if you stole something. You're very lucky Mr Choudhury is being so understanding; not everyone would be. Why did you take the needles?'

Rufus sniffled.

'Do you have an answer? Why did you take them?'

'I think I'll leave you with this for a second.' Kam stood up, giving the two of them their space as he went back into the classroom. Richard sat on the bench where Mr Choudhury had been and Rufus climbed up on his lap and started playing with his dad's glasses.

'Rufus, don't try to distract me. Why on earth did you want to steal the needles? And what's more, how are you going to make it right?'

'I wasn't stealing, I was borrowing. It's Rafe and Rupert, they're horrible, like really mean. Rafe is always horrible and Rupert told tales on me!' His voice was less sorry, more petulant now and Richard couldn't help but smile. He had never liked his older brother much either.

'Okay, so that's your motive, and big brothers can be ghastly sometimes, but you know what, they share your blood, and all your childhood memories. We have to treasure them.' Rufus snorted and Richard fought to hide his smile. 'What were you going to do?'

'I was going to stick them out of their beds, I thought if I just put them in like this then they'd never know they were there and... owwww!' Rufus giggled, his face lighting up as he used his hands to demonstrate intended angle and result.

'Hmmm. That's not okay, Rufus, really not okay. So how are you going to make it right?' Rufus's face fell; he had obviously hoped his dad would approve of his plan.

'Um... I won't put needles in their bed?' he asked hopefully.

'And?'

'And I'll say sorry to Mr Choudhury for fibbing and taking the needles when I was meant to be looking after them?' He queried his answer, a tone that suggested he would really rather not.

'Yep, exactly that. I'm going to have to tell Mummy though and you need to get back in that class now and apologize. Okay?'

'Do you have to tell her? She's still cross at me. She's going to take my fingerprints away and she didn't smile when I...'

Richard was keen to know why his son was in the doghouse with his mother but also knew Rufus was deliberately trying to eke out the time before he was sent back to class. Plus, he and Marion had always agreed on a united front with the boys.

'Well, she wouldn't be cross without reason, I'm sure she'll tell me about it when I talk to her about this. Now scoot, go and get the right thing done, young man!'

He tipped his son from his knee, ruffled his hair and went to hold the classroom door open so Rufus was not under any misapprehension about what he would be doing next.

'Love you, Dad,' he said in a whisper as he headed back in.

'Love you, son,' Richard answered, also in a whisper before closing the door and watching him head towards Mr Choudhury.

He turned to Rupert's classroom next. His teacher, Mrs Adams, was frightening, younger than Mrs Trunchbull but otherwise employing very similar methods and sporting an identical bun. He supposed that should be his next stop, although after this little escapade was half dreading what he would find.

He reached the door and leant his head against the glass to take a peek before he knocked. And breathed a sigh of relief. Thank goodness for that, he had one child at least who wasn't causing havoc. For there was Rupert up at the smartboard – long gone the days of scratchy chalk and a blackboard in schools – demonstrating to his classmates how to solve a maths problem whilst Mrs Adams watched and nodded.

No need to disturb that; he didn't want to put Rupert on the spot more than necessary and Mrs Adams was terrifying. He didn't want to test how she'd react to an unannounced visit.

He slid past towards Harmony's door. None of his children in here and only ten minutes until breaktime. He reckoned he could easily manage this, do as Rosy asked and then he'd be ready to win over the PTA.

As he opened the door he heard Harmony Rivers, the teacher charged with enriching the hearts and minds of Class Two, saying, 'And we all know what Zeus was famous for don't we?' in a rather arch tone.

Oh dear me; when he'd studied the Classics at his over-priced prep school – the second battle he had won with his mother was keeping his boys at home and educated in the village (the first had been marrying Marion) – they had a teacher who bordered on the perverse, who was very keen on what Zeus was good at, and it all seemed to centre on descending from the mountain in a disguise and into a young shepherdess or nymph, permission unnecessary.

He knew Harmony had her faults; he had witnessed the nativity the year she had been in charge as it descended into frenzied chaos as the universe literally gave birth on the floor to mark celebrating the winter solstice, no stable, star of light or virgins to be seen. Despite these facts, surely she wasn't going to teach a class of eight-and-nine-year-olds about rape and incest within the Olympian family. Was she?

He winced as he edged into the room, relaxing only as he heard the children shout out answers that were both correct and perfectly appropriate for a primary school classroom.

'He was like the king of the Greek gods, Miss.'

'He could throw lightning bolts and control the weather. Ka boom!'

'He had a winged horse called Pegasus.'

'Excellent, class.' Harmony praised the children and Richard felt his pulse slow back down; so far, so good. The teacher then noticed him in the doorway and waved him into the class. 'Hello, Mr Marksharp, do come in. How can I help you?'

'Hello, Ms Rivers, class,' Richard responded. 'I was in school, and Miss Winter said you were doing great things in here and I should nip in and see what you're up to.'

'Oh, thank you. They are a clever lot.' Harmony wrinkled her nose at him in return for the compliment; Richard felt a pang for not being strictly truthful but it had to be better than saying that Rosy wanted her kept on her toes.

'Is your... um... Marion with you?' She arched her body a little bit, to see around him into the hall to check. Richard managed to keep a smile off his face.

'No, you're quite safe,' Richard stage whispered and a titter arose from the children, making him feel lousy. He wasn't intentionally poking fun at Marion.

'Pull up a chair; we're learning all about ancient Greece.'

Richard nodded in agreement, easy now he realized he had overreacted when he had first come in. Of course she would be appropriate; teaching and content had moved on an awful lot since the eighties. That winter solstice celebration had merely been a one-off.

'It's a shame you couldn't have popped in this afternoon; we'll be making some Grecian red and black figure pots.' And with a smile she clicked on the smartboard to bring up some illustrations of typical examples, largely depicting domestic tasks in ancient Greece.

Richard nearly fell off his tiny child-sized chair as he examined the bottom left one intently. The one with men equipped with unfeasibly large phalli undertaking athletic events.

'So, class, who can tell me what they notice about these pots?' Harmony asked, whilst Richard shut his eyes, prayed for a quick escape and a normal heart rate.

Chapter Twenty-four

Richard was pleased at how well the PTA meeting had gone. Everyone was very welcoming, Jenny had insisted on keeping him full of coffee and biscuits and Serena seemed to take charge of the meeting, although she checked back with Jenny on every decision made. There was the odd moment of unease, when Jenny had offered her condolences on him and Marion, reinforcing the fact that their marital break-up was common knowledge. No hiding in front of these people and pretending everything was alright.

Even as things were at the moment, Richard was still clinging to the belief that this was a temporary blip. That Marion couldn't possibly break up their family because of a misunderstanding. But she was still spitting venom about how he hadn't been able to keep it in his pants at every opportunity they got without the boys present – and she was very definitely keeping those to a minimum, never letting them last more than three and a half minutes.

Richard knew he needed to find a way of getting her to listen to him, to convince her that her beliefs were not true, that he had been ever faithful both in thought and deed. He had considered roping in Claudia and getting her to call Marion and swear that nothing had happened. But even he knew *that* was a plan with a million flaws and he needed to find a better way. If he couldn't convince his wife of his integrity himself then perhaps he didn't deserve her.

He was hoping that his involvement in the school would not only help him have a better window into his sons' lives, but also throw the two of them together whilst the boys were safely confined to the classrooms.

With little faith in his own abilities at getting her to listen, he thought spending time doing the things Marion did, like the PTA meeting, would give him inspiration. All he had actually learnt was that Serena wanted to ring in the changes by making the parents' quiz night they were planning voluntary fancy dress – Marion would never have stood for that – and 'soap characters', past and present, was set as a theme. Jenny reminded everyone that it was wise to water down the alcohol; apparently Marion had been doing this for years, to boost profits and decrease drunken, disorderly behaviour by the parents, who, excited to be out without their children, would end up trying to fornicate on the gym mats.

He sent Marion a text after the meeting to see if she wanted to meet up so he could let her know how things had gone but received a terse reply about how Jenny had already done so and she *was* very busy. Which left him somewhat at a loose end. He supposed if nothing else he could go and google Frank Butcher costume ideas.

He headed back to Chase's, who had been good enough to suggest he move into his huge house, partly because that's what friends do but also because it did no harm to have it occupied when he and Angelina were away and they were away a lot. With most of Chase's business interests in the States – wellbeing investments, he called it, but in Richard's head anything that generated that kind of revenue was definitely a capitalist venture rather than an altruistic one – the blonde power couple spent an awful lot of time there.

Richard was grateful; it was much better than staying in Treporth Bay and he hoped it wouldn't be long before he got back to the marital home. Marion's misconception of what Claudia had been doing at his house couldn't last much longer. She'd have to listen to reason soon. Although even the thought of Marion listening was enough to make him chuckle a bit. As if.

Tonight, with Angelina away, Chase had organized a dinner party. The regular crew of Alex, Chase and himself – Hector had jetted back to Morocco – had been invited along with Matt Masters, who he liked immensely, and Dan the vicar, who he didn't know so well. He did hope the man's job didn't limit their freedom to speak as openly as they wanted, but figured meeting him and then deciding was probably better than leaping to conclusions. On the other hand, as a man of God he may well decide it was in his best interests to aid Richard's marriage, may have experience with other parishioners and have some useful suggestions. It certainly couldn't hurt if he could rope God onto his side.

There was a large van parked in the drive as he walked into the vast house – far too big for his tastes; it made him feel lonely – and he found Chase in the foyer directing a couple of men who were struggling with a portrait so huge that it could be used for pasting wallpaper. A portrait of Angelina.

'Oh, nice,' Richard said, thinking it was anything but. 'Does she not want to supervise you hanging it, make sure it's just right and things? Marion has such a good eye for these things, I'm useless, would have all the pictures wonky and not even notice.'

'That's what these guys and this is for.' Chase brandished a spirit level. 'She asked me to get it up before she got back from London. She was on morning TV today; you've just missed it. Twitter are blasting her for what she said about regional accents and people with home-dyed hair – it was a dig at the host, I think they have some kind of history, maybe a fallout on a celebrity cooking show years ago – but she never seems to mind the hate too much, says it keeps her profile and the bookings high. She said she has more articles and jokes on panel shows about her than the Pope and the Dalai Lama have combined. Terrifying, isn't it? What do you think?'

'That she shouldn't be allowed to do live television?' Richard queried, only half joking and deliberately sidestepping having to give an opinion on the picture. It was a *Marilyn Diptych*-like print – four colourful prints of the same image: Angelina's bottom, well her whole body, but largely a bottom, her back, hair and her hand held up to give the artist, and the viewer, the finger. 'So, this is a present for her from you?'

'Oh no, this is her engagement present to me.'

Richard failed to stop his laughter.

'I know, right?' Chase said, smiling himself. 'She says it's to keep me company if she's ever away, like this evening. But we both know it's a great big stamp of possession over the house and me; there's no one who is coming into the house and not knowing that she lives here. But if it makes her happy then that's good enough for me.'

Richard wasn't the only one to laugh as he viewed the portrait. It was the reaction of Matt, Alex and even Dan as they each entered the house that evening.

Richard found he immediately liked the vicar, one of those automatic things when someone walks into a room and you know instantaneously whether you love them or loathe them. As the men all settled in the kitchen around a vast table, Chase happily cooked for them. He was great at cooking and had been a massive foodie influence over both Richard and Alex at uni. The conversation soon turned to marriage, but to Richard's immediate relief, the focus was Chase. Whilst he was hoping to speak to his crack team this evening, he would prefer to have a couple of beers in him first. He had never been great at talking about his emotions and had a feeling that he may make a bit of a twit of himself this evening, that his carefully buttoned-up, public-school-educated gates may flood open in the company of men that he had known for ever.

'So congratulations are in order.' Dan started the conversation, raising his bottle to his host, who was busy chopping vegetables at whip-smart speed, making it a miracle that he still had his fingers.

'Thank you.' Chase stopped for a moment, to nod his head in acknowledgement. 'It is exciting; I had never much thought about marriage but when Angelina proposed I knew I wanted to spend the rest of my life with her so it was an immediate yes.'

There was a wordless battle around the table as every man sitting there struggled to keep their eyebrows under control. A lid for every pot.

'You're an absolute glutton for punishment. I love my sister, I have to – it's the rules – but honestly she is far from easy. And as to that' – Matt gestured back out of the kitchen and everyone knew he was referencing the painting – 'I don't think I can keep coming around if I have to stare at her arse every time I walk through the door. Most unsettling.'

'I'll drape a tea towel over it every time I know you're due over.'

'A tea towel? I don't think so. Like her ego, she needs a full-sized blanket to cover it and even then it's not quite going to get to the corners. A sail, that's what you need. I'll buy you a sail and some pulleys, that should do it.'

Chase laughed, put the knife down again and pulled his phone out of his pocket, pressing the voice recorder function. 'So Matt Masters, TV darling, are you saying that your sister has a huge arse, big as a boat?'

'No, I am not.' Matt bent over and clearly and loudly spoke into the phone, as if he were an elderly gentleman. 'But I am saying she has a huge ego, and I think that painting is merely a ploy to stop me visiting. And the whole finger thing, Ange, what would my fans say? You've just alienated my core base. Huh? Huh?' The men chortled as Chase put his phone back in his pocket.

'I shall give you some respite and not send her that until tomorrow.'

'See, this is why I'm glad to have you in the family – a man of good sense, bar the actual marrying her thing.' Matt smiled.

'Both of you are planning to get married this year. It's going to be a pretty romantic summer,' Richard said, his genuine joy for Chase and for Matt overriding the pinch of irony that his wife would be helping both.

'Ahh, yes, I was going to talk to you about that, Matt,' Chase said, artfully arranging the eeny-weeny slices of veg on a plate, throwing fish from the pan on the top, complete with crispy skin and a high-held chef-y drizzle of something citrussy and delicious. 'I'm so pleased we're both getting married but Angelina only just mentioned the timings the other day; she says she has set things up to be a double wedding in the summer. It took me by surprise and I wanted some time before I talked to Angelina about it, time to work out best possible alternative solutions. With you guys I can just come straight out and say it. I can't do that and had Angelina been thinking straight then she would have realized. We can't get married until next summer at the earliest, it's simply not practical, for either my workload, Angelina's or that of the majority of our guests. I have commitments in the States all throughout this summer; obviously I've rejigged so I can fly back in for your wedding but doing mine at the same time, not feasible. Especially if you look at our guest list. People need way more notice, they're coming in from everywhere. I don't know why Angelina didn't realize and I wanted to sound you out before I went any further but I think she just got caught up in the idea of a Masters wedding extraordinaire and didn't go past that.'

'Hmm, that's the exact same phrase Marion' – Matt paused and nodded at Richard – 'used when she came and pitched it to us.'

'I think Marion may have had a fair bit to do with it. How do you feel about not doing it this summer? Letting us have time to get properly organized, although I don't doubt Marion will already be all over it and I could probably get married on Wednesday if I asked her nicely.' Chase swapped a half-smile with Richard. The years between them all meant he was allowed. And she would be, he was only speaking truth.

'Truthfully, Chase, I don't want a double wedding. I told Marion it was a no and she fought a good fight, didn't she, Dan?' Dan nodded and Richard knew there was a wry smile on his face. 'Rosy and I have categorically ruled it out, but I suspect Marion thought she could still wheedle it through. However, we actually got a text the other day saying "I am listening to you", so I guess I have to hope she has finally heard us and stopped the double celebrity, mad paparazzi jerk-off that she was planning. I know she's excited to have your and Ange's wedding to plan. She just may not have mentioned the separate wedding thing to Angelina yet.'

'She will be excited; she never did get the wedding she wanted and I have a feeling she and Angelina may have similar ideas when it comes to a day to remember,' Chase remarked casually, causing Richard's head to jerk up from his food. It was true, his and Marion's wedding had been dictated by his mother, before he had fully developed the backbone to defend their wishes – a backbone that was encouraged by Marion and in full swing by the time it came to the choices of his sons' school. He had always known Marion's wishes had been sidelined to keep peace and he felt bad for it. He didn't realize his friends were aware of it as well. 'So, we're in agreement here, you and me. It's a big no to a double wedding this summer, but one of our own, which seems a much better idea to me. Especially as I have a feeling what you and Rosy want may be quite different to your sister's wedding wish list.'

Matt leant over the table and high-fived his brother-in-law to be.

'This is delicious, thank you.' Richard needed to say something and decided gently-gently was a good way to go about it. 'Marion does need to know that you guys have decided upon this. I think she is counting on your wedding to Angelina this summer to help raise her own profile and get her business established. Now I know, of course I do, as does she, that you must have things the way you want but I am worried about her. She needs to know sooner rather than later. It's not the money so much but for her self-belief; for her own esteem she needs to make a go of this business. She is so brilliant, so clever and she willingly put her career to one side to bring up our sons so now I want to step up and give her some support, and it feels weird sitting here watching you guys high fiving plans, which you are quite right to make, but will have the downside of disappointing my wife.' Richard took a deep breath; that was a pretty big speech for him.

'Okay, well there must be something we can do to help Marion so that our postponement doesn't hit her too hard,' Chase responded and Richard nodded. Tonight was meant to be about getting help from his closest friends to get Marion back but this was far more important; getting Marion help with her business seemed a much better, much less self-serving idea and with this group of men around the table he couldn't find better allies.

The focus shifted to Marion, with Dan saying the parish was pretty penniless but he would throw anything that paid and was church-related her way. Alex added that his fundraiser last year had been a disaster so he had breathed a sigh of relief when he heard Marion was running an events company; he'd meant to get in touch but just hadn't got around to it. He would get on it tomorrow. Matt promised to put in a good word with the Penmenna Hall owners, who were planning some big celebrations for next year; he was very happy to recommend her as a consultant.

Dinner finished, they decamped to Chase's mancave, complete with pool table, old-school arcade machines and bar, where things turned from the superficial to the slightly deeper and with Richard in the spotlight. It was the sort of thing that he dreaded, having all the attention on him and for something that he was finding difficult to manage.

He was open about how much he missed her and how he would do anything to have her back. All the men nodded understandingly, but it was as he was having a ferocious bout on Frogger with Dan laughing and cheering him on – Matt, Chase and Alex were clustered around the pool table, giving the two of them space – that he was given a little hope.

'I don't want to break a confidence and I can't say I have the answer to your problems, but it may be worth knowing that I think Marion would love to give your marriage another go; it's second-hand information having come from Alice, but Alice is a pretty good judge of character. I reckon it's worth hanging in there.'

'Oh.' Richard was a bit taken aback, and unsure what to say as an immediate response. He didn't know the man yet his marital problems were obviously a conversational topic in his house. Then he remembered he was in Penmenna, and that was exactly what happened in villages. Everyone talked and what they didn't know they made up. It wasn't done in a malicious way, he certainly didn't think that, it was just a bit disconcerting. He may as well embrace it. He wasn't exactly doing a great job of getting Marion back by himself. 'That is nice to hear, although I don't know if I dare believe it. She's pretty determined not to give that impression to me. I don't think I've seen her a single time since I've been back without her mentioning my inability to be faithful. It's not fair.'

Dan made a funny shape with his mouth and Richard realized how that sounded. It occurred to Richard that people may well know why Marion had left him, but they didn't know he hadn't done anything wrong other than be a naive fool.

'Let me explain that so I don't sound like a petulant child.' Dan looked a little uncomfortable, as if bracing himself for a cheater's lies. 'I let a colleague stay at mine whilst she was having problems with her flat. I thought it was a kind thing to do and, ironically, I thought Marion would be pleased. I swear I never touched her, never wanted to. I love my wife, Vicar...'

'Dan.'

'Dan, I love my wife, I've never cheated and never would. There is no one I want to spend my life with more, and that's even more true today than it was when we met twenty odd years ago. I think she is the most amazing person I have ever known: she's got grit and she made me a father to three boys who combine her chutzpah, intelligence and wit in the most perfect ways. But' – he paused to catch a breath – 'she thought I slept with my colleague, who deliberately set about sowing discord and creating fairly compelling evidence to imply that I had. I had *no* idea until Marion threw me out, none, and I arrived back in London to find this other woman cuffed to my bed in a last-ditch attempt to get my attention.' He was aware the chatter across the room had stilled. 'Obviously I kicked her out and suddenly understood why Marion was so furious but trust me when I say I had no idea.'

'He is pretty useless when it comes to women,' Chase chipped in, his pool cue now resting at his side. 'We have no idea how he managed to attract and keep his wife.'

'Clearly I didn't!'

'You're going to get past this. I'm sure of it. I've never seen a more adoring couple. It's frequently quite vomit-inducing. This will work out in time, I have faith. I don't believe for a second you've cheated on her.'

Richard turned to include the others in his conversation. 'I really haven't. I don't want to, apart from anything else. I literally have no impetus to sleep with anyone other than my wife, even when she won't have me. Like now.'

'This colleague, it wasn't…' Alex shuddered.

'Claudia, yup. You dated her, I believe.'

'Woah. Your wife set me up on a blind date, one. We had dinner and that was it and parted ways. She seeped poison.'

'You could have mentioned the poison bit before now.'

'To be fair I didn't know you were planning on moving her into your flat.'

'I didn't—'

Alex held his hands up. 'Yeah okay, bad joke. But I know you wouldn't have cheated on Marion and especially not with that viper. I can totally and utterly believe this has all come about because you are really freaking naive.'

'Thanks, I'm going to take that as a compliment. Now if only you could persuade my wife…'

Chapter Twenty-five

Six weeks or so had passed since Dan had given him a smattering of hope as to getting back in Marion's good books. The vicar's words – *Marion would love to give your marriage another go* – whirled around his head at all times. And to be fair she had been defrosting a bit recently. Not on his supposed adultery front but just in generally having him around.

In a remarkably short space of time her business was storming ahead. It would seem – and no real surprise – that her reputation preceded her. She was taken up with lots of bookings for events this summer, so much so that both Penmenna Hall and Alex were now on her books but rather as a favour to them than a necessity for her.

There were many upsides to this, but one of them was that she was happy to rely on him when the boys needed ferrying to and from things and he was enjoying a domestic role, preparing food that he knew they would like and cramming as much nutritional goodness in as he could for the people he loved. His reward was not just the obvious pleasure of the boys racing through his dishes but also the little half-smiles on his wife's face when she came home to find a warm dinner waiting for her, the dog walked, chores done, homework undertaken and the children happy.

Those smiles were so special.

She had also eased back a little on referencing Claudia at every chance she got. It had now been consigned to being one of those things they didn't mention. But the injustice of it still smarted. One day he would find a way to show her he had never cheated. One day soon.

Another difference was that he was now the one attending all Penmenna School events and beginning to realize exactly what was involved. He always thought he had been pretty on top of things, smugly knowing how the PTA worked – but he now had to accept that even with the best will in the world as well as all the things Marion had in place, it was more than a little chaotic. The fact that Marion had always ensured the smooth delivery of everything PTA related was further testament to her skills.

The parents' quiz night had descended into farce. Serena had decided that Marion's watering down of the alcohol was mean. She had learnt that lesson. Three Dot Cottons had begun brawling in the children's loos, Seth Armstrong had climbed the wall bars and then decided he couldn't get down even with Hilda Ogden shouting instructions in a very not-PG way, and Ken Barlow was caught out the back of the PE shed making out with Kat Slater. The children were so much easier to manage.

Then Pippa had persuaded him to be the Easter bunny. She had said there was no joy like the simple joy brought about by doling out chocolate to a whole school of children. He quite liked the idea of it, so had happily accepted. What the teaching assistant had failed to mention was the way children climbed, bit and gouged when it came to chocolate without a very firm hand to guide them. Most of the classes were fine, but Harmony's was terrifying.

Her constant repeating of the phrase 'It's not nice to hurt others whilst we express our feelings, our needs and ourselves, is it?' proved particularly ineffective. He wasn't convinced a mini caramel egg was worth gouging out someone's eye, but it would seem Class Three didn't agree. He couldn't help but point that out to an utterly unrepentant Pippa as she administered first aid.

The other thing Pippa had failed to mention was how a whole head-to-toe fun-fur suit had a very particular smell to it, or that it didn't have any convenient holes.

He had also thought he knew his boys inside out, was fully aware that they had a tendency towards mischief but were super smart and switched on with normal levels of sibling rivalry. He had, and he was reluctant to admit it, thought Marion's insistence on ferrying them from activity to activity was a little unfair, born of her insecurities because of her upbringing and tied to her high aspirations for her sons. He hadn't been convinced it was healthy, wanted them to be able to relax more, equating their busyness with the pressure his own mother had piled on with her 'failure is not an option' mindset. He was very much for a work–life balance and thought it was something he could encourage in Rafe, Rupert and Rufus now he was home more.

That had turned out to be a worse decision than dressing as the Easter bunny.

He had had no idea.

Marion clearly kept the boys busy as a crisis management technique. It wasn't because she *wanted* them to precis in Latin, cook sous-vide food successfully before leaving primary school and take on the most challenging beach breaks with confidence as he had thought. No, it was a necessary part of keeping them alive because he learnt that, left to their own devices, these three boys would create so much mischief that every crisis team in the county needed to be on constant high alert.

He had thought that a relaxed Easter holiday would be heaven on earth. He agreed with Marion that he would be the boys' primary carer, freeing her up to dash around the county finding perfect spaces, collaborating on exquisite menus and no doubt shrieking blue murder at florists when required.

By day four he was ringing around every club and tutor he had cancelled and begging them to fit the boys back in again. The incident back in February with Rufus stealing the school embroidery needles had nothing on the tricks the boys played upon each other given a few minutes' spare time.

One of them – and this was the trouble, the culprit was always hard to identify; the boys had a fascinating dynamic of screaming at each other, screeching accusations and then banding together in unity should Richard get too cross – had taken all the Oreos apart and resealed them with toothpaste.

Rupert and Rafe had worked together to convince Rufus that he wasn't smart enough to balance a glass of water on each hand. He dutifully placed his hands flat on the table for them to rest the filled glasses on and then screamed until Richard rescued him, once the boys backed away laughing knowing he couldn't move without spilling the water everywhere. Whilst he was stuck there they raced up the stairs and mismatched all his socks. This in itself wouldn't be so bad, but Rufus was the most like Richard and he liked order. He liked things just so and socks not in pairs was one of those little things that would drive him witless.

Then there were the printed-out fake adoption papers, left in the living room with Rupert's name written on which lead to the inevitable screaming – 'I wish I *had* been adopted!'

Rupert had then got his revenge by dipping onions into toffee and pretending he had made toffee apples as a peace offering. He laughed so much as his brothers bit into them that he actually slid down the wall clutching his sides.

How Richard had managed to get through the holidays without murdering at least one of them or turning to vodka as a breakfast choice, he wasn't sure, but he had done it. The boys went back to school tomorrow and had, for the last few days, been impeccably behaved. Richard wondered if it was partly due to him losing his shit, just a little bit one day, and calling them all monsters, but not in the affectionate way he usually did, more in an I've-bred-three-little-sociopaths-that-are-completely-incapable-of-behaving-in-a-civil-fashion kind of way. He had beaten himself up for days afterwards, not helped by Rufus's tearful response, 'Mummy *never* shouts.'

Ultimately he rationalized that the children did need to learn about the realities of life and the realities were that constant squabbling was going to push anyone, no matter how calm they usually were, over the edge.

They had behaved a bit better after that. They had never, never seen their father lose his temper. He was always just Richard but in Daddy form: amiable, wanting to please and – he hoped – kind. It seemed shouting, a tool he had always been very much against, was occasionally what was needed.

He opened the fridge door to prep supper as Marion had texted to say she should be home by six, and promptly burst into laughter. One of the boys – and he suspected Rufus, possibly with Rafe's help – had put googly eyes on all the fruit and veg in the fridge. The boys heard his laugh and came and sat on the stairs and watched him, shining with pride for putting a smile on his face. He couldn't help but feel smug with the contentment that one got when one's children worked together; it was rare and he wallowed in it for a bit.

When Marion came through the door, he had dinner bubbling away and couldn't resist taking her to the fridge. He opened the door, hearing the patter of feet a second time as their sons came to see her reaction. Marion burst out into a most un-Marion-like guffaw, pulling out the broccoli and waving it from side to side to make the eyes move, then following it up with a carrot and a pear.

The boys sidled over to join them and Marion edged herself closer to Richard as they all squished in front of the fridge, pulling out vegetables and putting silly voices on.

Despite it being such a family moment, Richard couldn't help but feel a frisson run through him. This was the closest Marion had stood to him for months and the very nearness of her, the smell of her was assailing his senses, making him both weak at the thought of how much he wanted everything to be right and strong at the thought of proving to her he was the man she wanted.

The boys eventually ran off after a three-act play that ended up with all the vegetables dead bar one very triumphant piece of baby sweetcorn and Marion headed up for a bath. It had become a daily ritual. She would jump into a bath whilst Richard finished off the dinner. Then he would either head out and back to Chase's large, and largely empty home, or be invited to stay if Marion was in a particularly good mood. He had wondered if the regular bath was something she had done to avoid spending time with him when this new routine of him being there and cooking had started. But whatever the reason was it made him happy having her coming down the stairs all relaxed and smelling of rose oil.

Today as she headed towards the bathroom, he heard a bedroom door shut upstairs and the pitter patter of feet on the landing. His eldest son, Rafe, appeared within seconds in the kitchen and pulled the door shut behind him, taking a seat at the kitchen table.

'That was nice, wasn't it?' he said in a voice and tone mature beyond his years. Certainly not the tone of a boy who had been a bit free with the toothpaste earlier in the holidays!

'It was,' Richard confirmed, knowing that Rafe was talking about all of them being silly together.

'It felt like old times,' Rafe added and Richard felt a pang. It did. His son wasn't wrong.

'I know you think I'm a child but I'm actually a young adult now. In just under four years I'll be able to get married, with consent obviously, join the armed forces and a trade union should I want to. And, oh, I almost forgot, I'll be allowed to drive a mobility carriage too if I need to, which quite frankly is an increasing possibility the older and eviller my brothers get. Just giving you context for my maturity.' Rafe delivered his speech with a very serious tone, no doubt also designed to demonstrate his wisdom.

'Okay.' Richard pulled out a chair, working hard to keep the smile off his face, and wondered where this was going.

'And I know even as a young adult it's probably not cool for me to offer advice to you but I'd like to, if you don't mind.' Rafe clearly had a lot he wanted to say, and was currently holding his father's eyes with the ferocity of a Rottweiler, bidding him to take him seriously. Richard had every intention of doing so. He had craved this sort of involvement in his son's life from the minute he held Rafe in his arms. This was the kind of family he pictured himself having when he was a child, tied in knots of repressed fury at his father's sky-high levels of not-giving-a-shit and his mother's obsessive neuroses and controlling, rigid parenting. His boys were going to be free to speak, their views listened to.

'I don't mind. I have a lot of respect for your opinions; you are a far better judge of both situations and character than many adults I know.' His mind went straight back to the parents' quiz night. 'So spill, what do you want to talk about?'

'You and Mum.' Rafe spoke clearly, plainly and still holding his father's eye.

Richard tried not to gulp. He wasn't expecting that although maybe he should have been. Oh shit. He really didn't want to be pulled into a conversation which may have the side effect of seriously pissing Marion off, yet neither did he want to not be as honest as he could be with his son. He was aware that the way he dealt with this could well influence how often Rafe came to him throughout his teenage years. He decided, as with most things, honesty was the best policy.

'Okay, what do you want to know?'

'What's going on? You move out, you split up and then instead of you being away all the time you're suddenly here and cooking dinner every night. I don't understand it. When you were together you were never here and now you've told us you're apart you're here all the time. And Dad, to be honest, I don't think it's just me that's finding it confusing. I'm grown up, but I think both Rupert and Rufus could do with very clear messages at this stage of their lives, and to me this is a clear case of mixed messaging.'

'Um… well, yes…'

'Hang on, let me finish. I want to tell you what I think so you don't feel foolish saying something that we both know isn't going to fly. If I tell you what I think first, then perhaps we could go from there.'

'Yes, yes we could,' Richard agreed and wasn't sure if he wanted Marion to hurry up and finish her bath and come and join them or take a long, long time, preferably until dinner had been burnt to a crisp and Rafe had become distracted by something else.

'Okay then. It seems to me a lot of distance built up when you were working away and then probably, but I can't be sure, there were some misunderstandings—'

'Yup, there certainly were,' Richard couldn't help but interject. His boy was so wise.

'Dad!' Rafe silenced him with a look, channelling his mother beautifully. 'And in most relationship break-downs, even minor niggles are due to miscommunications, people not being honest about things. I know this because I am sort of in a relationship myself now, as you may have guessed, and am frequently amazed by how Sophie gets so super cross about stuff that is quite frankly made up in her head. But the first thing I know about it is when she is spitting feathers at me, whereas if she had raised it with me before rather than snowballing it in her mind it would be a lot easier to sort out. How am I supposed to know that buying her a dress with flowers on was all the evidence she needed of me being a man restricted by outdated gender norms born out of my inherent misogyny? Eh? I just wanted to get her something she had liked online a few days before. And don't get me started on periods. Anyway, I'm getting sidetracked. But my guess is this is what has happened. The thing is...' Richard wondered if his son had some super-powered lungs; how on earth did he talk so much without once appearing to stop for breath? And also, exactly how adult was his child's relationship, because these were not things Richard was thinking about at twelve years old. '...you weren't just a couple, we're, *we're*' – he said it again for emphasis – 'a family and we need you to make it clear what's happening. We love having you here all the time but it's causing the boys to think you'll get back together. Are you? What *is* going on? We didn't really get much detail before, and we've given you space but now we need to know more.'

'Woah. Whilst what you say is wise – it really is and I am so impressed—'

'Do try not to patronize me.'

'Yup, okay.' Definitely his mother's son. 'But actually, we *can* be no longer together and yet still retain a friendly working relationship as we co-parent. That's what we're doing. And, yes I'm sad that your mother and I are not together any more but I'm proud of the way we are making this work anyhow.'

'Yeah but, Dad, it seems to me like you're bending over backwards to be accommodating and I love having you

190

around but maybe it's time you stood up and said what it is you want rather than just doing what you're told. Why did you split up in the first place? Are you going to get back together? Is that what you want? And if so, what can I do to help?'

Chapter Twenty-six

Marion came down from her bath feeling beautifully refreshed. No one had ever said before that working full-time was easier than being a devoted stay-at-home parent. She was very aware though that she had it easy with Richard stepping into the traditional role of home-maker and easier still by then getting the double bed to herself so she could spread-eagle out, no compromise needed.

Truth was she missed him in their bed, missed the way he curled around her as they fell asleep, feet entwined, knees tucked into knees, pelvis turned into pelvis and his arms wrapped around her giving them both comfort. A closeness she could never imagine having with anybody else. That feeling that there was nothing that could touch you, that you could sleep through the night, trip through life, with nothing bad happening to you all the time you were there, next to each other.

She couldn't fault the man he had been since he had moved back down to Cornwall. Her venture into self-employment would have been considerably trickier if it wasn't for his support. Being there meant work could be her sole focus so her business was going from strength to strength. She was worried that, if anything, she was a bit overbooked.

If it weren't for Richard's infidelity then her life would be perfect. He made no bones about the fact that he wanted her back, would do anything to have it so. And with every passing day the temptation was strong. It was hard not gently touching his leg under the table as the family ate, a hint of what she was planning for later clear in her eyes. It was hard not leaning into him as everyone chatted and giggled. But there was too much tied up here: obviously there was the utter betrayal of Richard touching and kissing someone else the way she had always thought was saved especially for her. Then add into that her baggage, her mother's stream of men through her life and his baggage, the way his father behaved, that all fed into the fear that if she forgave him now he could turn into his father and she, subsequently, would turn into his mother and they would both become parodies of the very things they swore they would never be, all those years ago as they lay under trees with textbooks open and a lifetime of hope and promise on their lips.

As she walked into the kitchen she was surprised to see Rafe and Richard caught in intense conversation, their subject matter clearly deep, both freezing as they felt her eyes upon them. That didn't bode well.

'That smells delicious, Richard.'

'Yes, it's not smelling too bad, is it? It's new, I've not made it before so it might be a bit experimental. You guys are my guinea pigs… squeak squeak.' Richard wrinkled his face up and wiggled his fingers as whiskers, his glasses moving up and down as he did so, and Marion's heart melted a little. He was such a fool. He shared a smile with her, a proper one where the eyes spoke far more than the words and she felt a shiver rush up her spine. 'Staying at Chase's is rubbing off on me. Even with him not there, a desire to cook is seeping through my skin by osmosis.

Here, have a taste.' He stood up from the table and moved to the stove.

Marion walked over and leant forward, mouth obediently open as Richard carefully touched her lips with the tip of the wooden spoon, just letting her taste the flavours without burning her. She found herself stepping in a bit closer and he repeated the action. It tasted so good; her senses were floored, not so much by the smell and flavourings of the food but by Richard's proximity to her, every sense alert and tingling.

It was muscle memory, had to be. Her body reminded by his proximity of the way he had made her feel before, time and time before, the honesty of their lovemaking, the vulnerability and the excitement. No one knew their way around her as he did and… she took a step back, remembering that Rafe was in the kitchen and flicked him a quick smile to include him and break the sexual tension boinging off the walls.

Had they been discussing her? How was the best way to find out? She started to carefully phrase a sentence in her head that would get a straight answer without putting either of them off. *It's not always about you, you know* pinged into her head. Bloody hell. That Alice and her evening visits and peppy texts had a lot to answer for.

Her train of thought was interrupted by her mobile trilling from her bag. She considered, just for a second, ignoring it and having dinner with her family. But her compulsion, the person she was, couldn't let it go entirely. She'd just have a quick look and see who it was.

Bugger. Angelina. She couldn't leave that. She'd been chasing her for weeks. There were so many issues she didn't know where to start; some input from the woman herself would be Very Helpful Indeed at this point.

'Darling, how are you?'

'Yes, yes, great thanks. And you?' Marion walked out of the kitchen, away from the smells of star anise and lemon, away from her husband and oldest child, just for a minute, into the living room as Richard called for the two younger sons to come down the stairs and eat. An odd feeling, as if she was on a piece of elastic, washed over her – her whole body was trying to ping back into the kitchen.

But business had to come first. What if Richard suddenly stopped being reasonable about everything and cut her off without a penny? She needed business to come first. Just until she had a squirrel fund entirely of her own making, to support herself and the boys.

'All good, having a fab time. People really do love Chase over here you know, it's like he's some kind of god. We had paparazzi scale the walls and fall into the swimming pool, hilarious.' Angelina babbled on, failing to ask, as ever, how things were.

As fond as Marion was of Chase, she couldn't help but remember Richard saying that Chase's self-positivity movement had done a lot of good but also smacked, just a teeny bit, of being a cult.

'Anyway, I'm not calling about that; Chase may be popular but he can also be an arse. Tell me, how is all the prep going?' Marion knew Angelina was referring to the fact that Chase had put his foot down, a rare but immovable occurrence, and insisted that not only should they let Matt get married in peace but that he was not prepared to tie the knot this summer, saying it was impractical. The woman had been spitting blood such was her fury when she rang her friend to tell her all of this a few weeks ago.

Marion had been split when she heard this news. She had been dropping hints – they hadn't been subtle ones – to every customer she had booked about her best friends Angelina Masters and Chase Cooper and how their wedding would be the height of summer sophistication, happening in Penmenna and organized solely by her. It would look pretty bloody bad if the wedding was shifted until next year.

On the flip side, she was getting closer to Rosy as they collaborated on cakes, shoes, hair, cars, everything. Which had led to her priorities changing. Having been forced to marry Richard in a ceremony designed by his mother, she had found herself wanting to make sure Rosy and Matt got the wedding of their dreams, with a couple of cute surprises thrown in. Chase's insistence that a double wedding was totally off the table made that much more achievable without Marion having to shoulder the blame.

Luckily Angelina's determination 'not to have my entire summer ruined' meant that Marion had been able to persuade Angelina to throw a huge party the weekend after her brother got married and had suggested using it to celebrate her engagement. Angelina was keen on the party but was being particularly diva-ish, constantly bleating that she wanted it as celebratory as possible but failing to give any further detail. She had however been pin-sharp in making Marion promise she'd oversee her wedding as well.

'Um, yes, that was why I left all the messages.' Marion answered Angelina's question and realized her tone was a little passive-aggressive so quickly changed it up. 'But you are always so busy, the price of being so terribly popular, no doubt.' And she tinkled down the phone.

The real Marion wanted to tell her that she was utterly unreliable, over-indulged and had zero awareness of others, but that would not be sensible.

'Oh, I really am,' Angelina replied, with no trace of irony.

'Quite. Things are going well, holding the party on your beach is a beautiful idea, very wedding-y. I would have loved that for my own wedding, so Cornish but desperately chic Cornish, polo-on-the-beach Cornish rather than Redruth Cornish. We've got three domes booked from Aidan's dad from school so even if the weather is vile, it is all covered. I'm so excited; I don't think you could have chosen a better location and obviously the beach will be immaculate.'

She wasn't sure how Jenny and Serena would feel about removing seaweed and making sure all visible stones were attractive ones but when she had planned it she'd assumed they'd be bored the first week of the holidays and would be grateful for something to do. Now though an annoying little voice in the back of her head was saying that she couldn't expect people to help for free and she may need to offer payment. That voice was dammed irritating and getting louder and louder as the weeks progressed.

Marion continued her rapturous self-praise. So far she had had to make every decision for this party, which ensured it would be marvellous but she was concerned it had very little of Chase and Angelina in it. 'The food has been tasted, such a shame you couldn't be here for that, and is going to be absolutely divine. Food of the gods; I have never tasted anything so... well, words don't describe it, but you won't be disappointed.'

'Fabulous, I knew I could trust you. You have such brilliant taste. You're my friend after all.' Angelina cackled and Marion thought she may well scream if she had to listen to that joke one more time.

'Excellent. The caterer is organized and booked, flowers and large plants done, thank you for choosing those, I would have picked that line as well and the plants are going to give us a structure, change the space completely. Exquisite. The one thing I am worried about, Angelina' – Marion took a deep breath and prepared herself – 'is that I'm having very few RSVPs back. And those that I do are saying they'd love to come but there simply wasn't enough notice.'

It was bad enough that she couldn't describe the event as the wedding of the year any more; having it as an engagement party was a barely acceptable substitution. A deserted engagement party, however, was not. It would not look good in promotional photographs and Marion needed to sort this out.

'Ah, okay. Yes, Chase did say that, it's why he wanted to move the date. I tell you what, let's keep everything as it is and I'll take over the guest list; don't you worry about it. Just trust in your taste and make it the best party you could possibly imagine, the most romantic, the most me, the most you.'

That sounded fishy. She had expected a full-on toy-out-of-pram level tantrum when she mentioned the paucity of attendees. The one thing that Angelina needed was attention from everyone and the more the better. Even one guest not going to her party should be enough to warrant a struggle the Gallagher brothers would be proud of.

'Are you sure? The guest list is often one of the most stressful bits. That is what I'm here for.'

'Absolutely fine. Although I've had an idea. An insurance so to speak.' Angelina's voice was a little high-pitched, strangled almost. 'How about you invite everyone you know and love' – that was a fairly small list – 'and get as many people as you can there, just in case.'

'That sounds bizarre. Why would you want my friends at your party?'

'Volume, darling, volume. We want crowds so big they dwarf a presidential inauguration.' Angelina added, 'You forget I'm practically American now; size is everything. Don't believe what anyone else has to say.'

'I think that maybe if getting guests in time is a problem…' Marion tentatively prepared to suggest moving the date again. Honestly, she'd be beating Alice into heaven at this rate, the pearly gates ushering her in with a triumphant chorus of trumpeting angels.

'Oh my God! Marion! I thought you were supposed to be working for me…' The snap was fierce.

'I am. And with your best int—'

'Shut up, you *stupid* woman. I'm not paying you to ignore me.' Wow, that was bold, even for Angelina. 'Just do as you're told and do it when you're told. It's really not that hard. I swear, staff!' And with a huff so loud the big bad wolf would have been impressed, Angelina slammed the phone down.

Chapter Twenty-seven

Richard was back in school again after the Easter holidays and as much as he loved his boys he was relieved to have a bit of peace again. Bounding up the steps into school, he realized he had missed it. He wasn't sure if it was the sense of community it exuded, or the sound of the children laughing from behind closed doors as they learnt, or the enthusiasm with which they bombed around the play-grounds in all weathers, hair flying behind them as they ran, bounced, skipped, jumped and ka-powed that made him love it so. He could understand why Marion had been happy to be involved for so many years. It represented a very different childhood to the one she'd had, and it must be a constant source of pride to her as she watched the children here being so carefree.

The PTA were meeting to outline their plans for the term, just to make sure everyone knew where they were going – aware that the quiz night and, to a lesser degree, the Easter egg hunt had been a bit of a wake-up call as to how events panned out without Marion's iron fist and death glares. Nothing had burnt to the ground but neither had they been stress-free affairs that any member of the team particularly wanted to repeat.

The May Fayre took place on the Friday of the last day of half term and as the biggest fundraising event of the year no one wanted to mess that up. It needed to run as smoothly as ever. And that was another of the things that Richard loved about this school. Yes, the PTA had a fair amount of in-fighting – probably less since his wife had distanced herself – and bickering about *really* petty stuff, but these parents turned up week in, week out to make sure their child's school was the best it could be. You didn't get that level of commitment in the City for anything that wasn't tied to a financial reward. Or, his recent experiences had taught him, a sexual one.

Shaking that memory off quickly, he headed to the staffroom to make a cup of coffee, only to find Alice doing exactly the same.

'Oh fab, I wanted to catch you.' She smiled over the coffee cups at him. He only knew Alice from around the school and that she was dating Dan, but had always been struck by her thoughtful manner, the way she considered everyone's opinions and every outcome before making her decision. He also knew that Marion occasionally, increasingly more so these days, had kind words for her. Rare and worthy praise indeed.

'Okay, anything I should be worried about?' he asked, very worried indeed. He hoped the May Fayre wasn't going to be a repeat of the Easter bunny fiasco and she was priming him to take on a role no one else wanted.

'Possibly.' She grinned at him and raised her eyebrows before casting a covert look around the staffroom and then guiding him by his elbow out of the communal space and towards the stockroom.

Oh dear, oh dear, what could she possibly have to say that couldn't be said by the kettle? This was not the impression he had of Alice at all. What on earth did she want him for?

He watched as she closed the door forcefully, but not before whipping her head around to check that no one had seen them. Door shut, she rounded on him and grinned again. He counselled himself not to judge until she had spoken.

'Nothing to panic about, honestly, Richard, you look terrified. It's just that we need to keep this on the downlow.'

'Keep what?'

'Good question. You see at the moment I'm looking for men. And a little bird told me that you have an exceptionally good…' Jesus Christ, was nowhere safe in this world? Was this what it had been like for women for centuries, with men pulling them into cupboards as if it were perfectly acceptable to think 'no' meant 'try harder'? His heart was pounding; he was all hot and bothered. What on earth was he going to do?

The door was pulled open and a triumphant 'Aha!' came booming into the room, swiftly followed by Serena, who he thought was alright despite Marion despising her in the run-up to Christmas. He trusted his wife's judgement though so was always a bit cautious around her – but today she was clearly going to be his rescuer.

'I saw you two run off and I thought what a wonderful opportunity to talk about—'

'Serena, I thought you agreed that maybe it was not appropriate to—'

'I changed my mind. I can't stop thinking about it. It would be a way of making amends, to myself largely. Please let me.'

Huh, maybe not his rescuer. This was insane. And rather frightening.

'Richard, stop looking so scared, honestly.' Alice turned her attention back to him. 'I only wanted to talk to you about your voice and singing in the community choir.'

He felt his shoulders relax. The choir, of course. Thank goodness.

'And I wanted to talk to you about Claudia,' Serena chipped in, despite a fairly pointed look from Alice.

Gulp.

'Right, to be clear you've dragged me into the cupboard because you want me to become part of your choir.'

'Yes, exactly that. Marion mentioned in passing that you sang and did so well. We are preparing some songs for Rosy's wedding, but in secret, hence the stationery cupboard. Obviously it means we can't ask Matt and Chase is overseas for most of the summer so we're down two male voices and you can tell that the harmonies are lacking. So, it's my mission to find a new male member.'

Serena sniggered.

'Oops, not like that obviously. Serena!' Alice shot her friend a look and he couldn't help but laugh. Marion would have snorted at that.

'I'm very happy to come along to rehearsal one day and see how it goes, but I'll have to fit it around me looking after the boys and Marion's work and so on.'

'Of course,' said Alice, 'I'm sure if you wanted to you could bring the boys along. Always good to have new voices. Annie and Ethel are helping me out with organizing it all and I'm sure they wouldn't mind...' She said this last bit as if she were talking to herself but out loud, and lacking a little conviction, her final sentence trailing off as if she doubted it.

'Okay, brilliant, thank you.' He turned to Serena. 'And what did you want to ask me about Claudia? I don't know how to make it clearer short of hiring a sky writer but I didn't sleep with Claudia, have never slept with her and never want to, and haven't seen her since I left London. How do you know her?'

Serena sank down onto the little grey safety step stool.

'Did Marion not tell you?' she asked.

This phrase filled him anew with dread.

'Did Marion tell me what?' he asked, knowing he was scrunching his face up with nerves as he spoke. He didn't think they had any secrets but then he had thought his marriage was as secure as a marriage could be.

'Um…' Serena looked up and then back and forth from Alice to Richard. 'About the letters and things before Christmas?'

'Nope.'

She took a deep breath and then… whoosh, words spewed from her mouth at great speed. 'Okay, please don't hate me, I hate myself for this enough as it is. I've been friends with Claudia since the year dot, you don't need to know all the details but I've felt beholden to her and her family since I was very little. I knew she was madly in love with you…'

'She was?' Richard couldn't help but ask, surprised. She had tied herself to his bed and everything but he hadn't read *love* into that.

'Yes, besotted. She wanted a man to treat her as well as you did Marion. She decided instead of finding one of her own she'd go straight to the source and fixed it in her head that you were the one she wanted. Honestly, she did not stop going on about it. I moved to Penmenna, nothing short of coincidence, and she started hassling me to help her. I refused time and time again but she hit me with the big guns, talked of how her family had practically brought me up and I wouldn't be anyone without their intervention, all pretty true as it goes but not kind to mention it; anyway, I caved. And I am so sorry. She got me to post poisonous little notes through your front door saying you were always away for a reason, that you were emotionally invested elsewhere, that sort of thing. It was an attempt to sow discord and drama in your relationship. I am so, so sorry.' She took a huge gulp of air and there were tears glinting in the corners of her eyes.

Richard believed her; her tone, her face, her body language were all riddled with mortification. He almost felt sorry for her until he remembered how odd Marion had been at Christmas, how they had squabbled time and time again and he hadn't really known why. Now it all made sense; now he could see how she had misread the situation between Claudia and himself – she had been set up for it. Months of being told he was being unfaithful and never ever breathing a word of her fears to him.

It all made so much more sense. Maybe he should have been crosser at Serena, but her words smacked of utter truth. He could well imagine how single-minded Claudia had been in getting her own way. He wanted to call Marion, reach out and talk to her about this. About how sorry he was that she had gone through that on her own, had lies fed through her door making her safe place, the place they had worked so hard to make their home, their sanctuary, invaded by mistruth and deceit. And to not feel able to talk to him about it…

'Okay, so what was it you wanted to tell me about Claudia today, based on the fact that you thought I already knew all of that?' he asked, worried about what else there was to come out. His tone may have been a little snippy but the fact that he hadn't known, had let Marion down so monumentally without even realizing, was stinging hard.

'She rang me over Easter. I've been eaten up with guilt for the best part of six months and she called all glib and guilt free and said she had met someone. I'm guessing it's not you, and that it's reciprocated this time. And instead of being glad for her, I was so cross. How dare she? I mean how dare she?' Serena had stopped sniffling now and started to look cross. 'She blithely ruins Marion's and your marriage, trashes the friendship I had with her simply because she wants her own way *all* the time, and I'm left sitting here being eaten up with guilt. Even though Marion appears to have forgiven me, I can't really forgive myself; I know better than that. It's really eating me up so I thought I'd approach you and say that I don't want to meddle...' Richard smiled; his experience was that that sentence always preceded a first-class level of meddling. 'But I did want to say if there is anything I can do to make it right, I will. I can try and get Claudia to ring Marion and say nothing ever happened if you like.'

Alice, who had been silent up until now, spoke.

'I'm not sure that is a good idea.'

'No, neither am I, but I appreciate the offer. The funny thing is that Marion has been saying all along that she needs proof that I didn't sleep with Claudia but how can you prove something that *hasn't* happened? I can't. But no, don't get her to call, I don't think hearing Claudia's voice on the end of her phone is going to put a smile on Marion's face. By telling me what you have today you have made more sense of things I was struggling to understand in my own head, so thank you for that. But if you want some kind of redemption and feel the need to do something to get it, then put your mind into finding a way I can prove that I didn't cheat. A way that doesn't make Marion cross but exonerates me. I haven't cheated, never have, and it's infuriating that I can't persuade the woman I love above all in this world of that fact. If you can help me with that, no matter what's gone before, you'll be doing me a good turn.'

Chapter Twenty-eight

The first half of summer term had whizzed by and before Richard knew it the May Fayre was upon them. He was as excited as a small child as he stood in the school hall and called Marion to update her. 'Hello, it's just me.'

'Yes, I know, Richard, that's how phones work.' Marion's voice perfectly encapsulated the ennui of dealing with the irredeemably stupid and made Richard chuckle.

'Of course. I promised I'd keep you in the loop. Tables are being put out, everything seems to be on plan so, so far so good.'

'Excellent, things should be fine. Jenny has been working alongside me for years; I can't see any problems… ooh hang on, they haven't put Alison near the Pimm's stall, have they?'

Richard snorted. 'Have a bit of faith, we're not brain-dead amoeba… oh hi, Pippa, yes, it's all looking good, isn't it?' He greeted his friend, gave her a thumbs up and turned his attention back to his phone. 'I think everyone learnt their lesson last year with Alison and there were talks of not having any booze at all after the quiz night but we've come up with a happy compromise.'

'Which is?' Richard couldn't help but grin at Marion's sharp response. She would always be this way, wildly untrusting of anyone else's ability to manage things as well as she could, but only doing so because she just wanted everything to be perfect for all those involved.

'Which is, Rosy and Lynne have taken over the Pimm's stall, the theory being that Lynne will draw people in and encourage them to let their hair down a little bit, but Rosy will be there as a visual reminder that letting your hair down is fine but getting totally inebriated and stripping to do a naked yoga pose in the middle of the school hall is a step too far.'

'You mock, Richard, but that did actually happen one year. Think of how many young minds have been scarred by the state of Judith's flapping bosom; I'm fully grown and still have nightmares. I am so relieved that our Rafe has gone on to have a functioning relationship – that woman could have done some damage.'

'That's not what you said a couple of nights ago. If I remember rightly you've been pretty rude about Sophie. Didn't you say she has the cold dead eyes of a serial killer?'

'I'm allowed to have some fun. I was under the impression that was the upside of having teenagers, or pre-teens. Is it not? And I was only joking; she's bright but hardly serial killer bright!'

'No, I guess it is fair reward.'

'But back to the school fayre – there will be something, there always is,' Marion insisted. He knew her anxious foreboding was about being prepared for everything, not because of a hopeless pessimism.

'I don't think this is a good idea, that's all.' A familiar voice from across the hall caught Richard's attention, causing him to stand up straight and cast a look around as he answered his wife.

'Well, maybe not this year, don't fret. Everything is okay. Hang on a minute… boys, stop right there. Shouldn't you both be in class?'

Rufus and Rupert, who were never seen together in school, looked up at their dad, pausing their tiptoe across the school hall. As they did so a girl from Rupert's class walked past them; Richard noticed her wink at his boys and slide into her classroom. In response to their dad's voice, Rufus had frozen to the spot whereas Rupert blithely answered, 'Yep, we're both heading there now. Just having a catch-up. Excited about the fayre, that's all, aren't we, Rufus?'

He nudged his younger brother so hard that Rufus, currently resembling a cartoon burglar caught in the act, nearly fell into the wall bars, but quickly righted himself and said, 'Yes, class, now. Excited. See ya, Dad,' before opening the door to his classroom and racing in as if he could not wait to dig his teeth into the ten times table. Hmmm.

'Was that our two?'

'Yes.'

'Together in *school*?'

'Yes.'

'What were they doing out of class?'

'No idea, they're back in now. I think they were just going to the loo.'

'At this time?'

'Yes, honestly, not everything is suspicious,' he reassured his wife, although something was very definitely niggling.

'Ha!' was her response. 'So, Pimm's stall is very sensibly covered. What are you doing, you never did say?'

'Oh, I'm on face painting. It should be fun.'

Richard held the phone away from his ear as raucous laughter exploded from the speaker.

'What's funny about that?'

'Oh, Richard. Rookie move, Richard, rookie. You'll see. Look, I think you're going to be fine; as long as no real changes have been made to the format I can't see why it won't be a raging success. You *will* have something happen at the last minute, it always does but I'm sure Jenny and Serena will have it covered. And Rosy is very capable with any last-minute catastrophes.'

'And I'm here.'

'And you're there and you are definitely very capable.' Her voice fell an octave as she automatically slipped into her sexy Marion voice, recovering herself very quickly as if she had surprised herself and making her tone brusque again.

It had certainly surprised him.

'I'm sure it'll all be fine, and I'll be on the end of the phone if needed. I'll try and pop in as soon as I've tied up everything here.'

Richard could feel her embarrassment coming down the phone; he understood it too. After so many years being *them* it was hard not to slip back into old ways. He would love nothing better than to slide back, but Marion had been resolute and whilst the two of them had the odd evening with the boys where it felt as if nothing had changed, it was abundantly clear that one thing Marion was never going to do was take him back. He kept it business-like instead of responding the way he wanted to; all the time he and Marion were chatting like this had to be better than back at the start of their break-up where things were tense, silent, resentful.

'We should all be fine; the only things we've changed a bit are the fire engine and we're having a bouncy castle. Oh, and Davinia is bringing llamas along with the horses this time.'

'You've what, she's what… this is madness. You cannot let llamas on the school field, they spit! Has anyone done a health and safety check to see what risks they pose? They're bound to be riddled with all sorts of parasites. You can't just willy-nilly agree to anything; it all has to be researched, planned. Honestly, I don't know what you're thinking. Where's Jenny?'

'Stop trying to micro-manage, love. She's just talking to the fire brigade about when they arrive.'

'Oh my God, you didn't agree to that, did you? She's been after the fire brigade for ages. Why do you think that is? It's not for the good of the children, let me tell you. She's obsessed. I swear she watches enough *Chicago Fire* to keep the series going just by herself. It's not healthy and if you want to have the children discover Jenny White on her knees in the fire engine before the fete's even been properly opened then so be it. I despair.'

'I'm sure that's not going to happen, Marion.'

'Are you? Are you really? Everyone knows the fire brigade come to school fetes to keep the mothers happy; their offspring clamber over the fire engine, the mothers imagine clambering over the firemen, pheromones are so high that even the flowers in the field are standing to attention and boom, in four years and nine months, admissions for Class One are through the roof and we need to build a whole new school.'

'I think that's a bit alarmist.'

'I know you do, which is why I'm finishing up here and coming to help. If this is already where things are at, you'll be in full-on disaster status within the hour. I'm on my way.'

'Really there is no need.'

'Richard, I know you are capable, articulate and good. I know you've been chair of the governors ever since darling Rafe was in Reception but trust me, you are still very naive as to quite how bad things can get and how quickly. As I said, I'll just finish up here, I'm literally around the corner, we're almost done and then I'll be with you.'

'Won't Jenny and Serena be cross that you're stepping on their toes?'

'Llamas *and* the fire brigade.' Marion made it sound as if she were talking to a toddler. 'I think it's for the best.' And his wife hung up the phone.

She just couldn't help herself, but he was sure that once she had arrived she would see that everything was fine. Which would probably make her a little bit cross. He was under no illusions that his wife would love to swoop in and save the day.

Jenny was currently chivvying everyone to set up the tables and the mini stage, clearly having picked up some of his wife's moves. Serena was chatting to Pippa's mum, Jan, who was setting up her cake stall along with Annie and Ethel. Richard went to join them for a chat before he faced digging through the supplies cupboard to find the face paints and sponges. The floor plan had him set up next to the cake stall, and he'd be sharing his space with Kam's sisters, who had come down to do henna tattoos, having been a raging success at last year's fayre.

The bell rang for break and suddenly the hall was swarming with children. Shoes racing, tappety-tap across the wooden hall floor, the girls in their summer checked dresses. A loud gabble of animation.

'Will you lot slow down?' Annie shrieked as Ethel grabbed hold of some globe artichoke plants and held them close as children swarmed by her. The majority of the pupils headed out into the playground as the sun had been beating down for weeks, heralding a perfect Cornish summer.

A few kids came trailing out of the boys' loos, making lots of eurgghh noises, ramping each other up with the drama that was occurring, one making a great show of holding his nose and shaking his head.

'Can we go over to the infant loos, Miss? These ones are blocked.'

'Really? Oh for goodness' sake! But yes, of course you can,' Pippa responded. She turned to the rest of the PTA. 'Hang on a minute, I'll be back in a sec.'

'I'll come with you.' Richard and Pippa wandered into the boys' loos to find every single toilet rammed full of green paper towels. Thick and clogged and with not one able to flush.

'Why do they do this?' Pippa said. 'Every couple of years, someone does it. We'll have to close these for now. I'll put up a sign; can you go and get Rosy to call the plumb—' Loud shrieks erupted from the other side of the hall and they raced to see what was causing such fuss.

'Erghhhh...'

'Miss, Miss!'

'That's gross!' A cacophony of girls' voices came from the other side of the hall where the girls' toilets were located.

Pippa raced across the hall to see a cluster of girls from Classes Two through to Four all standing at the cloakroom door that led to the girls' loos and making *yuk* noises. Annie had pushed some aside to take a peek and as Richard and Pippa approached they heard her say, 'Right, you little buggers, get back. Get back now.'

'This sort of thing didn't happen when we were at school.' Ethel was next to her, shaking her head. 'Little monsters. Things were very different when we had the slipper to scare us. Nothing wrong with some firm discipline.'

'We know your views on discipline,' Annie replied and the two women cackled.

'It's a good thing…' Richard started to say and then realized that a puddle of water was beginning to slowly seep out of the bathroom into the hall.

'I'll go and get Miss Winter,' Annie said, dragging Ethel away before any more views about Ethel's preferences escaped her friend's lips.

'I'll see what I can do in here.' Richard pushed the door open further and started to wade through. It wasn't a huge volume of water – moppable, he thought – but it was rapidly spreading and, as he looked in, was coming from the sinks which had been blocked, presumably along with the loos, and the taps turned on and left.

'Why would anyone do this on May Fayre day?' he asked Pippa, who had joined him. 'Surely everyone is excited for that. Why try and sabotage the school today?' He turned off all the taps and plunged his hands into the sink, pulling out sopping wet towels and placing them in a large bin. One sink cleared, he headed on to the next. The truth was he had felt a flutter of fear when he realized what had happened in the boys' loos, but Rupert and Rafe couldn't have done something to the girls' loos as well; it couldn't have been them after all.

It wasn't long before Rosy came through – four cleared sinks' worth of time.

'The plumbers can't come out until tomorrow morning. They've promised if they can free up any time then they'll do so and give me a ring but it's not looking good.'

'Oh my! Oh my! Oh my! *What-am-I-going-to-do?*' came the high-pitched shriek from Jenny, panic crammed into every syllable, the realization of a possible cancelled Fayre hitting her.

'Can we not call a different plumber?' Richard asked. Surely it was simple enough?

'Ah, you'd think so, but no. The insurance only applies if we use the insurer's nominated plumbers. And we just don't have enough wiggle room in the budget to countenance paying someone independently to come out.'

'Isn't Alisia's dad a plumber?' Pippa suggested as Richard emptied out the heavy and now sopping wet bin liner from the large bathroom bin.

'They're on holiday.' Rosy shrugged.

'I'm never going to live it down. What are we going to do?' Jenny sounded like she was going to start hyperventilating.

'Hey, hey, Jenny, calm the… calm down. *We* are going to find a solution together,' Serena said. 'This is not the end of the world.'

'It might be the end of my world.' Jenny sniffled in between taking deep, deep breaths. 'What on earth do you think Marion is going to say when we have to cancel the May Fayre? She'll never forgive me.'

'First of all, Marion isn't a crazy woman; she's hardly likely to lose her temper at you, you've not rammed the loos full of towels.' Serena tried to reassure the woman, whose shoulders were now heaving. Unfortunately, the silence and wide-eyed looks of all the adults now surrounding them didn't lend a lot of weight to what she was saying. Serena fixed Richard with a stern glare. 'Is she, Richard? She's not really running the PTA any more. We're going to get this sorted and she's never going to know.'

Jenny didn't look convinced.

Alice appeared from nowhere with a mop and bucket; whispers had traversed the school now and children were crowded around the doors that led to the playgrounds, peering through windows, to see the drama unfolding. A murmur rose amongst them as they realized that tonight's fun may be at risk.

'Look, aren't the infants' loos fine, over by Class One? Can't we just use those?' Ethel asked.

'And the staff loos, can we not open those to parents and let the children use the infants'?' Pippa suggested.

'It's possible but I need to check any legal responsibilities we have with the school open to so many people. We may simply not have enough toilets to cover the required minimum for this sort of event and have to consider another solution. But we might be okay; either way I am sure we will find a way around. Penmenna School has faced far bigger beasts than this and triumphed,' Rosy explained.

'What about the church hall?' Annie proffered. 'I think it's the stich'n'bitch this evening, but not until after the fayre and I can always move that into The Vicarage. Dan won't mind at all. He'd be happy to help, wouldn't he, Alice?'

'He would.'

'Thank you, that's very kind,' Rosy said. Jenny was still sniffling, breaking off her gentle sobs to make the most amazing nasal sounds that would make an elephant beam with pride.

Richard knew there would be a solution; he was just going to have to find it. The group of them stood around trying to problem-solve once the mopping had been done and all the sinks unblocked. Sheila popped up with a large plate, complete with doily.

'Biscuits for the troops. I'll get some of the older children to make some coffee and bring it down, since none of you have been able to have your break,' Sheila suggested happily, offering the plate around.

'No, you know we can't do that. I'm sure we'll all survive,' Rosy said firmly. Pippa harrumphed comedically as if her world would break without coffee.

Sheila was right, though; there was barely any time before the bell rang to signal the end of break. Then Richard's attention was caught by the sound of his youngest son's voice floating in through the playground door. 'It worked, it actually worked.' It sounded jubilant, as if he was jumping and punching the air.

Richard's stomach plummeted to his toes; they *did* have something to do with this! For goodness' sake, he was going to kill them. But as he turned to glance across at the outside door that led into the hall – as did the others, having noted a change in tone coming from the children's murmur by the door – he saw the pupils parting like the Red Sea when faced with Moses.

And there, striding in through the granite doorway like the Amazonian queen she was, stood the sexiest woman Richard had ever seen. Confidence exuding from every pore, dressed in a bright red snakeskin summer dress, matching kitten heels and with her hair cut and styled into a new, shorter, far edgier crop and with a slash of scarlet lips, markedly different from the Fuchsia Crush she had been wearing for years, was his wife.

She was magnificent.

Chapter Twenty-nine

Marion couldn't help the glimmer of a smile on her face as she marched up the steps, through the children and into the school cloakroom that led in turn to the hall. Walking into the hall, the first person her eyes lit upon was her ex-husband. Standing there in the dress-down clothes that he seemed to have adopted as his uniform recently, he was surrounded by other members of the PTA and the staff. She caught his eye; it would be hard not to – he was staring at her with so much admiration that it was difficult not to bask. It made her stand even taller.

She knew she looked good but she hadn't known how Richard would respond to the little changes she had made. She had told herself she didn't care; they were no longer together and he no longer had an opinion that she was going to listen to. But she knew as she saw him standing there that his opinion did matter. It mattered a lot and she was a teeny bit cross with herself for caring as much as she did. So much for her feminist ideals. But with a job – no, not a job, a roaring new business – and the changing way she defined herself, she was enjoying the shaping of her new identity.

She had always been proud to be both wife and mother, feeling they were seriously overlooked roles that were never given the status that they deserved. She didn't disagree with that now; she just knew she felt so much better doing what she was doing. Fresher.

And, a little upsettingly, because she knew it should be the last thing that she cared about, she was secretly over the moon that Richard liked the way she was looking. She was keeping that secret tightly close to her chest.

'Hello, everyone.' She attempted her breeziest tone. She had been trying to make some changes about how she dealt with people and had discovered that if she took the 'Alice approach', the more-flies-with-honey-than-vinegar thing, then people were even more helpful than they had been when she was putting the fear of God into them. That had always been so much fun. If people were willing to be told what to do then that was really up to them, but she had left a meeting recently at the Hall for Cornwall and overheard two of the employees talking about her, in a positive way. As if they liked her. It had made her feel as if her head was touching the clouds.

And now she was going to sprinkle some of the magic dust she had accrued all over Penmenna School, show them this Magical Marion rather than the Monster Mark-sharp which she knew for a fact they had been calling her for years.

Although she would have to be firm about the llamas. That was ridiculous.

Oh, and she may have to park herself at the fire engine, just to oversee things – obviously.

As she approached the group of adults clustered in the hall, she put a big beaming smile on her face and saw that Jenny had red-rimmed eyes, Alice had a mop in her hand and Richard was holding a very heavy-looking binbag.

'Everything alright?' she asked in as jovial a tone as she could manage without sounding like she should be sectioned. 'Jenny, have you been crying? Whatever for?'

Serena jumped in to answer. 'Jenny's fine, aren't you, Jenny? We've just had a bit of a hiccup with the loos.'

'Oh, my poor love, don't let it distress you. There's nothing we can't sort together.' Marion leant forward and stroked Jenny's shoulder. Jenny startled. Marion couldn't help but think Jenny was a bit of a tit who had failed to rise to a challenge, but continued working on the fake-it-until-you-make-it school of nice. If she kept doing it, it may become ingrained and even start to come naturally.

As to the chaos that greeted her as she made her entrance, truth was she hadn't really expected any better, but she did believe that bit about everyone pulling together to be true. Together the Penmenna School crew could probably sort anything. But having her at the helm, albeit only for today, couldn't hurt.

The bell rang, heralding the children back through the hall to their classrooms, the more confident ones stopping to ask what was going to happen, the others whispering behind hands and giggling as they trailed past.

She had missed their little faces. Their curiosity, their mischief.

Some of them saw her and, having obviously noticed her absence around school over the last few months, tentatively waved. It was funny how the children were less scared of her than some of the adults were. She flashed another conciliatory glance at Jenny.

'Right then, Marion and I will see if we can sort this,' said Richard, all assertive and masculine-like. She liked him when he took control.

'Okay, I'll go and see if we need to cancel the fayre, work out if moving it to the church hall is a sensible move and try and work out a plan. Should a miracle occur can you let me know, Richard, and then I can get back to what I was meant to be doing this afternoon,' Rosy addressed him before turning back towards her office.

'Of course, I will,' Richard answered, as if he had been doing this sort of thing all his life, being the heart of their community rather than working away in a slinky, high-powered office in London.

'Yes, we need to get back to class,' Pippa said and Alice nodded.

'But we're here to help, what do you need?' Serena added.

'Marion and I will try and troubleshoot this; are you guys happy to just keep prepping as if it is all going ahead for now and we'll have an emergency meeting at lunch and see which way the land lies? That way if everything is already out of cupboards and organized it's just a matter of moving things from one place to another. Oh, and Marion, do you know how Serena and Jenny can access the May Fayre playlist you complied a couple of years ago? We can't find it anywhere on the network.'

'Yes, yes of course. It's not on the network. I'll email it across now,' Marion said whilst looking at her husband, the easy-going man she had known forever who was taking charge so beautifully. Even if he had somehow managed to stick her on blocked loo duty. She was fairly sure in all her years at Penmenna that was one job she hadn't taken upon herself.

'Right, you and I can get stuck in. I'll go find some gloves. I'm sure Sheila will know where to find some.'

'I'm sure she won't,' Marion said darkly. 'Why have you got me cleaning loos?'

'Not cleaning, my love – oh, I wonder if they're in here.' He flung open the cleaner's cupboard and rifled. 'Aha! Brilliant, look there are heavy-duty gloves for you here, and a box of disposable ones here. The boys and I can take those.'

'The boys? Why the boys? Aren't they in class?' She realized her voice was pitched slightly higher than her new-Marion-who-is-friendly-and-chill-whilst-remaining-efficient voice was meant to be, but really!

'They are at the moment,' Richard agreed, a firmness in his tone that she hadn't heard for a while. 'But we're going to get them now.'

'To clean loos?' Marion could hear her outrage. Her soon-to-be-ex-husband wasn't some new confident man who pitched in to help; he was a maniac. Why on earth would her boys need to be dragged into this?

'Because I have a strong feeling our dear sweet sons are responsible for this. We just need to find out why.'

'My boys? Madness!'

'*Our* boys and highly probable. What I don't under-stand is why. Why would they want to mess everything up? There is nothing more important than your friends when you're young; why bugger up the May Fayre? It makes no sense. We both know they're naughty…'

She caught Richard glancing at the fury that she knew would be clear on her face.

'Yes, yes, I know. You'd say not naughty, terribly bright and not challenged enough.' And then he rolled his eyes and faux yawned.

Wow.

She would have had anybody else's eyes out. But his face was such a picture. She fought the chuckle rising up; someone needed to defend her babies.

'But you're convinced it's them.' Her maternal ire was starting to bubble. 'I'm sure they didn't have anything to do with this, Richard. And besides, what happened to innocent until proven guilty – where are you going?' Richard was, most irritatingly, walking away from her.

'To get a confession.'

This was ludicrous; what a waste of time. They should be looking for alternate venues or negotiating with the insurance company or using all their cards to get some emergency Portaloos installed.

Then she saw the looks on Rupert and Rufus's faces as her husband led them out of their respective classes. They were a mishmash of all sorts of emotion: she could identify fear, presumably at being caught; guilt, ditto; and yet some kind of jubilation mixed in, the two of them repeatedly shooting each other *we did it* looks.

They were as guilty as hell.

Chapter Thirty

It took a while. Firstly, Richard got the boys to crack. It hadn't been as hard as she would have hoped. Rupert held out, but Rufus was much younger and struggled under his father's rare, stern glare. Rupert remained mutinous, stony-faced and refusing to be drawn. Yet he gave away his guilt the minute he gave his brother a narrow-eyed *you're so dead later* look.

The whole family had pitched in and emptied and unblocked the loos. The majority of them hadn't been used so the job itself wasn't too unpleasant, the thought being far worse than the actuality.

Any warmth that Marion felt at seeing the family working together was quickly replaced with an all-over feeling of abject guilt. The boys had conspired to do something dreadful, ruining their and their friends' fun, all in an attempt to get Marion into school so she could see Richard in a setting outside of him cooking dinner and then leaving.

Rufus cocked up explaining, his emotion making it hard to work out what on earth he was going on about, so at the end of the toilet clean Rupert confided that they had hoped to get his mum and dad together in an out-of-house situation, try and force them together with a problem that needed solving, knowing that the two would have to actively collaborate rather than just rub along. They wanted to throw their mum and dad together, knowing Marion wouldn't be able to help but interfere. They also had noted how seamlessly their dad had slid into school and wanted their mother to witness that. Quite adult principles had gone into a remarkably juvenile stunt. But the fact was, if Marion and Richard hadn't separated the boys would never have dreamt of putting the May Fayre in jeopardy just to try and create a rapprochement.

The two of them, she and Richard, had kept it together and presented a united front of disappointment, sending the boys to Rosy Winter as soon as the toilets were unblocked where they were to explain that all the toilets bar two were now cleared and that they were responsible and were very, very sorry.

'I hope she tears a strip from them,' Richard said. For a man who was so kind, so compassionate about people, Marion never understood why he was harder on the boys than she was. Surely he could see that the boys were hurting, doing their best to resolve family difficulties. Well-intentioned, as she put it to him.

'Yes, but the thing is, Marion, I do understand why they do the things they do – I get it and it breaks my heart – but everyone who has ever done bad things from the dawn of time has a good reason for what he or she is doing; that doesn't make it right. The boys need to learn to fit in with society's rules, that when they are doing things to make themselves happy they need to look at how it's impacting others around them and then make a decision that is the best for the most rather than the best for them. And if our boys don't learn these lessons, as much as we love them, they're going to grow up into over-indulged and entitled sociopaths. So yes, I understand why they took the action they did but I also understand that it's our role to make them understand how to fit into society as a good man. So damn right they're admitting to their crime and then they will do whatever Rosy tells them and we will not step in to defend them, enabling them to get away scot-free because we feel guilty. Protecting them in the short term because we understand why they behave as they do may appear the compassionate option but may well damage them in the long term.'

Marion took a deep breath and looked over at her husband, the determination writ upon his brow, and fell in love all over again with his integrity, his resolve to stand up for what was right not what was easy. A rare trait, and one she frequently knew she failed at. This man, though.

'They can't be allowed to go to the fayre tonight,' she said to him, the two of them still standing in the hall but locked in each other, oblivious to the unpacking and organizing happening around them.

'Nope.' Richard scrunched his mouth and shook his head.

'Means we can't go either.'

'I know, I was looking forward to it as well.'

'You can go, you've been involved with this one. There is no reason for you to miss out.'

'No, there are plenty of face-painters to step in and the boys need to learn their actions have consequences; me missing out on something I wanted may well coun-terbalance their idea that they've won. I believe they'll feel bad about that and I have every intention of making sure they're aware of the fact that I had been looking forward to it.'

'I'll wingman you.'

'I know you will. We've always had each other's backs.'

'We have.'

Marion looked at him and everything was a crazy tumult. She wanted to lean into him so badly, rest her head on his shoulder as she always had, just be.

However, she couldn't. She had made the decision to walk away, and still believed that she couldn't give her permission for cheating, but oh my goodness she hadn't known the sheer physicality of being apart was going to be so hard. The keeping her body away from him, not just in a sex way – although she was definitely struggling with that side of things – but in a companionship way. Those little touches, the hand on the hollow of the back as you walk past, the tucking of a lock of hair behind an ear as you talk, the squeeze of a hand at any given opportunity: these she ached for. Here, standing so near to him, the two of them close because of their sons' appalling, effective plan, brought the hurt of it all to the surface. She stood torn between a whole mishmash of feelings, not quite sure of her next step.

'Mind you, I was quite keen on face-painting. I reckon that's some art even I could do.'

'Oh bless you, face-painting is not fun. It's several levels of hell, the first starting the minute the child tells you what they want and only ending when they realize that they just look like themselves but with colour on their faces as opposed to actually becoming Spider-Man or The Hulk. Trust me.'

'Probably.'

'I'll tell you what, if you really want you can face-paint me this evening.'

'Oh yes?' Richard raised his brows in tandem and smirked.

'*Face* paint.' She smirked back and then got a hold of herself, remembering a time when they had been at uni and painted each other's entire bodies blue for fancy dress, and then getting so carried away with the painting and the body bit that they never made the party anyway. Although they did have to throw the bedsheets out.

'Maybe we should do the boys as well, something they really don't like and take photos and post it on their social media.' Richard changed the subject, his face flushing as he remembered the same thing. At least so she assumed. He could be blushing for any reason, but they were fairly well attuned and she'd place money on this being why.

'I think that might start a revolution.' Marion realized they were talking in half-whispers, making the conversation intimate, indicating to both themselves and the outside world that this was just between the two of them. She could only imagine Rupert's response to the suggestion that they paint his face. The boy may only be ten but he behaved, the majority of the time, as if he believed he was in his thirties at least.

'The three of them banding together may be too powerful a force for the two of us to counter.'

'Oh God, we need to punish them hard.'

'We do. They need to know they can't do whatever they want; the end does not justify the means.'

'Should we saw their legs off?'

'It's their minds that are their problem.'

'Legs, arms and lobotomize?'

'Sounds more like it.'

'Hire them out as paid agent provocateurs?'

'Now you might be onto something. Although I'm not sure that's been a real thing since the nineteenth century.'

'Oh, it is. I think they just call them influencers these days. Seriously what are we going to do? Let's be practical, are there any jobs you need doing that you really don't want to do?' Marion asked her husband. She had already made them scrub the walls down the other day and was running out of punitive housework.

'I don't think I can get them to empty the gutters or cut that overhanging tree down.'

'No, maybe not.'

'Although I did see an article online the other day about a barber in America offering "old man" haircuts as a cruel and unusual punishment for children.'

'Shear my babies' beautiful locks?' Marion gasped in mock outrage.

'Two Friar Tucks, that'll teach them.'

She burst out laughing at the image. 'I wish I could say yes, but no.'

'We could always make them decide the punishments for each other.'

'That's not a bad idea; no one knows you better than your siblings.'

'Right? And I reckon we could trust them to be fair.'

'But we'd have to make sure they were punitive, not eat twenty jelly babies at once sort of nonsense.'

'They'll definitely try something like that. Eat nothing but profiteroles until you're sick.'

'Ah, but Team Marksharp Senior is still a match for Team Junior.'

'We are. Always. Forever.' And the two exchanged a look so loud the whole hall could hear it.

Chapter Thirty-one

Several weeks had passed since the night of the May Fayre, when Richard and Marion had successfully presented a united front against their two younger sons, and there had been a marked difference in how Marion had been treating Richard since.

Today was a perfect example. She had come home earlier than usual after spending the day shopping with Rosy and had started to cook, absentmindedly preparing enough for all five of them whilst he sat and chatted with her. She wordlessly slid his plate in front of him a little while later and neither of them ever addressed it but both knew, he was sure they did, that something had shifted, that their friendship seemed to be back.

The change between them made Richard so happy that he had been practically skipping everywhere over the last few weeks. He wanted *everything* back, but this was a jolly good step and the real first positive one he'd had. It had opened up his hope, sprinkled it with a little life and it was beginning to grow again.

Once dinner had been finished, he and the boys headed to the church hall for choir practice. Community choir had started as one of the boys' punishments. Richard had been adamant that they needed a greater understanding of how the world worked, the dynamics of working together and the pride in creating something as a group. Which is why the rest of their punishments were also based around the village, like community service but for primary school children and lasting until the summer holidays.

Alice had found them chores to do around the church and they were helping out at Memory Club, working with Bill Meacher weeding and maintaining the church grounds and aiding Pippa on the village's Feast Week committee. With that and their homework they hadn't had time to breathe, let alone get up to further mischief.

To compound the seriousness of it all, their tech had been confiscated until they got positive reports for each task they undertook, their PlayStation only returned after a month of good behaviour.

But to be fair to them, they had done all of this without too much fuss and actually enjoyed bits of it. So much so that Rafe had started to join them at choir.

With his three boys at his side, Richard entered the church hall and found everyone gathered and halfway through 'Amazing Grace'. Alice hadn't wanted to use the school hall as they practised for Rosy's wedding because she was having enough trouble keeping it secret from her boss as it was.

It had taken the choir weeks, no exaggeration, to choose the songs for the wedding. At one point things were getting so desperate Alice made them sing fifteen of the most popular hymns for weddings to try and see which ones sounded best.

The answer was none of them.

The choir had only formed at Christmas last year and carols were easy to master – everyone knew them and had been singing them since childhood – but with other hymns, even the well-known ones, the choir was a lot weaker. When they had run through 'Morning

Has Broken', Richard privately thought it sounded like the blackbirds were being baked into a pie rather than signalling the break of dawn. But listening to them now, a few weeks on, he felt a swell of pride; he wasn't sure how Alice had whipped them all into shape but somehow she had managed it.

He slid into the back of the group, handing each of the boys a song sheet complete with the words.

'Oh aye, look out.' Ethel paused her singing and greeted him and his family as they came and joined in. So much for Christian charity. Grace clearly wasn't saving Ethel today.

Annie, dressed head-to-toe in clashing scarlet and emerald, dug her in the ribs with her elbow. 'Now, now Ethel. Don't be a crosspatch; that's not like you. They've been good as gold for weeks and it's lovely to see the young getting involved.'

'The only thing those boys should be involved in is borstal.'

'They don't have borstal these days; you are more generous-minded than that.'

'*Amazing grace, how sweet the sound that saved a wretch like me…*' Everyone else was still singing the repeat verse but Richard couldn't help but listen to the conversation next to him.

'Not to them that don't deserve it. Don't be fooled by them singing all nice when we're all watching. I won't forget that kerfuffle up at the school in a hurry. I mean, I don't mind a bit of mischief, but that's something beyond that. Nickanan Night when we were kids never caused *that* much trouble.'

'Knockdown Ginger was never that much fun either. Give me scrumping any time of day; much more thrilling and a reward at the end as well, yum.' The two women cackled, all pretence at singing abandoned. 'I think it was romantic – they were only trying to get their mum and dad back together, everyone knows that. You can't blame them,' Annie continued.

'I bloody well can.'

'You're just cross cos we were out late last night.'

'Out? What nonsense are you talking?' Ethel, wearing her usual lace blouse and sensible skirt, looked at her more colourful friend and smirked. 'You'll be claiming next I was up half the night with a glow stick at that Rave in a Cave thing on the beach.' Then she winked. Richard had often thought there was more to Ethel than met the eye, and this conversation was proving it.

'Ha, I bet your ears are still ringing. I told you to wear those defenders and not to stand right next to the speakers. Honestly!'

'We were only there an hour.'

'An hour were long enough. I told you I didn't like that nonsense – *boom, boom, boom.* Had to listen to enough of it when I was living in Plymouth.'

'And I told you being old is about experiencing as many new things as you can before you die.'

'Some things I'm quite happy to never experience. I'd rather hoped the joy had more to do with regular cups of tea and a hot water bottle.'

Richard breathed a sigh of relief that they had changed subject.

With 'Amazing Grace' over, people were now talking amongst themselves, cramming a quick few minutes of gossip in before Alice got them practising the next song. He watched as Rafe dragged his brothers over to Ethel. Where was this going?

'Hello, I'm Rafe Marksharp, we've met lots before and I've been coming to choir for a few weeks now.' Rafe addressed Ethel.

'Yes. First time we met, I told you I'd chop your hands off with a rusty machete if you bothered Ethel's friend, Reg, again, but you've been alright ever since,' Annie remarked.

'You don't forget a threat like that in a hurry. My mum was furious with me, and I'm sure Reg will have mentioned that I haven't been back to Whispering Pines since. I miss it. Anyway, I know you also know my brothers.' He dragged his two siblings forward. Richard watched warily.

'Yes, Although I'd be quite happy to live out my days without seeing them again, dastardly little sods.'

'I know, I just wanted to explain that they have been very distressed by my parents' separation and were simply trying to reconcile the two of them. They're young and didn't think through the consequences of their actions but they have apologized to everyone and have been working really hard to make it right. They're happy to offer further apologies to you if you like, aren't you, Rupert and Rufus?'

Rufus looked fairly willing; he was getting good at apologies. Rupert slightly less so.

Richard decided now was the time to intervene, although he was also fascinated to see how this would end.

'Ooh, Richard, brilliant. So pleased to see you.' Serena popped up by his side, distracting him from the boys.

'Hi, Serena, good to see you.'

'You too. I'm glad you're here, I was hoping that you'd turn up this evening.'

'Oh, okay. Yep, me and the boys. Marion says hello to everyone; she's been so busy. She, Rosy and Lynne have spent the day dress shopping and now she's trying to organize the wedding entertainment. Matt keeps going on about getting a band called Blood of your Scrotum for one song and Marion is not convinced.'

'Oh dear! Well, I was hoping you'd be here and perhaps she wouldn't. That sounds weird but this is a bit delicate.'

'Oh?' Richard didn't like the sound of that. Serena tipped her head over to a quiet corner and reluctantly he followed. Half of him was itching to jump into the Ethel and Rafe interaction – he reckoned Ethel would only be happy once all three boys had been keelhauled and Rafe would only settle once Ethel was brainwashed into being a fully paid-up member of the Rafe-Marksharp-is-a-marvel fan club. At this point, he wasn't sure who was coming out the winner. The other half of him was fairly sure he didn't want the boys hearing whatever it was Serena had to say.

She slid out a folded piece of paper and passed it over to him surreptitiously. It felt like a drug deal. Just more church hall-y. Rather than put it straight into his pocket, he opened it up and saw it was a printout of a WhatsApp conversation. A conversation between Serena and Claudia.

'What is this?' It was a stupid question. He could see the answer. He just wanted a minute to process. And another minute to decide if he really wanted to read this. It felt wrong, as if he were eavesdropping, snooping or peering through people's curtains late at night. But yet the conversation was Serena's and she was handing it over to him, right now. Express permission given.

'I was chatting to Claudia the other day; I do so periodically. Although, to be more accurate, Claudia reaches out when she wants an audience and ignores everything else.'

'I don't know if I need to be reading Claudia's messages. Out of all the people in the word I should avoid right now, Claudia is probably at the top of the list. Why are you giving me this, Serena?'

'Like I said a couple of months ago, this is eating me up. She got in touch to talk about her new-found love. So, I thought I'd use the opportunity to push a bit, see if I could find that evidence you referred to recently. Take a look when you have a minute. You might find it useful.'

'Okay, thanks, I guess.'

'Do you think you'll use it?'

'I think I need to read it first but truth is, as grateful as I am – and there may come a time when I need it – things are going quite well at the moment. I'm hoping that we might be taking slow steps back to a healthy place, but I never did the things I'm accused of and I would like it if Marion got there by herself and realized that I *am* the man she thought I was.'

'I don't blame you, that would be the perfect solution, but the fact is, Richard, and you know this better than me, your wife is a pretty stubb— determined woman and you may need a little help. Just a little push. Maybe once she has proof that she was mistaken then she'll find it easier to walk back. Just saying.'

'A good point. But it feels a bit like an *aha!* moment, an ambush. You know, as if I were to jump out of a bush waving a piece of paper triumphantly whilst dressed like Robin Hood.' Serena looked at him oddly. Marion would have known what he meant. He tried again. 'If I give her this, it feels like I'm saying in a slightly aggressive way, "You were wrong and now you need to eat yourself up with guilt." Truth is we maybe needed something to shake us up. I have never seen Marion happier than she is running this business and I've certainly never been happier getting to spend my time down here, back with my boys. Even though I'm having to sleep umpteen miles up the road at my mate's house, I feel closer to the boys, more connected to family life, than I have done in ages. So maybe it has done us good. And I want to see how things naturally progress from here, see if we get where we need to be without throwing even more confusion Marion's way. But, having said that, I am really grateful that you've done this and it may well come in handy if my trust-in-destiny plans don't work out the way I envisage. I hope you feel fully off the hook now.'

'Not quite fully, but yes, it has made me feel a bit lighter. These messages aren't quite a full confession but they do make it clear that she hadn't had sex for quite some time before meeting Xavier, and that she has no idea why she was obsessing over unrequited crushes as she was.'

'I'll have a proper look when the kids aren't around. But thank you, I do appreciate it.'

At that moment, Alice clapped her hands to get the group's attention. 'Okay everybody, let's get back together. You managed to make that sound brilliant. Which is just as well as we don't have a lot of time left. Let's see, or hear even, if you can sprinkle some of your magic over "This Little Light of Mine" as well.'

There was a general shuffling as people got themselves back into one central body, Richard's walk back punctuated by Rufus running into his father's legs.

'Dad. Dad. Ethel says she's going to take me out sailing and show me what real life is like, I think that's what she said. Can I go, can I?'

Richard looked at Ethel's face; it was not flushed with compassion and a willingness to educate his young son. There was however a distinct look of mischief. He had a funny feeling Ethel may well have more in common with his boys than he had thought and he wasn't convinced that sending them off to sea with her was the most sensible idea.

Chapter Thirty-two

Serena: Thought I'd check in and see how Love's Young Dream is going?

Claudia: Ah, you came up in convo the other day. Perfect is the answer, perfect. He's so fabulous, not quite as tall as I would have wanted, but very rich. I can't always understand everything he says but I'm finding that it doesn't matter too much. We have the language of love in common. And he is besotted with me, besotted. You have to meet him.

Serena: I'd love to. Did you say he worked in finance too?

Claudia: Yes, but in the States, not in London. It's so nice to find a man who's a man. A real man, an alpha, not afraid to be in charge. He was magnificent the other night, simply doesn't tolerate poor service. I don't know why I've wasted so much time on mooching about over wimpy-ass betas. Complete waste of time. Anyway, you must come up and meet him. I was thinking this weekend, he's over so I've booked us a table for Saturday at eight. So excited for you two to meet.

Serena: I can't make it this weekend, so sorry. Am really happy you've found someone. Another time?

Claudia: You're always so flaky. Your best friend is IN LOVE after not having sex for ages! Years! Seriously, no sex since that airline pilot when we went on our girls' weekend away three years ago. And now I'm in love, I can barely walk which is definitely a win, and I want you to meet him. Just come. You're not still sulking are you?

Serena: Sulking? NO. About what?

Claudia: About that stupid letter thing. You should never have agreed to do it if you were going to make such a thing about it. Although I am a bit embarrassed about the fuss I made over that man. Especially seeing as he was too much of a coward to admit how he felt about me or do anything interesting. All that stupid 'I love my wife' shit. I'm not convinced he actually likes women at all. Xavier is a real man. In all ways!

Serena: I can't do this weekend. Maybe in the summer holidays if Xavier is around then?

Claudia: FFS! Must go. Will you stop being such a crap best friend and get your arse up here please! Table is booked.

Richard sat up in bed, his laptop playing documentaries in the background but paying zero attention to them. Instead he sat reading and re-reading this piece of paper over and over again. It felt weird reading someone else's messages but he could see that this, whilst not explicit, certainly implied his innocence. Or at least that Claudia clearly hadn't had sex for quite some time, not that he was sympathetic.

Should he show Marion? Should he use it as the proof she had asked for? It had literally landed in his lap as if it were meant to be used, but perhaps he should patch up his marriage differently, healing the rifts that must have already been there for his wife to consider that he had been playing away. Heal those rifts, create a stronger family base and prove the sort of man he was, not the man he wasn't. That was going to be his plan.

Chapter Thirty-three

It was mid-July and the sun streamed through the curtains, waking Marion before her alarm. She stretched, her usual morning stretch from tips of fingers to tips of toes, then reached over for Richard. It was her birthday and the two of them always made a great big family affair out of it.

Then she remembered: Richard was no longer there.

This would be her first birthday since she was nineteen without waking up next to him. She closed her eyes and took herself back to birthdays past, not madly healthy but on her birthday she was allowed to indulge, surely?

The past few months had been odd; things had very much changed in her life and she was wildly happy professionally. The business was taking off and she had been throwing herself into events all over the south west. She had bookings now from Devon, Exeter and a company in Bristol had even reached out recently.

Personally, she was pretty damn content. She had a firm female friend now for the first time in her life. She had always been the weird kid in school and then once she went to university she expected to be exactly the same, but instead she was suddenly popular, albeit only amongst the boys. A fresh start with none of her baggage apparent, no one there to remember that she was the smelly kid with a mother that the other kids called a slapper. At Oxford, the aloofness she had developed as a wall throughout her childhood now read as confidence rather than avoidance. Men were drawn to her and she discovered the joy of a new-found status as queen bee. It was something she had clung to relentlessly ever since before she realized, which she was only now doing at this point of her life, that there was joy to be had in being part of a group, joy in having a give and take friendship rather than being the leader.

She and Alice had become close, with the woman popping around at least once a week for a drink and a catch-up. Marion had found that instead of snarling when her doorbell rang, over time she had started looking forward to her visits, would buy in snacks, stock up on the wine she knew Alice preferred and get ready to share the things that had gone right that week, the things that had gone wrong and none of it with the expectation that she would have sex afterwards, so a bit like having your husband as your best friend but without the need to shave your legs.

Why was everything turning her mind to sex at the moment? Was this what happened? She knew full well that when married she had spent a lot of time thinking about sex and not always having as much as she would like, but when Richard would come home from working away, boy would they make up for it then. She had always assumed that single people had it easy, that whenever they felt an urge or an itch they could, quite literally, nip out and get it scratched. Having now been single for over four months she had learnt that that may not be the case. Or certainly wasn't proving to be for her.

Instead of a new-found sexual freedom, every man she spoke to was sadly lacking and after only a minute or two of conversation with them her desire to flirt was seriously dampened, turning into a strong desire to wind up the conversation and escape. They would reveal some flaw, something about themselves that just didn't measure up in her head and would put paid to any sexual flutterings she had in an instant. What was becoming abundantly clear was that no one measured up to Richard and that as other men spoke to her, she could only hear Richard's voice in her head telling her a story, laughing over a shared memory or anecdote, picture him brushing her hair from her face, his hand creeping up her leg, unbuttoning a button.

When push came to shove, the only man she wanted to reach out and touch her in any way was Richard. It was not helpful and she hoped it wasn't going to last long. At this rate she may never have sex again. That was not a thought she wanted to explore on her birthday.

Neither was the fact that Richard himself was being so goddamn adorable. Providing her with the perfect family she had always dreamed of. Being there for her and the boys, wordlessly meeting Marion's day-to-day needs without a quibble, no prompting or clues needed. Just stepping in and up and making sure that home was running smoothly, despite not living there any more, so when Marion would return after a hard day's work everything was in place to enable her to relax in the evenings and free for her work commitments in the day. He was like a nineteen fifties housewife; everything was done efficiently and uncomplainingly, and Marion was loving it.

'Choreplay' was a word she had heard recently and now she knew the truth of it. Having a partner doing the things that were needed and without the implication of it being a favour was remarkably sexually attractive. Everything Richard was doing made her want him even more than she had before. She wanted him beside her now, to help her celebrate her early birthday morning the way they always had, before the boys would wake and come in.

That was one birthday wish that wasn't so simple to grant any more and annoyingly was the one thing she wanted. If she could have Richard back, back in her bed, without having compromised her principles then she felt she would be the happiest, most fulfilled woman in the world.

'Raaaaarrrrrrrrrrr!' Her bedroom door opened and in rushed the three boys as if telepathically knowing she was awake. Rufus was the first through the door, battle cry escaping his lips, leaping onto her bed and straddling her, trying to peel her eyelids back despite the fact that she was awake and her eyes were fully open.

'Hello, you.' She grabbed her youngest boy's face and kissed it. You didn't have three boys and not learn how to respond quickly first thing in the morning. 'How are you this morning?'

'It's your birthday!' he screamed with excitement. Very close to her ear.

'Happy birthday, Mum.' Rafe and Rupert had followed their younger brother through the door, both too old to hurl themselves at her although Rupert looked like he was tempted to, just a little.

'Hello. It is my birthday.'

'And… ta-daaa!' Rupert and Rafe pulled presents from behind their backs, causing Rufus to yelp in frustration, jump off the bed – managing to whack Marion in the face with a very bony six-year-old elbow as he did so – and run back into his room, returning seconds later with a badly wrapped gift.

Marion sat in bed and opened the presents from the boys. Richard had always been good at making sure the boys knew how important it was to make a fuss of their mother's birthday.

This year Rufus had given her chocolates from her favourite shop, all the while hovering to see if he could have one, or two or six. Rupert had bought her a copy of the ancient *How to Win Friends and Influence People* – she'd read that at fifteen – along with *Trump: The Art Of The Deal*. Rupert was so business savvy, out of all her boys she imagined he would be the one to be a self-made millionaire by thirty, but she should probably schedule in a quick chat about appropriate role models. And Rafe, sweet Rafe, had given her a scented candle, a very grown-up gift from her very grown-up boy. He had explained that it was because he knew how she worried that the house smelt of dog whilst everyone knew Marion's house only ever smelt of clean linen and perfection so he hoped this helped put her mind at rest.

Once they had established that she was properly awake they brought up a breakfast tray with croissants, Lady Grey and blackcurrant jam, a single red rose at the side. Richard had trained them well. And presumably had something to do with all of this happening even though he was no longer obliged. She tamped down any emotion she might be feeling over Richard and ate her breakfast gratefully.

The morning progressed well and once the boys had all scampered back to their rooms she put on a new dress she had spotted in Fowey the other day. It was beautiful, *so* her; she was loving the recent revival of animal prints. They made her want to purr.

It seemed weird putting it on, getting ready without Richard to do up the zip, to turn her around, holding her hand and arm aloft as he twirled her, to appreciatively look her up and down and give her a gentle kiss on the top of her head, on her lips. Birthdays were always such family affairs, a day surrounded by those she loved the most.

With today falling on a Saturday she had changed her birthday meal to lunch rather than dinner, hoping a change may stop the pangs that she was feeling. She had hoped these pangs would have lessened with time but Richard's continued presence meant they seemed to be ramping up rather than dying a death.

She was taking the boys for a celebratory lunch at The Bay, a chi–chi restaurant in Treporth Bay. She imagined this evening she would probably drown herself in drink, get horny for her husband and sob herself gently to sleep. But for now, she was going to make herself look as glorious as possible, show her boys a fabulous time.

She figured they all had a clear hour for relaxing before they had to leave. As per birthday rules in their house that meant the children had to spend the next hour doing exactly what Marion wanted them to. She normally used this for further learning opportunities. Last year she had made them all watch a recording of *Carmen*. She had planned to escalate it to *Tosca* this year but hadn't got around to locating a version she could approve, so with a grin, the new more relaxed Marion chucked on *The Simpsons* whilst she glanced over the wedding insurance she had arranged for Rosy and Matt and made sure it was all in order. Rufus looked as if he had died and gone straight to heaven.

The boys were sprawled out on the living room floor, unable to believe their luck, when the doorbell rang.

'Shit! Turn off the TV, quick. Look like, I don't know, you're reading a book or something. Where's Darcy? Oh for God's sake, where's the sodding dog?' Marion hissed as she shut down her laptop and headed to peek through the spyhole to see who was at the door.

There at the front door was a gaggle of women: Alice, Sylvie, Rosy and Serena. She shot a quick look at her boys, who had obediently turned the TV off and grabbed books, although in Rufus's case it was *The Art of the Deal* and upside down. She supposed it was better than nothing. The doorbell rang again. She pulled the door open.

'Happy birthday to you, happy birthday to you, happy birthday dear Marion, happy birthday to you!' the women chorused as she stood there staring at them, almost paralysed by the unexpected nature of it. No one had ever turned up on her doorstep to sing to her before. Never.

'Oh, oh… um, oh.' Great conversational skills there. What was wrong with her? 'Come on in. This is a surprise.'

'A nice surprise?' Alice asked tentatively, her lips twitching as she fought her smile, as if now she was more familiar with Marion this was an inside joke they shared, a nod to Marion's slightly-brusque-but-developing friendship style.

'Yes, a nice surprise. A lovely one. Come on in, the boys are just um… reading.'

'We just thought we'd come and wish you happy birthday; shall I put the kettle on?' Alice said.

'Um, yes, that would be great. Sit down, sit down.' Marion waved her arm at the sofa. She had been to Sylvie's house many times, had even seen inside Serena's – fought inside Serena's – but couldn't remember a time she'd had either woman over here and realized it might well have been never. It had never crossed her mind to invite them. Why was that? Why had she not reached out to people and brought them into her home? Was it a confidence thing? A sanctuary thing? She had the confidence to push right on into their houses, but had she been protecting herself from letting them do the same? Keeping her space safe?

She realized that all the women had carefully wrapped gifts and both Sylvie and Serena, despite having faces wreathed in smiles, were sitting on the edge of their chairs a little nervously, as if they weren't sure they should be there.

Marion suddenly realized she had the power here; she could change the atmosphere by taking charge but in her new Marion way – more welcoming, less critical. She might not be able to pull that off. She'd give it a shot anyway.

She settled herself down on a pouffe and smiled across at them.

'It's so kind of you to nip in and say hello on my birthday, thank you so much.'

Simple words yet both women's faces immediately relaxed.

'We wanted to wish you a happy birthday, here.' Sylvie proffered the gift she held.

'And me,' Serena piped up and gave Marion a smile. Marion felt like her heart may burst.

Chapter Thirty-four

It had been an odd kind of day and yet strangely magical. Richard had started by sending a text to Rafe to remind him to set the breakfast tray out for his mum. He *sort of* had faith that the boys would give Marion a happy birthday morning but he just wanted to make sure. He had then spent the morning being dead anxious about how the day would pan out, his involvement and overstepping the mark before dressing himself carefully and heading out to drive the boys and Marion to lunch.

He had also worried about what was an appropriate present. In the past, part of the birthday had been him gifting Marion something slinky and expensive from Rigby & Peller, but he was fairly sure that lingerie was not something a husband gave his wife when they were separated, and that if he tried Marion would be furious at him for not listening. That was definitely something that had been a common theme when they were together. He hoped that what he had decided upon instead would put a smile on her face.

He hadn't been sure whether he'd be welcome or not today but the boys had insisted he come and when he had tentatively raised the question of whether he should join them for lunch or not, he had been surprised when his wife – *ex*-wife; one day he would add the ex automatically but he wasn't there yet – had said it would be nice for him to be there.

It had taken a fair bit to ask, anticipating the response to be *do sod off* so her positive answer, and indeed her smile, had been unexpected and made him feel warm inside. But not as unexpected as the gales of laughter he had heard coming from the house as he approached it.

Even stranger, once he was inside, Marion informed him that they had changed the reservation and now Serena and Alice would be accompanying them along with Jenny and Sophie, who were due to arrive at any minute – Sylvie had to get back to her ballet classes and Rosy was out with Lynne again for the final dress fitting. Rafe had given him a triumphant grin and Richard could well imagine that his eldest son had been just as surprised by Marion extending the invite as he was.

Their greatly expanded party had walked over to Treporth to The Bay and spent three hours at their table outside, a linen parasol protecting them from the heat of the midday sun, giggling, ordering, eating and drinking. Richard had kept pausing to look around the table, his anxiety utterly lifted – although that could have been to do with the booze and holiday feeling that pervaded the table – as he looked around at his family and the people gathered here for his wife's birthday. His Cornish life.

It was all so pleasing. He had always found the people Marion professed to be her friends a little brittle, on edge and not really showing their true selves. None of them seemed to stick around for long. And then there were those whose true selves were self-serving, self-promoting and narcissistic, Angelina being a great example, although he was warming to her over time.

But this, the people around this table now, felt right. Warm, lively, honest. Everything that made his heart happy and his soul dance. His boys were being witty, Rafe clearly besotted by Sophie but being respectful, caring as well as quick and funny, making him swell with paternal pride. Rupert and Rufus were joining in, also quick in their comebacks and participating as equals, able and happy to contribute.

And there was Marion. He was used to seeing her lording over everyone else and getting things done exactly as she wanted them, but today was different; today Marion was comfortable, joking, making actual jokes, and giggling like a teenager. And that was pretty amazing to see.

He had had a quick pang when he saw Serena. Had she told Marion what she had handed over to him? Would she tell her later today? But he had no control over Serena's actions. If she chose to throw a bomb into the mix he would deal with it there and then; there was no point expending any more worry on today. He was happy right now and he wasn't going to allow himself to lose that.

'Right, let's walk home across the beach instead of via the coast path; the tide is low and it's ever so sunny out there today,' Marion proclaimed as she pushed her chair back. 'And thank you, that was the best birthday lunch. Most unexpected to have you all join me. It made me feel really special and I can't tell you how much I appreciate it, especially as it's been a' – she didn't meet Richard's eye as she paused and he was glad for it – 'funny old year. Right, let's go!'

They collected jackets, scooped up bags, paid the bill and their party trundled off along the road, down the granite steps that led to Treporth Bay beach and in turn back to Penmenna. The beach was one of Richard's favourite things about Cornwall, but then that was true of many people. The sea, that gentle lapping beast that surrounded the county and blended into the background a lot of the time, that parents let their children play in at the water's edge with only half an eye on them, was actually the most powerful, most interconnected thing on the planet.

Richard loved to dwell on the fact that, whilst it could be millpond smooth here one day, the sea's fickle temperament could be creating deadly uproar on the other side of the world, the whole mood of it changing in an instant, becoming a grey, murderous and snarling beast in one place, serene and turquoise in another. He had always been fascinated by the multi-faceted power of it, the sheer vastness, creating within him a wary respect for the sea combined with an utter love for lying back and sculling along on a gentle day, looking up at the cliffs rising stalwartly against it.

Richard inhaled deeply, breathing in the smells of saltwater and seaweed drying halfway up the beach, scents that contributed to years' worth of memories and experiences, triggering an emotional response that felt like a homecoming. Walking along the beach now, his hand was itching to reach out and take Marion's hand, to pull her close to his side and chuckle with her as their boys raced ahead of them, but today instead he was watching her laugh with Serena and Jenny as if whatever they had said was the funniest thing on earth. He watched the blonde head of his eldest son as it leant in towards Sophie's, her curly dark hair – true good Cornish stock – bouncing off his as they walked, deep in talk. He watched his younger boys racing ahead to the rocks which separated the two beaches, which when the tide was out would be exposed, slippery with seaweed and crammed with rockpools and hidey-holes and all sorts of adventure for the inquisitive young mind.

'Hey.' He hadn't realized that Marion had stopped walking and was waiting for him, the hem of her skirt gently whipping around her knee as the breeze coming from the sea calmed the searing heat of high summer's shine.

'Hey.' He stopped alongside her, her friends thoughtfully wandering ahead.

'It's a lovely day, isn't it?'

'It is. It's your birthday, it should be a lovely day.' She shared a smile with him, her eyes holding his and he wished he knew exactly what it was she was thinking. If he had his way the next words out of her mouth would be…

'Are you busy now?' she asked.

Okay. He would've chosen something more dramatic, something along the lines of 'I was crazy to put an end to us. Let's start again; move back in this afternoon and we can be together forever.'

But he could definitely work with 'are you busy now?' Although he did hope this wasn't one of Marion's old tricks where he said no and then was landed with a hideous undertaking no one else wanted anything to do with.

'No, my day is free. I didn't know if you had any plans so I thought I'd keep things open just in case you needed me.'

Please need me. Any way will do.

'What were you thinking?' he said instead.

'I was thinking it seems a shame to end the day. Serena needs to get off – Rob had taken Josie out this morning and to the cinema this afternoon but she feels she should head back and do mother things. But Jenny and Sophie were planning to have some beach time today before Rafe highjacked their plans and I thought, maybe…' Tentative Marion; very interesting. 'Maybe we should make the most of the beautiful weather, a free day and all of us here. What do you think? Do you fancy spending the rest of the day on the beach with me and the boys and some of the others?'

Well that was a yes.

Chapter Thirty-five

Lying out on the sand, Richard was at his most relaxed. Jenny and Alice were sitting up on towels and discussing a book they had read lately, Marion listening intently and cracking jokes; the boys had a blanket spread out as a central point but they were racing around. Rafe and Rupert had lost their pre-adolescent ennui and were happily burying Rufus under a pile of sand and stones, using their hands as spades to the background of Sophie's cries: 'Be careful of his head!'

He could hear the caw of the seagulls and watched them soaring down to the water, swooping on an empty chip packet seconds after it was discarded by its owner.

The others began to drift off as the day got later, and soon it was just him, Marion and the boys. Everyone was languid, heavy-lidded after an afternoon in the sun and a long, long lunch.

'Thank you for going back to the house to get all the beach stuff.' Marion rolled over onto her side; he concentrated on keeping his eyes on hers, resisting the desire to glimpse down at her chest where the angle of her sundress now revealed the curve of her breast, peeking from its bikini. Okay, he had had a quick look; it was hard not to notice with her lying next to him all afternoon.

'No problem, it's been a really nice way to finish the day.' His head was lolled over to the side, his eyes still on her, his mouth curving up of its own accord. Pure pleasure washed over him, matching the rhythm of the waves.

'Who says it's finished yet? I do hope you're not planning on short-changing me on my birthday.' Marion quirked her face in her minxiest way.

'I wouldn't dare.' Richard's heart was racing although he kept his voice relaxed.

'Glad to hear about it. I'm getting a bit dopey now though. A touch too languorous.'

'I know what you mean.' He did. Although she had thoroughly managed to awake all of his senses with just a few words.

'Know what we should do?'

'Really?' Richard knew what she was talking about; was he feeling brave enough? It was pretty lovely lying here.

'Oh I think so – shall we see if the boys are keen?' Pure Marion. Steel. Her mind alight by a good idea. What she believed to be a good idea.

He couldn't say no to her.

'Can do.' Keeping it cool. Good work, Richard.

Marion had always liked swimming at the end of the afternoon, whereas Richard was a crack of dawn person, before the beach became crowded. But his wife – ex-wife – was adamant that the best time was when the sun had spent all day warming the water, when families were beginning to leave the beach to head home for dinner; that was when Marion liked to splash in the waves.

When he had first brought her to Cornwall she couldn't get enough of the sea and the sand. They'd be down here day and night, living off fish and chips, pasties, ice cream, cheap bottles of wine and the occasional joint. Somehow, that happy-go-lucky young thing had grown into a woman who worried more about getting sand in her clothes, smudging her make-up, having other people watch her and judge.

Today it would seem carefree Marion was back. He was pretty sure the sparkle in her eye was down to this rediscovering of her old spirit. Although it could be the peach Bellinis at lunchtime.

'Oi, boys. Are you coming in?' She nodded her head waterwards as she called across to their sons.

Oi? Ha! Who was this woman and what had she done with his wife?

'Nah, you're okay. We're happy here,' Rupert shouted over to them, answering for both of his brothers. Neither of whom seemed to mind. Their heads were bent over one of the graphic novels that Rafe had been reading. One that Rufus probably shouldn't be looking at if he wasn't going to grow up with the idea in his head that most women kept nunchucks in their boots and had boobs so elephantine they risked falling over.

Before he could try and distract his youngest son, his attention was grabbed by a woman racing past, wearing nothing but a scarlet bikini and a grin. No, she wasn't racing him? And without fair warning?

Of course she was. Cheeky mare.

Within minutes the entire Marksharp clan were in the water, the lure of both their parents laughing and jumping in the waves proving too much to resist. They splashed and kicked water at each other. The ball that Rupert had found abandoned in the cave earlier in the day came out and they played water volleyball. They spotted mini schools of fish swimming past, Rufus overjoyed that they would change direction based on his actions and captivated by the fact that if he stood still long enough they would swim through his legs as if he were a tunnel.

It seemed like only minutes had passed and yet at the same time as though this magical day had lasted forever. Eventually, as Rufus's lips had practically turned blue, they put their sensible parent heads on and dragged the boys back out of the water and made them dry off and warm up. Richard had had the foresight to pick up a disposable barbecue when he'd returned to Marion's house to collect beach things, and he began cook them all burgers now they had the beach practically to themselves. Marion had a point; this was a good time of day.

By the time the barbecue had burnt out, the boys were shattered. Richard scooped a sleepy Rufus up once all their stuff was packed away, while the older boys were sent off to grab a couple of pieces of litter that Marion had spotted on the beach. Normally people not taking their rubbish with them had her in a gibbering fury but today she just shook her head as she sent the boys off.

As they set off back from the sandy beach to the house, the boys walked ahead and talked about what powers would be the best to have in an everyday scenario. Would you rather be The Flash or Green Arrow? Marion and he walked side by side, wordlessly, and Richard knew that it might not be his birthday but still, it had been the best day he had had in a long time.

Marion turned the key in the lock and he prepared himself for the emotional stab when he had to turn away and head back to Chase's home. First, though, he gently carried Rufus to bed, stripping him down to his pants and patting the duvet into place around his youngest son's drowsy form as the older boys also prepared themselves for bed, their yawns contagious as they groggily brushed their teeth.

Coming back down the stairs he was surprised to see Marion relaxed on the sofa, Darcy in his bed by the side of her, a glass of wine in her hand and another glass poured for him.

'Stay and have a glass of wine with me?' Her question was unsure; his heart leapt. He slid down onto the sofa next to her in answer and reached for the glass.

'Happy birthday, love,' he said, the endearment slipping out naturally, as if just for a moment he had forgotten his exile.

Marion neither flinched nor protested, instead sinking her head back into the softness of the sofa. 'It's been an amazing day.' She let out a little laugh. 'Not what I expected at all to be honest.'

'In a good way?'

'Oh yes.' She now lolled her head to face his direction. 'Quite easily the best birthday in ages. I don't want it to end.'

'You're not tired?'

'Yes, but good tired, you know. Where you don't mind but don't really want to move.'

'Well don't move then,' Richard said and Marion made a nuzzling noise and closed her eyes.

'In all the hubbub earlier, I forgot to give you your gift.' He kept his voice quiet, reluctant to burst her calm.

'You got me a gift.' The smile widened on her face although she kept her eyes closed.

'I did. I wasn't sure of the etiquette but thought I'd risk it. Stay there.' Richard got to his feet and fetched the present from the side table he had popped it on earlier.

'You're a funny man. So stable and yet fond of risk.'

'I'm not fond of risk.'

'Sometimes you are.' The grin was radiating from her face now, head still back. 'Sometimes you like a little bit of danger.'

Five or six scenes of him and Marion being *Very Risky* flashed through his mind. He couldn't find any words. How to respond to that?

He didn't need to; Marion hadn't finished. 'I suppose that's what makes you so good at your job. Steady without being risk averse.' She paused. 'And what made you such a good husband.' Her delivery was matter of fact.

Had she just said that? Was she regretting asking him to leave? He sat down on the sofa, the gift on his knees. How to answer this best? He didn't want to screw things up, and misinterpreting the mood may well do that.

'I think… um, I'm glad that you—' His words cut short as Marion suddenly sat up, opened her eyes and looked directly at him. Her gaze was inscrutable.

'You're a good man, Richard. You really are. Now is that for me? Hand it over.'

He passed her the present and wondered if he should have included the WhatsApp printout Serena had given him. Would it have been the right time? Would it have spoilt the vibe that was now in the room, that had been building between them all day? Would he have changed Marion's birthday by making it about him and what he wanted? He had the paper in his back pocket; he had moved it from pair of jeans to pair of jeans since he had been given it.

No, this was not the time. She had just said what an amazing day she'd had. He wasn't risking that changing.

Marion put the gift to the side of her and reached over to him. She dropped her fingers onto his arm, lightly tracing the length of it with her finger whilst looking up at him. The sexual chemistry was off the scale. She flicked her hair and moved closer. She didn't seem that interested in her birthday gift. She did however have a very fixed look in her eye. What was going on in her head? *What* was she thinking?

Chapter Thirty-six

Marion was thinking of the hairs on his arms. She was thinking of how, further up, his upper arms had the most beautiful shape to them and led to his strong, solid shoulders. Shoulders she had laid her head on more times than she could possibly count.

Heat was rushing through her and the compulsion to reach out and touch him, pull him into her was strong. This man was amazing. He was patient. He was good. He never wanted more from life than to look after those he loved, to be a better parent, a better husband, a better person than his parents had been. It was one of the things that bonded them.

And he knew her like no other man did. Like no other human for that matter. He knew how her moods could be mercurial, he knew how she created a mask that she hid behind and he didn't judge her harshly for it. No, he supported her, built her up, made her feel strong, helped her believe there was nothing she couldn't do if she put her mind to it. And she did believe that.

What was more, he knew every inch of her body, where exactly his touch could make her tremble. Exactly the pace her body craved at any given moment, slowing down or speeding up in a way that was so attuned to her, like a sexual telepathy. Telepathy that only comes after a lifetime of loving. She knew if she ever were to find another partner the chances of them knowing her body so intimately was zero.

Her hand was now under the top of his T-shirt sleeve and he wasn't moving. He appeared frozen. That would not do. She could not bear to think that this man was no longer comfortable with her, was no longer her best friend who knew that he could, should be relaxed in her company. That the two of them were always meant to be. She was his harbour, and vice versa.

In this moment she didn't give a shit about Claudia but she did care about this man sitting in front her right now. The very core of him.

Her whole body was in a state of anticipation, nerve ends fizzing, memories of the way he had made her feel before coursing through her body as if they had a life of their own, as if her body were in charge here, not her head, not her heart.

She reached around with her other arm, placing it parallel, pushing his T-shirt sleeves up, her hands up, round and down. Reaching to stroke his shoulders, the top of his torso, that very part of him that gave her so much security.

This was no good; she needed more than this. She pulled her arms back down, taking care to trail her fingers as she did so.

She leant forward, grabbing the hem of his T-shirt. She locked eyes as she pulled it up, revealing his stomach, his chest, a tight smattering of curls, sandy blonde with a little bit of grey threaded through. Grey that signified all the years of their lives they had lived and grown together.

Wordlessly Richard lifted his arms up, allowing her to pull his T-shirt over his head, freeing him for her. She balled the fabric and threw it behind her, rising up a little from the angle she had been sitting at as she leant forward and ferociously claimed her husband's lips.

Chapter Thirty-seven

Richard was still on cloud nine several days later and floating from his temporary – hopefully very short-term – bedroom in Chase's house down to the kitchen where Chase, Angelina and Matt were all sitting around the kitchen table and chatting nonsense, a little get together to celebrate Matt's last night as a single man.

'Stop nagging!' Matt was saying to Angelina. 'I was really clear with Marion that I didn't want a stag party. I'm too old. If I can't be at home then sitting here, with Chase's den down the hall and my mates around me is a pretty good option. Much more civilized than a night in The Rat's Arse with Mickey and Andy trying to encourage me to drink twenty shots in as many minutes with Roger scowling at me over the pumps because I wasn't born here. It would be different if I was in my early twenties but my idea of a perfect evening is curling up with Rosy and Scramble and watching something together, not going from bar to bar in Newquay and vomiting on the beach.'

A woof came from under the table, where Scramble, Matt's dog who was never more than three steps away from his dad, vocalized his approval.

Angelina harrumphed. 'You can shut up. You're lucky I let you have him in here. Honestly, Chase, you should see the number of shoes that dog has eaten, I don't think...'

'You have mentioned it before.' Chase blew a kiss at his beloved. No one was in any doubt as to Angelina's opinions on Scramble and enforced euthanasia. 'I believe he caused indescribable carnage.'

'He did.' Matt joined in. 'Did things to her shoes that would have made Charles Manson blush.'

'Oh, you're all horrid. This really is the world's dullest bachelor party.'

'That's not true,' Richard said once he had grabbed a beer from the fridge and joined them at the table.

'It really is,' she assured him. 'Not like when Chase and I get married. Then you'll be having the biggest stag do known to man, won't you, darling? Paparazzi everywhere.'

'Will I?' he asked, not looking terribly committed.

'You will.' She nodded.

'Will he be allowed to burn that atrocious painting?' Matt asked.

'Ooh, yeah, okay, I'll have the biggest stag do known to man if we can burn the painting,' Chase teased his fiancée.

'Oh, I don't like you sometimes. Richard, tell us how things are going with you. Have you won back your wife yet? Presumably not or you wouldn't be here…'

Ouch. Angelina didn't even pause for breath as she continued. Probably just as well, as he had no idea what the answer was right now. 'Or is she too busy planning the most glamorous engagement and wedding the world has ever seen?'

'Erm… don't think that's my wedding she's talking about? My wedding that's tomorrow and the focus of this evening?' Matt asked devilishly, his lips playing on the top of his water bottle.

'Oh no, don't think so. Think it's the most glamorous wedding in the world, mate; that has to be hers, definitely not yours.' Chase chuckled.

'You're such arses. You wait, it's going to blow your minds! Anyway, my party has kept Marion very busy so I have found a way to make it up to you, Richard.'

'To me? That's very sweet but not necessary. Although I am a bit confused about your engagement thing, as I think is Marion. She's doing what you asked but felt getting her to invite everyone she knows was bizarre. Ah, perhaps I shouldn't have said that.'

'Oh, I've been so clever,' Angelina crowed, not making much sense but clearly not minding Richard's cock-up. Chase looked at her lovingly.

'As riveting and bordering on unbelievable as that might be, you'll have to excuse me.' Matt pushed himself up from his chair. 'The world's dullest bachelor needs to collect his best man from Newquay Airport. Jean-Jacques' flight should be in shortly; in fact he could well be flying over now. Wave, everybody.'

Everybody obediently waved skywards, bar Angelina.

'Stay and hear about my cleverness,' she said.

'Oh, sis, if I were to do that then by the time I got to the airport it would be time for him to leave again.'

'Sarcasm is the lowest form of wit, you know.'

'I do. I believe I've told you many times. Glad you were listening.'

'Oh, go away.'

'Don't forget Hector too, he'll also be on that flight,' Chase added.

'Will do. Can't guarantee to keep him in the car until we get here though and I'm still not sure what he's doing coming to my wedding.'

'He'll go anywhere for a free party. I think he quite likes it here, the whole Cornwall thing. It was kind of you to let him come. We'll understand if you need to push him out. Just make a note of where so we can grab him in the morning. I imagine Jean-Jacques has strong arms, together you'll be fine.'

'Is no one going to listen to how clever I've been?' Angelina genuinely looked close to tears. Matt blew her a kiss and walked out, and Chase leant over and filled her glass.

'Go on,' encouraged Richard.

'Well...' She took a deep breath now she had an audience. 'You know we were going to have our wedding with Matt and Rosy but they are a little selfish, not that I blame them,' she said in a tone that very clearly showed that she did, 'and Chase wanted us to wait until next year because our work diaries are simply insane...'

'You both have very important work to do.' Richard wasn't convinced of this but knew it would make her happy and he did expect that someone, somewhere felt a little better for reading articles about the woman sitting in front of him.

'We do. People don't often understand that, but we do. We lighten people's lives. Anyway, don't let me get sidetracked. So, I had already asked Marion to arrange our wedding, which I have now moved to next year but we kept a date for our engagement party instead.'

'Yup, clear on that bit,' Richard answered encouragingly.

'Good, so I've made her arrange the perfect party; she's inviting all these guests, people she knows, to help me out. There's no way all our friends could make it with so little notice. She's chosen the cake and the food and the music and everything. And every time she tries to query any details I just shout at her and put the phone down. It's hilarious, so much fun. She gets so cross.' Richard wasn't convinced this was fun.

'Haven't I been clever?' Angelina clapped her hands, like a performing seal looking around the room for approval.

'You haven't told him what's actually happening yet, love,' Chase pointed out and then took up the baton. 'So, Angelina and I were talking, after the night we all got together last time actually and she thought it was sad that you had that quiet, tasteful wedding your mother demanded instead of the crazed blow-out wedding that Marion had always wanted. I remember at the time she was so happy to be marrying you that she didn't mind compromising. She understood your dynamic with your mum and I was impressed then with how she sucked up her own disappointment and made the best of a day that was nothing like her, or at least nothing like her then. It's fair to say she's changed quite a bit since.'

'Yeah, she was amazing. I've always been so grateful for that. I think it was because her mother was so dysfunctional that she took my parents in her stride and made sure she made my life easier not more difficult. I still regret not standing up for that, for the wedding of her dreams.'

'Woah, don't be. Your mother was impossible. As resolute as Margaret Thatcher, about as empathetic and with an additional layer of steel. You've fought battles for Marion and the boys since then and won. You were still young when you and Marion married.' And Richard nodded, his friend of a lifetime seeing things he didn't realize anyone else but Marion saw.

'And you said you wanted Marion back; we think that's a really good idea so we thought we'd help.' Angelina couldn't let Chase have the spotlight a moment longer. 'So we have arranged for that day to be your renewal-of-vows day whilst sort of pretending it's our engagement party. But actually it's all for you two. Marion gets the wedding she always wanted, you get your wife back, Marion still gets paid for the work she's done and I'll write testimonials and let out pictures to the press saying she helped organize a party for us and everyone is a winner. Admittedly we thought you and she would probably be back together by now and this would just be the icing and the cherry on top. But you have just over a week. You'll have to get a move on. Why aren't you jumping up and down? Richard, Richard! Get your head out of your hands. This is a good thing, be grateful. Why is he looking like that, Chase?'

Richard couldn't respond as Angelina wanted. The idea was nice, sweet even, and he would love nothing more than being able to reaffirm his commitment to Marion in front of witnesses, especially Rafe, Rupert and Rufus, but he wasn't convinced that Marion was going to see it the same way. They had spent the night together but that didn't mean he was officially back, and the quickest way to mess that up would be to make assumptions. He was deliberately going slow, letting her make the decisions when she was sure it was right and she was ready. Neither could he keep this a secret from her, couldn't keep it a surprise as Chase and Angelina wanted. He was going to have to tell her and tell her soon, and she was going to go berserk.

Chapter Thirty-eight

Marion finished checking the church – the day was here at last – and started the short walk up to Rosy's cottage. This event was special to her; it was the first one she had booked and although the summer had proven that planning events was the perfect job for her – everything she had organized so far had been remarkably stress-free – she could feel her tummy flip-flopping as if she had a bellyful of goldfish.

As she marched up the hill, she quickly ran through everything in her head. She had nothing to be nervous about and what's more she was fairly sure she had given Rosy and Matt the wedding they wanted, an intimate affair. Not everyone needed a big brash wedding, and whilst she may have yearned for one she knew that the small one she and Richard had had proved rather lovely in the end. Just them in a bubble of their own. She hoped Rosy and Matt would feel the same about theirs. On a practical note, the suppliers had confirmed, all the final balances had been paid and she had Serena on the payroll and running a sub-team down at Penmenna Hall where the reception would be taking place; there was nothing that could go wrong. She was nervous, or her tummy was, because she cared. That was all. She wanted these people to have the most perfect day of their lives.

Letting Richard stay the other day had been playing on her mind as well. She loved him so very much, the bones of him and all in between but she had behaved rashly, impetuously, driven by her wants rather than what was sensible. She would have to think carefully about what she wanted the next step to be. Did she forgive or should she put the walls up again?

Marion pushed open the little wooden gate and walked up the path to the cottage. With the front door on the latch, she pushed it open and wandered up the stairs where she could hear a collection of female voices. She paused for a second – there was a bit of a funny smell coming from downstairs – she'd explore once she'd said her hellos.

If the day was on schedule then Rosy should be having a chilled glass of Prosecco under the watchful eye of her mother and sister, whom Marion had yet to meet, whilst Pippa painted her nails. Despite all Marion's best advice, Rosy had been adamant that Pippa would be doing her hair and make-up. If she didn't walk down the aisle with eyeshadow all colours of the rainbow and hair that was a backcombed mess then Marion would be very surprised. But the bride was the bride and today was her day. Marion could only offer options; if she wanted to leave her final touches to a woman who looked like a head-to-toe jumble sale then so be it.

'Hello, hello, hello.' She sang her greeting as she entered the room. It was exciting to be here.

'Hello, Marion, good to see you. Look, my nails are almost done.' Rosy turned and waggled perfect nude pink nails at her. So far so good. If Pippa could resist a lime green topcoat then all would be well.

'Beautiful, very tasteful. Well done, Pippa.' She made her praise sound heartfelt and was genuinely surprised. Pippa raised an eyebrow and made a low growling noise whilst Lynne, who was chief bridesmaid – another decision Marion thought was a bit dodgy – scowled at her. Marion grinned on the inside. She did get joy from winding some people up, and Pippa and Lynne were definitely upon that list.

'And you must be Rosy's mother – peas in a pod.' That was a lie; Rosy's good looks clearly came from her father's side of the family.

'Hello, lovely to meet you.' A woman wearing a lavender floral dress and vile lilac hat proffered her hand. Marion shook it and pasted on a big fake grin. And then repeated the motion with the younger but similar-looking woman standing next to her, in an equally grim outfit. Note to self: check outfits from all family members in future and make suggestions for outfits based on colour schemes and good taste. Perhaps she could get a taller member of the wedding party in front of them during the photos? No, no she couldn't. That was old Marion thinking.

'So, your wedding is under control and running smoothly. Everything has arrived and is in place now. I had a quick look at the church earlier and it looks beautiful.' She drew those last three words out, to emphasize how much she meant it. 'The pinks and blues of the roses, anemones and lisianthus are stunning, and the scent is wonderful.'

'Thank you, I'm pleased they work well. Matt thought they would,' Rosy said as she laid out the other hand for her final topcoat.

'I think today will be gorgeous, stress-free. But I'll just run through the order— what on earth are you doing here?' Marion halted her original sentence mid-flow as Harmony entered the room, wearing a hacked-up bedsheet with some kind of smouldering stick in her hand. It looked a little like a short stubby penis woven out of natural materials and set on fire. Marion had never wanted to learn more about Harmony Rivers than she had to, and waving around half a burnt eco-friendly dildo was proof that Marion had been right.

'Oh, don't worry.' Rosy was quick to reassure her. 'Harmony wanted to sage smudge for us as a wedding present.'

'Dear God, whatever for?' An awful thought crossed Marion's mind. 'You're not letting her do that in the church, are you?'

'I'll have you kno—' Harmony started to speak but Marion fixed her with a look and Harmony fell silent, affecting a facial expression like Darcy when he was caught halfway through wolfing down supper from the kitchen worktop. Harmony jabbed the smudge stick into the air aggressively a couple of times with narrowed eyes.

'Right, order of service. I know you know it but if we have a quick run-through… We'll walk to the church as you insisted, although I still think that's madness and should you change your mind then I can have the MGB GT you booked for the journey from the church to Penmenna Hall come early; you just have to say the word and I will have it here.'

'No, it's alright. I *really* like the idea of walking through the village to church. It won't take more than ten minutes; I've broken my shoes in like you suggested and it will make it special.'

'I've never heard of a bride who wanted to walk before,' Rosy's mum interjected. The woman had some sense, then.

'I know, Mum, but I want to… oh my goodness, Harmony!'

There was a loud squeal and a crash as Harmony, who had been flailing around the bedroom and had recommenced making ohm-ing noises, twisting, turning and chanting, suddenly tripped over the bridal shoes. She screamed as she fell, throwing her hands out to try and save herself, smouldering sage stick still in her hand. Marion's eyes whipped towards Rosy's wedding dress sitting on a seamstress's mannequin to keep it pristine and currently the only thing that was going to stop Harmony slamming hard onto the floor.

Quick as a flash, Marion moved it.

'Argggghhhh.' Harmony landed on the carpet next to the mannequin, clutching her sage stick, arms and legs akimbo.

'Oh my goodness, are you alright?' Mrs Winter and Lynne rushed over to help pick her up whilst Marion inspected the dress.

'For goodness' sake,' Marion snapped as she dropped to her knees to examine the damage. 'She's burnt a hole here, just by the seam. How in God's name are we going to get a burn out of silk? Trust you to spoil things with your bloody nonsense.' She pinched the smoulder with her finger, trying to stop it from spreading at all and then quickly huffed on the silk and dabbed it again with a damp finger to make sure.

'Marion!' Rosy interjected.

'Yes, I'm sure it was an accident.' Marion read between the lines. 'She didn't do it on purpose.' She supposed she didn't, but if she hadn't been here being daft then it wouldn't have happened at all!

Pippa shot Marion a look of agreement, as if she could read her mind and completely agreed that this was avoidable. They had never been natural allies but Marion

sneaked her a smile back. And added an eyeroll of camaraderie for good measure.

'Look, Mum can probably do something. If anyone can
she can.' Pippa moved away from Rosy and took a look.
'I reckon at a push I could just bring the seams in a bit
and fix it that way but Mum'd be even better.'

'Right, she's down at Penmenna Hall setting up for the
reception; I'll call Serena.'

It didn't take long for Serena to whisk over with Jan
in tow, who confirmed that she indeed could fix it and
exactly as Pippa had said. Marion had meanwhile kicked
Harmony out, saying, 'I am the wedding planner,' along
with 'How much smudging does one small cottage need?'
over and over again, louder and louder until she got her
own way.

'Hello.' Serena sidled up and stood next to her.

'Everything going well down at the Hall?' Marion
asked, her eyes on Pippa who had moved on to hair and
make-up. She was actually doing a remarkably good job
and had manged to create an up-do that looked like a
down-do with the most beautiful vintage bridal comb
on the side. It looked incredibly glamourous. Marion had
underestimated Pippa's talents. She wouldn't do that again.

'So, how are things with you and Richard?' Serena
whispered.

'Pretty good actually, he stayed over on my birthday,'
Marion confided, in a half-whisper out of the side of
her mouth. A thrill raced through her as she could pass
this nugget on to her friend. It had been quite a night.
Certainly one she wouldn't forget in a hurry; bits of her
that she hadn't known existed ached by the next day.
Aches that made her smile mischievously.

'I'm so glad to hear it. I knew you'd see sense and everything would be alright as soon as he showed you the evidence.'

'See sense?' That was a little rude. She paused before she asked the obvious next question. 'What do you mean by "evidence"?'

'The evidence I gave him, like he asked. You know, that he didn't sleep with Claudia.'

Marion turned to face her friend. 'What on earth are you talking about? Richard stayed over because I had a weak moment. We're not all reconciled in marital bliss and he certainly did not show me any evidence of anything! I'm not sure how you dare to make presumptions considering your role in the whole sordid affair.'

'I'm sorry, I misunderstood. Ooh, look, that's a lovely shade of blush Pippa's putting on Rosy. More Prosecco, anyone?' Oh, now she talked at a normal volume.

'No, no, no. You don't get off this easily. What is this evidence you're talking about and exactly how many people has Richard told the intricacies of our marriage breakdown to?'

Serena paled, as well she might. Marion was fully aware that there wasn't an answer that would appease her right now.

'Everything okay?' Rosy asked from across the room. That woman was like a hound on a rabbit; there was nothing she missed.

'All fine.' Marion smiled through gritted teeth, the fakery making her voice even more singsong than usual. She would not cry. She would not cry. But how many people knew now that Richard had cheated? The embarrassment! Had he told the whole village he had been unjustly accused? She could kill him. Mind you, Serena said there was evidence? So much for all his cries that evidence of something that never happened was impossible to get, but why not show her, why not tell her? Why was that man still keeping secrets?

Chapter Thirty-nine

The morning had raced by, all catastrophes averted. Jan had returned with Rosy's dress, the whole room's breath on hold as she slipped it over the bride's head, hoping that it would still fit and that the burn was fully disguised. It dropped over Rosy's outstretched arms, fell perfectly into place and everyone in the room let out a sigh of contentment.

She looked beautiful, Marion thought, caught up in the emotion of the moment, really beautiful. Her hair resting over one shoulder, the diamanté of the hair slide catching the sunlight as it poured through the window. The dress itself was high at the front, cut into a cowl and then swept away into the deepest V ever seen at the back, dipping right into the small of her back and framed with lace. Marion couldn't picture a better dress for the occasion, indeed would have quite liked one herself, in every shade under the sun. She could truly say never before had she envied anything from Rosy's wardrobe.

With the bride dressed, Prosecco drunk and oohs and ahhs bouncing around the room, Marion started to chivvy everyone out. The bride would need to leave for the church shortly and Marion had scheduled a ten-minute mother and daughter moment before that. When Rosy's mother descended the stairs to climb into the car, she had had a tear in her eye which she blinked away as she swept the bridesmaids, Rosy's nieces in sage green dresses with little wicker baskets full to the brim with rose petals, out of the house and into a waiting car.

Marion couldn't imagine her mother shedding a tear at the joy of her daughter marrying a good man. Although she was fairly sure Richard's mother shed the odd tear when she heard of their engagement.

Finally, it was just her, Lynne and Rosy and the photographer left in the house. She messaged Richard quickly.

> T minus three. We'll be leaving in three minutes. Get everyone into the church now. Any stragglers, shoot them. And why the hell does Serena know more about our relationship than I do?

She deleted the last sentence. Not helpful at this moment. She would take him to task for that later. She left the shooting bit in.

'Right then, are we ready? You look phenomenal, Rosy, really you do. There won't be a dry eye in the house.'

Bing.

> Everything fine here. So lovely actually. They sang 'You're Getting Married in the Morning' as Matt pulled up. Hector is proving a little tricky, practically pissed by breakfast, but I think I've got it all under control. Will get everyone inside now.

'Tell me about it. The only thing stopping me from streaming with tears right now is my fear of Pippa should I smudge this mascara,' Rosy said, bringing Marion back to the present. She definitely wasn't worrying about Hector right now. She'd sort him out later. He was relatively easy to deal with. A childhood of nannies meant she only had to quirk her brow disapprovingly and the man practically melted.

'I think you're right to be frightened.' Lynne laughed. 'She spent hours on those eyes.'

'And they look fabulous for it; now come on, let's go. I know it's expected for the bride to be late but there's no need to take the mickey.' Marion chivvied them out of the bedroom.

'It's all downhill, we'll have plenty of time. I can always run if I have to,' Rosy said with a mischievous lilt.

'I'm sure the world's best wedding planner will happily launch you over her shoulder if necessary and sprint to the church,' Lynne said. Marion narrowed her eyes.

'And risk creasing that dress, and mine!' She smoothed down her dress, a fire-engine red number – it was definitely Marion's favourite colour at the moment. 'Fireman's lifts cost an extra £500 and for that I'll do practically anything.'

'So I've heard,' Lynne joked and they shared a giggle. Was this a bonding moment?

'Chop, chop, do come on.' Marion managed to get them out of the front door – progress – down the path and into the lane leading towards the village, the photographer leaping about like a demented gazelle in front of them, skip, snap, skip, snap, with Marion grinning in every frame whilst daydreaming of ramming his camera down his throat. He may be the best at his game but right now he was like a mosquito begging for a slap.

It was the oddest bridal procession she had ever seen, Rosy walking in between Marion and Lynne, holding her dress up and out at the sides so it didn't drag on the ground and get grubby. She looked like she was about to launch into some kind of Tudor dance.

Marion could feel herself getting antsy as Rosy kept stopping to admire the colours of the trees, make cooing noises at the cows in the field and to talk to Bill Meacher, who had appeared out of his cottage and attempted to strike up a conversation. Marion was not having that.

'Off, go, go, go! We don't have time for you today.' She flapped him away, corralling him as if he were a sheep and waving Lynne and Rosy past.

'I say, Marion, I think—'

'Walk!' Marion barked and Lynne shot her another look.

'I've always thought you were a bit of a nightmare…' Lynne said.

Ouch!

'But today I have to admire your efficiency. We would have been stuck there for hours. Even growing up my mum told me to walk to the shop the long way around, avoiding the Meacher house if I wanted to be home by sundown. His wife was even worse, you know, had me pinned in talking about different widths of sewing thread for over half an hour once; I was ten and didn't know how to escape. If we had all just treated the both of them like rogue chickens that would have been a lot easier. I'm going to try that in class.'

They got to the centre of the village, Bill Meacher left a few hundred yards behind them looking a little confused, and they could see Penmenna church in front of them just as Marion's phone beeped.

All good, everyone in their places and ready
for the bride. Looking amazing in here. Love
you.

She wasn't dealing with that latter bit now but good to know the groom was in place.

She looked up from her phone and exchanged a smile over the bride's head with Lynne as Rosy began to work out what it was she was seeing.

'Oh my goodness, what? How? Oh my goodness!'

'Don't cry! Lynne admonished. 'Do you need me to dab your eyes?'

'Marion, how did you…?' Rosy indicated she didn't need Lynne and her bits of tissue, turning to her wedding planner instead.

'Oh no, it wasn't me. It was your matron of honour here and Alice, all them. Stop and listen.' They could afford a ten-second pause; Marion had scheduled it in. She'd been impressed when Alice had come to her and suggested this and looking at Rosy's face now had to admit it was really touching. She wondered if she could pinch the schoolchildren for other weddings in her diary.

In front of the church was what seemed like half the school's children with their parents standing behind them. They were everywhere, in the churchyard, all around the lychgate and sprawling out onto the pavements, lining the road for a good distance. The photographer was going crazy trying to snap the children and Rosy's face all at the same time. As Rosy, Marion and Lynne strained their ears to listen, they heard the children all singing Pharrell Williams' 'Happy' at the top of their little voices.

And all her tough-nosed resilience, all her I-am-not-going-to-cry went up in smoke, tears streaming down Rosy's face as she approached the children from Penmenna School, led by Alice, loud in voice as they sang their headteacher down the road, through the gate, across the churchyard and into the church.

It was so touching that Marion forgot, just for a minute, about how cross she was with her husband.

Chapter Forty

Richard wanted to seat himself in the church right at the back. He figured that Marion wouldn't come in until the bride was down the aisle and he wanted to grab her as soon as possible to warn her about next week. But he had to take up his seat beside his sons in the chancel with the choir. It was probably a good thing; if he tried to tell Marion now about Angelina and Chase's well-intentioned crazy idea she would probably screech 'you what?' at the top of her voice as Dan asked about just impediment.

The morning had been seamless so far. Things were pretty simple from the groom's point of view: Matt had given Scramble a long walk along the beach and then got dressed. It had been that easy. Although Richard thought he could see an edge of fear on his face underneath his usual customary charm and could empathize. He had spent his entire wedding day in abject fear that Marion wasn't going to turn up, that she'd realize the error of her ways and make a bolt for it, that his mother may have paid her off or hired a hitman to take out the woman she didn't deem fit for her son. He reckoned no matter how secure you were in your relationship, everyone had fears when the actual day came.

He had been over to pick the boys up fairly early on to free Marion to get over to Rosy's and had planned to tell her all about Angelina's ridiculous plan then but she hadn't given him a chance, instead pushing a bleary-eyed Rufus at him, saying, 'Must dash,' and leaving.

That could be interpreted in a myriad of ways. None of them particularly good. None of them implying that the night of her birthday – and what a night it had been – had been so life-affirming that she was planning on asking him to move back in. He didn't really understand the rules these days. It all seemed pretty straightforward to him; if you wanted to be with someone, cared enough for them to let them into your bed then surely, surely that was a sign that things were back on. He needed to discuss that with her later today as well. He was possibly as nervous as Matt at this point.

Sitting in the chancel, he could hear a huge chorus outside of the children singing. When the song finished, a huge cheer went up, and heads turned as the chords of 'Canon in D' struck up and they waited for the bride. People gasped as Rosy entered.

She had always been attractive but today she looked beautiful. Richard watched Matt's face light up, his eyes so shiny that Richard was warmed by the strength of his obvious love.

Two little girls came in before the bride, one scattering rose petals delicately along the nave, doing little ballerina skips all the way down the aisle – the perfect bridesmaid. The other one was slower and more interested in eating the rose petals than scattering them, stopping occasionally to spit the odd one out.

As Rosy reached the front of the church he saw Marion slip into the pew at the back. He wanted to be sitting beside her, squashing his knee up against hers in a show of solidarity and a promise of things to come. He imagined reaching out his fingers to interweave through Marion's, to bind them together with a gesture, here in the church as two others pledged their love. He cocked his head up, sending a great big grin all the way down the nave and in her direction so she would know how excited he was about them spending time together later, at the reception, masking his concerns about what he had to say.

She may be some distance away but she had the eyes of Superman – X-ray vision and super-sight – and she picked up on his look. And she wasn't grinning back at him. No, even at this distance he could see her facial features were very definitely snarl-like, not sending him waves of romantic hope in the least. Bugger, and this was before he had told her about next weekend!

–

Marion was pleased at the way everything was going so far, though she didn't want to be too jubilant with the reception still to get through; a lot of moving parts and people – it was always people that messed things up.

A voice at the back of her mind pointed out it was always people that fixed things and made them right too. It seemed new, kind Marion was well and truly implanted and as irritating as she might be, Marion had to concede it was a fair point. And not everybody was annoying; the children had been sweet singing on the way into church and that had been arranged by Lynne, who she very defi-nitely had never been a fan of but was now warming to.

Then as if to rub in the universe's capricious nature she caught sight of Richard, sitting up at the front with the community choir and trying to catch her eye. Okay, some people were aggravating and right now, as much as she loved her husband, Richard was one of them. *What* had he been thinking? Why on earth would he have something that proved he had never slept with Claudia and then *not* show her? She did not understand how that man's brain worked sometimes.

The service raced by, the vows and the exchange of rings only taking a matter of minutes. The bride and groom had gone into the vestry with Dan, Lynne and Jean-Jacques to sign the register and Marion needed to stop revelling in the romanticism of the moment and get on with her job. The choir were singing 'Amazing Grace', and it sounded all kinds of wonderful. Her eyes alighted for a second on her boys standing in front of Richard and joining in – such good boys, voices and faces like angels.

This wedding had been heavenly. She prayed – she was in a church so it seemed fitting – that the reception went just as smoothly.

Chapter Forty-one

Everyone gathered in the churchyard to greet the bride and groom as they exited the church after the ceremony. Richard's eyes darted left and right in an attempt to find Marion. Aha, she was there handing out rose petals to the guests ready to throw as confetti. Petals, he hoped, free from bridesmaid spit.

He was determined to see her, talk to her. Part of him knew that he should maybe wait until this evening, when the pressures of the day were relieved, but the other part of him was beginning to get a little resentful. He was so busy trying to listen to what Marion needed, respect what Marion wanted, that his own needs and desires were in danger of getting trodden underfoot, buried into a weave of earth and worms and roots, never to grow and flourish. Surely if he was working towards a fair partnership then what he wanted had to have a voice as well?

She was standing now, admiring her handiwork. She had persuaded the gardeners from Penmenna Hall to bring tools to the wedding, which they had stashed around the side of the church and were now held aloft in a guard of honour as the bride and groom left the church, hoes and spades rather than swords and sabres.

'Can you keep an eye on the boys a minute?' Richard turned to Annie and Ethel, who were standing next to him. Possibly not the best people to ask given their history, but leaving them to their own devices was never wise.

'Of course we will.' Annie smiled, her church bell earrings jangling as she did so. He had a feeling that he may return to find his sons tied to a crow's nest, having set sail to the Caribbean whilst Ethel stood on the dock rubbing her hands and counting the pieces of eight she had exchanged for his boys.

He headed over to where his wife was and stood beside her as she counted the cars lined up to take the wedding party to Penmenna Hall. His arm was itching to pull her towards him as he spoke to her – surely the other night meant it was okay to do that – so he reached out his hand and wrapped it around her shoulder. Instead of jumping and whacking him with her iPad she nestled in for a moment and breathed a sigh of contentment.

'You have done this so well. You're quite wonderful, you know.'

'That's nice of you to say; you've always been my biggest fan.'

'I've always had a good eye for quality. Look at this, tell me you're not proud of yourself.' He gestured at Rosy and Matt heading out from under their wedding arch, grins so wide on their faces, their eyes sparkling bright. They could not have looked any happier. 'You have made their wedding so perfect, so seamless and so them. I am so proud of you I could burst.'

'And not a stuffed swan anywhere.'

'Eh?'

'Sorry, a joke with myself. I had to give them the wedding *they* wanted. They wanted one that was quiet, reflected who they were…'

'You couldn't have done better. I know how you wanted this wedding to be. You've always been a fan of a big blow out event and yet you made this so personal for them.'

'Well, I get my big blowout event next week. Huge, glam and jam-packed full of celebrity if Angelina has come through on the guest list. Ooh look, there they are. Coo-eeee!' She waved frantically at Angelina and Chase; the golden couple looked up from their chat with Serena and waved back.

'Ah…' He squeezed her closer, wondering if he could keep her there forever, relishing the moment and worried he was about to mess it up. However, her body language changed in that moment, her back straightening and arching away from him before he had even started to speak. What had triggered that? She detangled herself completely from him now, her face unreadable. He needed to press ahead or he would never get this said. 'I wanted to talk to you about next week. There's something you don't know.'

'Oh, I *know* there's something I don't know. I know that. I had forgotten for an instant but trust me it's fresh again now.' Her tone had changed as she shifted her focus from Angelina, Chase and Serena and fully back on him, turning herself so she was now facing him, arms up and crossed against her body.

'It is? You do?'

'I do. We need to talk about it but we'll talk about it later, trust me. Today shouldn't be about being cross and I'm really very cross with you.'

'Cross with me?' That seemed unfair. He was putting her first and warning her and she didn't seem to be appreciating it.

'Yes, Richard. Now shush and help me. I need to start getting people in cars and up to Penmenna Hall or we'll get behind schedule.'

Richard knew he was looking at her as if he were a fish, mouth open and a puzzled expression on his face.

'Marion, just stop for a minute. Listen to me and then I'll help you with people and cars. Next week, it's not just an engagement party; it's a vow renewal ceremony, for you and me. I thought you should know.' He held his hand lightly on her shoulder, hoping that she was listening to him and not thinking of cars, numbers, people, routes, the things that she felt she should be worrying about now.

This time her mouth dropped open. She was listening. And she did not seem particularly pleased.

Chapter Forty-two

Marion took a deep breath as she sat herself slowly down on the wooden bench, perfectly placed just outside the orangery so she could see all of what was happening without being part of it. There was obviously something about benches and her this year. It felt as if she had come full circle, from a wooden bench on her old housing estate where this idea, the idea of her setting up in business had been born and now, where her most meaningful event of the year was taking place. The Marion that sat here this evening was a very different woman to the one eight or so months ago.

Everyone had eaten outside once they arrived at Penmenna Hall from the church, the tables winding through the trees with candles and tiny lights on them along with large tall clumps of gypsophila standing straight down the centre of the tables, making the whole thing feel a little bit like a fairy banquet. The tables were now largely deserted: a few children were gathered around someone's iPad; Alex and Sylvie sat taking a breather whilst looking achingly glamourous, him with a loosened bow tie and her looking like the elfin queen.

Marion took a sip from the glass of wine she had brought out with her and took in the scene that was playing out behind the glass of the orangery. The majority of people were sitting around up the far end in a plethora of comfy chairs clumped in groups whilst a brave few, Pippa and Kam, Annie and Ethel among them were dancing down at the other.

Sitting here now she could hear the music drifting about, dancing in the air by her ear, the sound of people laughing, the business of the day done with nothing left to do than celebrate with friends and loved ones. It was rather nice.

The air was floral as night-scented stock mingled with the aromas of jasmine, honeysuckle and phlox. She could see Rosy and Matt, Rosy leaning onto him as she took off one of her shoes and rubbed her foot; he supported her and whispered something in her ear, making her laugh and nod her head.

Hector was flailing around the dance floor, providing a picture familiar at weddings: drunken man with tie around head and bottle in hands, happily stumbling and being a bit of a tit, albeit a harmless one.

Rosy had kicked off her shoes now and she and Matt were in a slow dance, one just for the two of them, ignoring the up-tempo beat of the music around them. Holding each other's faces as their feet moved from side to side.

It made her feel quite emotional, the lump that had been in her throat as she sat down now fully formed. Those two were so in love. They reminded her of herself and Richard on their… oh and there he was now, coming into view. He was dancing with Rufus, in the middle of the floor, twirling him around as he always did her.

What the hell *did* she feel about him?

She'd been so cross this morning when she found out about Serena's evidence that supposedly proved Richard had not slept with Claudia, so cross at him for keeping more secrets. As for arranging a renewal ceremony, that was so out of order she couldn't begin to get her head around it. But now as she watched him dancing with their youngest son it was hard to feel too much anger. If she could just separate all her emotions out, work out which one was the dominant and why, and from there move on to what was the best thing for her to do next. How did she want to shape her life? Who did she want to be in it? Who did she want to be?

She recalled Alice's advice from a few weeks ago, that sometimes taking a moment for oneself was the best way to see clearly. Was this what she was doing out here now? Taking a moment for herself? She could certainly do with some help seeing clearly.

She was just coming to terms with Richard and her possibly getting back together. And then on the day she had to be calmest, most together, most professional, he had dropped a bomb on her. Telling her that her great big celebrity party next week, her I-am-Marion-Marksharp-and-I-can-arrange-the-chicest-the-most-glamourous-the-most-everything-party-ever party was not what she thought it was. It was going to be so embarrassing, professionally and personally, and in front of all the people Angelina had made her invite.

She could feel her breathing spiking. She tried to balance herself by looking back in through the windows of the orangery. She focused in on Hector again; he had just tripped over Scramble and was now scooping the dog up and trying to plonk a kiss on his mouth. Did that count as animal abuse?

Hector was a funny old thing. He represented everything she had believed made one successful in life. Born to privilege, he had everything his heart could ever wish for, and yet still she knew he had an ache inside there, an ache that money and status wasn't filling.

She had lost count of the amount of times he had made a pass at her over the years; he was an absolute fool of a man the majority of the time but there was a depth to him that many didn't see.

Scramble very definitely didn't at this moment.

Hector had asked her to run away with him more than once. She never had agreed of course, but neither had she objected to the attention. She would never have left Richard for Hector, not in a million years. Although it was his house she had run to, his advice she'd sought last summer when she and Richard were starting to struggle.

She had thought they were getting back on track. This year had been tumultuous, it had pulled her apart and forced her to build herself up and adapt and conquer but the last few months, she had almost been living her dream life, slowly making her peace with her husband, her family around her. And now, at the point where she was nearly ready, he had to have secrets from her, hide something else that had to do with him and Claudia, not show her the evidence she had so desperately craved. And then he'd assumed she was ready before she had said she was coming close, forcing her to do what he wanted and with the support of people she had thought were her friends. He could have Chase, that was fair enough but Angelina was hers, all hers. He didn't even like her that much.

'Hey, hey. You're going to snap that glass stem in a minute. Do you mind if I sit down?'

Marion looked up to see Pippa standing over her looking a little flushed and out of breath. She had been dancing but a minute ago. Marion wanted to say *no, no you can't, sod off*. Pippa was the one person left in Penmenna that she hadn't really gelled with over the last few months, the one who was always a step back, eyebrow quirked and looking at Marion with undisguised loathing.

Marion was aware enough to know that this was largely her fault. She had taken a swipe at Pippa at every possible opportunity over the years, and it was true some of her worse insults still made her smile but it hadn't been fair really; she suspected it was all born out of jealously. Jealousy that Pippa was so confident, had a perfect family and seemed to lack all the demons that plagued Marion.

Pippa sat, not waiting for Marion to answer. See, confident.

'I've been watching you out here; you look pretty stressed but you should be proud.' She paused and Marion sensed a reluctance, as if she wasn't sure of what she was about to say. She went ahead anyway. 'Is there anything I can help with?'

'No thank you,' Marion said shortly; the last thing she needed was Pippa's help. But then it wasn't that long ago that she was happy being an island, and yet she had learnt that having friendships, making connections was more rewarding than she had realized.

'That was snappy,' she said by way of an apology.

'Yep.' Pippa nodded. 'Why, though, why aren't you happy today of all days? You should be over the moon. Do you know what, all through summer I've been trying to take the burden off Rosy so I kept offering to help her with things.'

'You did help her, you did the hair and make-up and did a good job; your mum made and decorated the cake. I'd say it was definitely Parkin-heavy, this wedding.'

'Mmm. What I'm trying to say is that every time I asked if she needed something, if there was any way I could help, she replied *Marion's got it* every single time. And you had, you made everything so relaxed for them. Sitting on this bench on a summer's evening bigging you up seems really freaking surreal. That was not something I ever thought I would say to you, that's for sure. But maybe you've picked up too much, so as you helped Rosy I'm here to support you, so let me in. What's going on? Why that look in your eye on a night you should be bold with victory?'

Marion looked Pippa up and down; what harm could it do? And to talk to someone she didn't care about that much, maybe that would be liberating. She could always stop as soon as she became uncomfortable.

'Men. I don't expect you to understand.'

'Ha! I'm going to assume that's because I'm wildly happy with Kam rather than you having a personal dig at the people I dated before him.'

'Oh good God, no, you can shag who you like. I meant Kam, obviously I meant Kam.' Marion was mortified; she didn't mind being taken for a manipulative, power-hungry sociopath but she wasn't a bigot. She had never judged Pippa for her romantic partners; her clothes, yes, but not her choices of partner.

'It's alright, but trust me I understand what you mean. Yes, Kam is great but oh my goodness I've had my fair share of nightmares. Not that Richard is a nightmare – oh look, we're both getting ourselves into a pickle now.'

Marion smiled. 'Richard is no saint, let me tell you.'

'Oh, we've all seen him grope you under the table at governors' meetings, we know that.'

'Unnecessary but that's not what I meant. I thought I knew him, was convinced of it – and when I make my peace with the fact that he is a good man, a good role model and the person I want to grow old with, he does something duplicitous or self-serving and shakes my world all over again. I can't help but think I'm better off as I am, keeping him at a distance.'

'Look, Marion, no one knows what goes on behind closed doors, but duplicitous and self-serving doesn't sound like the Richard I know and have come to know even better over the last two terms. I'm not questioning the fact that you know your husband a damn sight better than I do but are you honestly looking at his behaviour rationally rather than emotionally?'

'Of course its emotional; it's my life, how can it not be emotional?' She should have known this woman wasn't going to talk any sense.

'True, emotion isn't a bad thing, but when it dominates us, pushes out rationality and impacts our life negatively then maybe we need to re-look at what we're thinking. I know that when my emotions, my fears and insecurities were telling me that Kam was a let-down and I reacted rather than thought, I made poor decisions. I guess that's what I'm trying to say. Don't do what I did.'

'I didn't mean to have a go, I didn't know that about you and Kam, but I'm trying, I really am. My mind just gets flooded with the injustices of what he's done, what he's doing and what he's planned.'

'Aha, the old wood from the trees problem. I can't wave a magic wand for you, Marion, but I can make some suggestions, if you promise not to whack me over the head with your glass.'

'Go on. I am willing to listen to anybody right now.'

'Anybody?'

'Well, obviously not Harmony but pretty much anybody else.'

'Okay, well this is a bit Harmony-like. Mindfulness; do you practise it?'

Marion tried not to lose her temper. Why did people always say this as if it was a miracle cure for everything and anything if only she tried hard enough? She recognized that Pippa was trying to help, but breaking that promise about her wine glass was proving difficult right now. She put her drink on the floor beside her and answered honestly. 'I hate mindfulness.'

'Okay, why?' Pippa asked.

'I tried, I did try but I found that I just couldn't switch off my brain. The minute I tried to concentrate on how my poxy toes were feeling in that moment then everything else just crowded in and made it impossible. It made me feel like I was failing at even this basic thing.'

'Yep, I get that. And it's okay, it's really common. Just acknowledge it and note it. Note what keeps popping up and stop fretting about it happening, it's all part of it. What keeps popping up? Anger?' Pippa asked and Marion moved closer to her on the bench. This was weird; it felt honest, but it was still weird.

'It might be easier if it were anger. I get sad. So sad.' She tried to cover up the honesty of her words with a little laugh.

'Why?' Pippa said so quietly that Marion couldn't be sure she had spoken at all.

'Why? Because I love him so much; he comes into a room and my heart pitter patters as if I were a teen. I want to reach out to him, bind him to me and never let him go. Every tiny crinkle and crease he has on his face, on his body, has been one that has grown with us as a couple. We have gone from being eighteen years old and madly in love to a pair of middle-aged parents and we have taken every step of that journey together and my heart wants to continue that. But – and it's a huge but, an insurmountable but – it's not just love that counts, it can't be, there needs to be respect as well. I respect him but recently… recently his behaviour has indicated that he doesn't feel the same.' She glared at Pippa as she said this, challenging her to oppose her.

'Are you sure? To the outside eye no one could possibly argue that Richard doesn't respect you. We are all so fed up of hearing what a bloody queen you are when quite frankly we, I, only ever get the rough side of your tongue and there's nothing very regal about that. Imagine I'm a judge in a court case: back it up, tell me how he doesn't respect you.'

'If he respected me why didn't he do as I say? Give me the evidence rather than keeping secrets?' Marion heard her voice squeak high, sounding indignant. Like a petulant child that wants to be heard. Was that what she was being? Was that what Pippa was trying to say? Were her emotions and insecurities letting her inner child, her hurt self, make the decisions?

Apparently not because Pippa wasn't giving her time to think that one through.

'Firstly, just because someone respects you doesn't mean they have to practise blind obedience. I would argue that the people that care about you are prepared to stand up and be difficult sometimes. Doing as you are told all the time is not a sign of respect but capitulation. Have you talked to him about this?'

'No.' Marion shrugged. That was a fair point. Marion had always liked to command blind obedience but she had never really respected it.

'Okay, well, talk to him about whatever it is you wanted him to do, find out why he didn't do it. If you love Richard, and I think you do and yes, if you respect Richard' – Marion nodded – 'then let him speak. Listen to him. Ask him why. What else? You're nodding and yet I'm not convinced you're convinced.'

'He told me today...' Marion didn't know how to verbalize it; her embarrassment was off the charts. 'He told me that next week's party at Angelina and Chase's house is actually a surprise set up to renew our vows. He's made a fool of me. Why on earth would someone organize that without asking if I wanted to renew my vows? I chucked him out; I'd strongly suggest that indicates that vow renewal is not top of my list of priorities.'

'Okay. I hear you.' Pippa paused and Marion looked at her, unfathomably desperate to hear what she had to say. Surely she had to agree. There was no black and white on this issue. Not saying yes to a renewal and having one scheduled; that was way too far for even newly zen Pippa and her mindfulness. 'And you're right.' Marion let out a sigh of relief. She was, she knew she was. 'But again, I'm going to say that doesn't sound like Richard. The man is such a love but let's face it, he wouldn't say boo to a goose in case he hurt the goose's feelings. Are you sure that he has done this? That there hasn't been a muddle? Again, loath as I am to tie this back to me—'

'Yes, you don't want to become narcissistic, dear,' Marion responded as quick as a flash, 'not an attractive look.' Pippa stopped and looked at her, brows arched. Okay, so they weren't that comfortable yet. Marion winked to show she was joking.

'What I was trying to say before you so rudely interrupted...' Pippa paused again. But this time to wink back at Marion. '…was that it may be worth taking it back a step, unravelling the truth of what's happened. It seems a very bold move for him and I suspect there's something else happening. Was this the party that is meant to be Angelina Masters' engagement party?'

'Yes, although she has been so difficult and has made me plan a huge, absolutely huge, party with half the guests being people I know, a handful of friends of hers and the rest are paid.'

'I suspect your answer lies somewhere there… ooooh, woah! Woah! What are you doing. Be careful!' Pippa interrupted her own answer to shout as Hector, in full flail mode, crashed out of the orangery and landed himself, pretty expertly, on Marion's lap.

'Hello, darling,' he slurred as he settled himself. 'Fancy a quickie?'

Pippa and Marion exchanged a look.

'Not now, Hector.' Marion tried shoving him off. It was not easy. He needed a little less booze and red meat and a few more salads.

'Hey, mate, why don't you come and sit between the two of us.' Pippa had moved up a bit and patted the free space next to her.

'Two of you, oh yes,' Hector slurred, shifting his not inconsiderable weight to the bench and managing to lay his head on Marion's shoulder at the same time. 'You've always been so lovely.' Marion didn't dare look at Pippa; she was fairly sure she wouldn't agree. 'Richard's always been so lucky. I would have loved to have been yours but even I know when I'm beat. Which is a shame. I should have tried harder to win you for myself. But you two were made for each other, made for each other.' At which point he leant forward and swayed a bit.

'You seem to be trying pretty hard right now,' Pippa observed.

'Oh no, you don't!' Marion tried to push him more forward; she recognised the signs.

Too late. Hector fixed her with a goofy smile and then vomited violently all over the ground in front of him, narrowly missing Pippa and Marion's shoes as they both swiftly drew their legs up and under and managed to avoid his sick.

'Jesus Christ,' Marion said, professional wedding planner side of herself abandoned as old and irritated friend took over.

'S'ry,' Hector slurred. 'Made for each other. Must sort it out.' His head slumped back on Marion's shoulder with not particularly attractive bits of spittle still on his chin.

'Friend of yours?' Pippa giggled.

'Not for much longer.' Marion tried to jiggle him along her shoulder.

'A wedding isn't a wedding without at least one drunken uncle,' Pippa observed sympathetically.

'Hmm. I need to get that cleaned up. You are a pain in the arse, Hector. Here, will you support his weight a minute?' Marion hefted Hector towards Pippa and stood up to go and get the bodily fluid clean-up kit; she knew it was sensible to have one. She considered using her walkie-talkie to call Serena whilst she watched over her friend and made sure he did nothing else to upset the night but knew it wasn't fair to get her friend to do something she really didn't want to have to do herself. Being new Marion definitely had its drawbacks.

As she stood, Richard came out of the orangery with a sleepy Rufus clinging to his hand.

'Hello, love, I've got to get him home; he's dying on his feet. It's been a lovely day though, well done. Obviously, I'll take Rafe and Rupert back with me as well.'

'Okay.' She ignored the 'love' bit; she didn't want to start a fight here. But honestly, he seemed to think that everything was more or less okay again, just because they had slept together. She needed to make it clear that she was still unsure of what was to happen between the two of them. 'I've got to get Hector into a taxi.'

'I'm not a child,' their mutual friend slurred, child-like.

'Oh, I know. I'd make you behave better if you were a child. Stay there.'

'Will I see you later to talk?' Richard asked, talking over the top of Hector, undermining himself next with, 'You'll probably be tired.'

Marion looked in at the orangery where Angelina was knocking back champagne like she was Oliver Reed, clocked Annie and Ethel, who were standing on one edge of the buffet table shrieking, 'R.E.S.P.E.C.T.' as the song played and then looked back at Hector, who was beginning to snore now, snore and dribble.

'Yes, Richard. I probably will be.' And she went to deal with the less glamourous side of being a successful businesswoman.

Chapter Forty-three

Marion was supposed to have had the most restful few days of her life. Richard had arranged to take the boys camping down west on The Lizard to surf. He wanted to give her time to recover from the wedding and time to prepare for the party. Marion had thought he was being daft when he suggested it. She didn't need time to relax; she had always subscribed to the sleep-when-you're-dead school of thought but actually it was pretty amazing. It would have been better however had she been able to relax properly. Angelina had refused to talk about her engagement party at her brother's wedding and had been resolutely ignoring all her calls ever since.

Marion had made the decision to just carry on getting the final touches in place, chasing up the caterers, the florists, the musicians to confirm just as she would have done if she hadn't found out the truth of Angelina's dastardly plan. But she wasn't finding it easy. Every step of the way was plagued by self-doubt, by that what-have-I-got-myself-into feeling that she had never really experienced before.

It had been such an exciting moment when Angelina agreed to let her host a party, had promised her a star-studded event to organize that would shriek glamour and shine. A real springboard for her business and an event she used to advertise herself and encourage other bookings. As the months had progressed Marion had become increasingly unnerved; every interaction she had with her supposed close friend added anxiety rather than resolving issues. And now there was this nonsense about it being a renewal of vows ceremony for herself and her ex-husband clouding the mix.

She was so conflicted; of course she had to do the very best she could. She wanted photos for her portfolio and her Instagram and she knew that regardless of motive behind the party it was going to look spectacular. She had just confirmed the fire-eaters and acrobats; there was no way it couldn't.

It was the social embarrassment though that had kept her awake over the past few nights. Now Rosy's wedding was done, and a roaring success, there was space in her mind for the panic to build about what next weekend would bring.

Everyone had been promised the party of the decade and up-close and personal access to Chase and Angelina. The fact that everyone present would think she had lied just so she could be the centre of attention as she made vows to Richard was mortifying.

She knew that people had thought badly of her before, but this was completely different.

She checked the lamb in the oven and dipped her finger into the hummus she had just whizzed up, but instead of excitement that her boys were due home in half an hour she was a whirling maelstrom of emotion, a lack of sleep amplifying her anxiety. It wasn't solely the impending embarrassment looming over the upcoming event that was causing distress; it was also the knowledge that waiting to deal with Richard until Rosy's wedding was out of the way meant that now things needed to come to a head.

She should never have slept with him on her birthday. They needed to sit down and talk and she suspected that today was going to be that day. She was a strong believer in facing things as they arose but the thought of talking to Richard was terrifying. Absolutely terrifying. She didn't know which way her mind was going and that in itself was bad enough; she had always been a woman who knew her own mind. Add in the thought of how she was responsible for making a decision that would grant Richard his every wish or break his heart, it was all too much. Just too much.

As she shut the oven door, her phone rang out. Glancing at it she saw it was Angelina. Aha, at last!

Best professional voice on – she didn't want her client to sense quite how anxious she was about next Saturday – she answered the call.

'Darling!'

'Darling! Just checking in to see how things are going?' Angelina squawked down the phone.

A whole lot better if I knew what the blazes was going on, Marion wanted to say but she restricted herself to a 'Fine, wonderful actually, everything is in place. It is going to be the most spectacular evening but I do want to talk to you, again' – she couldn't help but slip that in – 'about what the central purpose is?'

'You're throwing a party, Marion. A great big party,' Angelina said, with more than a hint of impatience.

'Yes, but what I'm s—'

'I do hope you're not going to disappoint me.' The darling-darling nature of Angelina's tone changed to pure steel. Honestly, it was impossible trying to have a grown-up conversation with this woman. 'I have invited my friends and you had better make it worthy of their time and energy. I rang to make sure everything was going well for you. This is a kind thing I'm doing and you just try to make everything difficult. People who make things difficult for others never get far in life, you know?'

Marion knew her face was a picture of taken aback confusion. Eh?

'I don't want to talk to you any more. Just get everything in place, turn up in your best dress. Oh God, please don't wear that leopard-print monstrosity. Animal prints were *so* last season; you're lucky I can guide you like this. I'll see you then. I'm trusting you, Marion, trusting you.' And with that she performed what Marion was beginning to think was her most perfectly honed skill and hung up on the call.

Oh, well that was alright then. None of Marion's perfectly reasonable questions answered but her professionalism and wardrobe harshly judged. Great, just great.

Chapter Forty-four

Marion was standing staring at her phone in disbelief when she heard the slamming of car doors. She moved over to the window to peek out and see if it was her boys returned home.

And it was; there they were leaping around the pavement as if they hadn't just had four days of Cornish beach life tiring them out. Rafe wasn't leaping quite so much, on the phone and no doubt talking to Sophie the minute he got back to Penmenna. Rupert was helping his dad unload their surfboards and Rufus was doing God knows what to the drain cover in the road. But for the moment Marion couldn't help it as her breath caught in her throat and she looked at all four of her boys together, all of them with their limbs lightly golden from the summer sun, their arms peeking out from the short sleeves of their wetsuits. Their hair was blonder after a few days spent on the beach and freckles on all four had developed, sprinkled across their noses and in Richard's case all over his face.

What was she thinking? Why was she creating problems where there should be none? This was what she wanted, this playing out in front of her right now. This family was hers; why would she endanger it? It was all she had ever wanted and now insecurities were making her push it away. With Rafe about to hit his teens she was aware that time was racing by and she needed to grapple back her family, make a decision that took them out of the limbo everyone had been in for the past months.

Woah! Before she carried on beating herself up, she stopped. *Be kind to yourself. You did this because you caught Richard cheating, you were right to do so, this is your heart talking, listen to your head.*

And what does my head say? she asked herself as she walked towards the front door, ready to greet the boys as they flew through it. *My head says talk to my husband, work out a plan and stick to it. This silly shilly-shallying doesn't fit with who you are. He is him, not his dad and you are you, not your mother. Be brave, be bold. Make your bloody mind up!*

'Mum! Mum! Mum! I did it, I stood up, not for long but I did it! I kept getting knocked over again and again. At one point I thought I was drowning, no two points, twice!' Marion smiled as she reached out to hug her youngest son to her.

'You almost drowned, twice?!' she said in a tone that echoed his excitement.

'I did! I did! But Dad says sometimes when everything is battering you down you have to dig deep, take a breath and try again, so that's what I did. I did it until I did it and I did it!'

Marion exchanged a quick look with Richard, who was trailing in behind, carrying some surfboards as the boys dragged in their camping trolley rammed full with all the heavy stuff.

'Did you have a good time as well?' She turned to Rafe and Rupert.

'Yeah, actually it was pretty cool,' Rafe acknowledged.

'Dad let us stay up until after midnight and the guy who ran the campsite lit a big fire and had a guitar and after our barbecue we went and joined him and sang. It was ace. And then the next night Dad let us go swimming at midnight, with torches in the sea. Although when the sun woke us up at dawn the next day I was tired so we had a lazy morning and do you know bacon tastes so much better on a barbecue and did you know that there is nothing, nothing in the world as sweaty as a tent?' Rufus was jumping up and down on the spot with excitement as he told of their adventures.

'Rafe's armpits come a pretty good second,' Rupert snuck in, but instead of being instantly punched on the arm, Rafe just smiled at him and raised his middle finger to stroke up and down on his face.

Why children thought their parents couldn't see that was beyond Marion, but for now she was happy that he had made his protest a non-violent one so she let it slide.

'I'm so glad you all had a good time. Lunch is almost ready so go get out of your wetsuits, rinse them and hang them up. Rafe you can use mine and your dad's bathroom and then come and grab some lunch.'

All the boys stopped to look at her, as if she had said something strange and Richard, on his fourth trip in from the car, flashed her a smile.

'Oh, before that go help your father. He wasn't put on this earth to be your packhorse. And clear up any sand you drop. And hang your shorties up to dry properly!'

'Neigh!' was Richard's contribution.

'Twit.'

'I know, but a happy one.'

'That's good to hear. *Are* you a happy one?'

'Yes, it's been a fab week; it was much more fun teaching them to surf rather than just booting them out of a car for lessons. Rupert is really good, you know.'

'Rupert is really good at everything.'

'True. But it was so nice to see them. I wish I had done this years ago.'

Marion sniffed when Richard said that. She must stop doing that; she didn't know why it happened. It was as if her nose wasn't prepared to let her not pass judgement on irritating stuff even though her brain was trying hard to let things go. But honestly the only things that had ever stopped him from doing it were his own choices.

'We need to talk, though, M.'

'I know, I know.'

'I think things have got so caught up, and misunderstandings have snowballed and... well, we just need to talk it out.'

'I know, I agree. Let's sort this out, have lunch, get the boys busy and then make time.'

'This afternoon?'

'This afternoon.' This was going to be fine. She had made it so much worse in her mind. It had to be done; it was like the dentist's, or giving birth – you kind of just had to accept it was coming and do it.

The boys soon came back downstairs in fresh clothes, and Marion pulled the lamb to bits, sprinkled some crispy onions and pomegranate on the hummus and grabbed the salads she had prepared earlier out of the fridge. As she looked down she realized she had made a feast. This was not a light lunch; this was an offering to the gods of domestic bliss. Maybe that was more telling than the runaway thoughts that had been dominating her brain. If she were to look at her actions not her thoughts, then her body was still playing out her desires to have everyone back together as one domestic unit.

So that was her heart and her body in agreement. If she could just convince her mind to slow down, to stop coursing around at 150 miles per hour, then maybe, maybe she could convince her head that this was the right path.

Richard had, wordlessly as was often his wont, set the table in the garden, and now the boys were ferrying out the huge bowls of food, Rufus pinching bits of cheese off the top of the whipped goat's cheese and tomato salad. She'd whipped goat's cheese, for goodness' sake; what more evidence did she need?

They all sat outside in the early August sunshine, the smells of Cornwall in the summertime wafting over them. There was a tang in the air of salt and sea, the aroma of pasties freshly baked in the butcher's jostling for space in the air, the ever-present noise of seagulls circling and the babble of families walking along Fore Street heading to the beach. She loved Penmenna and as she sat with her family in their garden, Darcy causing chaos as he ran around with a half-mauled stuffed toy in his mouth, pleased to have everyone together and outside, her heart felt as full and happy as was possible, her concerns about the coming weekend firmly pushed out as she revelled in this perfect summer day.

The boys chattered for ages about their time away, wanting to share every last bit of their adventures and making her heart swell – as well as surfing they had been crabbing, although Rafe made everyone put the crabs back as soon as they caught one. They had entered The Lizards' biggest sandcastle competition and been beaten into second place by a local team but had an honourable mention – 'Honourable, Mum, you've always said that's all you wanted for us and we got it!' Rufus exclaimed – and set up their own boules tournament back on the campsite that had enticed all the other campers in and to play.

Finally sated by storytelling, the majority of the food demolished, they drifted off, leaving her and Richard to pick over the remnants of lunch and exchange shy smiles.

'Lunch was delicious.'

'The sea gives everyone a good appetite. I'm so glad you had such a lovely few days; it's done the boys good – they've come back glowing.'

'And you? How are you? Did it help to have a few days on your own?'

'Kind of. But I've been having a hard time getting out of my head. And Angelina is being difficult – I don't know where to start.'

'Well, that you knew. It'll be over by this time next week and you'll have the most phenomenal photos for your social media to help with future bookings. But talk to me, tell me *why* you're trying to get out of your head? What's going on?' He reached for her hand and instead of snaking her arm back she extended her fingers and entwined them in his.

'I never really understood it before. You hear people say "stop overthinking and get out of your head and just trust" and it's never made much sense to me. How can you possibly overthink? Isn't thinking a good thing? But this week I've realized that my constant tearing everything apart and examining it in minute detail is hindering me, not helping me, and I guess that's what people mean.'

'I guess it is.' He squeezed her hand in a Richard way. An I'm-here-and-I've got-you way. She had missed this so much when he had been working away. And had been fighting it ever since he moved back. 'So, what are you overthinking?' His tone was curious and she believed he was interested.

'Are you fishing, Mr Marksharp?'

'Fishing?'

'Are you hoping I'll say it's you that's in my head?'

'Would it be so bad?'

'Yes, if it stops me getting on with my work.'

'And is it?'

'It's certainly playing a part. But if it makes you happy, yes you are taking up an awful lot of space in my brain. I miss having you here, miss having you in my bed.'

Wow! Where had that come from? She wanted to talk about next weekend, clear up the misunderstandings over their relationship, not make clumsy passes at him over the garden table!

'So, let's talk about that. And if I know you, this upcoming thing of Angelina's is eating you up. You can't help but be a bit worried. It's a big thing.'

'Yes. Yes it is. It was bad enough having her as a client, knowing that she will find fault on a whim but then you said that it was a surprise renewal of our vows and now I'm all of a dither.' Richard smiled; that was one of his phrases that had wormed its way into her everyday vocabulary. 'No! Don't smile. How dare you?' Ooh, she could feel righteous Marion kicking in, her crossness building. 'How *could* you? Our relationship is our business, no one else's. I would never have thought that you would have made such a leap, pushed me so publicly into making a decision…'

'Whoa! Stop. I have nothing to do with Angelina's party or her plans. I heard about her intention and tried to warn you. At no point would I ever, I hope, force anyone into anything. I think her intentions changed as time went on and this seemed to her to be a good plan once she realized that getting married in a hurry wasn't going to work for her and Chase. The way I see it, you and I need to talk things through; what Angelina is up to in the background does have an impact but it's not the key thing. We need to discuss the Claudia situation, we need to discuss what we both want for our future and see if it aligns but at no point have I, would I, force you into a vow renewal thing without telling you. Like the whole cheating mess, I'm put out that you think that I would.'

Marion sat and listened as he spoke, his voice calm, his words practical. She tried to process. 'So, hang on, what you're saying is that you didn't set this up with Chase and Angelina?'

'Of course not. And as soon as I found out what they were planning, and I believe they had the best intentions, as soon as I found out I told you.'

'Why? Why would they do it?'

'Honestly, I think it is misguided niceness on Angelina's behalf.'

'Angelina is never nice. She doesn't know how to be. How she and Matt are related is a mystery.'

'Right, exactly. She doesn't know how but clearly wanted to try and as a result has massively cocked up. And yes, Chase should have known better but I think he was so relieved that she wasn't forcing him to marry her this Saturday that he agreed to anything. On the other hand, there's also a strong possibility that their relationship flourishes precisely because he ignores most of what she says and does.'

'We don't have to go through with the renewal vows?'

'God, no, we don't have to do anything you're not comfortable with. I'm happy to stand up and shout to the world that I want to be married to you for the rest of my life, but you must do what makes you happy and not be bound by obligation or duty or social pressure.' His hand moved to her arm and started to absentmindedly stroke it. She leaned into him in return, a weight taken from her mind. He hadn't been behind this; she should have known. She wouldn't have to get up and be forced to make promises that she still wasn't sure on. She didn't want to bind herself to him again, not if he had cheated, and that hadn't been settled yet. That joy was next on the agenda.

'Okay.' She took a deep breath, still clinging to his hand, closed her eyes, and then blurted, 'I hear what you say about me trusting you. And I understand your point, you're right and to be honest apart from this blip, you've never done anything to demonstrate I couldn't trust you. But you know me, you know my history. No matter how secure I am as an adult I just can't seem to shake it off, that doubt that I'll become my mother, that belief that no matter what I do I'll never be quite good enough despite me trying my absolute hardest to make sure everything I do is the best it can be. I am trying, though, and talking this through is helping. But I am going to go somewhere now that isn't comfortable for either of us but it needs to be done.'

'Claudia?'

'Yup. You say you didn't cheat, you say now that there's evidence you didn't cheat and yet I haven't seen it. It feels like I'm on the outside. Somehow Serena knows about it and yet you haven't shared it with me.' She could hear herself; she sounded like a small child that had been left alone too long with the helium.

'Because it was Serena that found it, printed it out and gave it to me.'

'Printed what out?'

Richard took a big sigh. 'Serena printed out a WhatsApp conversation between herself and Claudia and showed me. Claudia is all loved up with someone and is trying to tell Serena how wonderful it is to be with someone who reciprocates her feelings. She goes on to say she's not had sex in years. I can't have had sex with her *and* have her be celibate for three years. Serena thought if I showed you then you would have the evidence you'd been banging on about.'

'I don't bang on, Richard.'

'I think you do, love, sometimes.'

'Why didn't you show me?'

'It felt grubby somehow, invasive, and like I said I thought you should have trusted me. Would it put your mind at rest to see it?'

Yes. Bloody hell, of course, had she not been asking for exactly this for months now? Did she need to skywrite it or paint it on her boobs? 'Yes!'

'Okay, hang on.' Richard stood up and slipped his hand into his back pocket.

'What? You've got it on you?'

'I've been carrying it around ever since Serena gave it to me, waiting for this conversation to arise.'

'I can't believe you waited all this time.'

'I didn't want to bog you down with us when you were working so hard to get things up and running with Marion Marksharp events planner.'

'You're a fool.'

'So you constantly tell me.'

'Well you are.'

'I must be, I'm still here.' Richard passed her the piece of A4 the message exchange was printed upon. Marion's eyes scanned it once, twice and a third time.

'She hasn't had sex in three years!'

'I understand it's not uncommon.'

'She says the most dreadful things about you. What a bitch! How dare she?' And then the realization of her error, the impact of her belief that he was a cheat hit her. 'You never slept with Claudia.'

'Nope.'

'I threw you out when you hadn't done anything wrong. You had been faithful? *You had been faithful.*'

'Yep.'

'Well why on earth didn't you tell me?'

'I think I did. Quite a lot. You said I was lying and you hit me with a vase.'

'I did and I really liked that vase.' Marion heard herself giggle. She was dreadful.

'So, what do you want to do about things now?'

'I don't really know. Since February my life has changed so much, and whilst I hate not having you here, I do like my new life. I like having focus and direction that isn't just about you and the boys. I know that makes me sound selfish...'

'No, stop right there. Wanting something you want to do for you instead of for me and the boys doesn't make you selfish; it makes you healthy. And actually, look at this last year: yes, you haven't been able to be as involved with the boys as you would be normally but has the world imploded? Have they all been seized by Scotland Yard? No, they've carried on being them. Sometimes they're evil little hellers, sometimes they are remarkably switched-on young men. But all the time they're yours and mine and all the time they make us proud. They're not toddlers any more, and despite your best intentions, they don't need you helicopter parenting...'

'Helicopter parenting? Do you even know what that is?'

'Yes I do. Because I've watched you do it for the last twelve years. It's time to let them grow up a little, let them do things by themselves.'

'Rufus is six!'

'Yes he's six, with two older brothers who are shaping up to be good – well, goodish – role models. Let us all pitch in, let it be something we all do together rather than something you control every tiny element of.'

'Hmm, they have been happy having you around more.'

'And I've been happy being around more. So, are you hearing what I'm saying? You can still have your new life. I will talk to Angelina firmly if you like and tell her this is just a party and whilst we appreciate her thinking of us we will do what we need to in our own time. This party will be fabulous, and I know that because I know you. You can still chase your dreams for yourself and I can help with the boys. I make no show of the fact I want to. And I make no show of the fact I would rather be living with you. Sleeping back in our bed, cuddling you after a long day. I'm happy to keep giving you time but now we've had this chat, now you know I didn't cheat, I need to know myself which direction you're heading in.'

He hadn't asked for an apology, he hadn't said anything she didn't know to be true and he had never been anyone but himself; it had been her that was out of kilter.

'Yours, Richard, I'm heading in yours.'

Chapter Forty-five

Richard moved his stuff back in that evening. It was amazing how fast he could move when he was motivated. And things had been rather nice ever since. With that pressure now lifted, Marion found her shoulders were a lot lighter, her brain no longer buzzing with anger, conflict or even guilt; it was only work that kept her awake at night now, but not for long. Not with the solid warmth of Richard next to her, his gentle hands reassuring her that all was good in the world.

However, during the day, Marion was focusing her all on Angelina's party. Which was happening tomorrow and meant she needed to get on site to oversee the set-up. She was just waiting for Serena and Jenny, who she had put on the payroll again for this event, and then they were going to head on over to Chase's and get things started. Chase and Angelina had hotfooted it to London to escape the chaos that the next few days would bring, giving Marion total free rein, which was exactly how she liked it.

She had said something similar to Richard as they woke up this morning.

'Mum.' Rafe crept up behind her just as she had seen Richard out of the door. He had taken Rupert and Rufus out, but Rafe and Sophie were coming to help her for the day.

'Mmm,' she answered, her concentration on her lipstick.

'Mum, can we talk for a bit?'

'Of course, but you'd better be quick. What is it?'

'It's a bit… don't be cross but I want to sit down and talk to you adult to adult but it will only take three, maybe five minutes.'

Marion held her tongue.

'Go on.' She sat down on one of the armchairs as he took another.

'We're all so pleased Dad is back. Obviously. But I couldn't help overhear you the other day…'

Marion gulped; this never boded well. Eavesdroppers really should learn more self-control.

Rafe continued, 'And I heard you and Dad talking about some plan to renew your vows.'

That could have been worse.

'Okay' – Marion drew the word out – 'and what do you want to say?'

'I want to say that I think it's a good idea; it would help us all. Make a marker to cement Dad being home full-time, but when I went to him and said this should happen he said he wasn't prepared to push you into anything, which is *so* Dad. So talking to you is the next step.'

Rafe took a breath and carried on, 'For Rufus and Rupert's sake, and Dad's, I think you should seriously consider the vow renewal thing. This is my plea for you to do that.'

'Your plea, eh?'

'Yup.'

'We haven't got much time.'

'From what I understand it's all set up, there's nothing left to organize.' Ah, he was quick. Out of all the boys, he was the most like her. Rufus was the most like Richard and someone had once described Rupert as the perfect blend of the two of them. She had always rather liked that.

'We'd still need to plan a bit, and surprise your dad rather than ask him, make it a big ta-daaa moment!'

'I thought you were against vow renewals as a surprise.' Gah. Could she get nothing past this boy?

'Oh… um, well in my instance yes. Obviously. But in this one, I reckon it's okay. I'll need help if he's not to guess.'

'I'm happy to take charge on that. And shall we get Rupert and Rufus in too?'

'I think that sounds like a team that I want on my side.'

The doorbell rang, interrupting their flow.

'That will be the girls; talk it over with your brothers and then we'll make some plans. I think this could be a really good idea.' She got up ready to walk towards the door. 'And thank you for coming to talk to me.' This had felt grown-up and she wanted him to know she appreciated it.

'Thanks for listening.'

'Can I get a hug?'

'Oh my God, Mum! Your timing! No. Sophie's out there.'

Marion chuckled as she opened the door. 'Hello.'

'Hello, hello.' Serena, Sophie, Alice and Jenny came in through the door. 'We're here and we're ready.'

'Excellent, let me just grab my shoes and my bag.'

'Ooh, first, Marion, we wondered if we could have a quick word.' Jesus! It was clearly a morning for it.

'It's August now,' Jenny said, looking at Serena for support.

And her point was?

'And you haven't said anything about the PTA,' Serena jumped in. 'It's the summer holidays but we had expected you to talk to us about it by the end of the summer term and let us know what you were thinking regarding its future.'

'Yes, its future,' Jenny reinforced. 'You've said you're stepping down, you've had us running things since February and now we want to know who is going to be in charge next year. September is a time of fresh starts so it made sense to us…'

Marion raised a brow in Jenny's direction, but just for fun. They were right, she did plan on keeping away from the PTA this academic year and they had survived, done well even, without her helping.

She looked at both of them, up and down, measuring them and ensuring there was a pregnant pause. Jenny had that look that resembled a small schoolgirl so on edge that she was about to wet herself any moment.

'Alice, it's good you're here, as the member of staff who forms part of the PTA, but you're right it's time I made my decision.'

'Which is?' Serena questioned.

'Which is that really…' She paused for a long time at this point, amazed that they hadn't worked out yet that the only power she had was what they willingly gave her. 'You don't need me to make a decision. It's not mine to make. I don't own the PTA; I never did. I may have thought I did and admit I was a *little* possessive. I do enjoy being in charge but that doesn't mean I am or that you have to carry on in the same vein.'

'I don't understand.' Jenny's face was the very picture of perplexity.

'If I were to be hit by a truck tomorrow, how would you run it?'

'We'd all pitch in, I guess,' Serena answered, a smile playing at the corner of her mouth.

'Right, so do that. Run it the way *you* want to. You can make it as egalitarian as you wish. If you both want to share leading it, then do that. If you want to appoint different people to have responsibility for different things, do that.'

'You're not going to tell us what to do?'

'I don't think I need to any more, and I think that says an awful lot more about me than you. It is yours; run with it and I shall cheer on from the sidelines and be a phone call away if you ever need me.' Marion beamed at them all as Alice stood next to her and squished her in for a hug as Jenny slumped to the floor in a dead faint.

Chapter Forty-six

It had taken days of setting up, months of planning but Marion was so proud of herself; the party was ready to go and everything looked phenomenal. The beach, the field and part of the huge manicured lawn that Chase had earmarked for the main body of the party were all set. The lawn had two big domes, one for the vow renewal ceremony which would later metamorphize into a dance tent, and one for dining with a huge bar at the end. There were jungle-sized plants shipped in, dozens of them, arranged to give a tropical feel and Marion had used them to make pathways, each leading to special areas to sit or to dance or whatever you wished. The main pathway ran down to the beach where there was another smaller dome as a bar, a stage set up for live music, a tequila tent and fire pits, bean bags and deck chairs aplenty.

She had spent all day at the site, stalking up and down and ready to bark orders at anyone who wasn't being efficient. But everybody was on task or ahead and kept smiling at her.

Sophie had slipped her hand into Marion's earlier today to drag her to the large dome where she and Rafe had been compiling a slideshow of Marion and Richard and were projecting it onto the walls of the tent. Marion had been so touched by both the effort and the effect that she had shrieked in a Jenny-like fashion and Sophie had squeezed her hand and said, 'You're alright, really.' A hard lump formed in Marion's throat, which she disguised by leaving quickly, marching around site and finding people to put chairs in rows in the dome.

With everything in place and guests due to arrive soon, Marion had slipped into Angelina's bedroom to put on her outfit for the evening, an ivory satin dress that clung in all the right places. She purred as she stoked her hands down her frame and looked in the semi-circle of mirrors that Angelina had in her dressing room. The fabric was a jacquard crocodile print, with the pattern barely discernible to the eye, shimmering out only if the light caught it right. It was also very tight, sleek. Richard was going to explode.

She was slightly concerned about the celebrant for her renewal but she had spoken to Angelina the day before to let her know of the small change of plans and how the renewal would be a surprise for Richard, not for her, as well as to check there was a celebrant in place. Angelina had shrieked, very annoying, and promised her everything was in place and she didn't need to fuss about details. Old Marion would have blown a gasket at that thought; this Marion figured that she would be surrounded by family and friends and could problem-solve in the moment if necessary. Plus Angelina hadn't hung up on her this time, which seemed to be the first in many months.

Her watch beeped; it was Rupert letting her know that Richard was on site and the boys had him in hand. It really wouldn't be long now!

Chapter Forty-seven

Richard was currently the happiest man alive, or at least thought he was. What had begun as the shittiest year of his life had turned on a sixpence and become the best. He was back with his wife, in the bosom of his family and no longer had the prison that was his job forcing him back to the coalface every Monday. Plus, he and Marion were practically honeymooning; he was so happy to be back and she felt pretty bad for kicking him out in the first place – he was fairly sure that wouldn't last long – but it was definitely giving their relationship a tinge of can't-believe-our-luck. He could live with that for a while.

He couldn't help but feel a little bit of a pang, though; today was the day Angelina had planned for their vow renewal, and he would have liked that. The opportunity to pledge his loyalty to the woman he loved and wanted to spend his life with. But with Marion not being keen, he wasn't going to do anything to rock the boat.

Today was her big day. She was going to prove to any naysayers that she could pull off two big events in two weeks, and do so fabulously. He had never doubted it and knew she didn't need him adding relationship demands at this point. She had been ever so slightly on edge as the day approached and a full bag of nerves by the time she dressed this morning. She was softer these days, less brittle, but as she kissed the tip of his nose as she left, she reminded him to dress his very sharpest, that she didn't want him showing her up. That was a tinge of old Marion.

She had taken Rafe and Sophie with her when she left, leaving him with Rupert and Rufus, who were behaving bizarrely. Rufus had been upstairs and got dressed in his suit – his suit! That had never been upon his body without a godawful fight – and then came and sat on the sofa repeatedly asking if they were going yet and was his tie okay? Instead of teasing him, Rupert had redone the tie for him – Rufus had tied it in four knots – and then encouraged his brother upstairs to play games whilst they waited, without any prompting from their father. He had been planning to take them to the beach for a quick swim this afternoon but they point blank refused. Even when he attempted to bribe them with ice cream.

When they did finally arrive at Chase and Angelina's, they were greeted by Hector, who took their car and valet parked it somewhere over by the old stable block. Richard's attention was caught by a helicopter whirring down low and looking for somewhere to land, presumably full of the very glam. By which point Rufus and Rupert had run off and were staring through the front doors – the house currently out of bounds – and laughing loudly.

'That picture is so rude!' Rufus was nearly wetting himself as he doubled over giggling and Rupert had lost his usual grown-up composure and had his nose up against the glass. Richard tried to move them away and around the back to the field were everything was happening. But his mind was playing its usual cruel tricks. What was Marion doing with Hector helping? Why had she asked him and not Richard? Richard felt a quick flash of jealousy and then reminded himself of how his wife had woken him this morning and took charge of himself. Hector was not a threat; he needed to stop worrying about him. Although the fact that Hector had winked at him as he took his car had set his teeth on edge. What was that about?

As he and the boys rounded the house to the back lawn they all let out a soft 'wow'. He had been here many times before, as had they, and it was always stylish but now it was completely transformed. There was buzz and noise everywhere. There were circus performers, fire-eaters and jugglers roaming all over the place, a mini orchestra outside the closest dome, waiters wandering around offering canapés and glasses of fizz. Richard could spot a bar across the way and asked the boys if they would like a drink but Rupert pulled on his sleeve instead and pointed to the beach that sat to the side of the property.

All day they had avoided the beach and *now* they wanted to head to one. He suggested they get a drink first but Rufus darted off, making that an impossibility. This was not how he had planned to spend his evening. He had foolishly assumed that with Rufus so keen to get here, he would be impeccably behaved when he did. Clearly, he still had a lot to learn.

There was a band playing on the stage on the sand and the boys stood around watching. Richard spied a tequila tent but shelved the idea for later. For now, he needed to find Marion, let her know he was here and see what she needed him to do. He was pretty sure a medicinal shot of tequila was not her plan for him.

He spent half an hour trying to find his wife but his boys kept leading him this way and that, claiming they had seen her, with Rupert spending a disproportionate amount of time with his phone in his hand. There were so many people here, it was hard to keep track and Rufus seemed high as a kite, the carnival atmosphere exciting him, darting off whenever something new and shiny caught his eye.

His own eye was also turning with frequency. Richard did not know much about celebrity but there were very definitely faces here even he recognized and not from just around the village. At one point he came across Lynne having a complete meltdown after speaking to one of the guests, a well-dressed willowy woman who hadn't heard that heels on grass or sand weren't a great idea. Alongside the generous smattering of the brightest and the best, the whole of Penmenna and most of Treporth Bay seemed to be here as well.

'Hi, if everyone could make their way to the large dome on the lawn… Angelina would like to say a few words.' Serena suddenly appeared – she should really be a cat burglar – repeating this message to every group she passed, chivvying them along to the huge tent.

Richard obeyed, aware he had been there an hour so far and still hadn't seen his wife.

It was unusual; she would normally be found at the centre of everything. But surely she'd be present if Angelina was making a speech? He turned to shepherd the boys but they were ahead of him, motioning him to catch up.

There were so many people here, all now moving along to the central point. He wouldn't be surprised to spot William and Kate in a minute; he had just seen two famous Saturday night TV presenters and a pop star who was supposed to be in rehab – or so Rupert informed him.

'Hello, hello, everybody.' Angelina tapped the side of a microphone and a burst of static shot across the field. Richard and the boys were inside the big dome now, all set out with chairs, and tried to edge their way forward, which was hard as everyone crowded in. 'Thank you all so much for coming; Chase and I are so happy to see you all here, at our home. Our nearest and our dearest.' She did a little head bow of meek gratitude. It didn't fool anybody.

Richard scanned the crowd. He wasn't sure who he could place here as being near and dear to Angelina, bar her brother, who was over in the corner, and Marion, whom he still couldn't see.

'We realized, sadly, that we couldn't get married before next year, but we can sure as hell celebrate our engagement.' She paused and then waved her hand in an upward motion to encourage a cheer, obediently delivered. She waved them down again.

'I also wanted to do that. I've seen the local head-teacher do it with her children in school but look at me.' She gestured, making them cheer again and then stopped them, gestured and then stopped. She was loving it.

Chase leaned in and whispered in her ear and she motioned for silence. 'I expect you know my brother Matt…' A spontaneous cheer erupted now, along with hollers and wolf whistles. Richard laughed, catching a glimpse of Matt's I'm-polite-for-the-cameras face. He refused to join Angelina on the stage despite her trying to wave him up. 'Matt got married last week and has stayed here for this but is off on his honeymoon next week, lucky thing. So romance is in the air in Penmenna and I… am… here… for… it. Those of you that know me well know I'm all about giving back…' There was a muffled crowd-wide titter at this. Ouch. But not enough to stop Angelina in full flow. 'Whilst today is about celebrating Chase and me and our love – and it's mainly about that, let's be honest – Chase's old friend from university wanted to renew his vows to his wife of many, many years, the best party planner in the world…' Richard winced; he wasn't sure Marion would like that term. 'Marion, who has made today happen and who organized Matt's wedding last week. So… I'm going to ask all of you to take a seat, bar the front three rows which are reserved for Penmenna people, you know who you are, and Richard, Richard Marksharp, would you come up here to the front.'

Richard couldn't see his boys, didn't know what on earth was going on and was thoroughly perplexed. Plus, he still hadn't seen his wife.

'Richard, now!' Angelina barked into the microphone.

There was a kerfuffle as people took to chairs, clearing the aisle as a photo slideshow appeared on the side of the dome. Photos of him and Marion from when they were eighteen through to them now and with the boys. As he looked up to the front of the stage which had now cleared, he saw Rafe standing at the end, suit and grin on.

He realized as he had been standing there in a state of shock, staring at the photos, that the front three rows of chairs were now filled with all his friends from school and the village. Rosy and Matt had taken a seat, as had Alex and Sylvie and Dan and Alice. Rufus's teacher, Kam, was also there with his girlfriend, Pippa – whom he would never have expected to turn up to anything that celebrated Marion. Next to them was Hector, Sheila, Serena and her family, Jenny and Sophie and Jim, Mickey, Andy and Roger from The Smuggler's Curse. Annie and Ethel. Even the butcher had turned up, as had Lottie from the corner shop. No sign of Marion though.

'There's more, now you're all seated. Today Marion and Richard will renew their vows in front of all of us…'

Richard couldn't keep the smile off his face; was this why the boys were being odd? They were part of this plan all along, knew that their mother and Angelina had planned this? He walked to the front to stand by his son; the photo stream had ended and he could not wait to see what was next. As to where Rupert and Rufus were, he stopped worrying and assumed they knew more than he did at this point.

'Hey, Dad, hope you don't mind. But I'm here to be your best man,' Rafe said in a low voice as Richard reached him.

'I can't think of anyone I'd trust more or rather have here up with me than you, son,' Richard said, giving him one of his trademark ruffles of his hair, and this time Rafe didn't duck. Both turned to face Angelina.

'Before we can kick this off, it looks like you're missing a celebrant.' She whooped. Yep, whooped.

'Dan can do it!' called Alice from the front.

Angelina gave her a terrifying look.

'Not necessary. As you know it's important to refresh your skills base frequently...' Richard was desperate to turn, just a little, to see Matt's face at this but resisted the temptation. 'So I am very proud to let you all know that I have undertaken online training and stand here today in front of you as a celebrant. I may not be able to get married myself today but marry someone else I can.'

Oh my God, in all his wildest imaginings he had never seen Angelina as the one to oversee their renewal.

'Now Marion was quite clear that she didn't want "Here Comes the Bride" because, as she says, everyone immediately thinks "fat and wide" and she is neither, so I chose this.'

The strains of 'She's So Lovely' played out, no hint of irony and with all of the first three rows singing along loudly, even Pippa, albeit a bit tunelessly. This time

Richard did turn and there, walking down the aisle in a fitted ivory dress, her hair styled within an inch of its life and carrying the biggest bouquet he had ever seen, Rufus and Rupert by her sides, was his wife.

Chapter Forty-eight

Marion took a deep breath as she stood outside the dome. This was both ludicrously exciting and also a bit terrifying. She had nothing to worry about. She just needed to keep repeating that. The boys had got Richard where he needed to be and now Rupert and Rufus were either side of her, determined to be as involved as their elder brother was, determined to give her away.

'You look amazing, Mum. Really special,' Rupert said, looking at her with love, before he peered around the tent opening and inside.

'You're always pretty but you look like a princess today,' Rufus added, squishing her hand and not wanting to be left out.

Rupert walked back to her side and passed her the bouquet that she had placed on the floor whilst she was waiting. It was huge. It would be a miracle if she didn't trip over it. Angelina had ordered it for her and it was as big and bold and brash as a floral bouquet could be. She loved it.

She could hear Angelina squawking on stage but wasn't sure exactly what she was saying. Then the music started; this was her cue. She could feel her heart beating as fast as a horse's gallop. She took a deep breath and Rupert and Rufus tugged her forward a little.

She was doing this. She had learnt a lot this year, about her life and how she wanted to live it. She wasn't going to allow herself to get into a jittery mess now. No, this was her moment.

As she walked into the dome and down the makeshift aisle, her hands clutching the bouquet, she heard the words to the song that was playing and, what was more, everyone singing the refrain.

'She's so lovely…'

Really? People were singing *this* for *her*? She realized that the dome was packed but it was the first three rows who were now standing on their feet, singing and clapping her down the aisle. She could feel a blush rise on her cheeks. She couldn't remember ever blushing before. She kept walking, one foot in front of another, not letting the emotion of being accepted, being supported by her chosen community, her chosen family, run over her. She kept heading towards Richard, the one who had always been there for her, through everything. Solid, unchanging and ever committed. She pulled strength from him as he watched her walk towards him. His smile lit up his whole face, the crinkle around his eyes as he beamed at her. She loved that. His gaze made her feel beautiful, special, as she was in his eyes and he was in hers; like there was no one else who mattered. She reached him; the boys low-fived each other and then stepped back to take their seats.

It was still feeling a little surreal standing here, next to the man who had stayed by her side throughout, despite her most extreme faults when she was at her most anxious, through her rejection of him and all their marriage stood for. He was still here and his eyes were still lit with love.

What Angelina was doing on the stage though was questionable. This was meant to be Marion and Richard's moment; for all her friend's generosity, shouldn't she have buggered off by now?

She flicked a quick glance across at him as they both stood there, happy and secure and wanting to proclaim their love, solidify their bond in front of all these witnesses. And there were a lot of them. Marion knew she had invited lots of people, paid for some particularly glamorous ones to keep Angelina sweet but still, there were a lot of people crammed in here and all their eyes were on her and her husband.

'Dearly beloved…' Angelina intoned in her best vicar-like voice, a hint of mischief in her tone that she couldn't quite disguise. Surely not! Marion lifted her eyes to those belonging to her friend and felt the giggle rising all the way from her tummy and spilling out over her lips. Of course. There was no way Angelina wasn't having a starring role in this.

The service progressed swiftly. Marion had wanted it as close as possible to the traditional service, so as not to pile pressure on Richard for a ceremony he had been told wouldn't happen. However, she knew that when it came to the vows, she had some things she wanted to say.

Richard had held her eyes as he said his 'I will' after Angelina recited the vows and she knew he meant it, as he always had, with every fibre of his being. Now it was Marion's turn.

'Marion Mildred Marksharp.' She would never forgive her mother for that middle name but no one, not even Pippa or Lynne, giggled at it. 'Will you take Richard James Algernon Marksharp to be your husband? Will you love him, comfort him, honour and protect him and, forsaking all others, be faithful as long as you both shall live?'

'I will.' Marion's voice rang out, pure and clear and loud.

'Curses,' Hector mumbled in a stage whisper, winking when she turned her head to glare at him, giving a thumbs up to Richard and making those around him chuckle.

Marion wasn't finished yet. She turned to face Richard and reached for both his hands. 'Richard Marksharp, you are the most amazing man. I love you with all my heart, my soul and my body, and in front of all these people I pledge my loyalty to you, here, now and forever. I haven't always been easy to live with and I'm learning more and more every year. But the one thing I can swear will remain unchanged is my determination never to let you go again. You are part of me, the better part of me and I shall cherish you every single day I am alive. Thank you for being in my life, thank you for giving me *our* boys and thank you for showing me how to love.' She let out a sigh, so, so happy in this moment with the man she loved beside her forever, the boys they had made between them as invested in their celebration of love as she was.

Before she knew what was happening, Richard, somehow channelling Cary Grant, swept her off her feet and into his arms with the most passionate kiss. As she gave in to it, she heard the crowd behind her push out their chairs, take to their feet and roar with joy. The whole community of Penmenna there to celebrate the love between Richard and Marion Marksharp.

Acknowledgements

It feels strange to be sitting and writing the final acknowledgements to this series. *The Cornish Village School* were my first ever books, and writing them has been so much fun. The characters have made me giggle, and whilst I can't believe I'm saying it, I'm going to miss having Marion in my life every day.

The writing community has been so supportive along the way and I have to give the biggest thanks to all the bloggers out there. Your kind words about these books have been so important, so helpful. They kept me going when I was having treacle-slow writing days, when my brain felt completely empty. Three in particular have turned up for every book, supported me endlessly on social media and made me smile – so whilst this is a huge thank you to all book bloggers, it's an especial thank you to Bernadette Maycock, Rachel Gilbey and Grace J Smith.

A big shout out to my agent, the incomparable Hayley Steed for all her support throughout. She is a shining light who always has my back.

My editor, Emily Bedford, has been so much fun to work with, our comment streams make me giggle. And another big thank you to all at Canelo who helped *The Cornish Village School* come into being.

Then of course there are those people in my personal life. Rob and Andrew, who I have dedicated this book to,

344

are two of the people I love most in the world. Ann, who is ever true and never seems to mind my constant barrage of questions, is wise and good and stuck with me for life. Jane and Sandra came into my life because of a shared love of writing and have become the best of friends. And, as ever, Namdi, Jack and Katharine who I love with every single spot of my being. Thank you to all of you for being the most supportive bunch of people and making me feel lucky every single day.